STAGE 3: BRAVO

Ken Stark

STAGE 3: BRAVO
Copyright © 2018 Ken Stark
All Rights Reserved

www.kenstark.ca

Copyedited by Eeva Lancaster
Cover Design and Formatting by The Book Khaleesi

Books by Ken Stark

STAGE 3 SERIES
Post-Apocalyptic Zombie Thrillers

STAGE 3
STAGE 3: Alpha
STAGE 3: Bravo
STAGE 3: Charlie
Billy, the Kid (A Stage 3 Short Story)

HORROR NOVELS

Gaia's Game
Arcadia Falls

SHORT STORIES

Horrible Little Nasties
Who's Going to Feed Johnny?
Jitters
Killing Joe Prince
Dead Weight

Audiobooks

Arcadia Falls
Gaia's Game
STAGE 3: A Post-Apocalyptic Zombie Thriller
Stage 3: Alpha
Stage 3: Bravo
Who's Going to Feed Johnny?

AVAILABLE on AUDIBLE

ABOUT THE BOOK

The world went blind.
Then it went mad.
But the Virus has one more trick up its sleeve...

Hank Mason had nothing left to lose.
But then came Mackenzie. And then came Sarah. And then came the others.
Though these seven souls had somehow survived the first days of the epidemic, every minute of life in this new world came at a price.

Thrown into a relentless battle against a population turned feral on one side, and desperate men willing to do anything to stay alive on the other, the only question remaining was...

How much were they were willing to pay to survive?

Now, those precious few are in a desperate race to save one more lost soul, and time is running out. The clock started ticking the moment they pulled into that forgotten little corner of a world gone insane.

Every second brings them closer to death.
They'll have to find a way out... or die trying.

WHAT READERS ARE SAYING

"Author Stark takes readers on a suspense filled journey in this apocalyptic saga. This one's a page turner with some brilliant insights as to what caused the deadly swarm, highly recommended!"

~ Amazon 5-star Review

"When a book about zombies and gore makes you cry, you wonder whether the book is really about the zombie apocalypse or whether it's about relationships and humanity. And... you know you've found an outstanding author."

~ Amazon 5-star Review

"Stage 3: Bravo reveals a few details we didn't know in the previous books. I don't want to give away spoilers, but the author's use of technology and science to explain what happened both with the illness and people fleeing it is creative and well thought out. I wish more authors found such creative uses and hindrances for the tech that surrounds us.

~ Amazon 5-star Review

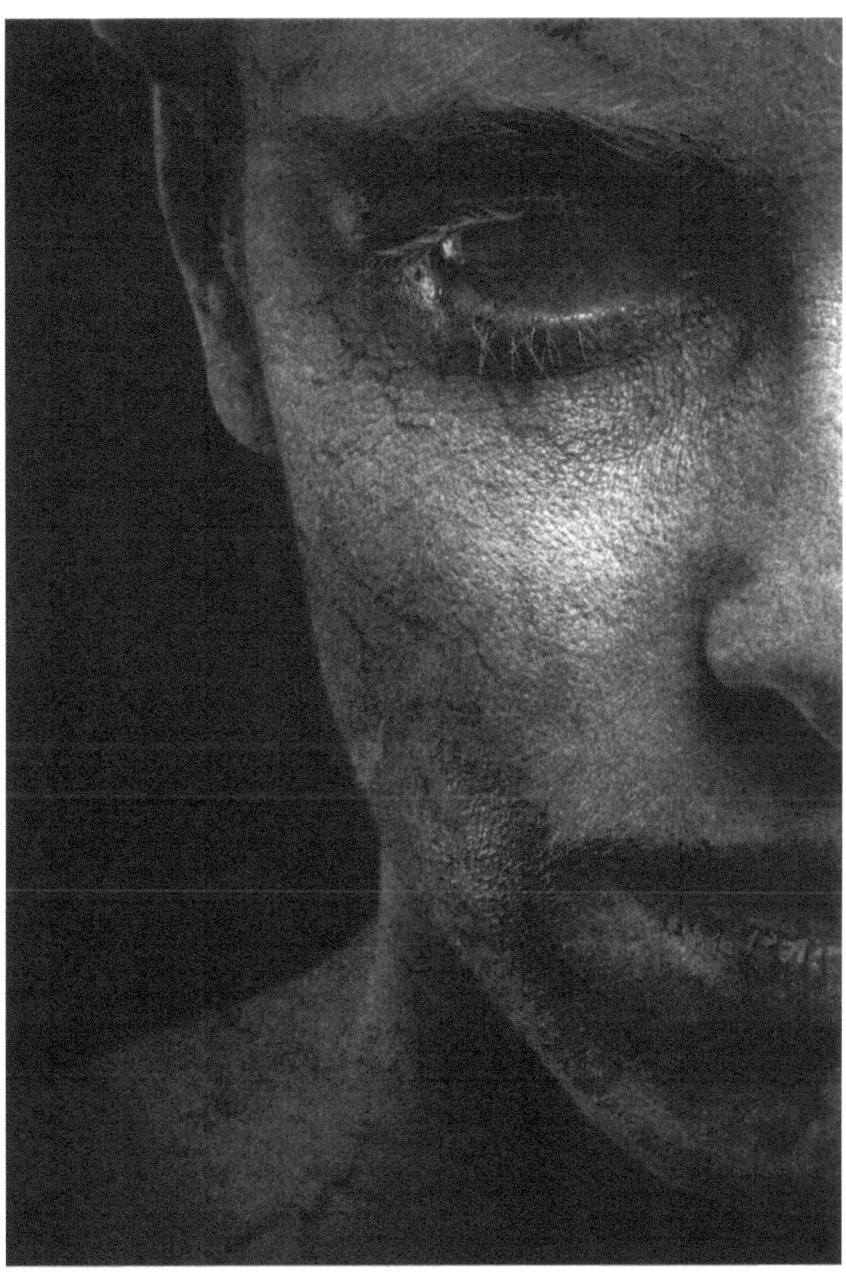

CHAPTER

I

Move, and you're a dead man."

He froze in mid-stoop at the sound of a gun being cocked next to his ear. Several seconds passed before he chanced a quick peek through the corner of his eye, and when his skull somehow remained miraculously unperforated, he dared to turn it a fraction of a degree to get a better look.

Legs. A man's legs, fitting the voice. Grubby jeans, worn almost through at the knees. Work boots beneath, spattered with mud and blood and what might have been dismissed as water had he not caught the faint whiff of gasoline.

"I'm no threat to you," he told the man, "I'm just..."

"I know what you're *just!* You and me and everyone else in this world, all of us left are *just!*"

The voice was firm, but with a little tremor at the end. A hint of fear. Not much. Just a trace. Just enough to make a trigger finger twitch.

Several more seconds passed with neither man moving,

1

neither man speaking, then the man bent at the waist offered an almost casual, "Do you mind if I straighten up? My legs are starting to cramp, and my back is killing me."

"You move one inch, mister, and you won't have to worry about your back anymore. *I'll* be the one killing you."

Huh. There was a little rasp in the voice he hadn't noticed before. And calling him 'mister.' Both earmarks of an older man. Sixties, probably. Maybe older. The work boots were his from before. The blood was new, but the mud wasn't. And he hadn't bothered to scrape the boots clean, so it was something he was used to. Not a city man, then. Outdoorsman. Farmer, maybe.

"Look, friend, I'm just trying to make my way in this world, same as you. How about you take that gun away from my head, and I'll just back out of here nice and quiet, and be on my way?"

The old man snorted. "Mister, I don't know who you think you're dealing with..."

"Well, that's just it, isn't it? I don't know *you*, you don't know *me*, and because we don't know each other, you'll be more than willing to pull that trigger and remove the better part of a stranger's brain."

"Damn straight," came the gruff reply.

"But you haven't yet. I've been entirely at your mercy for the better part of a minute, and you have yet to murder me. If I might be allowed an observation, what that hesitation generally denotes is that someone hasn't quite given up on his fellow man just yet."

"Hesitation?" the older man growled.

"Poor choice of words. I apologize. Let's call it a pensive pause then. Clearly, you are capable of defending yourself, but you're not unwilling to take a breath or two to fully consider other avenues. Does this person necessarily have to die for me to be safe, or would a simple threat be enough? Well, I can assure you that in my case, neither one is required. You've staked a claim here, and that's good enough for me. It's a big city, and too few people left for us to be fighting over scraps."

The gun barrel nestled directly behind his ear. Too big to be a handgun or a rifle. Only a double-barreled shotgun could cover that many square inches. Twin barrels, then, side by side. Two shots, two triggers. An old-timer's weapon, but perfectly capable of turning his head into mist.

"Listen, friend, you are obviously an intelligent man..."

"You don't know me, remember?" the old man huffed.

"No, I don't, but stupid died quick," he said, sharply. "So clearly, you're an intelligent man. But in the interest of cooperation, could I offer you a word of advice before you pull that trigger and spray my brains all over the floor? Take it for what it's worth, accept it or not, but I feel compelled to let you in on two points of strategy that will undoubtedly serve you better in the future. They might even save your life one day. Who knows? Do you mind?"

The old man made a sound somewhere between a snort and a laugh. "Sure, mister," he said, "Why don't you let me in on these deep dark secrets that might just save my life?"

In a single motion, the younger man bolted upright, batted the gun aside with a thick forearm, and snatched the weapon right out of the older man's hands.

"Number one: don't get so close, especially with a long-barreled weapon. You can kill a man as easily at fifty feet as you can at three."

"A–and number two?"

"Number two: if you plan on killing someone, don't talk about it, fucking *do* it."

STAGE 3: BRAVO

The old man didn't move a muscle. He stood there, ramrod straight, locking back his shoulders and looking the other man directly in the eye. He was afforded the briefest glimpse down the twin barrels of his own shotgun as it passed in front of his face, then the weapon was pointed in the air, the hammers were eased back down, and the gun came to rest on a thick, muscular shoulder.

The younger man took a moment to stretch the kinks out of his back, then he gave the barest of nods and stuck out a big, meaty hand.

"My name's Hank. Hank Mason. Most people call me Mace."

The old man trembled as he took Mason's hand, but his grip was as strong as iron.

"D–Daniel," he managed at last. "Daniel Thorogood."

"Pleased to meet you, Daniel." Mason allowed a quick smile. "Any relation to *George* Thorogood?"

"Not that I know of," the old man said as if he'd been asked a thousand times before. "Y–you're not going to kill me?"

"I wasn't planning to." Mason shrugged. "Why? Should I?"

"No, you shouldn't!" Daniel answered most emphatically. "But that was a hell of a chance you took. I might've blown your head clean off."

Mason allowed a self-satisfied smirk. "Well, sure. But you see, there's a third point of strategy I didn't get the chance to tell you. Number three: don't go anywhere without someone watching your ass."

Another figure stepped out from behind a row of boxes and took a bead on the old man down the barrel of an assault rifle. It was a woman. Late twenties. A full foot shorter than

4

Mason, and with a short crop of dirty-blonde hair.

"Daniel, this is Sarah. Sarah, Daniel."

"Uh, h–how do you do, Sarah?" the old man said, doffing an imaginary cap as only someone his age could do without looking ridiculous.

"Pleased to meet you, Daniel," Sarah said politely enough, but the rifle didn't move an inch.

"You know, it's funny," Daniel said off-handedly, suddenly no longer nervous and even almost cracking a smile. "I was never very good at math. My old teachers... well, they had an awful time with me. You see, I was forever getting everything all *bass-ackwards*. I think the modern term is dis... uh, dyslexia? Is that it? Anyways, I could barely figure out two plus two. I guess maybe that accounts for me figuring out the third deep dark secret before figuring out the other two."

With that, yet another figure emerged from out of nowhere and levelled a Winchester rifle directly at the back of Sarah's head.

It was a girl, barely out of her teens. Slim. Pretty. Long, dark hair tied back in a ponytail. To Mason, she looked like she'd be right at home leading cheers at a varsity football game. But the hard glint in her eye and that unwavering gun bespoke a willingness to do whatever she had to do to survive.

He gave the slightest of nods to Sarah, and she dutifully lowered the barrel of her weapon to the ground.

"This is my granddaughter, Jesse. Jesse, I'd like you meet Mace and Sarah."

"Pleasure," she said politely, sighting down the rifle to the exact center of Sarah's skull.

"Now, remember what Mace said, Jesse," the old man cautioned her. "Don't get close enough for someone to snatch your gun away."

"I won't, Grampa," the girl replied sweetly.

"And if you plan on killing someone..."

"Fucking *do* it," she said, just as sweetly.

Mason knew when he was beat. He raised his free hand in surrender, lifted the shotgun slowly off his shoulder, and handed it butt-first back to Daniel.

The old man took it, but instead of aiming it back at Mason, he simply propped it up on his own rather more spindly shoulder.

"Alright," he said, "now that the niceties are over, the question remains. Just what are we to do about this situation? Now, you seem like decent enough folks, but the second we lower our guns and let you walk away, what guarantee do we have that you won't return?"

"There are no guarantees in the apocalypse, Daniel," Sarah said, grimly.

Mason happened to spot an orange crate nearby, so he said, "May I?" and without waiting for a response, he kicked the crate to its side and lowered himself onto it with a heavy sigh. "Okay, so the way I see it, Daniel, the problem is this. If you do us the courtesy of not decorating the walls of this establishment with our grey matter, how do you know that we won't come back with the intention of killing you and your lovely granddaughter and stealing everything you have. I suppose it's too much to ask that you trust us?"

"Reckon 'tis," the old man scoffed.

Sarah came to Mason's side and he scooted over to give her room on the crate. Jesse made no move to stop her, but the barrel of the Winchester followed her every move.

"You know," Sarah said, squeezing her slender backside in beside Mason, "Mace and I were in very different places when this whole thing started. I don't mean geographically, but *emotionally*, you know? I'm a nurse, so my entire adult life has been dedicated to learning how to heal, how to repair, and how to administer to the sick and injured. I actually made it my life's work to help my fellow man when they needed it most. As for Mace," she tutted, putting a tender hand on his big, beefy shoulder, "well, let's just say that Mace had a somewhat different outlook. But you know what, Daniel? This new world of ours demands a great deal from a person. I don't think anyone left alive would consider themselves unchanged. But it doesn't all have to be negative. Look at us! I started around here, and Mace started somewhere down... here," she said, raising one hand high in the air and putting the other very near the floor. "But circumstances being what they are, we both changed, we both adapted, and now we're both about... here," she concluded, her hands almost meeting in the middle.

Mason patted Sarah gently on the knee and continued the narrative. "I've only known Sarah for a short time, but I've come to know her quite well. She's a real people-person, you know? Always happy to make new friends, always willing to help out, always eager to lend a hand, always ready to run to someone's aid in times of need. And how did the universe pay her back? With pain. Loss. Heartbreak." He finally rested the hand on her knee, and they shared a look that spoke volumes.

"I'm one of the lucky ones, Daniel, because I actually *gained* from the experience. Just a short while ago, I would have gladly shot you both in the head just for being in my general vicinity. But I've since come to a new awareness. While the rest of world was losing its humanity, I actually found a tiny bit of mine buried so deep down inside of me that I had no idea it was even there. And with that discovery came a new outlook. I realize now that not everyone is bad. Certainly *some* are, but not all. So now, I will actually give that other man the benefit of the doubt. I will actually take a breath or two before condemning that man to death."

The girl notched the Winchester a few inches to the right, precisely level with Mason's eyes. "You're in a strange position to be talking about shooting someone in the head, Mace."

"I think you missed the point, Jesse," Mason spoke to the girl as a patient father might. "But that's probably my fault, so I apologize. I'm still getting used to this whole *communication* thing. My point is simply this. Shit happens, and life ain't fair. This universe doesn't give a flying fuck about you or me or Grandpappy Daniel or Sweet Fat Fanny Annie. Good people suffer, and assholes win the lottery. It's always been like that, and it always will be. Shit happens, Jesse, and not one goddamn bit of it is fair."

Daniel looked at Mason long and hard, then he narrowed his eyes and asked, "You sure that's the point you want to be making just now, Mace? Didn't you just say—"

"I know, I know," Mason cut him off. "I just said that I've become a better person, but trust me, it wasn't for the good karma or to get a better shake or to earn points in the afterlife. Truth be told, I was dragged kicking and screaming into this new way of thinking. But I *have* changed, Daniel, and I'm glad I did. I believe it has made my life richer. In a way, you could even say that this particular unrepentant asshole won his own personal lottery."

"Well, good for you," Jesse snorted. "But since shit ain't fair, I guess it won't surprise you if I just play it safe and shoot you both right now?"

Mason gave her a broad and genuine smile.

"You're cute, Jesse. Smart. Strong. Resolute. I truly believe you would do whatever you had to do for the sake of your grandfather."

"Damn right," she said back, as cold as ice.

"Then you should probably lower that smoke-wagon." Mason's smile remained as he turned to the old man. "I apologize, Daniel, but I missed one last point of strategy. If you're going to have someone covering your ass, *six* is always better than one."

With that, five more shadows coalesced out of the darkness, and there was a chorus of clicks as five separate guns were cocked.

"Daniel, Jesse," Mason said, obligingly, "I'd like you to meet our friends. This is Christopher, Inez, Beverly, Addison, and that adorable little thing behind the Tommy gun almost bigger than she is? Well, that's Alejandra, and believe me when I say, you do *not* want to get on that girl's bad side."

"Fuckin' A," Alejandra purred.

Daniel looked around at the guns bristling in from all sides, and he lowered his shotgun to the floor with a sigh.

But Jesse was something else altogether. She kept her rifle pointed directly at Mason, and she even had the balls to shout out to the room. "Drop your guns, all of you! I swear to *Christ*, I'll kill them both!"

No one moved, but then there came one last *click!* from behind, and Jesse deflated like a tire. She slumped her shoulders and lowered the rifle, then she slowly turned around to see who could have possibly snuck up behind her without so much as a breath of sound.

It was a dog. An Irish Setter the approximate size of a pony, its head cocked to one side and watching her with utter fascination. Beside the dog was a girl. A pretty little thing with bright green eyes, a big messy tangle of curly red hair, and a snub-nosed .38 revolver, presently pointed right between Jesse's eyes.

"Did I say six?" Mason said. "Sorry, Daniel, I meant seven. I guess I was never very good at math, either."

CHAPTER

II

The Peterbilt was parked against a pair of concrete abutments forming a narrow alcove outside the front door of the building, so Mason discounted the handful of creatures pounding away on the far side of the truck. He came out carrying a twenty-gallon jug in each hand as easily as another might carry pillows. He lowered one to the ground and began pouring the other into the metal tank on the big truck's side.

"Are you sure?" Addison had to ask, barely managing to drag along a third jerry can. "There's a lot of supplies in there. These truck stops used to stock everything from adult diapers to ammunition. There's probably enough Slim Jims and beef jerky in there to feed us for weeks!"

"We already have enough to feed us for weeks," Mason reminded him. "The important things now are water and fuel, and not necessarily in that order."

"Well, add toilet paper to the list," Addison said, thumbing his glasses up his nose and taking a moment to properly adjust his sweater-vest. "And as indelicate as it sounds, you might want to survey the women for what they might need by way of... uh, you know... feminine hygiene products and the like."

A definite sourness passed over Mason's face. "Why don't *you* ask them?" he said, setting the empty jerry can aside and hoisting up the second. "I wouldn't even know how to bring the subject up."

Addison allowed a smirk. "Sure, Mace. But just so I'm clear, you will face down a man with a shotgun without batting an eye, you'll put your life on the line for veritable strangers on the say-so of a woman you just met, and you'll wade into a swarm of alphas with nothing more than an oversized stick, but *this* is where you draw the line? Asking a woman if she needs a tampon?"

Mason could only shrug. "It's... different."

Addison cocked an eyebrow. "Dude, we share living quarters. We've all seen each other in various stages of undress. Hell, we've seen each other pee in the middle of the road, for crying out loud!"

"And your point?" Mason asked gruffly, manhandling the third eighty-pound jug of fuel as if it were a toy.

"No point." Addison forced a noncommittal shrug. "No point at all. Everyone has boundaries. Boundaries are good. It's just nice to know where yours lie." He hid a grin and turned to go, but then he met Sarah and Mackenzie coming in the opposite direction and he could hold it in no longer. "Tampons! *Ha!*" He laughed aloud as he passed them by.

Sarah spared a curious glance back at the retreating man, but Mackenzie's attention was focused where it usually was – namely, on her big Irish Setter. The two were inseparable. Where Mackenzie went, so went Clancy, though he went now with his nose to the ground, panting happily away as he sniffed out the myriad scents of this new place.

It had been accepted as gospel that no one in the group would ever be unarmed, even in sleep, so Sarah and Mackenzie each had a gun on their hip and a rifle slung over their shoulders. Sarah's rifle had once belonged to another man, but it was hers now, and though the thing was as big as a howitzer, she could wield the massive weapon like a surgeon's blade.

Mackenzie's was smaller, thinner, lighter, but no part of the pairing had to do with the tiny hands or underdeveloped muscles of a ten-year-old girl. No, that slim-barreled .22 might not have looked like much, but with a sharp eye on the sights and a hundred-round magazine to keep it fed, that unassuming little rifle had saved their collective asses more often than all the other weapons in their arsenal combined.

They both came up behind Mason in full conversation, and Mason heard Mackenzie say as they approached, "It's too bad. I like them. Especially Jesse. She's awesome!"

"Mack, we can't go around picking up every stray we come across." Mason interrupted the conversation with a huff, setting the last empty jerry can aside and screwing the lid down tight on the fuel tank. "We don't have the food, we don't have the water, and we sure as *hell* don't have the room."

"Oh, c'mon, Mace!" the girl snarked back. "We have lots of food and lots of water, and we can *always* make room."

As usual, when dealing with Mackenzie, Mason found himself completely at a loss. Somehow, this tiny little girl not only knew the right thing to say, but she always found a way to say it as if she were the green-eyed conscience riding on his shoulder. Fortunately, even as he struggled for some way to upend her entirely rational statement, Sarah stepped in with an arm around the girl's shoulder.

"They don't want to come with us, Boo. They want to go home," she said, then she flipped a glance up to Mason and told him without apology, "Yes, I made the offer. But don't worry, Mace, they have no desire to join our roving band of misfits. All they want is to get back to Pescadero."

"And what's in Pescadero?"

"Weren't you listening? No, I guess you were out draining the last diesel from the tanks by then. Well, Daniel and Jesse live in Pescadero. They have a strawberry farm down there. It's just the two of them. Apparently, they hadn't been away from the place in months, so Jesse finally convinced her grandfather to come to the city to get a break. And... well..."

"They chose the worst day in all of history to go on a road trip," Mason finished the thought, but then a sudden notion had him arching an eyebrow. "So, what did he tell you about this farm of theirs. Is it fenced? How big, do you think? Did it sound like a good place to spend a couple of days?"

After. He didn't tack on the word *after* because he knew he didn't have to. Did it sound like a good place to spend a couple of days... *after*? *After* he'd led them all on a snipe hunt. *After* this ridiculous quixotic adventure was over. *After* the few of them who survived this wild goose chase were back on the run. And just like that, he realized why he and Sarah and none of the others ever, *ever* used that word. By tacit agreement, the very concept of *after* was anathema. By definition, that simple word encompassed not only every single second of life from this moment on, but every hope and every dream any of them would ever have. But just as everything before was smoke on the breeze, everything after was a deception. There *was* no after. There was only ever a *now*. The exact length of time from one heartbeat to the next.

"I didn't ask, Mace. It's their home, not a drop-in center for wayward orphans."

"I'd sure like to see Jesse again." Mackenzie turned her big, green eyes up to Sarah. "Can I ask if it'd be okay? Can I?"

"You can ask, Boo, but don't get your hopes up. Even if Daniel says it's alright, we might not be anywhere near."

After... Mason added inside his head.

The girl's lips turned down in the beginnings of a pout, but just as she opened her mouth to complain, she suddenly snapped it shut again and held up a finger for silence. She pointed under the truck just as Clancy started to growl, and just like that, Mason produced a seven foot length of solid re-bar from out of nowhere, Sarah swung her rifle off her shoulder, and all three of them took several steps back from the truck.

"Only one," Mackenzie hushed, crouching down on her haunches to get a clear view under the truck.

One of the modifications they'd made to the big Peterbilt was a sheet of aluminum welded to the bottoms of the fuel tanks on either side, in order to avoid just such a situation. But they'd had to strike a bargain between safety and utility. Christopher had argued for a floor-length skirt, but Mason couldn't abide the idea of getting the truck hung up on a curb or a median. So, they'd struck a deal. They'd gone with a midi rather than a maxi. The half-length sheet of metal helped, but it still left a pretty good gap between skirt and ground.

Mason crouched down, and sure enough, there it was. He didn't know where Mack had come upon her supersensitive Vulcan hearing, but he'd long ago stopped doubting its efficacy. Just like she'd said, a single alpha was crawling under the truck with room to spare.

STAGE 3: BRAVO

He and Mack used to refer to these things as 'wilders,' but Sarah's name for the living dead monstrosities had quickly been adopted by the entire group. It might not fit any better or roll more trippingly off the tongue, but he couldn't argue that the name 'alpha' held considerably less dire overtones than 'wilder.' And so 'alphas' they'd become by consensus.

This used-to-be man crawling toward them under the truck was still clinging to life, so it was an alpha. *Acute Loss of Frontal-lobe Activity. Acting Like a Fucking Animal.* Either way, the name fit. This poor bastard struggling along on its elbows should be curled up in a ditch somewhere, waiting to die. But the virus that ate away its higher brain functions kept it going right up to the end. So on it came, snapping its jaws and clawing blindly at the air, even as it spilled its guts along the ground.

Mason assessed the alpha's speed and strength, and quickly did the math. Not an immediate threat. Wait thirty seconds until it clears the skirt, then skewer it through the head. Easy-peasy. But then he'd just have to drag it clear, and why make more work for himself? So, kill it while it was still under the truck, then. The gun on his hip would do the job, but every alpha for a mile around would hear. Alright then... crawl under the truck and meet the alpha halfway. Or better yet, turn Clancy loose and let the faithful hound finish the thing off.

No. Both were feasible, but both held risks, and as far as Mason was concerned, risks were the things you took when you had no other choice.

He uttered the single word, "Mack," and in a flash, the tiny girl had her rifle off her shoulder and up to her eye. A tiny finger flinched, and a little red spot appeared between the alpha's eyes. No explosion, no sound that would echo like cannon-fire through the streets, the .22 went off with the abbreviated *snap!* of two hands clapping, and the creature collapsed to the ground, perfectly still and perfectly silent.

Mason stayed in a crouch and looked past the dead thing to four pairs of legs on the far side of the truck. Behind them, more were coming. He counted seven. Two alphas probing. Two more hobbling along as best as they could. The other three were echoes.

Echoes. That name was Sarah's, too. He and Mack had dubbed the dead things 'creepers,' and the name fit them to a T. But again, they deferred to the less provocative nomenclature. Echoes were clinically dead, so with no air in their lungs, there were no snarls and no howls. The only sounds they made came from the shuffling of their feet and the gnashing of their teeth. But with the virus at the helm, these unliving horrors were utterly relentless. They came, no matter what. They were drawn to the nearest human like moths to a flame, so there was nowhere to hide. Lying low and maintaining noise discipline might keep the alphas guessing, but the dead things always came.

Always.

"Want me to clear the rest of them?" Mackenzie asked, as sweetly as another child might ask if she could help set the dinner table.

Mason heard a crunch from behind and tossed a glance over his shoulder to see the old man just emerging from the truck stop. "No, it's okay, Mack," he said, giving her as gentle a fist-bump as anyone had ever given. "Why don't you go hang out with Jesse for a bit? Maybe there's something they need that we have."

The girl's face lit up, and she flung the .22 back over her shoulder with an abbreviated, "K!" But before she left, she turned her face down to Mason's and said, "By the way, Mace, where would you be right now if you didn't pick up strays?"

Without waiting for an answer, she spun on her heels and hurried back inside.

Her words were like a hard smack on the back of the head. *Where would he be, indeed?*

Sarah offered him her hand. "She's not wrong, you know."

"Is she ever?" Mason scoffed, letting her pull him to his feet.

The old man arrived and half-doffed his imaginary cap at Sarah, then he stretched out a hand to Mason. "I owe you a debt of gratitude, Mace."

Mason pretended not to see the proffered hand. He turned his back to the man, stepped up to the truck, and slid the seven feet of rebar back into its cradle behind the cab.

"You don't owe me a thing, Daniel," he said over his shoulder, cracking the driver's door of the Peterbilt just enough to retrieve the twin of Mack's .22 rifle from beside the seat.

"Oh, but I *do*, sir! I most assuredly *do*! Why, here I thought I was doing a decent job of it, but I guess I was just fooling myself all along."

"Nonsense," Mason said, folding himself cross-legged on the ground and bringing up the .22's sights. "You kept yourself and your granddaughter alive in a virtual shit storm. In my book, that makes you something of an expert." He lined up his sights on the knee of one of the alphas pinned to the far side of the truck, and fired a single round. The creature dropped to the ground, howling and snorting with rage, but a second round sent pin-balling around the inside of its skull silenced it.

"Not at all, sir, not at all!" Daniel protested, one eye keenly turned to the gathering swarm. "We came to the city because I love Jesse dearly, and she does so much for this tired old man without a single complaint. So when she said that it would be nice for us to get away for a day... well, there's nothing I wouldn't do for that special young lady."

Mason coolly set his sights on another knee, and followed it up by drilling a hole through the bridge of a dainty little nose.

"We know the feeling, Daniel," Sarah offered with a smile.

"Yes, I'm sure you do. Mackenzie is a remarkable girl. But what I'm trying to say is... Jesse and I... the two of us... well, I try to do my best, but we are both wholly out of our element!"

Mason took down two more alphas in quick succession and ended their snarls with another pair of handclaps. "We're *all* out of our element, Daniel," he said, taking aim on the more distant alphas and dropping all four with as many shots.

"Oh, but Mace," the old man said, almost pleading now, "we are barely clinging to life! There are times when we are holding on only by the very tips of our fingers! We have no idea what we're doing at all, or if what we are doing is right!"

The echoes were too close for Mason to get a headshot from under the truck, and since it often took two or three rounds to a knee or hip to get one of them on the ground, it simply wasn't worth the ammunition.

He stood up, leaned the rifle against the cab, and turned to face the old man. "Daniel, *all* of us are barely clinging to life. *All* of us are hanging on by our fingertips. Believe me when I say that no one alive knows what the hell they are doing, and I can speak from personal experience that there's no way on God's green Earth that we can possibly know whether or not what we are doing is right. If you're looking for advice or a pep talk or a pat on the back, brother, you've come to the wrong place."

The old man looked to Sarah, but she merely shrugged. "Yeah, he's a bit of a work in progress."

Just then, a young man came out of the building. Tall, lean-muscled, young enough that his clean, handsome face might never have seen a razor, and with an AK47 slung over his shoulder.

"Hey, guys," Christopher said around a long piece of licorice dangling from his mouth, "Beverly found a camp stove in the back, and my mom says she has all she needs to whip up a big batch of spaghetti. So, she just wants to know if we're leaving right away or if we have time to eat. And not to tip the balance one way or the other, but everyone's pretty hungry, and you know how Alejandra gets when she's hungry. I'm not sayin', I'm just sayin'."

Mason looked from the licorice bobbing from the young man's mouth to the rest of the pack clutched in his hand. It took a few seconds, but Christopher finally got the message and let Mason help himself.

"You can tell your mom to put the kettle on, but then come back and bring Alejandra and Addison with you."

"Yeah? Whatcha got going on?"

Mason hooked a thumb over his shoulder to the far side of the lot where two big rigs were parked, minus the trailers. Christopher nodded his understanding, but Daniel screwed up his face and gave his bald head a shake.

"I don't think so, friend. I had the idea of swapping my old pickup for one of those beauties, but they're locked up tight and no keys anywhere. Hey, any chance you know how to hot-wire one of them babies? Why, if you could do that..."

Mason stopped him right there. "I'm not after the trucks, Daniel. I'm after their fuel."

"But if you could hot-wire one of them..."

While Mason stewed, Sarah answered in his place.

"We don't know how to do that, Daniel."

"Yet!" Mason aimed a stick of licorice at her like an accusing finger. "I'll figure it out eventually. There's just so many damn wires and stuff..."

"I know," Sarah said, giving him a motherly pat on the back. "You'll figure it out. Eventually..."

"It's a bit of a sore spot," Christopher hushed to the old man, but one look from Mason sent him scampering away.

Before he got far, Mason called after him, "Hey, see if you can find a couple of buckets while you're at it. The bigger the better."

Christopher stopped just long enough to fake-salute. But just as he started off again, another call halted him in his tracks.

"And if you find any Kit-Kats while you're digging around in there, I call dibs!"

Christopher threw him a wink and a grin, and he disappeared inside.

"How much do we have?" Sarah looked to the empty jerry cans.

"This tank's nearly full, but I'd sure like to have both of them topped-up before leaving Ingleside. The last thing we want to do is run short in the middle of the bottleneck."

"Oh, Gloria," Sarah said, patting the metal fuel tank as tenderly as she would an expectant mother's belly. "You certainly are a thirsty bitch."

The old man watched them both with something akin to

awe. At last, he produced a well-used handkerchief from his back pocket, drew it across his brow, and gushed, "My word, I wish I knew how you do it."

Sarah cocked her head. "Do what, Daniel?"

"How you make it look so easy. You've built this amazing team around yourselves, and you just make it all look so... so *easy!*"

They both scoffed at once.

"My friend, *none* of this easy," Mason said, almost in a laugh. "We might look calm right now, but we're paddling like hell just below the surface. Believe me, Daniel, absolutely no part of this is easy, and God help us if it ever *becomes* easy. In fact, if you ever cross paths with someone who isn't scared shitless every waking moment and tormented by nightmares every night, you'd best put a bullet in that man's head. Because I can guarantee you, he is a worse monster than anything else you'll ever come across in this world."

"And we didn't build a team, Daniel," Sarah hastened to add. "We made friends. It's that simple. We made friends."

Sarah laid a hand on Mason's shoulder, and Mason's hand went up to embrace it. It was such a natural, tender display that someone who didn't know their history might have thought they'd been together for years. And apparently, Daniel was one of those people.

"Well, it's a fine thing that you two still have each other," he said, idly thumbing the gold band on one calloused finger. "My Ida passed from this life too many years ago to count. To tell you the truth, though, I'm almost glad. Oh, many's the time I would've done anything the good Lord asked to have her back with me, but with the way the world is now, I wouldn't wish that on my worst enemy, let alone someone as sweet as my Ida. She was like you, Sarah. She couldn't wait to meet new people, make new friends. Why, she had me put up a stand by the side of the road so she could sell baskets of fresh strawberries to folks passing by. But it wasn't about making a few extra pennies. She liked people. She genuinely *liked* people. And if someone stopped by, more often than not they'd end up in my sittin' room with a glass of lemonade and a plate of cookies."

The hands came off of Mason's shoulder, but they didn't part, and neither Mason nor Sarah made a move to correct the old man's assumption. In another life, Mason could easily have seen himself falling in love with Sarah, and he could imagine his other self living a peaceful, happy life with this incredible woman and her amazing daughter. But in this world, he wasn't *in love* with her, he simply *loved* her. Not as a wife, not as a girlfriend, not as a sister... but he loved her deeply and sincerely. And so, he was quite content to hold the hand of the woman he loved and let the old man think whatever he wanted to think.

"She sounds lovely," Sarah said at last.

"Oh, she was that," Daniel replied with a little catch in his throat. "She was that, and more…"

The barest crunch of gravel signalled the return of Christopher, this time with two others in tow; Addison in his sweater vest and dress pants, hitching his Buddy Holly glasses high up on his nose, and Alejandra in her leather jacket and skin-tight jeans, torn at one knee. Christopher set a pair of ten-gallon metal buckets on the ground near the Peterbilt, and they all gathered around Mason as he explained the mission. They listened to his every word as he laid out the plan, and when no one voiced any concerns or offered any suggestions, the entire team went back to work.

First, Sarah swapped her Howitzer for the .22 rifle and

took a position over the roof of the Peterbilt, with one foot inside the cab and the other braced against the open door, giving her a clear, 180-degree view of the lot. Then the others unslung their long-barreled weapons and left them leaning against the truck in favour of what they'd come to call their 'SBDs.' For Alejandra, it was a machete as long as her arm. Christopher had come across a long-handled hatchet somewhere along the way, and he'd since added some counterweight to give it the perfect balance. And Addison carried a unique weapon that he'd crafted himself and had lovingly dubbed 'The Nut-Buster.' It was a wooden baseball bat with a slot cut in the end, into which he'd fitted a ten-inch, shark-toothed blade from a circular-saw. A bolt through the middle of the blade and enough epoxy to choke a horse later, and the Nut-Buster was born. Silent but deadly indeed, and sharp enough to cleave through solid bone.

With one final pat on Clancy's head and a cautionary, "Not this time, Clance. You stay here and watch our backs," Mason grabbed the three empty jerry cans, Christopher took the metal buckets, and Alejandra led the way through the open door of the truck, across the cab, and out the other side. She flung the door open hard enough to bowl over a female echo, then she leapt down and finished the creature off with a slash through the skull. Addison followed and immediately joined in on finishing off the last two echoes, then they took up positions on either side to act as sentinels as Christopher and Mason emerged and sprinted across the parking lot.

Mason picked one of the two trucks at random and tapped lightly on the fuel tank. He grimaced, swore inside his head, and scurried around to the tank on other side. He tapped again, shot Christopher a grin, and positioned one of the buckets under the tank. The gas cap was locked, but even if it weren't, there were better ways of getting at what was inside than sucking up a mouthful of diesel fuel through a hose. With a single thrust of his blade on the underside of the tank, the fuel started to trickle. With another thrust to open up an air hole on the top of the tank, it literally gushed.

The bucket was filled in seconds. In a carefully choreographed move, Mason swapped the full bucket for one of the jerry cans, and Christopher lit off back to the Peterbilt as quickly as he could while spilling as little of the fuel as possible. Ten seconds later, he ran back with the empty bucket and sent Mason away with a full jerry can. Over and over, they took turns making the mad dash to Gloria, and when the gush of fuel slowed back to a trickle, they moved to the next truck and repeated the process.

The sentinels only had to act twice in those first minutes, and both times, the duty fell upon Addison. The first was a slow-moving echo, and a single blow from the Nut-Buster was enough to cleave its skull open all the way down to the bridge of its pert little nose. Then an alpha came charging in, screeching and clawing wildly at the air, so he wrenched the Nut-Buster free, took two light steps aside to let the thing hurtle past, and swung around backwards to catch the alpha in the lower back, just above the waistline of its little black cocktail dress. The creature continued to slash its perfectly-manicured claws even as it fell, but with its spine neatly severed, it could only crawl along on its elbows, gnashing its jaws and snarling like a jungle cat. One final blow ended the noise, but then another sound took its place as three, then four, then *five* alphas appeared out of nowhere and came charging in from both sides.

It just so happened that Mason had been running back with an empty jerry can when one of the alphas came straight at him from around a corner, so he used the nearest weapon at hand to defend himself. He swung the jerry can as hard as he could and caught the alpha on the side of its head with a resounding *clang!* but it barely fazed the creature. He hit it again, and then again and again, but he knew that he was only buying himself fractions of a second. But at last those fractions of a second added up, and he finally had the time and space to deliver a crushing kick to the alpha's knee. There was harsh *snap!* as the knee folded backwards, and as the creature teetered on the very brink of collapse, Mason pulled a knife from his belt and drove it up under the alpha's ribs, straight into its heart.

He looked to Alejandra and saw her slashing away like a lumberjack, hacking one leg deeply enough to spray a fountain of blood, then chopping another creature's hand off at the wrist before delivering a second blow that split the alpha's belly wide open. As the thing's guts unspooled onto the ground, she gave it one last whack to the neck, then she returned to the other creature spewing blood from its femoral artery, and calmly and deftly removed its head from its body.

On the other side, Addison had just taken down a spry teenaged alpha with the Nut-Buster through its throat, but when he lined up a similar shot on a little old female hobbling in on a shattered ankle, the alpha stumbled at the very last second and the saw blade drove straight through its gaping mouth, opening up its cheeks like a zipper. The creature's upper plate went flying, and its lower plate lodged at the back of its throat, yet it still came at him, snapping its gums and doing its best to snarl through a Joker grin that quite literally went from ear to ear.

Mason hurried the last few yards to find Christopher safely tucked between the big rigs, hurriedly screwing caps onto the other two jerry cans as the last of the diesel fuel trickled into a bucket. Mason grabbed both of the cans and motioned for Christopher to take the half-filled bucket, then he flicked his head back toward the Peterbilt and mouthed the single word, *"Go!"*

And that, Christopher did. He was young and he was fit, but the sloshing bucket slowed him down enough that Mason passed him by at a gallop and had the jerry cans shoved all the way across the floor of the cab before Christopher arrived. He took the bucket while Christopher hauled himself in, then he gingerly handed it back, careful not to spill a single drop.

That done, he went to the rear of the cab and unsaddled his own SBD. At seven feet long and two inches thick, the rebar had to weigh fifty pounds or more, but in Mason's hands, it might as well have been weightless. He gave it one quick spin as easily as twirling a feather, then he went to help his friends.

Addison and Alejandra were holding their own, but it wouldn't last. More alphas were coming, as Mason knew they would. The sounds of battle *always* brought more. Take down one and three took its place. Take down three and a dozen came. Take down a dozen and you'd better be prepared for all of Hell to come crashing down around your ears.

A quick count showed seven more coming at a run, but it was too late for Addison and Alejandra to break off from the fight and run. If they ran, they'd die, so this had to end, and it had to end fast.

Mason waded fearlessly into the path of the oncoming swarm and caved in two skulls in the time it took him to take a single breath. The three of them met in the middle then, and fought for all they were worth, while Sarah took aim over the hood of the Peterbilt and picked off any late-comers with a handclap. Barely a minute passed before the parking lot was littered with a dozen or more bodies, and the embattled trio could finally take a moment to catch their breath.

But they didn't have long. Five more alphas appeared from out of nowhere in a rage, and judging by the chorus of howls rising up from all around, Mason knew that the shit-storm had arrived.

He gave the signal, and all three of them ran for their lives.

Alejandra got to the truck first, but she stood guard until Addison arrived, huffing and puffing, and only once he had heaved himself in did she follow. Still, she waited in the door-way in a crouch while Mason clubbed one last alpha to dust, then she scampered across the cab as Mason leaped in and slammed the door shut against the swarm.

As the creatures raged and howled and pounded against a solid wall of grade-A Detroit steel, he squeezed his big frame awkwardly through the cab and out the other side. Sarah met him with a smile and a hug as he alit, Alejandra offered him a fist-bump and a high-five, and Daniel came up to him with eyes wide, jaw slack, and hand shakily extended.

"My word, Mace. If that was simply a group of friends taking care of each other, I pity the poor bastard who tries to do you harm."

Mason produced one last piece of licorice from his shirt pocket, popped the end of it into his mouth like a cigar, and shook the old man's hand.

"*I* don't," he said, slipping the rebar back into its cradle.

CHAPTER

III

So, you're risking your life to find a friend? That's very noble of you, Mace. And it speaks highly of you all!" Alejandra scoffed as she slid a sharpening stone down the length of her machete as gently and lovingly as if she were petting a dog.

"Every minute in this living Hell is a risk. What difference if we risk our lives here or there?"

No one raised a word of objection, Mason included. It might have been because most were busy eating, and Mason himself was trying like hell to wind spaghetti around a plastic fork and failing miserably, but in reality the question was perfectly valid. The entire world was a war zone. They were fighting for their lives every second of every day. What possible difference did it make where they fought?

"I wish I could offer everyone some fresh bread to sop up the sauce, but I'm afraid all I could find were crackers."

This was Inez. Christopher's mother, head chef, and ersatz mother of the entire group. Tall, stately, proud, the woman was as quick with a smile or a kind word as she was with the revolver on her hip.

"It's delicious, ma'am." Jesse beamed a smile. "I can't believe this came from a jar. It tastes better than homemade!"

"Well, aren't you sweet! Thank you, Jesse. The magic in any meal is always in the spices."

Mackenzie was knee-to-knee with Jesse, but she leaned even closer and whispered, "She has like a *thousand* little jars. She calls it her Chemistry Set."

Jesse's giggle was infectious enough to spread to the others, but it didn't last long.

"It's important to know for sure that our loved ones are dead," Beverly offered her own opinion to Daniel. "It doesn't make them any less dead, but at least we know."

And with that, the mood dropped like a stone.

Beverly. Poor, damaged Beverly. As far as Mason was concerned, the woman had been through more than any mother should ever have to bear. She hadn't just lost her child, she'd seen it torn to pieces by the swarm. She tried to hide her pain and fear behind a tough-as-nails facade, but Mason knew better. The horror of that experience had left a scar on that poor woman all the way down to the core.

With everyone suddenly and suspiciously focused entirely on their dinner, Mason spoke up to break the awkward silence.

"Becks means a lot to me, Daniel. Well, I suppose I should say that she *meant* a lot to me. Either way, she was a big part of my life, so yes, I have to know."

"And you're okay with this are you, Sarah?" Daniel asked, rather hesitantly.

Sarah popped an expertly wound ball of pasta into her mouth and laid a gentle hand on Mason's knee. "Of course!

Whole-heartedly!"

"Becks had a place in the Mission District," Mason offered, scowling at Sarah's success with the spaghetti while he was having none of his own. "But the whole block was gone, burned to the ground. Might've been a gas leak, or maybe just a candle that got knocked over. Whatever. But the last call my phone registered was from her parents' landline in San Bruno, so I assume it was her. She must've gone there when we, uh... *after* we... Well, anyway, if she's anywhere, she'll be there."

Again, he'd left a word out. A single word. *Alive*. If she's anywhere *alive*, she'll be there.

For the first few days after this whole thing started, in those few moments when he'd thought about Becks at all, it had always been in the past tense. He'd already had time to relegate her to the past after she left him, then the world ended to seal the deal. And from then on, the past really *was* the past. Dead. Buried. Forgotten. It was enough just to try staying alive for one more day or one more hour or one more minute without dwelling on what used to be. But then the strangest thing happened. A tiny little girl managed to teach him the power of hope. He began to think of a possible future, and with it, little bits of the past began to bleed through. It was only then that he realized what a double-edged sword this thing called 'hope' really was.

Did he believe Becks was alive? No. Of course not. The odds were infinitesimal at best. If she was at home when the world ended, she'd either been torn to shreds or turned to ash. Even if that last call had been from her, all the way down in San Bruno, the odds were exactly the same. Becks was dead, sure as shit. She couldn't *possibly* be alive. No way. Not a chance. There was no way on Earth she could still be alive. And yet, through it all, one abiding, *insane* thought kept nagging away at the back of his mind.

Could she be?

"Normally, it would be a twenty-minute drive," Addison mumbled between mouthfuls. "But with the highway blocked and the surface roads not much better, it's taken us two days just to get this far."

"We know about the roads, don't we, Grampa?" Jesse sighed.

"Oh, indeed we do. You were quite right to use the term 'bottleneck,' Mace."

Mason tried one last time to get more than two strands of spaghetti onto the plastic fork at a time, then he gave up completely, threw the fork over his shoulder, and reached into his back pocket. Like a magician pulling a rabbit from a hat, he whipped out a good-old stainless steel fork, and as the others looked on in varying degrees of surprise and amusement, he set about emptying his bowl.

"Where do you keep the parmesan cheese?" Addison asked, deadpan. "In your snood?"

Mason ignored him.

"It won't be easy, Daniel, that's for sure. With the I-280 out, we'll have to slug our way through one of a half-dozen surface roads between Lake Merced and the hills. It won't be so much a bottleneck as a gauntlet."

"I can attest to that," the old man harrumphed. "We got this far and could go no farther. My idea was to stock up on what supplies we could, then try going up around the lake. I don't much like the idea of backtracking so far, but..."

"Bad idea, Daniel," Sarah said, cutting him off.

"One way in, one way out." This from Christopher.

"Never go anywhere unless you have a back door," Beverly concluded. Suddenly disinterested in her dinner, she laid her bowl aside in favour of a pull from a half-pint bottle of scotch.

Mason levelled a scowl at Beverly, but not because she was drinking. Hell, he was no stranger to the bottle himself. In fact, there were times when he'd thought it'd be best for all concerned if every one of them maintained a perpetual semi-buzz as they wandered through this hellscape. No, he scowled at her because the bottle was one of *his*.

But the scowl was fleeting, ultimately. Beverly was part of the team, so what was his was hers. The pistol on her hip and the shotgun slung across her back were from his own personal armory, so she was welcome to his booze every bit as she was to the guns. Perhaps even more so, if it helped to numb the pain.

"I reckon that leaves the canyon road out, too," Daniel sighed as he set his bowl on the floor, then he remembered his manners and turned to Inez with a warm smile. "That was absolutely delicious, my dear. A hot meal was a godsend. Thank you so very much!"

Inez waved the compliment away. "All I did was boil water and open a few jars. Point me in the direction of a proper kitchen and turn me loose, and I'll show you some *real* cooking!"

"Spaghetti sure beats the snot out of cold soup and dry cereal *any* day," Jesse said, eliciting a cute little giggle from Mackenzie.

Clancy had already had his dinner, but with so many discarded bowls lying around, he began snorfling his way from one to the other, gobbling up what was left and licking the bowls clean. Far from being scolded, he was greeted with head pats and neck scratches from everyone in turn.

"Well, there's enough food in here to keep you going for

a while," Mason said, finishing off his meal with a flourish, then licking the fork clean and slipping it back into his pocket. "You're welcome to it all. You can even take the camp stove, too. And if there's anything you need that we might have, we'll see what we can spare."

A distinct sadness washed over the old man's face as he gave Mason a single nod. "That's very generous. Thank you, Mace. Thank you all for being so very kind."

Another awkward silence then, until Mackenzie turned to Mason and asked what the rest of them were undoubtedly thinking.

"Can't they come with us, Mace?" she asked sweetly.

Mack was the first child he'd ever really known, but he'd recently come to suspect that every kid must be born knowing how to say things in just such a way to cut like a knife through every adult's heart.

He saw Jesse look to her grandfather, and though she said not a word, he caught a hint of something behind her expressionless face. Fear? No. That wasn't it. Not exactly. Desperation, maybe? No, that wasn't it, either.

Then he had it. It was such a new thing to him, it was no wonder it'd taken him so long. The girl was looking to her grandfather with hope. She *hoped* he would give in. She *hoped* that it would somehow work out. She *hoped* that they wouldn't have be alone anymore.

Watch how tightly you hold that double-edged sword, sweetheart… he told her inside his head. *When that sucker cuts, it cuts deep…*

"Mack…" he started to say, but Daniel put up a hand to stop him.

"I'm sorry, my dear," he said to Mackenzie, "but we really do have to get home."

"Why?" Alejandra butted in, taking a moment to remoisten the whetstone with a gob of spit. "You leave the water running or something? *Madre... what's* at home that's so much better than anywhere else in *esta locura?*"

"It is *home,* my dear," Daniel informed her, clearly and precisely. "It is *home.*"

Addison slurped up the last of his spaghetti, and with a quick look into the pot on the stove and a resultant sigh, he laid the empty bowl down for Clancy to lick clean.

"So, what then?" he said, ruffling the big dog's ears. "You guys'll live on strawberries and goat milk for the rest of your lives?"

"Actually," Daniel had a sudden inspiration, "now that you mention it, the Montcliefs down the road have goats. I'm sure they would have fared just fine with ten acres of open field, even if Terence and Judith had been less fortunate. Have you ever tasted goat's milk, Addison? It is surprisingly sweet!"

"Hey, Grampa, what about the Johnstones?" Jesse said, displaying more of that pesky *hope.* "They have chickens, don't they?"

"Indeed, they do!" Daniel gave his knee a slap. "And the Bertronellis have pigs, the Wittickers have horses, and I believe there might even be a cow or two within walking distance. So there you are, Addison! Milk, eggs, bacon, transportation..."

Addison turned to Alejandra as she held her machete to her eye to check its edge. "Actually, it sounds pretty good."

She replied with an indifferent sideways head-bob and slid the blade back into its sheath. "Not bad," she admitted at last.

All of a sudden, it sounded not bad to Mason, too. In fact,

it sounded a whole lot better than not bad. Until now, he hadn't wasted a moment's thought on what they would do... *after*. That single word held so much promise and so much horror that he hadn't allowed himself to even consider it. But the way Daniel described that impossible future with such conviction, an *after* seemed almost within reach. He didn't go so far as to imagine himself in that idyllic world, but he put Sarah and Mack and the rest of them there, and that image brought him a certain amount of peace.

If he could do that much for Sarah and for Mack and for the others, he could die happy. He need only imagine Mack and Clancy frolicking through the grass and Sarah standing on a porch, laughing at their antics, to know how much he suddenly wanted them to have an *after*. He even considered declaring right then and there that he should go on to San Bruno alone and that they should all go with Daniel and have that idyllic *after*, but even as he considered the idea, he knew it would never happen. Sarah would never allow it, and Mack would never allow it, and that would end the debate. Then he considered how low the chances were of finding Becks alive and whether or not there was any point in trying at all, but that road was a dead-end too. As long as there was a shred of hope of finding Becks, he had to try.

Careful how tightly you hold that sword, Mace...

"You're all welcome," Daniel said at last, burying the blade even deeper. "Most of the property is open, but two acres around the house are fenced, and I'm sure a few strong backs could expand that acreage considerably."

Secretly, Mason hoped that at least some of them would snap at the bait. Inez, maybe? She was a fifty-year old woman. Surely, she'd be more comfortable milking goats than fighting for her life. And Beverly? Poor Beverly had been through enough. Would anyone blame her if she opted for cows and horses over alphas and echoes? If even one of these incredible people took Daniel up on his offer, just *one*, then Mason could consider his life well spent.

But then Mackenzie spoke up and drove the blade straight through his heart.

"We have to find Becks," she said, and Mason could almost hear her adding the silent words, *or die trying...*

CHAPTER

IV

With the highway turned into a parking lot, the options were few. Mission Street flanked the I-280, but that way was jammed, too. The only other option was John Daly Boulevard heading west, but they'd passed by it the day before and Mason hadn't had to look beyond the burned wreckage of an ancient pile-up to know that Daly wasn't going to cut it.

"So, what then?" Sarah asked, struggling to fold a blanket-sized map into the appropriate square. "Brotherhood Way to Lake Merced? Daly to Fairview Drive?"

"I have another idea," he said, cranking the big truck to life and throwing it into gear. "You'll want to buckle up. It might get a bit bumpy."

"I don't think I like the sound of that..." he heard Christopher whisper from behind.

Mackenzie corralled Clancy into the sleeper cab, and she and Inez and Christopher braced themselves as best they could as Mason set out with two other vehicles close on his tail.

The first was an old pickup, like something out of an old episode of The Waltons. Chevy. Mid-forties, if he had to guess. It belched the occasional puff of blue exhaust, but by Daniel's reckoning, it had never let him down before, so it wasn't about to now. The second was a beautifully-restored 1969 Mustang Mach 1 with Alejandra behind the wheel, Addison hanging on for dear life beside her, and Beverly huddled in the back seat. Mason remembered Alejandra getting all gooey over the Boss 9 engine and forged steel cranks when she discovered the vehicle on a hoist at one of their safe houses, but she'd failed to mention the 300-watt sound system filling the trunk. Even before they started, Alejandra pushed a button and the music started blaring, and Mason couldn't complain one iota. They were safely wrapped in a shell of strong American steel, and he had to admit that if there was a better way of shouting out to the world, '"We're still alive, motherfuckers!'" he didn't know it. Besides, who on Earth would be stupid enough to tell the Latina spitfire to turn down the tunes?

Mason pulled the Peterbilt out of the parking lot to the opening twangs of an electric guitar and a stand-up bass, then the unmistakable voice of the great Chuck Berry howled out of the Mustang.

I bought a brand-new air-mobile... It was custom-made, 'twas a Flight De Ville... With a pow'rful motor and some hideaway wings... Push in on the button and you can hear her sing...

Mason cleaved effortlessly through a pack of charging alphas and bashed a half-dozen abandoned vehicles easily aside, thanks in no small part to one more alteration they'd made to the big truck's design. He had dismissed Christopher's suggestion at first, but after a lot of scrounging and considerably more experimentation with a welding torch than either of them would care to admit, they'd eventually managed to affix three big metal struts to the truck's chassis and cover them with two plates of heavy-gauge steel. It was crude and it was ugly and it shot their gas mileage to hell, but Christopher had been spot-on correct when he'd extolled the virtue of the thing. What they had now was a cowcatcher, as strong and as solid as any that might have graced the nose of any old-time steam locomotive.

The abandoned cars peeled off to either side, and Mason pulled the Peterbilt onto Brotherhood Way. The incongruously named road was more of a highway, and as such, it had become as much a parking lot as every other major route out of the city, complete with its compliment of the dead and undead. During the panic, there were always some poor fools who'd opted to remain in the relative safety of their vehicles rather than face the desperate mobs outside, not realizing that they were locking themselves *in* with something far worse. All it took was for Mom or Dad or little Becky-Sue to get sick, and the rest of them were turned into chum. Some of those family-killers had managed to escape by clawing madly at the doors and getting lucky with a door handle, but not all. Even as Mason took to the shoulder to skirt the worst of it, he could see alphas raging away behind tempered glass streaked and spotted with ancient blood.

Just then, and in a display of the worst timing imaginable, one of those imprisoned alphas was whipped into a frenzy by the sound of Gloria's big motor, and chose just that moment to break free. A door popped open, a teenaged alpha in a blood-stained hoodie burst out, and Mason drove blithely into it, pinning it against the door, then ripping the door completely off of the car. The sight elicited a moan of disgust from

Inez and an excited little *whoop!* from Christopher, but that one alpha was hardly alone. Everywhere the big truck went, it acted as a gigantic dinner bell, stirring up alphas for miles around. They came from behind, they came from in front, and they came from every direction in between. They stumbled, they fell, and they ran blindly into one impediment or another, but they never stopped coming.

Never.

Mason kept the Peterbilt as close to the shoulder as he could, but even so, he continually had to push vehicles out of the way. Some were unoccupied, some weren't, but he treated them all with equal disregard. If it was a small enough car, he would simply maintain speed and punt the vehicle out of the way. If the vehicle was heavier or in a tangle with one or more others, it required a more delicate touch, so he would slow to a crawl and use Gloria's considerable muscles to bulldoze the lot of them to one side or the other. At one point, he came across a van and an SUV wedged solidly against a light pole, and they steadfastly refused to budge. But by backing off and coming at them from a slightly different angle, they finally rolled clear, crushing two alphas in the process, and at last there was room to escape the parking lot.

He bounded the truck down an incline, opened up space for the others through a cluster of cars, and made a hard left onto a side street. It looked more like an access road than a thruway, but it was clear enough that he could finally pick up speed again.

Sarah tried to follow their progress on the map, but she was having little success.

"Thomas More? Is that what the sign said?"

As she folded and refolded the map, Christopher piped up from the back, "Hey, I saw that movie! Richard Burton, right?"

"Mmm... Now *there* was a good-looking man," Inez purred.

Mason checked his mirrors and saw the swarm falling behind, and with the road treed on both sides, he couldn't blame Alejandra for rolling her window down and hanging out an arm. On the other hand, Daniel and Jesse kept the windows of the pickup closed tight, and he couldn't blame them either.

Soon enough, the access road ended at something resembling a paved footpath. Someone in the back hushed, "Uh oh," but Mason didn't stop. He slowed just enough to make the turn, then he swung the wheel to the right and made that footpath his own. Branches slapped against the windshield and threatened to tear away the mirrors, but then they broke into the open and Sarah barely had time for a quick, "Uh, Mace?" before the truck peeled off the path and onto a bright green lawn.

"Anyone up for quick round?" Christopher laughed aloud as Mason steered them straight down the middle of one of the San Francisco Golf Club's immaculately-groomed fairways.

He ploughed over a pair of alphas in garishly-patterned pantaloons and tore up a hundred square feet of grass as he swerved around a sand trap, and as he launched an abandoned golf cart high into the trees, the music from Alejandra's red rocket switched tracks. Whether it was a sly dig at Addison or a random pick of the MP3 player, Mason hadn't a clue, but it was a song he knew well, and he couldn't help but sing along.

Well, that'll be the day, when you say goodbye, Ye-e-es that'll be the day, when you make me cry-y, You say you're gonna leave, you know it's a lie, 'Cause that'll be the day-ay-ay when I die...

Inez joined in, then Christopher, and finally Sarah joined in too, and with all four of them doing four distinctly off-key Buddy Holly impressions, all Mackenzie could do was hang on for dear life and laugh as if it was the funniest thing she'd ever seen in her life.

Mason swerved the truck around a copse of trees and cut across two more fairways, rolling over countless dead and undead along the way, and tearing up hundreds of yards of the finest and most expensive grass in all of San Francisco, then he took a hard left and skirted between two particularly deep sand traps.

At last, he maneuvered the monster truck through a final tangle of trees as easily as if he were on a dirt bike and emerged onto a narrow path barely wide enough to accommodate Gloria's girth.

One quick turn later and they were on a green-belt between two housing complexes, and alphas suddenly came screaming in at them from both sides. The big truck slewed and skidded on the grass as Mason took intentional aim at as many creatures as he could to clear the way for the others, then he cranked the wheel hard, bounced over a curb, and drove onto and through an empty baseball field. He stopped on the pitcher's mound just long enough to make sure that the Walton-mobile was keeping up and to allow the low-riding Mustang to creep gingerly up and over the curb at a crawl, then they were off again.

The twists and turns through this suburban Hell had Sarah continuously folding and unfolding and refolding the map, but even after spreading the whole thing out on the dashboard and still unable to make heads or tails of the thing, she finally gave up. She crumpled it into a ball and threw it out the window with a snort, eliciting an amused giggle from

STAGE 3: BRAVO

Mackenzie and a roof-raising howl of laughter from Inez.

They crossed under the I-280, and Mason finally pulled the truck over. He keyed it off and waved an arm through the open window, and dutifully, Alejandra cut the music just as Country Joe and the Fish were telling everyone to lay down their books and pick up their gun.

The old Chev pulled up to Gloria's flank as Jesse rolled down her window.

"That's Mission Road up ahead," he called down to her. "If I were you, I'd stay on that road as far as possible. It'll take you all the way down to Burlingame, and hopefully the highway will be more open by then."

Before Jesse could relay the message, Daniel leaned across to the passenger side and doffed his imaginary cap. "I know the way from here, Mace. Thank you so very much! I wish you the very best of luck, my friend. *All* of you! And if you happen to be anywhere near Pescadero..."

Mason counted more than a dozen alphas closing in, so he waved his goodbyes and put the truck back into gear. But then Sarah leaned over him and stuck her head out the window.

"You both be safe!" she shouted down to the old pickup that suddenly looked incredibly tiny. "Take care of each other! Always!"

"We will!" Jesse called back, her eyes suddenly filling with tears.

Sarah receded, and again Mason waved his goodbyes, but then Mackenzie appeared from out of the back and crawled bodily over him to the window.

"Jesse!" she fairly howled, "Jesse! Will you teach me how to milk a goat?"

A tear streaked down the girl's face, but she still had to

laugh.

"Sure! I'll have to teach myself first, but then I'll teach you!"

They gave each other a little wave, and the Chevy pulled slowly away. It swung around the corner, and just like that, Daniel and Jesse were gone.

Mackenzie crawled off Mason's lap and into Sarah's, and the inside of the Peterbilt was suddenly deathly quiet. Mason considered any number of things he could say that might lift the girl's spirits, but ultimately, he said nothing. Sarah didn't say a word, either. She simply tucked Mackenzie's little face into her neck and stroked her hair, then she reached a hand out for Mason, and that simple touch said more than either of them could ever convey with words.

At last, the gathering swarm was close enough that Addison began waving frantically for them to get the show on the road, so Mason eased the truck forward with one hand on the wheel and the other tucked into Sarah's. And as he did, Country Joe and the Fish returned at full volume.

And it's five, six, seven, open up the pearly gates. Well, there ain't no time to wonder why, Whoopee! we're all gonna die...

CHAPTER

V

Suburban Hell, indeed.

Never before had those words been more apropos.

Like so much of the Bay Area, San Bruno had been a city planner's wet dream. Row after row of cookie-cutter bungalows, all conforming to strict community standards. A postage stamp of grass cut to within an inch of its life, not a single shrub or flower stinking the place up unless expressly authorized by committee, and nothing as incongruous as a wind chime or a lawn chair, or God *forbid*, a child's swing-set anywhere in view.

On a regular day, Mason regarded this sort of neighbourhood much like he did one of those multilevel birdhouses. Just like purple martins in their condos, these people crammed themselves in, one on top of the other, and they got along only through a mutually agreed-upon social convention. An obligatory wave to the neighbour across the way. Empty garbage cans removed from the curb forthwith. TV sets turned down after eight pm. If little Suzy or Billy or

Bobby was having a birthday party, every other kid on the street had to receive an invitation whether they were friends or not. As long as the rules were followed, the flock got along just fine, but when the shit hit the fan, the rules of a polite society didn't just break down, they went up in a funeral pyre.

As Mason weaved the truck through that suburban Hell, the way in which those final days unfolded was all too evident. Here, a body crumpled across a curb. There, an entire family splayed out around a little grease spot in an empty driveway. On this side of the road, a soccer mom in a minivan, slumped over the wheel. On the other, a child's body hanging half-in and half-out of a shattered front window.

Fucking humans... Mason muttered inside his head.

It was always the same. People rallied around marches for the climate and for equal rights and for gun control, they tweeted the shit out of government overreach and civil injustice and banning the ivory trade, and their Facebook pages were all about love and sunshine and rainbows and unicorns. But just beneath that carefully-crafted mask of civility, every human being on the planet was exactly the same. Shake their cozy little world, and out came the caveman.

That nice guy next door has food, so take it! The couple you play canasta with every Saturday has a van full of fuel, so make it yours! The girl across the street who babysits your kid is home alone, so get over there while her parents are dying elsewhere and help yourself!

Christ, it was always the same. Always. Mason generally regarded the human race as he would a swarm of flies buzzing high above the dinner table. They were annoying, but as long they kept their distance, he did his best to tolerate them. But the minute they drifted down and became anything more than annoying, he'd gladly swat the whole lot of them out of existence. And now, as he gazed out upon the crystal-clear evidence of mankind at its worst, he would have given anything for the mother of all fly swatters.

Mackenzie was watching the carnage from Sarah's lap, and Sarah made no attempt whatsoever to shield the child's eyes from the horrors all around. As she'd expressed to Mason not twelve hours before, speaking in whispers as Mackenzie slept, this was *her* world now, every bit as much as it was theirs. And perhaps even more so. With any luck, she would be living in this hellscape long after they were dead and buried, so she had to know it all. And indeed, this *was* her world now. *This*, right here.

Certainly, the girl had seen death and destruction before, but this was something else. Most of this carnage had happened in the first days of the panic, long before anyone had heard of stage 2 or stage 3 or wilders or alphas. This was man's inhumanity to man at its most unambiguous, and the horrors mankind was able to mete out on its own far exceeded the savagery of any swarm.

A man lay across the threshold of an open front door. The door was splintered on one side, undoubtedly kicked in with the same boot that'd then proceeded to stomp him to death. A dead woman and baby lay in a driveway in front of a vacant garage, the child in a broken little pile and the mother crushed by the wheels of her own car, stolen by another. A naked girl lay spread-eagle on an overgrown postage stamp of a lawn, her torn clothes scattered all around, save for the brassiere they'd used to strangle her life away still coiled around her neck.

The images went on and on, and aside from the occasional gasp from Inez or hushed curse from Christopher, they went on in silence. Mackenzie said not a word, nor did she betray any emotion whatsoever. She simply sat there in Sarah's lap, taking it all in.

At one point, Mason shouldered a minivan aside, filled with rampaging shadows and tiny bloody hands clawing at the windows, then he drove up onto the sidewalk to avoid a cluster of miniature bodies in the middle of the road, all of them still in their Little League jerseys. When he bounced down on the other side, he crushed an old woman's body to pulp under his wheels, then two alphas appeared from a side street and he accelerated into them, flinging their broken bodies to either side with the cowcatcher. And through it all, Mackenzie didn't bat an eye.

At last, he swung the truck around one last corner and slowed to a crawl. This was the street. Mason had only been here once, for an ill-conceived Thanksgiving dinner that had ended with him and Becks' father almost coming to blows, but that street and that house were forever etched in his mind.

And there it was. A simple little bungalow among a hundred clones. Mason pulled up in front of the house, keyed the truck off, and did the math.

The front door was closed. Garage door, too. A double gouge had been torn into the postage stamp lawn. And most importantly, someone had scribbled a big X on the front door of the house with a black marking pen. In the top quadrant of the X were the numbers 7-6. In the right quadrant, an X with a square drawn around it. In the left, the abbreviation DS 5871. In the bottom quadrant was 3 - ?, and below that, an arrow pointing west and the word 'Skyline.' And so the story was told.

"She's not here," Mason said aloud.

"What?" Inez howled from behind. "How can you possibly know that?"

STAGE 3: BRAVO

Mason took no offence at her tone, nor at Christopher squatting down between the seats and huffing, "What you got, Mace, X-ray eyes?" He simply laid out the information, point by point.

"Becks' old man had a Camaro. She showed it to me once. '67. Lovingly restored. Great for cruising around town or tearing up the race track, but wholly impractical for escaping the city with a wife and daughter and a few cherished possessions."

"I've seen how men are with their toys, Mace." Inez raised an eyebrow. "If you're talking about cherished possessions, seems to me that car would be number one."

"Not for a practical man like Becks' father. Too low, too loud, and too thirsty."

"The garage door," Mackenzie said distractedly.

"That's right, Mack, the garage door," he told her, then he explained it to the others. "The man was a cop, so he would've kept doing his job right up to when things truly went to shit. By then, the power would've already been out, so even if he was stupid enough to try to flee the city in a fifty-year old muscle car, he wouldn't have been stupid enough to stop the car and risk life and limb just to close the garage door."

"And you figured that out too, Mackenzie?" Inez asked her, sweetly.

"She's wise beyond her years," Sarah answered, almost automatically.

"As well," Mason went on, "the man was meticulous. I mean, just look at this house! Not a blade of grass out of place. Not a single drop of oil in the driveway. Not a single leaf in the rain gutter. But there are gouges in the lawn right up to the front door that look suspiciously like tire tracks. Now, being a sergeant with the SBPD, he would've been assigned his own squad car. Those tire tracks were obviously made when he came back for his family, too hurried and too scared to give a shit about his perfect little lawn."

"Okay, Sherlock," Christopher nodded, "I'm with you so far. So what's with the graffiti on the front door? They don't look like dancing men to me."

Mason didn't get the reference, but he carried on, even as three alphas emerged from behind a house somewhere farther up the street and came howling down the middle of the road toward them.

"That's a code FEMA uses when they've searched a building following a natural disaster. It's commonly referred to as an 'X-code.' The numbers on the top of the X are the date. July 6th. That's the day Mack and I found each other. The day Sarah's hospital was overrun..."

"The day the world ended," Inez grumbled.

"The symbol on the right? That 'X' inside a box? That's FEMA code for 'do not enter.' The left side of the X is to identify the searcher. In this case, Detective Sergeant Gary Hansen wrote his own badge number. The bottom of the X is for how many living or dead were found in the structure. In this case, there were three survivors and a question mark for the dead."

"Three survivors!" Sarah hooted, "That means Becks *was* here! Oh, thank God!"

"Don't go thanking him yet," Mason said, not wanting to take hold of that double-edged sword quite so tightly. "That third person could have been anybody. Mother-in-law. Neighbor. Paperboy. Hell, it could have been *anybody*."

Sarah didn't push it.

"Alright, Mace," she said, "So, three survivors and a question mark for the dead. The only way a question mark makes sense is if the place was overrun, which also accounts for the 'do not enter.' But what's with the arrow, and what's 'Skyline'?"

"Skyline College is a couple of miles away. Clearly, the man was familiar with FEMA protocol, and being a cop, he would have been well-acquainted with the community's disaster preparedness plan. I can only assume that Skyline College was designated as an emergency shelter, and the arrow is to tell anyone who cared that that was where they were heading. The only question is whether or not they made it."

In fact, that wasn't the only question. Not by a long shot. But there was no point in bringing up the hundred or so others presently banging around inside his head. He shouted a few clipped words down to Addison and saw Alejandra's thumb stick high up over the roof to tell him she'd understood. Beverly's face appeared at the side window, but only long enough to throw the empty scotch bottle in the general direction of the charging alphas. She sank back into the shadows, and Mason thought no more about it, but then the muzzle of a shotgun snuck out through the open window behind Addison, and everyone was too slow to react.

The first explosion caught them all by surprise. and had them jumping in their seats and reaching for their own weapons. Poor Addison was the closest to the shot, so he suffered the most. He hit his head on the car's ceiling, then he instinctively ducked away from the window, nearly landing in Alejandra's lap.

"*Puta madre!*" Alejandra howled, shoving him back.

As far as Mason was concerned, few weapons were more awesome than a twelve-gauge shotgun. Every shell sent eight .33 calibre rounds downrange at nearly two thousand feet per second. Close up, they could cut a man to bits. At fifty yards, they could take down two men standing eight feet apart. For someone with indefinite aim or shaky hands or a snootful of scotch, they were most certainly the weapon of choice. A truly awesome weapon indeed.

But Jesus *Christ* were they loud! If the .22 was a handclap and the Glock on his hip a cannon, that damn shotgun was a nuclear bomb! Yes, Beverly got lucky and took down one of the alphas with a single hit to the chest, but two more came chasing after the explosion from a side street, and then two more after that.

Beverly pumped the shotgun, and before anyone could stop her, she fired again. A second alpha dropped to the ground twenty yards away, but it hadn't been a clean kill, so the thing took to crawling along on its elbows, squealing like a feral pig and dragging its shattered legs behind.

Finally, Alejandra wrestled herself out from under Addison and reached over the seat, snatching the gun away from Beverly. The woman cursed a blue streak and tried to grab the gun back, but nobody won a tug-of-war against Alejandra. Mason couldn't hear every word of the ensuing shouting match, but at last, the shotgun was passed to Addison and he clutched it in his tight little hands, telling Beverly, "No, no, no... You can have your toy back when you learn how to play nice!"

The drama was over, but it had come at a hefty price. The first wave of alphas crashed into the Mustang just as the windows were cranked shut, and more surrounded the Peterbilt like a pack of rabid wolves. Behind them, more were coming. And behind them, more still. And it wouldn't end there. Those nuclear blasts would bring every alpha from miles around.

Mason turned a scowl toward Sarah, but she only shrugged.

"She's scared," she said, simply.

"We're *all* scared," Christopher reminded her.

"It's what you do when you're scared that matters," Inez chimed in.

Mason said nothing and keyed the truck back to life. There was a series of bumps and snaps and the barest skidding of tires as he rolled over the vanguard of the swarm, and there was one frightening moment when a creature bounced up onto the hood of the Mustang and began clawing away at the windshield, but eventually the numbers started to thin out and everything was silent inside the truck, save for the occasional sound of an alpha coming apart on the cowcatcher.

No one spoke for some time, but then Mackenzie looked over from Sarah's lap and fixed Mason with her big green eyes.

"Beverly was stupid, and stupid gets people killed," she said, as coolly as if she were commenting on the weather. "We should leave her behind. Or maybe we should just shoot her."

CHAPTER

VI

The rest of the drive was made in total silence. No doubt, Christopher and his mother were wary of stepping into what was already a supremely awkward situation, so they sat there silently, hand in hand, as the world swirled by. As for Mason, there was certainly some of that as well, but the main reason he kept his mouth shut was because he had no idea how to respond.

Mack had a cold, clear grasp of the world she'd inherited, and she wasn't wrong... entirely. Beverly had just done a very stupid thing that put them all in danger, and Mack was simply looking out for herself and for Sarah and for the others. Okay, fair enough. Good for her. But did one dumb move earn Beverly a bullet in the head? Was that the way this world worked now? Well, this was *Mack's* world, so maybe she knew better than any of them. Hell, maybe *she* should be in charge and he could just follow blindly along. Come to think of it, if she *were* in charge, they'd be skipping through strawberry fields in Pescadero at this very minute instead of picking their way through suburban Hell, and that wouldn't be a bad thing at all.

He cast a quick glance to Sarah, hoping that she would say something to Mack and he could follow her lead, but she said nothing, and Mason couldn't blame her. After all, what was the right way to handle this? Tell her she's wrong? Tell her she's *right*? She was neither, and yet she was both. This world of hers was fucked up six ways to Sunday, so who knew what was right anymore?

Hey, Sarah... he said inside his head. *Don't kids just say the darnedest things?*

The drive should have taken minutes. Hop on the 280, across to the 380, jump off at the Golden Gate Cemetery, and a straight shot to Skyline Boulevard. But sticking to surface roads had them back-pedaling and circling around and cutting down back lanes so often that Mason's internal guidance system was stretched to its limits. It took the better part of an hour just to reach a vast suburban maze that Mason knew would get them there, then another two hours to get through it. And of course the swarm came and the swarm raged and the swarm clawed at the truck and at the Mustang, and no matter how many fell beneath the wheels or were thrown to the ground like rag dolls, they just kept coming.

At one point, Mason got so turned around in the maze that he had to drive onto and through an elementary school yard, dragging a twenty-foot section of chain link fence behind like the tail of a kite, then he had to hop a little berm and manoeuvre the big truck between two houses without an inch to spare. He and Sarah both reached out and folded the side mirrors in, but even so, Gloria had to peel entire sections of aluminum siding away and bulldoze a wooden fence into kindling before she was back on the road. And still, the creatures came.

All along the way, Mason kept watch to make sure that the Mustang was keeping up, and every time he checked, he saw Beverly's shadowy head bobbing around in the back seat, and he wondered. Then he'd toss a glance to the seat beside him and see that precious little girl curled up in Sarah's arms, and he'd wonder some more.

But then he took one last bend in the road, and all of those thoughts vanished in an instant. A long, flat road running north to south stretched out across their path. This was Skyline Boulevard. Beyond it, he could just make out the top floors of several buildings at the end of a curved, double-lane road. They were out of suburban Hell, at last. This was Skyline College. They were there.

Well, *halle*-fuckin'-*lujah*...

There were muted cheers from Inez and Christopher, and a quick check of the mirror showed Addison pumping his fist excitedly, but a nagging unease stirred deep down inside Mason's belly as he crossed the road and started down the aptly named College Drive. He wasn't exactly sure what he'd expected to find here, but as the college rose into view and he was afforded a better look at the buildings and the grounds, he realized that what he'd actually been expecting could be summed up in a single word.

More.

He'd expected more.

Maybe not military helicopters and machine-gun nests and barricades, but he'd expected more. Simply that. More.

He pushed a little Prius out of the way, then stopped the truck again to have a good, hard look at the place.

A home field proudly proclaiming the name 'Trojans' was positioned at the front of the complex. Beyond that were a couple of practice fields and a baseball diamond. And beyond that was the college itself. Nine or ten squat buildings clustered around a central concourse.

And aside from that, nothing. Nothing whatsoever. No army. No marines. No ambulances. No emergency shelters. Not even a single tent where that elusive Red Cross nurse would greet him with a coffee and a donut.

He scanned every inch of the place, and apart from the bodies and parts of bodies littering the fields and the baseball diamond and the concourse and the rest of the grounds, he doubted that there was a single bit of difference between what this place had been before and what it was now.

"It happened too fast." Sarah finally broke the awful silence. "Before they'd even decided it was an emergency, it was already too late."

"Too late," Mackenzie echoed, barely above a whisper.

Christopher came up between the seats to have a better look. "One day, it's a flu bug. The next, it's Armageddon."

"I didn't dare hope out loud," Inez admitted, sullenly. "But deep down, I was still hoping."

"Too late," Mason hushed.

"So, what do we do now?" Christopher asked. Then, he laid a finger on the side of his head as if he'd just had a revelation. "Hey Mace, I happen to know about this little strawberry farm in Pescadero—"

Sarah cut him off. "We still have to look," she said, ending the debate before it could begin.

Alphas were already tearing across the fields and down the road and out from suburban Hell, but Mason let them come as he sank deep in thought.

The math was simple. If he had been in Becks' father's shoes in those first few days of bedlam, he would have taken one look at this place and given it a wide berth. Too many buildings. Too many people. Too few ways in and out. An emergency shelter after an earthquake, fine. But not now. No way. Not unless the army had already taken over the place with all their little tanks in a row. But figuring out the kind of math that went on inside someone else's head wasn't always easy, so he put himself to the task of answering a decidedly difficult question. Just what the hell would his ex-future-father-in-law have done?

Of course, the first consideration was the man's intelligence. He'd only met Detective Sergeant Gary Hansen once, and loathe as he was to admit it, he found him to be a highly intelligent man. One didn't make the rank of Detective Sergeant by chance, after all. And besides, stupid died quick, in which case, the man was already dead and he'd taken his whole family with him. So, alright then, let's say that this smart man had managed to keep his loved ones alive long enough to get here. What then would a clever man, a clever *police*man, do when he arrived at a theoretical emergency shelter and found nothing?

He would have radioed in, of course, but by then he would've heard only static. And the power was out, so no cell towers and no phones. So what does he do? He has his family in the car, the city has gone mad, the roads are nigh impossible to navigate without a big rig and a cowcatcher, there's no help coming, and he has zero contact with the outside world. So what does he do? What does this clever man, this clever *police*man... do?

He threw a signal down to Addison and roared the big truck to life, wheeling it directly onto the football field.

"If they're alive, they're here," he said, just that simply. "If they're not here, they're dead."

STAGE 3: BRAVO

Not surprisingly, not a single objection was raised, and all eyes were suddenly glued to the windows as Mason pulled the truck onto the practice field. Alphas came thundering in from all sides to either rage against Gloria's flanks, be crushed beneath her giant wheels, or come apart like sock puppets on her cowcatcher. A quick glimpse in the mirror showed the Mustang faring no better, but it could have been much worse, Mason knew. If this had been one of the big universities, or if it hadn't been summer, the swarm might easily number in the thousands. So all things considered, he considered that dozen-plus almost a blessing.

Two more alphas tore across the field directly in front of the Peterbilt and exploded against the cowcatcher, and whether Alejandra took that as inspiration or she simply wished to relieve some of Mason's burden, she suddenly tore past them in the Mustang, shaking alphas loose like a dog shaking off fleas. One alpha slid under the car and had its legs crushed to pulp, and another happened to come dead center and was met with somewhat more permanent results, then Alejandra set upon what appeared to be a personal crusade to destroy the rest. She slid on the grass, executing a perfect back-end drift that knocked one little cheerleader-alpha high in the air, then she came back at the swarm and tore straight through the thick of them. Two more bounced off of the grill and one flew up and over the roof, then the car skidded to a stop on a wide lawn on the other side of the concourse and spun around, kicking up dual pinwheels of soil. It picked up speed with the roar of a lion and took down another two alphas in spectacular fashion, then it slewed about in another 180-degree turn and sent one more cartwheeling over the roof.

And on and on it went. She tore down one side of the truck

and up the other, and when two or three creatures happened to be close enough together, she lit into a series of donuts that had them bouncing this way and that off the Mus-tang's back end. She tore back across the road, aiming the car into and through those few that remained, then she came barreling back at full speed, and with a quick turn of the wheel and pull on the handbrake, the car spun a full 180 degrees and parked itself precisely parallel with the Peterbilt, not three feet away. A hand came up, a thumb was raised, and the Mustang fell dutifully back behind Gloria as if nothing at all had happened.

"Lord have mercy..." Inez breathed.

"It must be past lunchtime," Christopher offered, humorlessly. "That girl gets hangry..."

Mason pulled the truck onto the main concourse and followed it up to and between the first two buildings. One building had the high-windowed aspect of a gymnasium. The other was filled with office cubicles. Administration, probably. Neither showed any signs of life. No barricades. No boarded-up windows. Nothing.

Up ahead was just more of the same. No army trucks. No soldiers. No emergency vehicles. Just more dead buildings in a dead city.

He realized then that it was pointless. This place was no sanctuary, and it never was. His mind began to run wild with speculation on what this might mean for Becks and her survival and for any hopes he might once have had of knowing one way or the other, then a single echo stepped out from the corner of the gymnasium to be crushed into paste under Gloria's wheels, and he suddenly realized what he should have spotted the second they'd entered this place.

Something was wrong with the picture. Well, not *wrong,*

exactly. To be precise, something was *missing,* and it wasn't the machine gun nests or the Red Cross tent or the girl with the donuts. While everyone else was looking to the buildings and to the windows and everywhere else at once, Mason focused his attention on the concourse itself.

There were spatters of gore everywhere, and much of the concourse wore a patina of old blood turned brown by the sun. It was evidence of the carnage that must have gone on here in those first few days. Such sights were familiar now. Unremarkable. So commonplace as to almost border on the mundane. But this place was different. Something here was made resoundingly conspicuous by its very absence.

"Where the hell are the bodies?" he finally said aloud, but before anyone could respond, the concourse opened into a wide courtyard and the question answered itself.

"Jesus, Mary and Joseph..." Inez gasped as the truck squealed to a stop.

There *were* bodies here.

Lots of bodies.

Too many bodies to count.

But where they were normally scattered about wherever they fell, someone at Skyline had done some housekeeping. Now the bodies were stacked, but not in a haphazard fashion as if someone had simply dragged them aside to keep the way clear. No, these bodies had been put to use. The courtyard was enclosed, save for wide gaps between most of the buildings, and someone had taken it upon themselves to close off one of those gaps by stacking dead bodies across it like sandbags.

It was a grisly sight, but an endlessly fascinating one as well. Four feet high and several bodies thick, that single wall might represent a hundred or more corpses. A cloud of flies as thick as smoke hovered over the carnage, and beneath them, more than a few fat, slovenly rats fed at their leisure. Sarah directed his attention to the other side and he saw another such wall in the first stages of construction, between the administration building and the next one in. As he watched, one of the bodies shifted, and a single over-stuffed rat the size of a house cat emerged. The animal threw one snarl at the truck and lumbered casually away.

"I don't like this..." Christopher said from the back.

Mason was way ahead of him. This wasn't the work of a few desperate survivors in those first days. Some of the bodies were so fresh that the blood still glistened wet where it had pooled.

Sarah's back stiffened, and she scooted Mackenzie off of her lap. "Mace?"

He was already on it. He stomped the clutch and slammed the truck back into gear, but before he could make another move, a masked man suddenly appeared on the other side of his window with a gun aimed directly between his eyes. Then another appeared on the other side, with a gun trained on Sarah. Then more masked men rushed out to cover both the Peterbilt and the Mustang, and his heart sank in his chest.

Not a word was spoken inside the truck. There was no need. They'd all discussed every imaginable what-if scenario at length, up to and including what Mason had dubbed their 'failsafe.' And on that failsafe, they had all agreed most vehemently. If there ever came a point where they were outmanned and outgunned and the only options left were to either surrender or die, every single one of them would choose the latter. They would rather die fighting than live a few more minutes or a few more hours or a few more days at someone else's feet. With a crystal-clear understanding of all the horrors mankind could mete out on its own, the consensus was, 'If we're going down, we're going down together.' And now, looking out at the guns bristling all around them, Mason knew that moment had come.

He didn't say a word. He didn't have to. They all understood the situation, and they all knew how it worked.

They'd wait for him to make the first move, then all hell would break loose. Some might die, maybe all of them, but no matter. Better that than the alternative.

His hand came slowly off the wheel and drifted down to his lap, making the face behind the gun flinch. The man had a bandana or kerchief covering much of his face, but there was no hiding the youth in his eyes. He was young. Early-twenties. Maybe even younger. Pupils dilated. Skin blanched. Sweating, but not from the heat. Classic acute stress response. Fight or flight. The punk was scared, but the pistol in his hand didn't waver an inch, and his finger was white on the trigger. Scared or not, the punk wouldn't hesitate to put a bullet in his head.

Mason crept his hand down to his thigh and felt the grips of his pistol against his wrist. If he'd been alone in the truck, he would have made his play right then and there. He'd duck back to buy himself a fraction of a second, whip out his gun, and fire blindly through the door. But the moment anyone started to shoot, they'd *all* start shooting, including the man on the other side of the truck with a gun trained on Sarah. He'd only have time to get off a round or two, then Sarah would die, and Mack would die, and the rest of them would follow. And so, in that awful eternity of fractions of a second, he did the math.

The twenty-something punk was scared. Scared shitless, but trying hard not to look it. The man on the other side was the same. A fresh-faced kid. Scared, but lethal. One more masked man standing in front of the truck like a fool. Slender. Willowy. Tiny, even. Around the Mustang, three more. One on each side and one standing stupidly behind. All of them had handguns. No automatic weapons. Single shots only.

Good.

The truck was still in gear. If he kept his hands off the wheel to put them at ease, then pop the clutch and slam the gas pedal to the floor, he might catch them by surprise. Maybe the punks on either side would take that microsecond to grab for a handhold instead of pulling the trigger. Or maybe not. That part was out of his control, so he didn't give it a second thought.

Whatever happened from then on was up to fate. So, okay then. Floor the accelerator, duck, turn the fool in front of the cowcatcher to hamburger, and come up with all guns blazing and hope for the best.

The three men covering the Mustang would start shooting as soon as Gloria roared, but none of those idiots had ever come across anyone like Alejandra before. The girl was smart, and she was quick, and she was every bit as ruthless as Mason. Right now, she'd have one foot on the brake, one on the gas, and her hand resting idly on the gearshift. At the first sign of... well, *anything*... she'd throw the Mustang in reverse and bring up her Tommy gun, and then God help those motherfuckers with what she'd do next.

Mason eased his other hand from the wheel and laid it casually on his left thigh, inches from the door. When he popped the clutch, he'd throw open the door and give the punk one more thing to worry about. It might even buy him another microsecond.

He spared a glance out of the corner of his eye and saw

STAGE 3: BRAVO

Sarah with her hand resting lightly on her own door handle, so as usual, she was right inside his head. A faint chuffing of metal against leather coming from behind. Inez and Christopher drawing their weapons and getting ready. And as for Mackenzie, she was crouched between the seats, wiping fake tears away from her eyes with one hand even as her other hand crept slowly toward the revolver on her hip.

Jesus, that girl! Here she was, staring death in the face, and she was putting on a show just on the off-chance that it might buy them another second.

Alright then. They were ready. All of them. They were ready to fight, and they were ready to die.

He crept his hand an inch closer to his gun and got ready to pop the clutch, but just as he was about to make his move, a man came out from behind one of the buildings, waving his arms in the air and hushing orders to the ragtag army. Mason's first instinct was to use that moment of confusion to his advantage, but he held off, and just like that, the guns at both windows suddenly disappeared and he was left gaping at the oddly familiar figure storming up to the truck.

He slid the gearshift into neutral and popped open his door as the twenty-something punk with the gun stepped back to make way for the man who was clearly in charge.

"Are you fucking *kidding* me?" the man growled, every word dripping with contempt.

Mason greeted Detective Sergeant Gary Hansen with a derisive snort.

"Good to see you too, Gary. Somehow, I knew it would take more than Armageddon to kill a stubborn prick like you."

CHAPTER

VII

Turn that damn motor off, asshole!" Hansen stood on the step, snarling up at Mason. "I said, turn it off! *Now!*"

Reluctantly, Mason complied, then he threw a thumbs-up to Alejandra, and the rumbling Mustang was silenced. With that, Hansen gave a quick series of hand signals to the others, and the masked men spread out, taking up positions at all four corners of the courtyard and lowering their bandanas. It was only then that Mason had a good look at the gunmen. All of them were young. *Too* young. The twenty-something punk looked to be the oldest of the lot. The rest were just kids. Eighteen. Nineteen at the most. And not all of them were men, after all. The one that he'd envisioned turning into hamburger on the cowcatcher was a girl. Tiny. Pretty. Nose full of freckles. The kind of girl who might've just walked out of a Coppertone commercial.

And as he watched them spread out, every single one of them did a most curious thing. Every single one of them tucked their handguns away and brought out another weapon from behind their back or from over their shoulder or from a clip on their belt. It was their own version of his own group's SBDs, but that wasn't the curious thing. What caught Mason's attention was that while the twenty-something punk slipped his pistol carefully into a holster on his hip, the others were entirely casual about how and where they put their own guns. Waistband here, back pocket there, and then the girl with the freckles slipped her own 9 mm pistol into the breast pocket of her shirt, and Mason finally got it.

"Son of a bitch..." he said aloud.

That firearm had to weigh three pounds at least, but the shirt barely sagged.

Hansen followed his gaze and smirked. "That's right, asshole. Colleges aren't exactly known for their weapons stores, so I took a page out of John Dillinger's handbook."

"The guns are fake..." Sarah breathed, dumbfounded.

"You sent children into harm's way with... with *toys?*" Inez screeched from the back, then she came out and stared daggers at the man. "*Toys?!*"

"Not *toys*, Madam," Hansen corrected her. "Some were carved out of wood, some were moulded from plastic."

As she fumed and sputtered, he ran a quick eye around the other occupants of the vehicle. He glared at each of them in turn, softening his expression ever so slightly at the sight of pretty little Mackenzie, then the snarl returned in full as he settled his glare back on Mason. "I hope you'll do these *children* a favor and make as much noise backing the hell out of here as you made on the way in, asshole," he said. And with that, he stepped down from the truck and became a traffic cop, waving the Mustang back.

"No! Gary, wait!" Mason jumped down from Gloria and

was immediately met by the point of an arrow.

It was the kid who'd been on Sarah's side of the truck. Young. Smooth-faced. He looked like he'd be more at home on a skateboard than in an armed camp. But his hands were steady, and the metal bolt in that ridiculous homemade crossbow looked like it could bring down a buffalo.

"Gary, I came here looking for Becks," Mason said past Sk8rBoy, but at the mere mention of her name, a lump rose up at the back of his throat and all he could do was plead. "Just tell me she's alive, Gary. Please, just tell me Becks is alive."

He watched the man's shoulders slump and saw his chest rise and fall in a sigh, and as that lump in his throat grew into an all-consuming anguish that threatened to burst his heart from his chest, he heard a timid voice from behind him hush a single word.

"Mace?"

He spun on his heels, and there she was. Tall, slim, and with a mane of ebony hair framing a face so beautiful that it might have inspired Alexandros to carve the Venus de Milo.

It was her. It was Becks. And yet, there was no running into each other's arms. No embrace. No teary-eyed kiss that went on and on. They simply regarded each other across a ten-foot gulf that encompassed a million miles of heartache, and Mason finally found voice enough to say, "Hi, Becks."

The girl forced a smile and looked to the sky, sending her mane of hair into a mad whorl and Mason's heart into a tailspin. There was a time when he'd considered that toss of the head adorable. She'd want to go out, he'd want to stay in, and she'd smile and look to the sky in a 'What am I going to do with this man?' kind of way, and it made him love her even more. But flash forward a year, and that move became something else. She'd ask another couple over for dinner, he'd spend the evening grumbling, and she'd smile and look to the sky, and it would take days to get things back to where they'd been. By the time another year vanished, he'd say one of his usual stupid things, she'd smile and toss back her head, and then she'd walk out. And on one of those times, she never came back.

Just then, the freckled-faced girl gave a little whistle like the chirp of a bird, and everyone in Hansen's underage army readied their SBDs. Becks put a finger to her lips and went running to where the girl was stationed on the far side of a building with a concave front that made it look as if a giant had taken a bite out of it. Mason was about to follow, but Detective Sergeant Gary Hansen cut him off at the pass.

"Alright asshole, you've seen her," he snarled. "Now, how about you do her a favor and get your ass out of here?"

With that, he ran from one of the youngsters to the other, whispering to each of them in turn with a calm hand on the shoulder or a confident pat on the back, then he ran off after his daughter. Mason had a full second or two to decide his next course of action. Really, though, he didn't need those seconds. Not where Becks was concerned. And in any event, the decision was made for him when both vehicles emptied out and seven more bodies rushed to join him.

Without any instructions from Mason, the group immediately fanned out to all sides.

Mackenzie gave Mason a tiny fist bump and cautioned him, "Watch your back, Mace," then she sprinted off after Sarah, Clancy in tow.

The last to go was Addison. He handed Beverly's shotgun to Mason with a petulant sneer, corralled the woman to his side, and dashed off with his Nut-Buster in hand.

Mason tossed the weapon in the truck, grabbed his rebar from its sling, and ran to join Becks and her father.

By then, Becks was armed with some kind of spear, the freckle-faced girl had a homemade crossbow up and ready, and Hansen had assumed point position halfway between the buildings, brandishing what looked to be a baseball bat studded with spikes. Perhaps thirty feet separated the two buildings, but someone had driven or pushed several cars across the far end to block it off. One of the cars looked suspiciously like an unmarked police cruiser, so Mason had to offer at least a tacit salute to the bull-headed prick in charge of the place.

As inevitable as the tide and as relentless as time, echoes had already gathered two-deep on the far side of the barricade. They pressed up against the cars and pawed at the glass and clawed at the air in the silent scream they all shared, but with no active brain function beyond that which steered them toward humans, they were like insects stuck in amber. Still, Mason had seen firsthand how the laws of physics worked. Pile enough water behind a dam, and the dam eventually breached.

But the reason for the freckle-faced girl's whistle wasn't the echoes. The arrival of two new vehicles at Skyline had apparently not gone unnoticed. Only a sliver of the surrounding area was visible from this vantage point, but in that narrow rectangle of space, he could see as many as a dozen alphas closing in. And worse, two of the creatures were tearing across the parking lot in full charge, directly towards the barricade. Presently, they slammed into the echoes and proceeded to tear them apart, but in their fury, they actually succeeded in lifting two of the dead things off of their feet and throwing them bodily over the hood of one of the cars. Mason immediately charged in, weapon at the ready, but in the few seconds it took him to cover the distance, the job was already done. Both invading echoes were down, and Hansen's baseball bat dripped gore from a dozen bloody spikes.

Even so, the alphas continued to rage, and one of them was beginning to claw its way across the hood of a rusty old Honda pinned against the police cruiser. Hansen took a step toward them, but then he seemed to have second thoughts. He lowered his weapon to the ground, leaned his weight fully upon it, and made a grand gesture of sweeping his arm from Mason to the alphas, as if inviting the newcomer to come join the fun. It was an utterly derisive display, but Mason wasn't interested in playing games. He launched himself onto the hood of the Honda and set to work.

One swing of his fifty pounds of rebar cracked the closest alpha's head open like a walnut, another swept two echoes aside, and a third skewered the second alpha straight through the heart. With both alphas down, another man might have ended it there, but fired up by a flood of emotions he would have had a tough time even putting a name to, Mason was nowhere near done. He took one more swing to open up a gap between the echoes, then he vaulted off the far end of the barricade and took the fight to the swarm. He swung, he hammered, he pummeled, he kicked and he stabbed, and less than a minute later, the last creature crumpled to the ground in a tangled, bloody heap. Mason took one last look around, then he planted a hand on the hood of the Honda and vaulted cleanly over it without so much as a laboured breath.

He didn't know quite what response he'd expected from Hansen, but he wasn't at all surprised when the man spat on the ground and growled, "If you're done showing off, asshole, now's a good time to brighten our day by fucking off."

Before Mason could respond, Becks appeared between

them, planting the back end of what he now realized was a javelin into the ground.

"Daddy, why don't you give us a minute..." she said, and when the man looked about ready to explode, she pursed her lips and added a rather more petulant, "In *private*, Daddy..."

The man scowled daggers at Mason, but he left without another word, and Mason finally found himself in a place that he'd never allowed himself to truly believe he would ever see.

He was with Becks. She was alive! She was here! She smiled at him, and it was real! Then her eyes misted over, and that was real too. He half-expected her to dismiss it all with a look to the sky and a whorl of hair as she walked away, but she didn't. She stood there at arm's length, and she smiled at him.

"It's good to see you, Mace," she said at last. "I'm glad you're okay."

"Me, too," Mason managed, but then he fumbled for the right words to correct himself. "I mean, I'm glad you're okay too. I almost feel like I should take back some of the shit I said about your old man. I mean, he got you all here safe and sound, so..."

Aww, damn...

Becks' look said it all. Something was missing. Or rather, some*one.*

Barbara. Becks' mom. She should be here, but she wasn't. And now he could see it in Becks' eyes and in that single tear rolling down one delicate cheek, and for perhaps the first time since all of this madness descended, Mason knew what it was like to feel genuine sorrow. He'd only met Barbara twice. Once at the Thanksgiving dinner from Hell, and once again when she'd come to the city to visit her daughter and insisted on Mason joining them for dinner at Fisherman's Wharf. Unlike Detective Sergeant *Pain-in-the-Ass* Hansen, Barbara had been a warm and loving person. He'd liked her. He'd genuinely liked her. She had been a sweet and gentle woman, every bit like the daughter she'd raised.

"I'm sorry—" he started to say, but Becks cut him off.

"It was quick," she said, wiping away that one tear and allowing no others. "That's all a person can ask for these days, isn't it? I've seen a lot of death recently, Mace, and quick ain't bad. It might be the best any of us can ever hope for, right?"

On a wild sea of emotions, he took the only safe tack. "Probably," he said, then he looked back to the little freckle-faced girl with the homemade crossbow, and he had to ask, "Is that all there is here? Kids? No army? No FEMA? No other cops?"

Becks shook her head. "You're seeing it all, Mace. Seven in total. The school was on summer schedule as it was, and most of the students and faculty had taken off long before things got bad. There might have been sixty or more when we got here, and Daddy tried his best to get them into some kind of order, but most didn't listen. They were all spread out in this building and that, hunkering down like they were waiting for someone to come and rescue them all. Daddy finally convinced twenty students and one teacher to come with us, and we barricaded ourselves in the Science Building. And from there, we had a front row seat as the '50s tore the rest of the place apart."

Mason knew the term. '50' was short for '5150' – a section of the California Welfare Code dealing with involuntary psychiatric holds. '50' was also California cop slang for a crazy person. But beyond this other term for alphas, he picked out one considerably more pertinent word and echoed it back with a wince.

"Twenty?"

"Twenty students and one teacher. But most got stupid," Becks snorted, sounding far too much like someone Mason knew all too well. "Some got scared and ran, others just got scared. And now we are seven. But every death taught us something we didn't know before. We learned early on that if we were very, *very* quiet, most of the '50s went away on their own, mostly chasing after someone else to rip apart. They're attracted to human sounds, you see? So, once we figured that out, some of the boys began to sneak out and scrounge for supplies while the '50s were... uh, *otherwise occupied.* We used chains and ropes to seal the doors of the buildings that were overrun. After that, a few of the more creative kids hobbled together a few weapons, and we fortified our little Alamo. And we were doing alright, at least for a while. But then the *other* things came.

"We didn't get it at first," she said, hardening her expression. "We just didn't understand. We thought that maybe the worst was over, that the virus was running its course and making the infected sicker and slower. But then we saw it with our own eyes, and there was no denying it. Dead people were coming back to life. *Hundreds* of them, all around. At first, we fought them the same way we fought the others, but they didn't die because they were already dead. So a few more of us were killed before we figured the rest of it out. Tell me, Mace, how does a sane person wrap their head around dead people coming back to life? And if they can somehow manage that impossibility, how the hell do they *remain* sane?"

To that, Mason could only shrug. "Maybe the only way we to survive an insane world is by embracing the madness."

The sound of metal-on-metal made them turn as one to the barricade. Another echo had arrived. The first in the next wave of a sweeping tide that would never end. But wait... No, he recognized the gold watch on the creature's wrist, the one now rattling against the side of the police cruiser. It was a Rolex. Ten grand if it was a penny. And the suit. Armani. Tailor made. He recognized the dent in the side of the thing's head, too. He'd put it there not two minutes ago. Well, apparently, he'd gone a little light on Armani, but he'd soon fix that. He took a step toward the barricade, but Becks stopped him.

"My turn," she said simply enough, and in one quick, fluid movement, she brought up the javelin, drove it through the creature's eyeball all the way to the back of the skull, and drew it back before the thing had even begun to fall.

"Two weeks ago, I didn't have the stomach to put a worm on a hook," she said without a trace of emotion. "Now, I can do that and not feel a thing. I guess I'm embracing the madness after all."

CHAPTER

VIII

T he middle of the courtyard was a battlefield of its own, but one that might have played out in the mannerly confines of a public library. Mason's people were mixed up with Hansen's underage army, and all of them were arguing and cursing, but every single bit of it was being done in a hush. For all the world, they resembled an irascible and belligerent group of parents having it out while their children were asleep in the next room. So hushed were they that all of their voices together barely rose above the background hum of flies buzzing around the body wall.

Sarah was at the front of the pack, face to face with Hansen and making up for the lack of volume by gesticulating wildly in the air. Mack was at her side as usual, but when the girl saw Mason reappear, she and Clancy broke away and went to him at a run.

"That mean man says we have to go, Mace," she whispered up at him, then she had her first real look at who he was with and she asked, almost in a huff, "Are you Becks?"

STAGE 3: BRAVO

Predictably, Becks dropped to a knee and beamed a smile at the girl. "My name is Rebecca," she said, holding out a hand, "But my friends call me Becks, so you can too. And by the way, that *mean man* is my father."

Mackenzie took the hand, but only fleetingly. When she failed to offer her name, Mason obliged.

"Becks, this is Mack. I can honestly say that she's saved my ass more times than I can count. This big beautiful mutt is Clancy, and I can say the same thing about him."

"Well then I owe you, Mack," Becks' smile widened, "and you too, Clancy."

At the sound of his name, Clancy rushed into her arms and happily exchanged kisses with this woman he'd just met, but Mackenzie spoke up to set the record straight.

"Only Mace and Sarah call me that."

An ordinary person might have been offended, but not Becks. Mason knew how much she liked kids, so he wasn't at all surprised when she stopped fussing over Clancy long enough to say, "I'm sorry, Mackenzie, I truly am. I didn't mean to be so forward."

Mackenzie sized up this new woman, then she too reacted exactly how Mason could have predicted. "That's okay," she said, cracking a smile at last. "I guess I don't mind if you call me Mack."

And just like that, with so many big, beautiful hearts coming together, the three of them couldn't help but be instant friends. But not so the others, apparently. One or more of the voices rose above the background buzz, and Mason hurried over, bearing the others along in his wake.

"It's a big place!" Sarah was trying to stand nose to nose with the man, but it was more like nose to clavicle.

"And in this big place," Hansen answered back, "we

occupy precisely one building. *One!* We don't have room, we don't have supplies..."

"*Chido!*" Alejandra growled from somewhere around his sternum. "We'll make our *own* room!"

"With *guns?*" Hansen growled back, "You'll win the battle and lose the war!"

Before things could get any more heated, Mason and Becks stepped between the warring parties.

"Now, listen..." Mason hushed, surprised as hell to be the voice of reason for once. "It seems to me that we have three options here. One, all of you can come with us. It'll be a little cramped, but we'll manage." Several people on both sides voiced their objections, but he ploughed on. "Two, we can all go our separate ways and take our chances. We've made it this far, so maybe we'll make it for another week or so. Or maybe not." Again, a voice or two rose up, but not nearly as vociferously. "Or three," he said at last, "we can work together, we can share our food and share our weapons and share our know-how, and maybe, just *maybe,* we can keep from beating the crap out of each other long enough to survive."

Having said his piece, he kept his mouth shut and prepared for the fur to fly. But, it didn't. In fact, there followed a long pregnant silence broken only by one voice; that of the twenty-something punk.

"And *then* what?" the punk huffed, hoisting something that looked suspiciously like a farmer's scythe to his shoulder.

"Then we'll decide what to do next," Mason told him, matter-of-factly. "We'll go through our options, discuss the pros and cons of each, and everyone will have a vote."

"A vote?" Hansen snapped. "Listen, asshole, there won't be any votes here. *I'm* in charge, and what I say goes!"

"Say what?" Alejandra sneered up at him.

"Uh, that's not how we do things, Officer Friendly," Addison said, thumbing his glasses high up his nose.

"That's never gonna happen," Sarah told him outright. "Most of us have been down that road before, and we're not about to go down it again."

"Not for nothin'," Christopher seconded.

"We'd rather die..." Beverly concluded for them all.

Hansen targeted his glare at each and every one them in turn. "Well then, by all means, get back in your vehicles and vote on which way you're going to haul your asses away from here."

"Daddy...." Becks purred, and as it was with every father facing down every daughter since the beginning of time, there was never a doubt as to the outcome.

He huffed and he puffed and he scowled and he snorted, and then he relented. But only just.

"Fine!" he growled. "The damage is done, so you might as well stay the night. But you will do exactly *what* I tell you, exactly *when* I tell you, and exactly *how* I tell you, is that clear?"

"Daddy..." Becks tried again, but this time, her father was resolute.

"No, Rebecca! That's the way it is! My house, my rules!"

"Oh, I've heard *that* one before," Christopher mused under his breath, earning him a gentle cuff on the back of the head from his mother.

"Mace, we don't need this... this *tamarindo*," Alejandra said, sheathing her machete. "You wanted to find your *bomboncita*, and you did. Good for you. Congratulations. She's alive. So invite the pretty girl along, and let's get the fuck out of here, huh?"

Becks looked at Mason as if she'd never seen him before.

"What? You came all the way from the city just to find me?"

"I had to know," he told her, honestly.

"Yeah," Alejandra snorted. "He had to know if you'd been eaten. *Yet!*"

"*Ally!*" Inez tsk-tsked from the sidelines.

"And we came with him," Beverly chimed in.

"Because that's what friends do." This from Christopher.

Becks took it all in, and she came close to reaching out for Mason's hand. But ultimately, she didn't. She looked to each new face in the crowd, her back stiffening ever so slightly at the sight of the beautiful young woman holding the equally beautiful girl to her side, then she turned back to Mason and told him what he didn't need to be told.

"You have some incredible friends, Mace."

"Yes, I do," Mason agreed without reservation, his eyes wandering over her shoulder to the image of Sarah and Mackenzie huddled together with Clancy.

Apparently, this was all Hansen could take.

"Alright, alright..." he growled. "Dark's coming quick, the natives are getting restless, and you're breaking my fucking heart. You say you have food and water in that monster truck of yours?"

"Enough to fill that fat donut-hole of yours, *tamarindo*," Alejandra snarled at him, apparently still itching for a fight.

Hansen glared down at the Latina spitfire, and there was something almost akin to a glint in his eye as he snarled back, "*Cuidado, peleonera. Sigue hablando de esa manera, y podríamos ser amigos...*"

For the first time since Mason had known her, Alejandra was at a loss for words.

Fortunately, Sarah filled in. "We have more than enough, and we'll gladly share. But about this whole 'my way or the highway' bullshit..."

Hansen cut her off with an upraised hand, but even as he responded to Sarah, his eyes never left Alejandra's. "Fine. For one night only, I declare this a democracy. *Esta bien, peleonera?*"

Alejandra nodded, grudgingly and not a little disconcertedly. "*Esta bien, tamarindo.*"

"Alright then," Hansen said at last, motioning for his band of underage guerrillas to lend a hand. "Grab the shit, let's get inside, and we'll worry about tomorrow, tomorrow."

As always, none of Mason's group moved until Mason gave the word, and as always, Mason looked to Sarah for final confirmation. But as always, they were in total agreement. She nodded, and Mason passed it on.

"Agreed," he said, setting everyone in motion.

As he turned away from Becks, he had the fleeting sensation of long, slender fingers just barely kissing his hand, but then they were gone as if they'd never been there at all.

CHAPTER

IX

Mason suggested moving both vehicles as close to the Alamo as possible, but Hansen hissed, "Don't you fucking *dare* fire that monster truck up again!" and that put an end to it.

The Mustang and Peterbilt were left where they were, and Alejandra, Addison, and two of the boys stood guard while the rest of them off-loaded supplies. Five minutes later, three more echoes had been added to the body wall, and the door to the Science Building was closed behind a burgeoning group of fifteen souls.

Bottled water and granola bars were shared, then a propane stove was brought out and placed on a lab table, and Inez marked the entire area as off-limits. But then one of the college kids found a stash of licorice and chocolate bars in the supplies, and all she could do was laugh and let them help themselves with gentle admonishments of, "That'll spoil your appetites, kids!" all to no avail.

The new arrivals broke into two groups to explore their

new environs, and the college kids were only too happy to show them around. As far as they were concerned, it seemed, this new-found alliance made them all instant friends, despite Hansen's blustering, and if those frightened young people needed anything now, it was friends.

In truth, though, the exploration didn't take long. It was only a two-story building and there wasn't much to see, but Mason came away from it with his mind put somewhat at ease.

There were far too many ways in and out of the Alamo for his liking, but he had to give due credit to Hansen's attention to detail. Every door had been well secured, and any room with a window lower than chest-height had been sectioned off and secured. The building appeared to be well and truly safe, but it had its drawbacks as well. It was all classrooms and labs, so the accommodations were spartan. The students had long ago raided every closet and every locker for clothes and jackets enough to fashion themselves beds of a sort, and they'd also scrounged a few buckets small enough to fit into a toilet for their sanitary needs, but there was one accommodation sorely lacking in this last bastion of humanity. There was precious little water. The biggest ocean on the planet was less than a mile away, and these people barely had enough to keep themselves hydrated, let alone clean.

"There's lots of stuff in building six, but it's crawling with '50s," one of the boys offered, wistfully. He was eighteen at best; stocky, muscular, and with a hint of peach fuzz on his chin.

Mason could easily imagine him on the football field, but he held a spiked baseball bat as if it were second nature.

"What's your name, kid?" Addison asked.

"Uh... Richie, sir."

Addison thumbed his glasses higher up his nose. "Well, it's a pleasure to meet you, Richie. But if you call me 'sir' again, I'll give you an atomic wedgie you'll be plucking out of your butt crack for a month. And believe me, kid, having been on the receiving end of many myself, I am somewhat of an expert in the field." The boy chuckled, and Addison smiled back. "So, where's this building six?"

"Right next door," the boy answered. "There's the Fireside restaurant and a coffee shop, and a book store that sells snacks. There's all *sorts* of stuff there!"

"Is that the building with the bite out of it?" Mason asked.

Again, the chuckle. "That's the one, sir... uh... *Mace*. It *is* Mace, right?"

"It is," came the reply. "Richie, this is Addison, Alejandra, and Beverly."

The freckle-faced girl had accompanied them all the way, but only now did she speak. She sidled up beside Alejandra and offered her a pretty little smile and a soft, "Hi."

Alejandra replied with a grunt and a jut of her chin.

Richie introduced the two others in his group. "She's Teddy, and this is Willy."

"William!" The other boy reminded him with a scowl. He was the Sk8rBoy who'd met Mason's descent from the Peterbilt with the bolt of a crossbow.

"Alright, William," Mason said. "So, which one of you wants to tell me why you haven't cleared building six and liberated all of that... *stuff?*"

"Are you kidding?" Richie hushed a howl. "There's gotta be a hundred '50s in there!"

"No way there's a hundred," Alejandra scoffed. "Not unless someone propped open every door and sang a few choruses of Ave Maria."

"She's right," Addison agreed. "Chances are, a few got in and ran rabid, and Officer Friendly was just too scared to go in after them."

"Hey!" Sk8rBoy snapped. "Gary ain't afraid of nothin'! There were twenty or thirty dumb-asses in that place who thought they knew better than him, so they stayed put. Then one of them got stupid and the place was overrun, so even if it was only a few that got in, they're *all* '50s now. Get it, Tubby?"

At that, Addison grabbed the kid by collar, and he didn't so much as bat an eye when a crossbow came up to meet him at nose level.

"First of all... *William*," he said, as calmly and deliberately as a teacher explaining a math problem to his densest of students, "my name is not Tubby, it is Addison. Secondly, Sheriff Woody has every right to be scared when his only backup is sawed-off little shits like you, still waiting for their testicles to descend." The boy screwed up his face as if he were about to fire back, but Addison neatly cut him off. "And thirdly, *William*, if a handful of alphas got into building six, those twenty or thirty dumb-asses would have been turned into salsa, not more alphas."

"We tied the doors closed after that," the freckle-faced girl, Teddy, hushed to Alejandra. "No one in, no one out."

"Good work, *chica*." Alejandra gave the girl a fist-bump, and Teddy offered a poorly pronounced, *"Gratzias."*

Alejandra said nothing, but Addison cooed, "Aww, it's so cute when they try," to no one in particular.

They met up with their other half in short order, and from all accounts, the entire building was much the same all over. It was safe, it was secure, but it was woefully lacking in basic supplies.

Names were exchanged all around, and Mason was finally introduced to the twenty-something punk behind the gun at his window. He was tall, thick, not as heavily-muscled as Richie, but close. The man's name was Donn. Donn with two Ns. On this point, twenty-something was most adamant, and Mason could only nod his understanding as their hands met for a single abbreviated shake.

"Good to meet you, Donn," he said, careful to add the second 'N' in his head, just in case the kid noticed.

Now that Mason had a close-up view of the punk's weapon, he realized how close he'd come by calling it a scythe. It might once have started out as the cutting blade on a rider-mower, but some heavy-duty filing had turned it into a long, hooked, incredibly *lethal*-looking blade, and then it'd been affixed to what had probably once been the handle of a spade. The war-scythe looked heavy, but Donn with the two Ns handled it as easily as a whisk broom.

The last boy finished the introductions. His name was Diego. He was smaller than the others, and instead of a home-made crossbow or club or war-scythe, he appeared to be armed only with a child's slingshot, albeit a little bigger than most, and with a wrist-strap for support.

"*Qué onda, muchacho,*" Alejandra said to him, but the kid only stared back at her, looking utterly lost.

"I'm sorry, ma'am," he said, rather timidly. "I don't speak Spanish."

Alejandra scowled and said nothing.

"*I* speak Spanish... um, *un pico*," Teddy tried, beaming a smile.

"No, you don't," Alejandra told her flat out, erasing the smile.

"Alright." Detective Sergeant Gary Hansen put an end to

the chatter. "Diego, William, I believe you're on patrol. Richie, how about you go top-watch and see how much damage our... *guests'* arrival has caused?"

The man's words and tone both rankled Mason to the core, but he didn't take the bait. Instead, he offered a quick, "I'd like to see that for myself," and followed along after Richie, sparing a moment to share a look with Becks and another with Sarah and throwing a little half-wink to Mackenzie.

They passed down a short hallway and turned into a side corridor, ending at what looked to be a closet. But this was a closet with a difference. An access ladder ran up one concrete wall, all the way to a hatch set in the ceiling. Richie stopped long enough to collect of pair of binoculars from a hook and drape them around his neck, then he took the ladder in hand and led the way up. Once at the top, he unhooked a bungee cord and cracked the hatch open for a quick peek, then he eased it wide open and waved Mason up.

The view from the roof was incredible. To the west was the Pacific Ocean, as wide and calm and placid as if nothing at all had changed in the world. It was only a mile away, with a road winding down the six or seven hundred feet of the hill, all the way to the Cabrillo Highway paralleling the coast. It was a *desperately* beautiful sight, if one looked past the container ship run aground next to the pier and the columns of smoke rising from a dozen different fires.

To the south was Sweeney Ridge, a vast landscape of trees and brush that went off into the distance as far as the eye could see. A hiking trail led away from Skyline and branched off in several directions, but even without the binoculars, Mason could see bodies littering the trail and several echoes bumbling their way through the brush.

"Mr. Goode convinced a few of the others that they'd be able to get out that way," Richie offered, somberly. "But they were wrong."

Dead wrong... Mason corrected him in his head.

To the north and east, things were just as Mason had seen since the beginning – a sheer and unrelenting horror show. He let Richie do his proper scan of the surrounding suburban Hell, then he gratefully accepted the binoculars to have a closer look for himself, and what he saw through those lenses was proof that Hansen was right. That big thundering Peterbilt and roaring Mustang had indeed put Skyline in danger. Alphas from miles around had been drawn to the noise, and it was only Hansen's quick insistence on silencing the dinner bell that had kept the place from being entirely overrun. When the motors were turned off, any alpha outside of a whispered earshot had been left suddenly adrift, and thankfully so.

There were hundreds. Literally, hundreds. From a mile away and right up to the college itself, not a square yard of real estate was left unoccupied. Most were in a state of vigil, heads down and standing as still as statues, but some were probing, and it was these that most concerned Mason. Probers were nothing but trouble. They would stumble along, following any sound or smell that might conceivably have come from a human, and they would follow that trail until it petered out or until the suspected prey gave itself away. If the former, they would return to vigil, all that much closer. If the latter, they would charge, and it was game over.

And there were echoes there, too. *Always*, there were echoes, chasing after humans like moths chasing a flame. The more humans, the bigger the flame. Now that two smaller flames had become one, every echo in San Bruno might well be converging on that blaze.

Richie set off along the edge of the roof to check the immediate perimeter, and Mason followed. Already, four new echoes were bumping up against the car-barrier, and a dozen others were converging on the building itself. The front of the building was still open, but it wouldn't be for long. He counted no fewer than five open corridors into the courtyard, so echoes and alphas alike were bound to get in. Indeed, when he and Richie finally returned to the hatch and hunkered down in hushed conversation, Richie confirmed as much.

"The DBs fill the Quad every night, and we clear them out every morning."

DBs. More cop slang. DB was short for Dead Body. Not as emotionally charged as *creeper* or as poetic as *echo*, but it was certainly on point.

"We tried piling up desks and tables and whatever else we could get our hands on, but it was never enough. And every time they knocked something over, the noise would bring the '50s at a run. So now, we just let them gather through the night, and when morning comes, three or four of us drop down from building eight to clean them out just as quiet as you please."

Now, Mason understood something he'd seen on his trip around the roof. One corner of the building came close to the corner of another, presumably this building eight. A running start might allow an able-bodied person to jump the gap, but someone had taken the liberty of laying two heavy planks across the gap, side by side, to form a bridge. He gave that other building a good look and saw three ropes hanging from the roof, all the way down into the courtyard.

"Dangerous work," he said.

"So's breathin', these days," Richie replied.

Mason couldn't argue.

"How many?"

"Yesterday, eight. Today, twelve. They just keep coming."

"And you add the bodies to the wall?"

"Better than leaving them scattered all over." The kid shrugged. "Might as well put them to use."

Again, no argument.

"There's a dozen or more cars in the parking lot and a few more on the street. Couldn't you—"

Richie cut him short. "It's not that easy. Do you know how to hot-wire a car, Mace?"

Mason's lip curled as if he'd just tasted something decidedly sour. "No. It's on my list."

"Well, neither do we. And even if we did, modern cars have built-in antitheft technology. Unless it's an older model, even if you get the car started, the steering wheel and gearshift lock in place."

"Locks can be broken." Mason gave it one last shot.

"Not quietly," Richie replied, and the subject was well and truly dropped.

Mason fell silent for a few moments to wrap his mind around the problem, but barely had he begun to work through the math when Richie spoke up again.

"Gary doesn't like you much," he said, turning up one corner of his mouth in a half-grin.

"No, he most certainly does not," Mason snorted. "I assure you, the feeling is mutual."

"You knew him from before?"

"I knew his daughter."

"Ah!" Richie tossed back his chin. "I get it now."

Mason narrowed his eyes. "You get *what*?"

Richie shrugged. "Hey, no father is ever going to like any man who dates his little girl."

"Not even a college football star?" Mason quipped.

"What, me? Naw, Mace, I can hit a baseball pretty good, but I can't throw a spiral to save my ass. Skyline doesn't even have a football team. Anyway, I came here for their Surgical Technology program, not to play ball."

Again, the narrowing of the eyes.

"You want to be a doctor?"

"Hell, no. A surgical technologist delivers patient care before, during, and after surgery. I wanted to help people, but I've never had any desire at all to be an actual *doctor*."

Mason digested it all, then he gave the boy the sagest piece of advice he might ever have offered anyone in his life.

"Good for you, kid," he said. "From my experience, someone who can swing a baseball bat is gonna last a whole lot longer in this world than any doctor."

CHAPTER

X

"They won't be able to smell my cooking, will they?"
Mason returned from the roof to find Inez huddled over the stove, looking like she was ready to throw herself onto it like a live grenade if he gave the word.

"There's a good wind coming off the ocean and all the windows are shut," he reassured her with a gentle pat on the back. The contents of the pot looked a little like lumpy oatmeal. But looks were often deceiving, especially where Inez's cooking was concerned. "That smells great, Inez. What is it?"

"*Canned* chicken, *canned* corn and *canned* milk," she sighed. "My stars, what I wouldn't give for some fresh produce and a nice cut of beef!"

"You and me both, sister," Mason agreed, helping himself to a spoonful of whatever it was.

As the others began to drift in, Inez directed them to form a line, starting at a stack of paper plates and plastic utensils to her left. Then she carefully doled out a healthy ladleful of lumpy oatmeal onto each plate as it passed, along with a goodly pile of boiled rice.

"If it tastes as good as it smells, Ma'am, you'll be the star of the day," Hansen said as he passed, flipping her the most threadbare of smiles.

"That's sweet of you to say, Sergeant Hansen. Thank you." Inez returned the smile in full. "But my name is Inez, and you'd better use it if you don't want to find yourself going to bed hungry."

Through the titters of a few of the college kids, Hansen reached out a hand, and Inez took it. "Well, it's a pleasure to meet you, Inez," he told her honestly. "Please, call me Gary. And on behalf of us all, I would like to thank you for this wonderful meal."

The tittering stopped immediately, and the college kids all came together in a muted chorus of hushed hurrahs, plastic forks held high in salute.

Inez accepted the praise in her usual fashion. She cocked an eyebrow and cautioned them, "You haven't tasted it yet. You might just change your minds," that raised another round of hushed laughter.

Once everyone was served, Clancy included, Inez helped herself and took a stool around one of two central lab tables, and as the others ate, she gently folded her hands in her lap and bowed her head in silent prayer.

Christopher immediately bowed his head, and when the others saw what was happening, one by one, every single one of them followed suit. The last to do so were Mason and Alejandra, but when even the hard-boiled Detective Sergeant Gary Hansen finally laid down his fork and bowed his head, they shared a shrug and submitted to their fate.

"Lord, we thank you for this bounty, and we thank you for bringing us together in these troubling times," Inez prayed in a hush. "We thank you for every day we have on this good Earth, and we ask in Jesus' name that you look over us that we may all have another tomorrow. Amen." With that, she opened her eyes and beamed a smile at all of them, adding, simply, "Thank you."

"You could've asked for a few sirloin steaks before hanging up the phone," Mason quipped, eliciting a growled, *"Asshole,"* from Hansen and a subsequent, *"Daddy..."* from Becks, sitting between the two.

Mackenzie was on Mason's other side, with Sarah beside her. Christopher and Beverly had claimed the last open seats at the main table, so Addison and Alejandra had been relegated to the kids' table next door with varying degrees of acceptance. Apparently, Teddy had taken a shine to Alejandra, and even now, she was more interested in regarding the girl with awe than with the food on her plate. But Alejandra was having none of it.

"You have a very a big gun," the girl said, running her eyes over the Tommy gun on Alejandra's back and clearly desperate to strike up a conversation.

When Alejandra failed to respond, Addison did so in her place.

"You wanna see big guns?" he said, striking an exaggerated Mr. Universe pose. "Just look at *these* guns!"

All of the kids laughed, but Alejandra just went on eating.

Small talk followed, mostly kept to its own table, but then the discussion became more focused. There was certainly nothing like individual tales of woe among these people who had just met, but Sarah described San Francisco in general and their group's flight south, and the college kids took turns detailing the running of their little piece of the world.

"So the courtyard fills up every night, and you send children down to clear them out every morning." Beverly picked that one single detail out of the infinity of horrors, and scowled across at Hansen like an angry Rottweiler. *"Children?"*

"Young lady," Hansen laid down his fork and returned every bit of the scowl, "Beverly, is it? Well, Beverly, these people you see here are no longer children. They are warriors, in every sense of the word. Why, back in the thirteenth century, they'd already be considered middle-aged, and every single one of them would have had a dozen battles under their belt."

"This isn't the thirteenth century," Beverly hissed at the man.

"Isn't it?" Hansen huffed back, and when no one at either table was able to come up with any kind of argument to the contrary, a deafening silence fell over the room, broken only by Addison's hushed, *"Awkwaaard..."*

"Why don't you shore up the defenses?" Christopher said at last. "You know, like the man said, build a wall. A great, *great* wall..."

"Oh, yeah?" Sk8rBoy William snarked back. "With what? Good intentions?"

"There's all kinds of stuff here, right? Tables? Desks? Chairs?"

"We tried that," Richie offered between bites.

"There's just not enough," Becks explained. "Even if we stripped the place of every desk and every table and every chair, it would only be a stumbling block. They'd barge through it in seconds."

"But a building is more than its contents." Inez had a sudden epiphany. "Desks and tables sure, but there's more here, right? Doors, walls, floorboards..."

"And nails to put it all together!" Diego added excitedly.

"Hey, my dad used to do that. He'd tear down old buildings from the inside out, and what he didn't re-use, he'd sell."

"Even nails?"

"Are you kidding? There's a lot of money in that old crap. He once sold an old toilet for five hundred bucks!"

Most of the kids laughed, but the whole idea got Mason's mind working, and Hansen's too, apparently. The man looked around the room, but now he did so with fresh eyes. Mason saw him doing the math, and he had to give him credit for not dismissing the idea out of hand. In fact, he had to confess that he had actually started to see the man in a somewhat new light of late. Yes, Gary Hansen was a bull-headed, opinionated, self-centred prick, but he was most certainly intelligent, and deep down, Mason was beginning to suspect that he might actually give a flying fuck.

Sound like someone you know, Mace?

From out of nowhere, he felt Becks' hand curl into his, and suddenly, all other thoughts were forgotten. Barricades, alphas, echoes... even the blustering, pig-headed-but-possibly-giving-a-fuck Detective Sergeant Gary Hansen. In that moment, all Mason knew in the entire world was Becks' hand in his, just like it had been so many times before.

Before...

The very notion of the word was like a cold slap across the face. There *was* no before. There was only ever a now, and in that most evanescent moment of now, everything was different.

He could feel Becks' hand in his, he could feel her long, slender fingers and the warmth of her flesh, but something had changed. Hell, *everything* had changed. He had already had time to resign Becks to the past, back when the thought of a past actually meant something. Back when he could look at photographs of the two of them together and smell her on his pillow and feel her ghost beside him as he cried himself to sleep. But that past was long gone, and any *after* the two of them might once have had was gone right along with it.

Her hand lingered for a moment longer, and then it slipped away. So, apparently, she had sensed the change as well. Or maybe she had simply sensed the change in him. Either way, with her hand slipping away from his, he began to feel the first fresh pangs of an old wound reopening in his heart, but then Mack leaned in from the other side and put her little hand on his elbow, and he was brought back to the here and now.

"All good, Mace?" Mackenzie hushed.

"All good, Mack," he replied automatically, then he leaned over and buried his face in her tangled mop of curls and gave her a gentle kiss on the top of her head. "Yeah, Mack. All good."

"You sure, Mace?" Sarah broke in, and when she caught his eye, he knew that she knew. She was inside his head, same as always, so he could see his own concerns reflected back in those big blue eyes.

Whether it was all good or not depended entirely on what they did next. The description of life at Skyline was done, and the future was clear. This sanctuary couldn't last. The arrival of Mason's group might have accelerated the end, but it was an end that had always been coming. They could debate imaginary options until they were blue in the face, and it wouldn't change the outcome. *Fuck* the great, great walls, and *fuck* building six. Either way, they'd only be delaying the end by an extra day or two. At most.

If they stayed, they'd be dead – wall or no wall, *stuff* or no *stuff*. Eight echoes yesterday. Twelve today. Tomorrow, there'd be twenty. The day after, there'd be too many to clear. And once that tipping point was reached, they'd be trapped in the Alamo and those DBs would pile up like gruesome snowdrifts until the windows finally gave way.

So that was it. They had to go. Hansen was sunk deep in thought, and Mason knew that he was debating that very question. Surely though, the man had to be able to see the writing on the nonexistent walls. Despite Mason's feelings toward him, Hansen was no fool. Surely, he could see that this place was a death trap.

So now came the moment of truth. Mason knew exactly what their next step should be, but it wasn't his call to make. Not here. Not now.

Or at least, not yet.

Hansen was sitting ponderously quiet as he mulled over the whole situation, and Mason used those few moments to come to another conclusion. If the man opened his mouth and anything but the right words fell out, this little social experiment was done. He and Mack and Sarah and all the rest of them would be gone at first light tomorrow. Sooner, if possible.

He laid down his fork and waited for the man to speak, and while he waited, Clancy snaked his way under the table and came up between his legs, resting his big head across his knee. Mason scratched the big dog between the ears and patted his head, and he waited. And when Clancy abandoned him for Mackenzie who was more certain to pass him a bite of food, he waited still.

At last, Detective Sergeant Gary Hansen made up his mind, and no one hung more on his every word than Mason.

He leaned forward, ready for the worst, so he wasn't at all surprised at what came out of the man's mouth.

STAGE 3: BRAVO

"We have to clear building six," Hansen said, just that simply.

Well, shit...

CHAPTER

XI

Huh?" Christopher looked up from his plate. "What's a building six?"

"It's the next building over," Teddy said with a little tremor in her voice.

"The one with a bite out of it," Mason added through clenched teeth.

"Didn't someone say that every building here was overrun?" Beverly looked across to the kids' table. "Doesn't that include building six?"

"It does," Becks answered, though not easily.

"Yes, building six was overrun, but we're going to clear it," Hansen announced, calmly resuming his meal.

"Uh... and *why*, exactly?" This, from Sarah.

"There's food over there. Water. All manner of supplies."

"We have all that in Gloria," Addison jumped in, "which, I don't hesitate to remind you, is parked just beyond your building six."

"He's right." Alejandra aimed her fork at Addison and

her glare at Hansen. "We should make a run for it while we can."

"Damn straight!" Christopher agreed most vehemently.

Inez scowled at her son's use of language, but she didn't disagree with the sentiment.

"It does seem wise, Gary."

Hansen didn't even bother to look up from his plate. "I'm sorry Inez, but my house, my rules."

"Well, so much for democracy..." Beverly scowled.

So, that was it. Game over. Just as there was no arguing with stupid, there was no reasoning with the pig-headed. Though Hansen could never be lumped in with the former, he was the absolute *epitome* of the latter. If the man's mind was made up, a truckload of dynamite wouldn't be able to move it an inch. So it was settled. Come morning, Mason would take his merry band back on the road and leave this stubborn, hard-assed son of a bitch to his own doom.

All eyes were on Mason, but he pretended not to notice.

"Can't you see that Skyline is a lost cause?" This was Sarah again. Not yet giving up on trying to move the unmovable.

"Little lady, one thing I learned in the navy is that you don't abandon ship until your feet get wet. The second you trade that big, dry ship for an open-air lifeboat, the clock starts ticking, so you do everything possible to keep the ship afloat for as long as you can."

Christopher dragged a hand through his hair. "Uh, dude, I hate to break it to you, but you're already treading water and the sharks are circling."

"All that's missing is the *frickin'* lasers," Addison tacked on, eliciting at least one nervous giggle from the kids' table.

Mason had lost his appetite entirely, but he continued to

pick at his food as he tried to wrap his mind around a problem he wouldn't have imagined coming in a thousand lifetimes.

Hansen was a dick. He'd known it from that first over-the-top, iron-fisted handshake two years ago. He'd declared it to Becks in a fit of pique on more than a few occasions since, and he'd seen absolutely nothing in this new incarnation to change his mind in the slightest. The man was a dick. A grandiose, bull-headed, know-it-all dick. If he was so willing to throw his life away, then so be it. But Hansen wouldn't just be throwing his own life away. He'd be killing his daughter, too.

With that realization, Mason almost reached for Becks' hand so that he could feel her long, slender fingers intertwine with his own once again, but he couldn't bring himself to do it. So he sat there, staring down at his plate and dragging a plastic fork through rice turned suddenly sodden as he turned his mind to the others so intimately involved in this unimaginable drama.

The kids. The college kids. Would they listen to reason and abandon this place, or was Hansen's Kool-Aid just too strong?

It didn't take long to get an answer.

"We've done alright so far," Sk8rBoy William huffed.

"It's been no walk in the park, but we wouldn't be alive if it wasn't for Gary," Richie seconded the motion.

The others said nothing, but their body language spoke volumes. As scared as they were, each and every one of them would stick with Hansen. They'd go on plugging leaks in a boat already on the bottom until every last one of them was fish food. And as much as Mason wanted to grab them by their collective necks and shake some sense into them, he couldn't blame them one bit. After all, Hansen had kept them alive in a world gone mad, so why the hell would they take someone else's word over his? In fact, Mason would have lost respect for them if they had.

And with that revelation came another.

Hansen was a dick, but he was willing to go down with his ship for one reason and one reason only. His family. Becks. Richie. Donn. William. Diego. Teddy. They were his family now, every bit as much as Sarah and Mack and all the others were Mason's. And just like Mason, he'd never put his people's lives in the hands of another.

Right, wrong, good, bad, us, them... they were all just words now. Meaningless, empty words from a dead world. Just as hollow and insignificant as those other words – past and future. There was only ever a now, and in the now, seven souls were going to end if he didn't do something.

He ran the math a dozen different ways, but all he saw was death. Even when he cheated the values, the outcome was always the same. Two days. That's how long they had. Two days at the most, and even that second day was a long shot. They might once have had more, but not now. He'd seen to that himself by charging Gloria in here like a bull moose on steroids.

He instinctively reached out for Mack and Sarah, and as always, their hands automatically parted to include his. And as he drew strength from that unfathomable bond, he came to a decision.

Building six had lots of *stuff,* the kids said. Enough to keep them going for weeks. Until Mason and his crew arrived, clearing that building and liberating all of that *stuff* was the only smart move. Now that things were so much worse, Hansen was only hedging his bets. His family needed supplies, so why not grab them now while they had the manpower? If these new people fled off into the darkness afterward, all the better. They'd take the bulk of the swarm with them, and things at Skyline would be better than they'd ever been.

Fuck! Hansen was even smarter than he'd thought. The man was damn-near brilliant in his cold-bloodedness. He was looking after his own people, and perfectly willing to sacrifice the lives of others to do it. If Mason wasn't so impressed, he might actually have been appalled.

But maybe Hansen's ruthless cunning wasn't wasted after all. If they could liberate some of that *stuff* and set these kids up better than when they'd blundered in, it would be far easier to convince Sarah and the others to leave them behind. And, he had to admit, it might just make it easier to convince himself.

His mind made up at last, Mason gave him the only answer he could.

"Alright." He gave his assent to Hansen, and by extension, to the entire group.

"Seriously?" Christopher scoffed. "Like, we're seriously going to do this?"

"Mace, there's no—" Addison started to say, but he didn't get to finish.

"Me, Addison, Christopher, and Alejandra will go in first," Mason said, not looking up. "Crossbows, slingshot and .22s on the roof. Once the building's secure, the snipers can cover everyone else as they come across. Then we'll all cover the snipers as they follow up."

Despite the capitulation, Hansen remained his usual self. "Negative. Me, you and Richie go in, and Teddy and William will cover us with crossbows."

"Bullshit!" Alejandra railed at the very notion. "We're a team! We know each other's moves! You can't just throw a bunch of people together and hope for the best!"

STAGE 3: BRAVO

To his credit, Hansen actually considered her argument, and though it clearly didn't sit well with him, he ultimately relented.

"Fine, *peleonera*. Like Mason said then. But I'm going too, and everyone else stays put. Once the building's clear, we'll fall back and return as a group."

"Too big a risk," Mason said. "Why make the crossing twice?"

"You afraid, big man?" Hansen challenged him with a smirk.

"Only an idiot wouldn't be," Mason told him without a hint of shame. "But your house, your rules. I guess we'll do it your way."

"Fine," Hansen growled.

"Fine," Mason agreed again, scowling.

"*Fine!*" Hansen barked, concluding the ridiculous interplay.

"Well..." Addison sighed aloud. "It sounds like everything's fine."

They all ignored him.

"Uh... I don't suppose there happens to be a library in this building six?" Sarah asked, looking across to the kids' table.

"The library's in building five," Teddy answered her. "It's the next one over."

"There's a bookstore in six, though," Diego chimed in. "That's where we get all our textbooks."

"Any chance they'd carry the American Medical Journal?"

"Uh... dunno." Diego shrugged. "Maybe."

"How about magazines? Science Life? Anything like that?"

Now, Donn with two Ns stepped in. "I think I've seen Science

Life in the bookstore, but if it's not there, the library will have it for sure. They get all kinds of magazines no one ever reads."

Sarah withheld comment.

"Do they keep all the old issues? The one I want is from a while ago."

"Uh, I honestly have no idea…" He shrugged.

Sarah turned to Mason and told him, point blank, "Mace, I want that report. If it's not there, I want that magazine."

"A little light bedtime reading material?" Christopher asked.

"It's something Jim Lambert said. He thought it might help explain the virus."

"A little late for that, don't you think?" Beverly growled, dropping her fork onto an unfinished plate, and with that, all eyes went to the two women. Out of the corner of his eye, Mason saw Mackenzie glaring daggers at Beverly, and no wonder. If there was anything more dangerous than coming between a mother bear and her cub, it was coming between this fiery little cub and the closest thing to a mother she would ever know.

Sarah took the time to choose her words very carefully. "No, Beverly, it's not. If we can figure out what the virus is and where it came from, maybe we can find a way to beat it. If not, at least we'll have a better idea what we're dealing with."

"And will any of that bring my Amber back?" Beverly's voice hitched, her eyes suddenly welling with tears. "Or Albert, or Devi, or even your *precious* Jim Lambert? Will it put everything back to the way it was, Sarah? Huh? Will it?"

Mason cautioned her, "Beverly, lower your voice," but the woman seemed beyond caring.

STAGE 3: BRAVO

"Why, Mace? Are you afraid they'll hear me?" he howled.

"Yes, I am!" he admitted, honestly. "Absolutely! Beverly, right now you are putting all of our lives in danger, including the lives of these children. If you have something to say, please use your inside voice."

"Haven't you heard, Mace?" she snorted derisively. "These aren't children. They're warriors!"

It wasn't much, but Mason caught it. Tiny fingers slipping away from his and Sarah's and moving toward a sheathed knife strapped to a tiny hip. He reached casually across and recaptured Mackenzie's hand, but he could actually feel the girl's rage in her tight little grip. And as she squeezed his hand nearly hard enough to cut off the circulation, he wondered...

If he let her go, which would she do? Would she launch herself across the table like a feral cat, or excuse herself from the table, wander slowly around behind the woman, and calmly and coolly slit her throat?

Jesus, would that sweet little girl really commit cold-blooded murder just that easily? But he already knew the answer. Of course, she would. And so would he. And so would Sarah and Alejandra and Addison and Christopher and Inez. Beverly was part of this ersatz family, but no one in this new world had a blanket amnesty. Back in the old world, families disagreed. They argued, they fought, and that's where the line was drawn. But in this new world where lives hung by the most tenuous of threads, lines blurred easily. And sometimes, the sneaky bastards had a way of disappearing altogether.

So what did that say about Mack, and what did it say about him, and what did it say about every single one of the others? Were they bad people because they were perfectly willing to kill one of their own, or were they good people because they would do the unthinkable to save the rest of the family? Ultimately, Mason knew that answer, too. They were neither. They were survivors, and in this new world of the damned, a survivor was all anyone could ever hope to be.

Fortunately, the point was made moot, at least for now. Beverly reached across the table and took Sarah's hand as the tears began to pour.

"Sarah, I am *so* sorry," she bawled quietly, her voice in a whisper. "Mace, all of you, I am *so* sorry..."

Sarah said nothing. She simply held her friend's hand and joined her tears with a few of her own.

Mason felt Mackenzie's tight little grip loosen, so he knew that her rage was gone, just like that. And as Inez and Sarah put their arms around Beverly from either side, drawing her in close and tut-tutting in her ear, a new calm descended.

The college kids finished their meals in silence, then they drifted quietly away and set about dismantling their make-shift beds enough to make extras for the new arrivals. Eventually, Inez ushered Beverly away to a corner where a few jackets and bits of clothing had been laid out, and she stayed there with her, holding her tight and matching her tear for tear.

Christopher rose to his feet, saying, "I think I'll have a look around before turning in," but he hadn't taken two steps before Hansen called after him.

"Just make sure you keep moving, kid. The front doors are glass, and we don't want DBs piling up."

Christopher's back stiffened. "Thank you so much for imparting that little pearl of wisdom, Officer Hansen. While I'm gone, perhaps you might wish to suck a bag of dicks."

Hansen's lip curled, but he held his tongue.

And now there were five. Five people sitting around a table in a most awkward and deafening silence. But then Clancy stuck his big head in Mackenzie's lap once again, and all eyes went to that sweet little girl handing her giant of a dog bits of food from her plate and giggling every time he took them as gently as lamb. Sarah and Mason shared a grin, Becks smiled from ear to ear, and even hard-assed Gary Hansen had what might best be described as a disturbance at the very edges of his perpetual scowl.

It didn't last long, though. When the last of the handouts had been given and received, Sarah announced, "Okay, let's get you two settled," then she led both girl and dog away.

And now there were three, and a more awkward silence there had never been. At last, Mason felt Becks' hand sneak back into his, and his breath caught in his throat.

In trying to look anywhere at all other than directly at Becks, his wandering eye happened to alight on Mack and Sarah, settling on the barest excuse for a bed in the far corner. Mackenzie was fussing over Clancy, exchanging kisses on the snout with generous sweeps of his huge tongue, then Sarah gave them each a gentle kiss on the forehead, and they all laid down, cuddling together as always. And as always, a spot had been left open for him on Mack's other side.

"She's quite the girl," he heard Becks say, and only then did he realize how long his gaze must have lingered on that idyllic little scene.

"She is," he agreed whole-heartedly, then he added an all-too honest, "They both are," and felt Becks' hand slip away.

"I see," she said, barely audibly.

He turned bodily in his chair to face her while doing his best to ignore her father's pasty mug looming up in the background.

"No, Becks, I don't think you do. I came across Mack on that very first day. I thought I was saving her life, but in reality, she was saving mine. Without her, I don't know where I'd be, but it wouldn't be anywhere good. That precious little girl saved my very soul, and then she went on to quite literally save my ass more times than I can count. And I can honestly say the same thing about Sarah. She's not my *girlfriend*, she's not my *lover*, and she is in no way a replacement for *you*, *b*ut I can honestly say that I love them both with all my heart."

Becks took it all in, then she dropped her chin and hushed, "And me?"

He put a pair of fingers under her chin, raised her head, and it was all he could do to not lose himself in those beautiful dark eyes.

"Becks, I will *always* love you. In spite of everything that's happened between us, I fought my way through Hell to find you, and I promise that I will continue to fight all of Hell to keep you safe. But if there's one thing I've learned, it's that we have to live in the *now*. No promises, no regrets, no past and no future. Whatever we had is gone, and whatever we might have from this point on is an empty promise. But I can honestly say to you, Becks, that it is *damn* good to be with you, right here, right now."

Becks leaned forward and kissed him, and despite her father snorting and grumbling away behind her, Mason revelled in that moment he'd thought gone forever. When their lips finally parted, the two of them shared a gaze that might have lasted for all of eternity, then Mason abruptly stood, announced to them both, "We have a big day tomorrow," and went off to the sad little excuse for a bed in the corner.

With Becks and her father looking on, he slipped off his boots, kissed Mackenzie on the head, and stretched out beside her and Sarah as if he'd been doing it for a lifetime.

"She seems nice," Sarah hushed from the other side of

Mackenzie, quietly enough not to be overheard.

"She is," Mason replied, just as quietly.

"Her old man's a piece of work, though."

"He is that. I guess some people never change."

"Some do," Sarah whispered one last time, and Mason could almost feel her elbow in his ribs.

He'd thought Mackenzie was already fast asleep, but she managed to coo a drowsy little, "Do you love her?" and he could only thank his lucky stars that it had apparently been with her last waking breath.

Her breathing slowed and deepened, she gave one last stretch like a tiny, sleepy kitten, and she was out like a light. Mason raised his head to look across her to Sarah, and they shared the sweetest of smiles, then they both laid back down and Mason was left alone with his thoughts.

Do I love her, Mack...? He asked himself the question again, and the last thought he had before sleep came to claim him was, *Yes, Mack, I do. I do love her. Almost as much as I love you and Sarah...*

CHAPTER

XII

The echo had been female at some point, but aside from one pendulous breast exposed between tatters of a bloody Trojans sweatshirt, nothing much was recognizable. Most of the flesh was gone from its face, the only hair remaining was a gore-matted clump of what might have been blonde, and the entire area between sternum and crotch was a gaping void.

The creature stared blankly in at Mason with its one remaining eye, snapping its lipless jaws and pawing at the glass, and it wasn't alone in the Quad. Echoes had gathered during the night, and now as many as eight were pressed up against the front of the building.

It could have been worse, Mason knew, and once again, he had to give credit where credit was due. By arranging their sleeping quarters in the back of the building, Hansen had all but ensured that the greater mass of echoes would collect precisely there, as close to the flame as the moths could get. A quick run from one end of the roof to the other, then a dash across the gangplank to building eight, and they would buy themselves a full minute or two before the swarm could manage to reorient itself.

Mason gazed out at the broken little female, and he spared a moment to wonder who this girl might once have been. Had she been pretty? The small stature and team sweatshirt suggested youth, so he concluded that she must have been pretty. Young girls were *always* pretty. It was only when the world started to beat them down that they lost that buoyant glow of youth. So, had this pretty young girl been someone's sister? Someone's daughter? Someone's lover? Had someone cared for this shattered little girl the way he cared for the only three girls he'd ever loved?

A splash of blood across the glass washed away all such thoughts, then two more splashes from two more echoes creased the glass, and it was all he could do to make out the close-cropped hair and wide shoulders of twenty-something Donn appearing beyond the blur, his massive war-scythe dripping with gore.

Mason uncoiled the last links of chain from the door and slipped quietly through, followed at his heels by Christopher, Alejandra, and Addison, all with their SBDs.

Most of the wet work had already been done. On Hansen's insistence, he, Donn, and Richie had taken on the task of clearing the Quad. It was a ritual they had performed every morning for the better part of two weeks, and Mason would be the first to admit that they had honed their skills to razor sharpness. Barely had a foot silently struck ground at the end of a rope before half a dozen echoes were quietly dispatched.

But even so, it was only the start of the battle. As the light of humanity shifted, so did the swarm, and though the wave of echoes was blocked on one side by the car-barrier, another wave began cresting around the west side of the building like a veritable tsunami.

It started with two, then three, and then came the torrent, and it was all they could do to swing and swing and swing again. Mason clubbed one little male over the head, cracking its skull open like an egg, but he hadn't even pulled the rebar free before another was on him. He gave the creature a ferocious kick to the knee that dropped it to the ground, then he speared it through one temple and out the other like a shish kebab.

Beside him, Alejandra was chopping away with her machete, and as always, what she lacked in height, she more than made up for in guts. If the echo was under six feet tall, she would hack at its neck, either severing its spine with the first blow or slowing it down enough for a second whack to do the job. If the creature was too tall for such a manoeuvre, she would chop it off at the knee to bring it down to her level and lay into it without mercy.

Addison and Christopher were side by side, cleaving away with Nut-Buster and hatchet, and Hansen, Donn, and Richie were giving it everything they had. All of them were big and strong and powerful, so it rarely took more than a single blow to turn a skull to mush. Only once did Mason see any of them falter, and that was when Richie missed his target by a few degrees and one of his bat's spikes got wedged between two vertebrae in a particularly big echo's neck. But Donn was quick to react. He decapitated the creature with one mighty swing of his war-scythe, then he planted a boot between its shoulder blades so Richie could yank his weapon free.

But even as the fight raged, every bit of it was done in a vacuum. There were no warning shouts, no grunts of exertion, not so much as a laboured breath. When they got winded, they gulped air instead of panting. When a bit of detritus splattered into an open mouth, they didn't spit, they wiped it away with the sleeve of a shirt. And when they simply grew too tired to fight, they fought on anyway, without a single whimper.

Sarah and Mackenzie were on the Alamo's roof with their .22s, but they were holding their fire. Teddy was up there too, with her crossbow as big as her, but she didn't release a single bolt lest the twang of strings give them away. Diego, though, was under no such limitations. His slingshot was as silent as a whisper. The boy stood stock-still on the very edge of the roof with the fanny-pack on his hip full of ball-bearings salvaged from wherever-the-hell, and he quickly proved the weapon to be far more than a toy. The kid's aim was spectacular, and the slingshot was powerful. Every slug he fired found its mark with more than enough force to penetrate a skull, and like a .22 bullet, once that ball-bearing entered the skull, it rattled around and around, turning the echo's brain into Swiss cheese.

One after another were felled, and every bit of it was done as quietly as Sunday prayers. Soon enough, the tsunami turned back into a river, then it slowed to a trickle, and Donn and Richie were left to mop up while the others set off on the next phase of the plan.

Four others emerged as silently as ghosts and took to covering the backs of those quietly making their way to building six. Becks had her javelin, Sk8rboy William had his crossbow, Inez toted Alejandra's Tommy gun, making her look a little like Ma Barker, and Beverly had been given the honor of wielding Sarah's kukri on the express condition that she resort to the gun on her hip only if it was absolutely necessary. At one point, Mason actually considered relieving her of the gun entirely, but he couldn't bring himself to do it. Firstly, Beverly was a valued member of the team, and despite a bit of a meltdown, he trusted her to follow orders. More to the point though, he knew full well that her gun might very well save one of their lives – his own included.

And then there was Clancy. He'd been held back until phase one was complete, but now he came charging out, ready to join in on the fun. He came up to Mason first as if reporting for duty, then he tossed his head in the direction of Donn and Richie dealing with a straggling echo, and he bared his teeth. A single gesture from Mason, though, and he stayed dutifully at the man's side, with his nose in the air and a keen eye on the perimeter.

Mason led the way up the concourse, took a handful of concrete steps as silently as a cat, and found himself directly in front of where a giant had taken a bite out of building six.

The entire front of the place was glass, with a glass door at either end, and another in the middle. The doors had been secured from the outside with 2x4s shoved through the handles and tied off with rope, and a good thing, too. Already, four echoes were trying to claw their way out, and by the look of their ravaged bodies, they weren't alone in there. Mason crept up to the nearest door and shone his flashlight as far into the darkness as it would reach, and when nothing else appeared, he did the unthinkable. He brought up his fifty pounds of rebar and rapped on the glass with a gentle *tap-tap-tap...*

At first, there was nothing. The echoes continued to bumble along, but beyond that, nothing moved. But hadn't it? There was one fleeting moment where he thought he might've caught the slightest shifting of darkness against darkness, so he tapped again, this time just a little harder.

It started as a subtle trick of shadows at the very limit of his flashlight. He wasn't sure at first that he was even seeing anything at all, but then the shadow grew, a howl arose from within, and a big male the approximate size of a mountain gorilla came charging across the foyer, crashing into the glass directly across from Mason.

Anyone else would have reacted. A flinch. A gasp. A backward step. But not Mason. He stood perfectly still as the creature thundered into the glass, thrashing and clawing and drooling a bloody red foam from its rabid, snapping jaws.

Mason gave the signal, and Addison, Alejandra, Hansen, and Christopher joined him, leaving Becks, William, Inez, and Beverly to protect their rear. As the trio of echoes followed the shifting light in awkward, stuttering steps, one of them happened to bump directly into the alpha, and the creature immediately turned on it, giving Christopher the precious few seconds he needed to work the ropes free from the door, slip out the 2x4, lay it on the ground as if it were Ming china, and slowly and quietly ease the door open.

Mason was the first one in, and barely had he set foot across the threshold when a second, smaller alpha appeared from out of nowhere and came charging directly at him. Normally, he would have held his ground and let the alpha to come to him, but to do so now would block the way for the others, so he launched himself at the creature and met it halfway, driving several feet of rebar through its snapping jaws and directly out the back of its neck. While the others took care of the big male and the remaining trio of echoes, he lowered the dead body gently to the floor, planted his boot on a blood-soaked t-shirt declaring 'I'm Not Like The Other Girls,' and *shhlucked* the rebar free.

Now came the hard part. The five of them were alone in an enclosed space currently occupied by an unknown number of alphas and echoes, they had no cover and no reinforcements, and they not only had to clean out every last one of those creatures, but they had to do so in absolute silence. Though alphas were not attracted to the howls of other alphas, it wasn't uncommon for them to probe toward those sounds, so they also had to do it quickly. All it would take was for one of those hundreds of alphas outside to probe a little too far, and one of his compatriots would have to act. Maybe it would be the twang of an arrow, or maybe the handclap of a .22, but it would be enough. That single unmistakably human sound would bring the entire swarm down on their heads, and behind them would be more. And behind those, more still.

Mason didn't have to signal the others. They all knew the plan. Addison and Alejandra split off on their own toward the stairs, and he, Hansen, and Christopher fanned out, just as a little old echo came stumbling around a corner. As if they'd practiced the manoeuvre a thousand times, Clancy weaved his big body between the creature's legs, dropping it to the ground, and Christopher made quick work of it with his long-handled hatchet. But as always, what began as a trickle soon turned into a torrent. Two more echoes came at them and were silently and summarily dispatched, then an alpha came probing from out of nowhere and the probe suddenly turned into a charge. The quick change caught Hansen by surprise, and Mason almost made the mistake of rushing to his aid, but another alpha came barreling out of a back room just then and made straight for him, howling like a banshee and clawing wildly at the air.

This time, Mason waited for the creature to come to him.

STAGE 3: BRAVO

He raised the rebar to his shoulder like a batter at the plate, and when the moment was right, he stepped into the swing and caught the alpha across the bridge of its ugly pug nose. The almighty blow sent the creature high into the air in a backward somersault and slammed it into a wall, minus the top part of its head.

And they kept coming. A tiny teenaged alpha bearing another in its wake. Then another. And another. Then three more echoes, and three more after that, then two young alphas as big as redwoods. And as the torrent came, the team fought on without a sound. Not a single grunt. Not a single groan. Not so much as a harshly drawn breath. The muted sounds of battle drifted down from above, so Mason knew that Alejandra and Addison were in a fight for their lives as well, yet he heard not a peep other than the abbreviated howls of alphas or the tell-tale *crunch!* of metal on bone.

At last, the torrent returned to a trickle and the trickle died away, and just like that, there was no one left to fight. The three of them split up and took to searching the main floor from one end to the other, but aside from a single scuffle from the direction Hansen had gone, it seemed that the job was well and truly done.

Mason carried the search to the farthest corners of the main floor, but even with Clancy snuffling around every corner and under every door, he came across only one more creature.

It was an echo, but only just. It had been a girl, no older than seventeen. Dark, almond-shaped eyes. High cheek bones. Slim. Tiny. Little more than a hollowed-out shell. The alphas had fed well, and now this poor, broken little thing didn't have enough muscle mass left to move. She clawed desperately at the floor, but couldn't quite manage to crawl her way out of a puddle of her own blood and gore and urine. Clancy growled at the thing, but then the growl turned into a single plaintive whine, and he sat on his haunches, looking from the echo to Mason and back again.

Mason said the first words he'd uttered since leaving building seven, but he did so in a whisper so light that he could barely hear it himself.

"I'm sorry..." he hushed to the tiny little echo, then he gently placed the tip of the rebar between those big, dark, almond-shaped eyes and leaned his weight onto it until the creature stopped moving.

With that final act, the brutal drama was played out. Mason returned to where they'd split up, physically spent and emotionally exhausted, and he was soon joined by the other four, with every haggard face reflecting the same disposition. There was no celebration, no round of handshakes and no pats on the back. They simply gathered together and made their way back to the door.

The defenders outside had been given instructions to fall back into building six if things got too hairy, so it was a good sign that they hadn't. But as Mason came close enough to see the Quad, it became readily apparent that their backup hadn't exactly been idle. Six new bodies now littered the ground; some with great gaping wounds, one crumpled in a heap with its head lying several feet away, and at least one sporting a single round hole in its forehead the approximate size of a javelin point. He also noted that Beverly had her shotgun back over her shoulder, but he couldn't really blame her for scampering back to the Peterbilt to retrieve it. She hadn't done anything quite so stupid as actually using it, so what the hell. Besides, maybe he'd been wrong to keep it from her in the first place. That big scattergun was more of a security blanket than a weapon to the woman, so maybe her having it would be good for them *all* in the long run.

As Christopher secured the door, Mason allowed one last lingering look at Gloria. In another reality, he and the others were there right now, piling in and making their escape. But not in this world. Not here. Not now. He briefly considered amending the plan on the fly, but to do so now would be a stupid move, and stupid died quick. And so, having done the math in as short a time as it took him to blink, he signaled to the others and started back to the Alamo.

They didn't travel in a bunch, but instead fanned out across the Quad. Only once did anyone have to act, but the echo was in such a ravaged state that a single swat from Alejandra's machete put it down for good. It was clear sailing after that, and they made it all the way down the cement steps and almost to the doors of the sanctuary before the end came. Richie and Donn were holding the line well, and were just in the process of clubbing a fat, bald alpha into the ground when the alarm was raised. It came in the form of a short, sharp *twang!* from Teddy's crossbow.

Damn! It had been too much to hope for, after all. Whether it'd been the abbreviated howls from building six or the muted sounds of battle from the Quad, the swarm had finally grown inquisitive, and that fat, bald alpha signaled the end. For all Mason knew, it might've been the first of the swarm to probe this far, or it might've been the tenth, but if Sarah had given little Teddy the go-ahead to fire, it meant that more were coming. *Lots* more.

He didn't have to get his group moving. They all knew precisely what that single twang meant, and they hurried along double-time. But then a handclap sounded from up above, and they all froze in place as if they'd just heard their own death knell.

"Inside!" he hushed to the group, fairly propelling Inez and William through the doors. "All of you! Get inside! Now!"

As always, when the end came, it came quickly.

One second, Donn and Richie were beating an alpha into pulp, and the next, they were staring wide-eyed into the abyss, seemingly rooted to the spot. Another alpha crashed into Richie, sending him flying backwards, and Donn was forced to chase after the thing, creeping his war scythe up its back in successively damaging blows until he could finally skewer it through the skull with one final, decisive swing. But then another came charging around the corner, and they were both caught flat-footed. Donn fended off the creature long enough for Richie to struggle out from under the dead alpha, but by the time he was back to his feet, another was almost on top of him.

Sarah picked off both alphas, then she and Mackenzie opened up on the gathering swarm. The barrage of handclaps was too much for the rest of the creatures to ignore, and a great raucous chorus of howls and snarls rose up as Mason called out to the two boys, "Donn! Richie! Move!"

They were both blanched with fear, but a second call from Hansen got them moving.

"Guys! Get your asses in gear! *Now!*"

And that they did.

By now, all four snipers were raining holy Hell down on the swarm, but it would always be a losing game. Teddy went through her crossbow bolts in seconds, then Diego's fanny-pack was emptied and he took to kicking up loose bits of gravel from the rooftop for extra ammunition. Mackenzie and Sarah kept up the barrage, but Mack's 100-round magazine ran dry just as the vanguard of the swarm tore around the corner, and it was all Mason could do to throw Hansen through the doors and barrel in after him, wrapping the chain back around the handles and holding up his hand for absolute silence.

No one uttered a word, but a half-dozen guns came up, bolts drawn, hammers cocked, and fingers on the triggers. And rightly so. Even secured, the door was made of glass. One lucky hit and the whole swarm would be in. Several of those huddled inside even went so far as to hold their breath, releasing it only when the first few alphas tore obliviously past, but as the Quad filled to capacity and bodies began slamming into bodies, the swarm turned from tearing itself apart to directing their rage on anything and everything within reach, including that very breakable glass door. Mason and Hansen both grabbed for the handles as if they might be able to keep the swarm at bay through sheer force of will, but with a shared grimace, they ultimately relented and herded everyone back upstairs. Only Alejandra, Addison and Christopher stayed behind. Those three would be their Tail-end Charlies, staying put to cover the doors. And if worse came to worst... well, Mason didn't dare let his train of thought carry him that far.

Once upstairs, Hansen helped himself to Sarah's Howitzer and made a move back down to join the others, but Mason caught him by the sleeve and whispered something in his ear, and he relented. As Hansen stuck Becks to his side like glue and went to each of the boys in turn to get them ready for a probable invasion, Mason huddled Inez and Beverly together and hushed to them both, then all three of them began turning the place upside down. At last, they tied a white lab coat into a bundle, and Mason ran with it down the hall and up the ladder to the roof.

By the time he emerged from the hatch, Mackenzie and Sarah had replaced their spent magazines with full and were down on their bellies on each corner of the roof, taking careful aim at the alphas nearest the door. Diego was still kicking up loose bits of gravel and doing what little he could to help, but when Mason arrived and waved him and Teddy over, he tucked the slingshot into his back pocket and ran to his side, Mason opened the bundle and spread the contents at their feet, and both kids raised a curious eye up to him.

It was a mishmash of odds and ends they'd grabbed at random. Glasses, tin cups, mugs, and, being the college's science building, there was a wide array of beakers and flasks and great bulbous things that looked a little like giant light bulbs. In a few clipped words, Mason told Diego and Teddy what to do, and he didn't have to tell them twice.

Mason went first. He'd had some experience in distracting a swarm before, so after signaling for Sarah and Mack to hold their fire, he picked up one of the big light bulb-looking things and hurled it as far as he could. It smashed to the ground close to the Peterbilt, and every alpha within earshot spun around toward the sound. He threw another in the same direction, but the swarm shifted at the very last second and the glass exploded against the back of a little female's head. It wasn't what Mason had been aiming for, but the result was just as effective. The alphas nearest the unfortunate creature tore into her, and the ensuing melee brought others.

After careful consideration, Diego selected a metal tray. The thing looked far too big for someone so small, but the boy had talents that went well beyond slingshots. He hauled back his arm like a champion discus thrower and let the tray fly, and it sailed far out over the swarm before finally clattering against the side of a building on the other side of the Quad.

As always, distracting the swarm was a double-edged sword, every bit as sharp and deadly as that ever-elusive thing called 'hope.' Not enough, and you accomplished nothing. Too much, and you were liable to bring the world crashing down around your ears. It was a game of subtleties; a lesson that the kids picked up on immediately. Teddy's first attempt was with a ceramic mug emblazoned with the words 'World's Greatest Dad,' but her aim was off and her throw was weak. It landed barely thirty feet into the swarm and succeeded only in drawing some of the more distant alphas closer. But she was a quick study, and her next throw was spot on. She hurled a glass beaker to the far side of the Quad with the precision of a quarterback, and with all three of them keeping it up for several more rounds, the crush of bodies against the Alamo lifted appreciably.

When Mason was satisfied that their priority had been met, he waved Sarah and Mack back across the gangplank and herded everyone into the hatch. As the last one down the ladder, he found Sarah, Mackenzie, and Clancy waiting for him at the bottom.

Sarah shook hands with Diego and Teddy, giving them both a well-deserved, "Good work, guys." then she threw her arms around Mason's neck and graced him with a kiss on the cheek. Mack gave each of the college kids a fist-bump, then she held up her tiny fist for Mason.

"Not bad," she said, receiving the gentlest of fist-bumps in return.

"Thanks, Mack. I'll take it." Mason said with a smile. But once Mack left with the others and only he and Sarah remained, his smile instantly vanished. "I guess things didn't go quite as planned," he said, wiping a smudge of someone else's blood from her cheek.

"They rarely do. Did you clear the building?"

"Yes, but fat lot of good it does."

"Was there food? Water?"

"We didn't exactly have to time to take inventory, but Addison said that the restaurant looked pretty well stocked."

"Did you see a bookstore?"

"In passing, but again, we were a little rushed. Did you see the size of that swarm? Getting to Gloria now is going to be damn near impossible."

Just then, another voice growled from behind, "Aww, are you going to take your ladyballs and go home, tough guy?"

Mason spun around to see Detective Sergeant Gary Hansen's trademark sneer, and it took every fiber of his being to not immediately remove it with a right cross.

"Great plan, Gary," he huffed, " Fucking awesome."

Hansen shrugged. "Hey, the best laid schemes o' mice and men, asshole."

"Yeah, well your scheme didn't just go awry, Gary. It brought the whole goddam house down."

"No, *you* did that!" Hansen aimed a big fat finger at Mason's chest. "You and that monster fucking truck of yours."

"Hey! He was trying to save your daughter!" Sarah roared.

"Who didn't need saving!" Hansen roared even louder.

"And how were we supposed to know that? Besides, if you'd just waited five more seconds before sending out the cavalry, we would've been on our way instead of standing here having this stupid *fucking* conversation!"

"Well, how was I supposed to know—" Hansen cut himself off, and Sarah stabbed a finger right into his chest.

"Exactly," she said, leaving Hansen to chew over that one

single word and all that it implied as she stormed out of the room.

Hansen stewed and said nothing, but Mason had to give him a modicum of credit for at least appearing to ponder the point.

"Spunky gal," he grumbled at last.

"I'd love to be there when you tell her that," Mason said, dryly. "So, you got any more bright ideas?"

Hansen's sneer returned in full.

"Just one, tough guy... If that mountain isn't going to come to Muhammad, Muhammad had better get his ass in gear and get over to that mountain!"

CHAPTER

XIII

A re you kidding me? That's gotta be thirty feet!"
Everyone was spread out along several windows overlooking the spit of land between the buildings, and aside from a strangely sanguine Hansen, nobody much liked what they were seeing. The car-barrier was keeping the swarm out, but it was also keeping them *in*, and a dozen or more alphas were already in full probe between the Alamo and building six, with thrice that many standing vigil, danger-close. And just a few short yards south was the Quad, now home to hundreds more, just waiting for a human sign. A dash across that thirty feet of open space wouldn't just be damn near impossible, it would be suicide.

"More like forty," someone from the back said in a hush.

"If you'd have listened to me, we'd all be over there right now," Mason growled, not trusting his temper enough to even look Hansen's way. "Or better yet, we could be miles away."

"And if ifs and buts were candies and nuts..." Hansen

snarked. "C'mon Einstein, if we'd done it your way, we'd have come up a few men short. No way we all could've gotten over there en masse."

To be honest, Mason had run that particular what-if scenario through his mind a dozen different ways since his little blow-up with Hansen, and as loathe as he was to admit it, the old bastard was right. The only reason the five of them made it at all was because everyone else was covering their collective backsides. If they'd all gone together, more than a few of them would have laid claim to their own bloody little patch of Skyline real estate that would be theirs forevermore.

"So we went through all that for nothing," Addison harrumphed. "The building's clear, but we can't get to it. Spiffing."

"Not exactly, Poindexter," Hansen gruffed, dabbing a fat sausage of a finger at the glass. "That's our way in, right there."

It was a door. A side door to building six. Metal. Set into an alcove. No latch on the outside. Mason had seen it earlier, but had immediately discounted it.

"Why the *hell* didn't you point that out before?" Beverly snapped at Hansen. "We could have gotten in that way instead of going all the way around the whole damn building!"

"Not likely," Sarah answered for him. "That's an emergency exit."

"So? We've broken into those before."

"Not quickly. And for *sure*, not quietly."

"So what the fuck good is a locked door?" This from Alejandra.

"You know, you might have thought to mention it, Ranger Smith," Addison threw in. "The least we could have done was unlock it while we were there."

Mason knew what the old man was going to say before he said it, and his blood started to boil.

"And so I did!" Hansen crowed, a smug grin curling the corners of his mouth.

Alright. That was the last straw. It was one thing for the man to put his own people first, but this was something else entirely. This was Hansen using Mason's people as alpha fodder, just so he could carry out some secret agenda. The distinction might be thin, but it was there, and suddenly, Mason wanted nothing more than to wipe that smug grin right off that ugly fucking mug. He covered the distance in two strides and came nose to nose with the man.

"You should've said something," he growled. "If that was your plan all along, you should've told us."

Hansen returned every bit of Mason's glare. "And then what? *Vote?*"

"Here we go again..." Inez sighed.

There was a time when Mason would have ended this with Hansen on the floor, searching for his teeth. Even now, he was hard-pressed not to return to the good old days.

"Alright. That's it, Gary. No more. This one-man show of yours is over. Now, granted, we all share the blame for the mess we're in. Well, alright. Shit happens. And if you've got a way to *unfuck* the situation, then okay. Good for you, and good for us all. But from now on, you will lay your cards on the table, Gary, you got me? And I mean *all* of them. Believe it or not, someone here might actually have a better idea than yours. Or maybe someone knows something you don't. We can argue, we can debate, we can come to blows if that's what you want, but *all* of our lives are on the line here, so we *all* get a say in how and why we risk those lives. Understand?"

He turned away from Hansen's smug puss before his anger

made him do something he wouldn't regret in the least, but for the first time since he'd known bad-ass Gary *mother-fucking* Hansen, the man didn't have an immediate smart-ass comeback.

Then Becks gave the old man her patented, "Daddy..." and the deal was sealed.

"Yeah, sure, whatever," Hansen snorted, and Mason tried to find peace in the fact that it was probably as close to an apology as the man had ever come in his life.

"Uh, so did this master plan of yours include how we get from here to there through a mosh pit from Hell?" Christopher asked.

Hansen grumbled under his breath, then he admitted, "Not exactly, no," and to save face, he added a rather less contrite, "But it also didn't include *you* people bringing in every 50 in the county!"

"Daddy..." Becks cautioned him again, and he acquiesced. Barely.

"Alright, fine! I'm sure none of you noticed, but there's a door exactly like that one right below our feet, one floor down. Almost a straight shot from one door to the other. Thirty... okay, make it forty feet. Forty feet and we're in, easy as pie."

"Easy as pie," Teddy echoed in a nervous hush.

Addison raised his hand. "*I* noticed..."

"That's one bitch of a pie," Alejandra said, slapping Addison's hand back down.

"Oh, c'mon, *peleonera*. You can outrun a swarm over a distance of forty feet, can't you?"

"Luckily, I don't have to outrun the swarm, *tamarindo*," she snarled, flipping him her middle finger. "I just have to outrun *you*."

As the back and forth continued, Mason sank deep into thought.

It was a damn crazy idea on the face of it. Fifteen people, half of them kids, crossing forty feet of open ground through a swarm numbering in the hundreds. It would be wholesale death and destruction. Slaughter on an epic scale. The whole idea sucked balls in a way that balls had never been sucked before, but for the life of him, he couldn't see another way.

They had to get out of this place. Not just out of the Alamo, but out of Skyline. This place was done. It might have been able to last another day or two before they'd blundered in full throttle, but not now. He and Hansen had both seen to that. Hand in hand, they'd dug them all into this shithole, and the shit was rising fast. They had to go. Period. And *stuff* or no *stuff*, the only way out was through building six. It was halfway to Gloria, and she was their only real way out of this mess.

He turned back to Hansen and leaned so close that their noses almost touched.

"Alright, Hansen, we have no other options now, so we'll do it your way. But I promise you, if any of these people get killed because of your need to be a know-it-all prick, it'll be on you, and I will take it very, *very* personally."

Hansen was half a head shorter than Mason, but he somehow managed to look him straight in the eye.

"You got a deal, big man. But the deal goes both ways. *Copy?*"

It was all Mason could do to not react in the way he so very much wanted to.

At last, Sarah put a hand on his shoulder and turned him back to the window, and Becks led her father away, grumbling about monster trucks and tough guys and the fucking nerve of some assholes.

"Possible," Sarah said, watching the swarm below and doing her own math.

Mackenzie came up between them to have a look for herself, and her shadow barged through after her. Mason gave Clancy a scratch between the ears as he propped his big paws on the windowsill.

"Doubtful," he answered back, plainly.

"Aw, there's not so many," Mackenzie said, her little nose pressed to the glass.

Mason buried his hand in her abundance of curls and turned her head to the right so she could see the rest of the swarm packed into the Quad.

"Oh! Okay, yah. That's a lot..."

"No other choice," he hushed to Sarah.

"Nope."

"One step closer to Gloria."

"Yup. Like jumping from stone to stone across a river."

"A river filled with piranha. With bears on your ass. Through a swarm of killer bees. With a Sharknado bearing down."

"Fair enough," Sarah smiled, however briefly. "Our people on the flanks, kids in the middle?"

"I guess. But lots of variables. No guarantees."

Sarah put her hand on his shoulder. "You want guarantees, Mace? Get AppleCare."

"Ain't no guarantees in the 'poc'lypse," Mackenzie chirped from below.

He ruffled her big mop of hair. "No, Mack, I guess there ain't. So how do *you* think we should do it?"

To no one's surprise, the girl shrugged and said simply, "The only way we can, Mace. No way through but through."

The smell of fresh coffee drew the rest of the crowd away from the windows, and even Mason peeled himself away eventually.

Inez rationed out what little her old-fashioned percolator could hold, telling them all, "Sorry folks, all we got is black," as they all took their seats around the central tables.

Mason waved off the coffee and took a seat next to Beverly just as she produced a fresh pint of scotch from one pocket or another. Even as he wondered just how much of his private stock she'd helped herself to, and where she could possibly be keeping it all, she passed it over and he poured a full quarter of its contents into his mug.

"If we wait, some of them might go away," he heard Teddy say, meekly.

"Not a chance." Donn shot the idea down. "Not unless someone else draws them away."

"What if we made a big noise ourselves?" Diego suggested. "Like, a *big* noise! Something that was sure to lure them away?"

"Anything loud enough to lure them away would only bring others in," Addison reminded him through a sigh.

"It's all a trade-off now," Mackenzie added, barely above the background howls.

Sarah ruffled Clancy's ears and asked on the off-chance, "I don't suppose anyone has an iPod or a phone?"

The question was met with silence.

Mason scowled through a mouthful of scotch. Of *course* no one had a working phone. They'd used up all the batteries in those first horrible days, trying to get through to their loved ones. Families. Parents. Friends. Anyone who would tell them that everything was going to be alright and that they weren't alone. If they could have seen far enough into an unimaginable future to save a bit of battery life for a moment like this, every single one of them would've likely slit their own wrists.

"We'll only get one shot at it," Alejandra said at last. "Anyone left behind to cover our *culos* is gonna be left behind for good."

"So it's a blitz, then," Addison summed up. "No snipers, no spotters. One big rush."

"All or nothing," Christopher said to his mother.

"Just like always," she said back.

"*Chido,*" Alejandra huffed. "I'm getting sick of just sitting around."

Over the next hour, Inez kept the dribbles of coffee coming, Mason helped himself twice more to Beverly's bottle, and they talked out a plan. Everyone offered their input, no one was excluded, and nothing was deemed too ridiculous to consider. Hansen sat out most of it in a kind of self-imposed exile, but once they had a plan that might be considered shitty-ass at best, he offered the occasional grunt of advice. And when the plan was slightly less than shitty-ass but as good as it was ever going to get, they ran through it again and again and again until everyone understood not just their role, but the role of each and every member of the team. For this craziness to have any chance at all of working, they all had to be in perfect lock-step, so Mason went through it again and again and again until even Detective Sergeant Gary *my-way-or-the-high-way* Hansen was forced to give it his official snort of approval.

Sk8rBoy William split his remaining crossbow bolts with Teddy, Sarah bestowed her Howitzer upon Hansen, and Inez relieved Mack of her .22, and once they were as ready as a bunch of school kids and civilians with a slightly-less-than-shitty-ass plan could ever be, Mason saw to one last order of business by stuffing a knapsack with what might eventually become useful. He then allowed the rest of them a minute or two to gather whatever possessions they considered too dear to leave behind, but aside from guns and crossbows and SBDs, nothing else was deemed to be worth those extra few pounds.

Addison and a couple of the boys wolfed down a granola bar or two, and most of the group had a last gulp of water, but the rest of their meagre stores were left behind as they padded single-file down the steps to the main floor. Once there, Hansen led them to the side door, and Mason clearly heard Beverly hitch a gasp in her throat when she saw a chair shoved between push bar and door to keep it secure.

He didn't have to wonder what was behind that gasp. Sarah had told him everything. That simple chair through the push bar must have brought back a flood of memories, up to and including a child being torn from her arms. But to her credit, she didn't say a word, nor did she produce the bottle to dull the pain. She sniffled once, wiping away a tear before it could form, then she swung the shotgun from her shoulder and clicked off the safety.

Hansen had one last look at the troops, then he carefully removed the chair and pressed as slowly and as gently on the push bar as he could. With one tiny squeal and a subtle *shnick!* a pencil-thin crack of light appeared. He put a cautious eye to the crack and stood there unmoving for several anxious moments, then he pushed the door open a little further, and a brilliant shaft of sunlight bathed fifteen anxious faces.

At last, he stepped aside and let Alejandra and Sarah squeeze through, out into the swarm.

Sarah hadn't taken more than five steps before coming to a halt. She was so close to two alphas on vigil that she could have reached out and touched them both. A dozen others were danger-close on all sides. Then the swarm shifted, closing off any possibility of retreat, and she was trapped. A single step in any direction would mean death, so following the plan, she stood there as still as a mannequin, kukri in hand, and waited.

Alejandra didn't get much farther. She managed to creep slowly around a cluster of alphas on vigil and sidestep a big bastard probing toward the Quad, but then she came face to face with two more on vigil just as all other avenues closed off, and just like that, she had nowhere else to go. She brought the machete up over her head in a two-handed grip, then she too froze in place.

The next ones out were Mason, Christopher, and Addison. All three spread out as best they could, but barely had Christopher and Addison taken a dozen steps each before they came to a stop. Mason held his breath and sidled sideways to sneak between two big males, bringing him just that much closer to Sarah, but then he could advance no farther, so he too stuck to the plan and froze like a statue.

And then came the super-weapon.

Mack and Clancy came bounding through the door and set off into the swarm as if they'd been let loose in a playground. Clancy bowled over the first alpha he came across and wound himself between the legs of another to upend it, while Mackenzie began running in circles around two others with just enough clicks of her tongue to get them both to break from their vigil. The creatures snarled and clawed after the sound, but the girl stayed always just one step ahead, and when they finally became so twisted up with each other that they both fell to their knees, they happened to be close enough to Christopher that a quick double-blow from his hatchet finished the things off.

It didn't have to be Christopher. It could have been anyone. But that first strike was the signal. All at once, five statues came to life and tore into the swarm in their own way.

Alejandra was the butcher. She plunged the machete into an exposed neck, cleaving it through almost to the bone, then she spun around to deliver a straight slash across a second creature's trachea and gutted a third before any of them had even stirred from their vigil.

Sarah was the consummate surgeon, and her kukri was the scalpel. A slash to a neck here, an uppercut to an armpit to open the artery there, then the barest nick to a nerve cluster to deaden an arm so she could get close enough for a slash across a slender thigh, and three creatures fell as one.

In his sweater-vest and glasses, Addison could have been mistaken for a high school teacher, but with his Nut-Buster turned loose, he was nothing less than a barbarian. That saw-toothed club was an awesome weapon, and after taking down a spindly old male with a kick to the knee, he turned the thing loose, hacking and pummeling and slashing his way through four more alphas with as many blows.

Christopher had a style all his own. He was an artist, wielding that long-handled hatchet as both a scalpel and a bludgeon. If a head or neck presented itself, he'd hack it through like a slender Paul Bunyan chopping at a sapling. If not, a slice under an arm or into a crotch worked just as well. At one point, he even used the wooden handle of the hatchet as a weapon, ramming the thing between the creature's jaws to buy himself the second he needed to draw his knife and slit the thing open from navel to breastbone, then he turned to the next.

As for Mason, he was quite simply a wrecking ball. With

STAGE 3: BRAVO

that fifty pounds of rebar and more than enough muscle to back it up, he quickly turned every alpha within reach into pulp. He swung, he bashed, he beat and he stabbed, and all of it without breaking a sweat.

It was a flurry of activity that lasted little more than seconds, but already, a dozen or more alphas lay dead or dying in no-man's land. But it hadn't happened in a vacuum. Every alpha within earshot picked up on the sounds, and when they came close enough to fall to kukri or hatchet or rebar, others came. And as the sounds of battle grew, the rest of the swarm went from probing to charging, and it took all five defenders working in concert just to hold the beachhead. They clubbed, they slashed and they pummeled, and with every clang of metal on bone attracting more and more of the swarm, at last there came a tipping point, and on Mason's signal, the rest of the fighters came pouring out in a flood.

Those with crossbows fired bolt after bolt, Diego took careful aim with his slingshot and made every bit of gravel count, and everyone with a spiked bat or war-scythe or javelin let fly at anything that moved.

Mason kicked into overdrive and lit into the swarm without mercy. He drove his weapon straight through a chest and used the momentum of yanking it free to plunge the back end of the thing through the throat of another. He brought it up in an arc to connect with the chin of female in full charge, then down again to split another skull in two. Another swing to splinter a little teenaged alpha's spine, then a backswing to crush in the side of another's head in a spectacular spray of blood and bone and gore.

Suddenly, the door to building six seemed a mile away. Seven, eight... no, *ten* alphas were between him and it. He bashed, he kicked, he speared and he stabbed, and with every prodigious swing of his rebar, two or three times as many were there to fill the space. He hadn't advanced more than a few steps before he began to question the entire operation, but it was too late to call it off, and there was no time for half measures. So he waded into the thickening swarm and gave it all he had as if it were the last thing he would ever be able to do on Earth. He advanced across no-man's land one step at a time and one dead alpha at a time, and just when he thought he could advance no farther, a little blur of red tore past with a series of chirps, and half of the swarm between him and the door suddenly disappeared.

It was Mackenzie, coming to his rescue once again. And where the girl went, her shadow was sure to follow. Sure enough, no sooner had he thought the words than Clancy came tearing in to trip up a pair of big alphas and grab a third by the ankle. There were the distinct sounds of bones breaking, then the thing fell face-first to the concrete, spraying out teeth like Chiclets, and Mason stepped blithely over it to have at the next.

He brought up the rebar and pounded away, and six mighty swings later, he was only ten feet from the door. He bashed a big female over the head and Clancy led another past at just the right angle and distance for him to clothesline it across the throat, and now he was only nine feet away. Then he picked out a distinct series of handclaps above the roar as alphas on either side of him grew ugly red freckles between their eyes and crumpled to the ground, and now he was only eight feet away.

With the car-barrier holding back the tide at one end and everyone fighting for all they were worth to stem the flow from the other, the crush of bodies between the buildings actually seemed to thin. But such things were illusory at best.

STAGE 3: BRAVO

Even as Mason skewered a bespectacled old male through the chest and clubbed a tiny child into dust, he knew that it was just a matter of time. Even now, the main body of the swarm was picking up on the sounds of battle, and as a solid wall of teeth and claws began charging in from the Quad, the last desperate phase of the plan was put into play.

Alejandra calmly stepped up to face the advancing swarm, machete sheathed and Tommy gun settled into her shoulder, then Christopher joined her on one side with his AK and Addison on the other with his Bushmaster, and when Beverly arrived with her shotgun, the stage was set.

On an unspoken signal, the foursome opened up, and while Christopher and Addison took precisely-aimed shots at individual heads in the crowd and Beverly's scattergun wreaked a havoc all of its own, Alejandra simply mowed the creatures down like wheat. Like a tiny female version of a '30s era gangster, she stood her ground and sprayed the swarm with a hail of bullets, but there was nothing haphazard about it. Where another might have shot wildly and hoped that the awesome power of the weapon would do all of the work, Alejandra kept her eyes on the sights and made every one of those .45 calibre slugs count. She quickly emptied the fifty-round magazine, then she calmly exchanged new for old and tore into them again, and with the swarm forced to stumble awkwardly over so many of the dead and dying, the bodies piled up like driftwood.

As soon as the barrage of gunfire erupted, Mason ran for the door, clubbing one more alpha into the ground and shouldering another into the side of the building hard enough to have it slump to its knees at the trailing end of a streak of gore. The creature tried to struggle back to its feet, but then the back of its head suddenly exploded in a puff of red, and Mason cast a quick look over his shoulder to see Hansen coming at a run, firing Sarah's howitzer from the hip.

Becks was right behind her father and trying to keep up, but she was in a battle of her own. She was running at one alpha with another on her tail, and Mason's heart skipped a beat when he saw her stumble. But the stumble was a feint, and when the two creatures came crashing together where she had just been, she drove her heel into the solar plexus of one while simultaneously thrusting her javelin through the eye of the other, and as one alpha gasped for breath and the other spasmed on the ground, she yanked the weapon free and plunged it into two exposed throats, silencing them both.

Mason flung the door open, then he and Hansen took to each side of it, shouting back to the troops, "This way! Now! *Move!*"

In prearranged order, Teddy, Diego, and William came running for the open door with Richie and Donn covering their flanks. Richie made more than a few alphas pay for getting too close with a bat to the head, but Donn simply outdid himself. He raged against one alpha after another, and by the time the younger three had crossed the threshold, the war-scythe was literally running wet with gore. He and Richie followed the others in, then the defenders started falling back in turn, closing the circle tighter and tighter. Inez went next, then Beverly, then Becks came close enough for Hansen to grab her by the arm and shove her in, then he stepped up to the firing line and emptied clip after clip after clip to cover the retreat.

Christopher went next, Addison piled in after him, and with the end so near, Sarah finally signaled to Mack and Clancy to get inside before jumping through after them.

Now, the only ones left outside were Mace, Hansen, and little Alejandra, still tearing the swarm apart, piece by bloody piece. At last, Hansen grabbed Alejandra by the collar and dragged her kicking and screaming away from the carnage, and Mace was alone once again. He took three mighty swings and caved in three more skulls, then he spun on his heels and all but hurled himself through the door.

Barely had he cleared the threshold before Hansen threw himself into the door to slam it closed, and there followed several anxious minutes where the outcome of the world's deadliest shoving match remained undecided.

The swarm crushed in on one side of the door, and Hansen, Mason, and Addison threw everything they had at the other. They forced it back, inch by inch, and at last there was the subtle *shnick!* of a lock clicking into place, and everyone crumpled to the floor to pant away their exhaustion.

"We made it," Becks said.

"Ev... Everyone?" Mason managed between furious gulps of air.

"Everyone, Mace," Addison panted. "I counted. All present and accounted for."

*Well, halle-*fuckin'*-lujah...*

CHAPTER

XIV

When they could move at last, fifteen beaten and battered souls dragged themselves upstairs and took over the Fireside restaurant. While some collapsed exhausted into one of the many overstuffed chairs or long couches, others made straight for the kitchen to see what it had to offer. One sniff at the walk-in refrigerator kept them all at arm's length, but they soon found enough canned and packaged goods left behind to feed an army.

On Hansen's orders, the bodies of the dead were carted upstairs and dropped one by one from a window. Over a ton of biomass rained down onto the swarm, and it ended with Mason taking sole custody of a tiny, hollowed-out body and sparing it just an extra fraction of a second before heaving it out with the rest of dead. Once that gruesome task was done, a kind of normalcy descended over the place. Bellies were filled, thirsts were slaked, and when it was discovered that several toilets on the main floor still held water in the tank, few in the group declined the opportunity to avail themselves of an actual working toilet. It was an hour of revelry and a waste of potable water like the world had never seen before, but it was hard-won and well-deserved, and Mason didn't raise a word of objection. In fact, when it was his turn to squander his three gallons of water, he did so without a second thought, even grabbing a magazine from the bookstore on his way down to keep him company. Twenty luxurious minutes later, he stepped out of the men's room to find Sarah coming down the hall with a smirk on her lips.

"*Omni?* Really? I had you pegged more as a *Sports Illustrated* guy."

"Only the Swimsuit edition. Hey, it says in here that Elon Musk believes we're living in a simulation. Think there's a chance he'd spring for the 'no living dead' upgrade?"

"Doubt it. Fucker probably hopped the last rocket to Mars. But listen... I couldn't find *JAMA* in the book store, but I did find this." She held up a magazine, keeping her place with a thumb stuck between the pages. "It was tucked all the way to the back of a bottom shelf behind *Crocheting Monthly*."

"Is it the right one?"

"It is, and it tells quite the story."

"About the virus?"

"Yup! Well, maybe. I'd need to see the actual *JAMA* report to know for sure, but I can see why Jim thought there might be a connection."

Mason looked at the cover. *Science Life*, it read in bold script. Beneath that, a woman in a white doctor's coat, posing before an array of lab equipment that would have made Dr. Frankenstein weep. She was pretty. Asian. Mid-forties, probably. Big dark eyes, high cheekbones and thick, pert lips that would have looked better in a smile than in the staid, expressionless set of an academic.

"Hardly the face of evil."

"Hardly," Sarah agreed, and Mason thought he saw just a glimmer of remembered pain wash through her eyes as she regarded the woman's Asian features. "Apparently, Professor Chan was one of the world's leading oncologists. I've never heard of her, but it says here that she and her team were on their way to developing a new method of fighting cancer."

"Cancer? What does a cure for cancer have to do with the end of civilization as we know it?"

"I'm not sure, but it seems that there was a viral component to her research."

"A virus? To fight cancer? Sarah, I'm no doctor, but is that even possible?"

"It doesn't seem likely," she shrugged, "but using mold to fight infections didn't seem likely until Alexander Fleming left a window open."

"Okay, so what of it? You already knew it was a virus, so how does that help? Do you think you can beat it, now that you know what it is?"

She dashed his hopes before they could form.

"Sorry, Mace. Not a chance. This is just a magazine article, not a scientific paper. It doesn't even identify the particular strain of virus, let alone how it might've been used in the research."

"So, how do you know it has anything at all to do with... well, *anything?*"

She flipped the magazine open to the saved page. "Because I haven't told you the most interesting part. Listen, these are Chan's own words. 'It shouldn't have worked, but it did. After years of trial and error and more disappointment than I could have imagined, we had finally done the impossible. It was only a single organism, but with the successful bonding of the tech, I knew in that very moment that the future of modern medicine had been changed forever.'"

Mason stared blankly down at her.

"Uh, Sarah? I know that you think you're making a point, but you're really not. Care to dumb that down for me? Like, *way* down?"

She gave him a smile that would have melted any man's heart.

"The operative word here is '*tech*,' Mace."

Again, the blank stare, but before Sarah could utter another word, Teddy came bounding down the hall, nearly breathless.

"Mister Mason?" she panted. "Uhh... Sir? Sarah? You guys'd better come quick..."

Fearing the worst, Mason grabbed his weapon from where he'd left it leaning against the wall, and he and Sarah charged after her. But when the girl ought to have led them downstairs to repel an invasion, she turned and ran *up*stairs, her ponytail bouncing every step of the way. Once they reached the top, Mason could see the reason for her concern, but it was hardly the stuff of nightmares. Sarah sheathed her kukri, Mason deposited his rebar against the doorframe, and they both stood there, dumbfounded.

Alejandra and Hansen were standing nose to nose, or as close as Alejandra could reach, surrounded on all sides by the others. Hansen was as red as a beet, and though she was outmatched by a foot and a half and a hundred-odd pounds, Alejandra looked like she was itching for a fight. Thankfully, there was nothing as foolhardy as a raised voice among them, but this was clearly no friendly meeting of minds.

"What the hell...?" Mason cursed just loudly enough to get everyone's attention. "Can't a guy even take a shit without you two coming to blows?"

"This *tamarindo* is more *gallina* than man." Alejandra glared at Hansen, spitting the words up at him. "He thinks we should stay here and sit on our hands. Maybe he expects Prince Charming to come and save the damsel in distress, huh?"

"All I said is that maybe we should wait a day or two!" Hansen towered over the girl, returning every bit of the glare and more.

Becks was at her father's side with her hand on his arm, pleading, "Daddy, please!" but when she tried to pull him away from the stand-off, he rudely ripped his arm away and snorted down at Alejandra, "If you were a man, *peleonera*, I'd knock you on your ass."

"Go for it," the girl hissed.

For a long, pregnant moment, it looked like Hansen might do just that. His fists clenched and unclenched, his muscles tensed, and a vein on the side of his neck pulsed red with every beat of his heart.

Addison was at Alejandra's side, and though he knew better than to come between a bear and a jaguar about to throw down, he hushed in her ear, "He's not worth it, Ally." then he looked to Hansen and cautioned him, "She'll whoop your ass, dude..."

Finally, Sarah stepped between the two, shoving them both apart.

"Seriously, *this* is what we're doing now? Jesus *Christ*, it's like high school all over again! For all we know, we might be the last human beings on the face of the Earth, and you two want to get into a pissing contest? *Christ!*"

"*She* started it," Hansen snarled down at Alejandra.

"No, *you* did," she said, sending every bit of his snarl back up at him. "You started it by opening your big fat *boca!* We go when Mace says we go. Not one second before, and not one second after. Got it?"

"Oh, I get it, *peleonera. El jefe habla, saltas.* He speaks, you jump." He looked past her to Mason. "So, is that it, tough guy? You call this shit a democracy right up until you tell everyone exactly what to do?"

"That's not—" Mason tried, but Alejandra cut him off with a growl.

"Damn straight, *pendejo.* That man says jump, I jump, because I know he has a good reason for me to jump. And if you were half as smart as you think you are, you'd jump too."

"Hey, if you want to follow the great Hank Mason through the gates of Hell, that's fine by me. *Chido, peleonera.* But I'm not about to put my life in the hands of that... that *jackass!*"

His voice had become a roar with that last, and though he immediately clamped his mouth shut, it was already too late. A general howl rose up from outside, and with it came a renewed pounding and clawing against the walls.

Sarah turned a weather eye to the stairs, then she swung back and focused all of her fury on Hansen.

"Make no mistake about it, Hansen. Yes, every single one of us would follow that *jackass* through the gates of Hell, absolutely and without a second thought. But that's not the way it works." Hansen was about to respond, but Sarah shut him down. "I know, I know... here's the part where I say that we wouldn't have gotten this far without Mace, and you say that he's the reason we're in this predicament in the first place, then I remind you that we'd already be fifty miles away if you hadn't sent out the SWAT team after us, and then I get so pissed off that I knee you in the balls. But what it really boils down to is this... For whatever reason, you can't stand Hank Mason, and that's it. Now granted, the man is a little rough around the edges..."

"A *little*," Addison laughed to himself.

"...but just so you know where we all stand, *Detective Sergeant*, every one of us owes that *jackass* more than we could ever repay. He saved my little girl's life, then against all odds, he saved mine...."

"And mine," Christopher threw in.

"And mine," Inez echoed.

"And mine," Beverly said, albeit with a quiver in her voice.

Addison put a thumb to his chest and declared, "And mine," then Alejandra growled up at Hansen with her own, "And mine, *gallina*," and this time, the man let the insult slide.

"And though he had every reason *not* to," Sarah went on, "that *jackass* then came all the way down here just on the slim chance that he might be able to save the woman who *ruined* his life. So, you should thank whatever god you believe in that that *jackass* was ever born, Hansen, because he probably just saved your fat wrinkled ass, too!"

"Well, she didn't exactly *ruin*..." Mason started to say, but that was as far as he got.

Sarah dabbed a finger into Hansen's chest. "Every single *motherfucking* one of us would be dead if it wasn't for Hank Mason, and that includes you! Maybe not today, maybe not tomorrow, but you'd be dead all the same."

Now, Hansen responded, and he did so in a subdued roar.

"Now see here, little lady..."

Sarah's face blanched, and she came so close to Hansen that their noses nearly touched. "Call me 'little lady' again, ass-hat. I fucking *dare* you..."

"Good *Christ!*" Becks grabbed her father by the arm again, and this time she didn't let go. "Don't you see it, Daddy? Doesn't everyone? Hey, Sarah, you want to know why Mace and my father are always at each other's throats? Why they absolutely can't stand one another? It's because they're both smart and they're both strong and they're both as stubborn as a God damn mule! *Jesus*, Daddy, don't you get it? You and Mace are *exactly* the same! And I'm not talking flip sides of the same coin, either. No, no, no! You two are the same side of the same *damn* coin! My *God*, how blind must I have been? Three billion men on the planet, and I picked the one man who was a carbon copy of my father. My *father! Jesus*, how screwed up is *that?*"

In the supremely uncomfortable silence that followed, Hansen and Mason locked eyes for a moment, then they looked awkwardly away and let their gazes drift anywhere at all but directly at one another.

"It actually makes a lot of sense," Christopher hushed to Addison. "You know, in a creepy Freudian kind of way..."

"I totally saw it from a mile away," Addison hushed back.

Becks took her father's hands in hers, and with the sweetest of smiles, she told him what Mason would've ripped his own heart out to hear just a few short weeks ago.

"I love you, Daddy," she said. "You know I do. But know this, too... From now on, wherever Mace goes, *I* go."

"What?" Hansen squawked. "You finally dumped that asshole to the curb after two years of his bullshit, and now you'd rather stick with that very same asshole over your own *father?*"

Becks looked at Mason and then at Sarah, then her eyes drifted down to the little girl with a tiny arm thrown over

Clancy's back, and she spared her the sweetest of smiles. She turned back to her father then, and with what Mason could only imagine as a witch's brew of emotions boiling away just beneath the surface, Becks remained Becks. Brave, resolute, and with a heart of pure gold fixed firmly to her sleeve, she skewered Hansen to the spot with her big dark eyes, and one corner of her mouth turned up in a sly grin.

"In a fucking heartbeat."

As Hansen's mouth gaped wordlessly open and closed like a dying fish, Alejandra delivered the killing blow.

"A blind man could see this place couldn't last, *tamarindo*," she jeered. "So what kind of man does that make you, huh?"

"Of course it couldn't last!" Hansen roared in a sudden blast of fury, heedless of the renewed howling from all around. "I'm not an idiot! I knew from the second we drove in here that this place was going down. But what was I going to do, head for the hills, same as everyone else? Take my little girl and my bottled water and my can of beans, and run? Is that what I should've done, *peleonera*? Should I have turned my back on sixty-plus frightened children and left them all here to *die*?"

With that, all of the fight seemed to drain out of him. He gave Mason one last glance out of the corner of his eye, then he stepped away from the others and lowered himself into one of the overstuffed chairs as if he might never have the strength to pull himself out of it again. Becks took the chair immediately adjacent and reached across the divide to take his hand.

"Oh, Daddy..." she cooed, wiping away a single tear.

Suddenly, everyone was at a loss for words. No one more so than Mason.

STAGE 3: BRAVO

"I'm sorry, my love," Hansen spoke to his daughter as if they were the only two people in the room. "I knew it was only a matter of time, but there were so many lives at stake that I couldn't let myself think it. I mean, I couldn't just leave them all here to die, could I?"

"Of course not, Daddy. Not you."

He reached across to brush a bit of hair from her face. "Even when we were down to seven, what was I going to do? Draw straws for the few I could stuff in my car?"

"Of course not, Daddy..." she said again.

It started with Richie. He broke away from the pack, stepped right up to Hansen, and offered the man his hand.

"I didn't know..." he tried to say, but then he stopped fishing for the right words and told him, simply, "Thank you for saving my life, sir."

Hansen tried to wave off the words, but Richie stuck to his guns and kept his hand out. Finally, Hansen took it, saying nothing in return.

And with that, each and every one of the college kids filed past and offered Hansen their hand, and to Hansen's credit, he shook every one of those hands even though he clearly didn't think he deserved it.

"And mine," Donn said.

"And mine," William echoed.

"And mine," little Diego said, puffing out his chest.

"And mine," Teddy said last.

Then Inez appeared, and saying not a word, she bent down and kissed him lightly on the cheek.

At last, Alejandra presented herself before the man and told him, *"No lo sabía. Quizás no eres tan malo después de todo."* When he cocked an eyebrow at her, she added with a shrug, "You know... *para un tamarindo.*"

154

He may have forced the chuckle, but the smile was real when he replied, *"No cuentes con eso, peleonera."*

She returned the smile, gave the man a nod, and Mason thought he might even have seen her throw him a wink as she peeled away.

Suddenly, those wide, overstuffed chairs looked like heaven to Mason. He made his way toward the big fireplace that gave the restaurant its name and plunked himself down in the chair closest to the hearth. Before he'd even kicked off his boots, he found Mackenzie crawling into his lap, Clancy curling up at his feet, and Sarah taking the seat next to him. And with that, everyone else found a seat – some sharing, some opting for a spot on the floor, and two of the boys, Donn and little Diego, perching themselves on the hearth directly behind Mason as if they were his own personal Praetorian Guard.

"So, what do we do now?" Teddy asked no one in particular.

Mason was perfectly content to let someone else answer the question. Hell, now that he understood Hansen just a little bit more, he'd even be willing to let the old man decide the next step. But as his eyes wandered about the room, he suddenly realized that everyone was looking at him as if waiting upon his every word, and he suddenly felt the full, ponderous weight of responsibility drop on his shoulders like a ton of bricks.

Just yesterday, it seemed, he was all set to single-handedly take on a world gone mad. He'd do his best to wring that bastard's neck, and if he got his own neck wrung in the process... well, so be it. He would have died on his own terms and with zero regrets. But now that he thought about it, maybe he *did* die that day, after all. The old Hank Mason was allowed to die a quick, ignominious death, and in his place emerged a new Hank Mason. A *better* Hank Mason. A Hank Mason who was somehow worthy of the friendship and devotion of wonderful people like these. And not one bit of it would have happened if the sweet little thing tucked under his chin hadn't dared to teach an unrepentant asshole a damnable thing called 'hope.'

He found a spot between Mackenzie's fiery-red curls to give her a kiss on the head, and he told her, silently, *You people think I saved your lives? Trust me, sweetheart, you've got it all bass-ackwards...*

"I'll tell you what we'll do, Teddy," Hansen finally answered the girl's question. "What we'll do is, we get the fuck out of here, and we never look back."

"Fuckin' A," Alejandra seconded the motion.

"Uh... and how do we do that..." Diego piped up, "...exactly?"

Mason had been harboring a dark thought all morning, and now he heard himself saying it out loud.

"I could try to fight my way to Gloria," he suggested, but it was met with immediate and impassioned opposition.

"No!" Sarah, Mack, and Becks all shouted at once, loudly enough to get the swarm back to howling.

"You *can't*, Mace," Sarah said, reaching out her hand.

Instinctively, he took it, and as their fingers intertwined, he could see Becks out of the corner of his eye, trying very hard to look anywhere at all but at them.

"No, you can't," she said into her lap. "You'd never make it, Mace."

"Hey, if the man wants to go, let him go," Hansen said, trademark sneer quickly making a comeback.

It might have been meant as sarcasm, or maybe not, but

for a second or two, for just the briefest of moments as he met Hansen's eye, Mason actually considered going for it. But then Mack raised her pretty little head and looked up at him with the most plaintive eyes he had ever seen in his life, and all such thoughts evaporated away in a single, fluttering heartbeat.

"You wouldn't leave me and Sarah, Mace..." she cooed. "Would you?"

He kissed her lightly on the forehead and tucked her back under his chin. "No, of course not, Mack."

The words had come almost automatically, but with the girl's tiny body relaxing back into his and Sarah's slender hand embracing his own, he knew how much he'd meant them. He'd meant those words with every fiber of his being. He would never leave them. Not while he still drew breath.

"Not now and not ever, Mack." He kissed her again. "Not for anything. Ever."

As Hansen turned up his nose as if he'd just caught a whiff of something foul, Donn jumped to his feet, declaring, "I'll go, Mace! I'll fight my way through those '50s!" But barely had the words left his mouth than Diego jumped up, shouting, "No, I'll go!" followed immediately by Richie standing and declaring, "No, I'll go!"

Jesus...

Mason had known big men in his life. He'd known strong men. He'd known men who would chew the world up and spit it out and shit on whatever remained. But out of all those big, strong men he'd ever known, not a single one of them had half the balls of these college kids.

"No!" he said, shutting the whole thing down before anyone else could volunteer to throw their life away. Then he directed another, "No!" squarely at Alejandra, knowing that she would lay a beat-down on anyone about to sacrifice their life for hers, just so she could go in their place. "No one's going *anywhere!*"

"But Mace," Diego tried one last time, "the needs of the many outweigh the needs of the few..."

"...Or the one," Addison finished the quote, much to Diego's surprise. When Diego looked to him, he cocked an expert Vulcan eyebrow and said, "Hey kid, I was a Trekkie when 'Trekkie' was still an insult. But trust me, we're nowhere near the Kobayashi Maru yet, so just maintain standard orbit."

"*Mierda...*" Alejandra narrowed her eyes at Addison. "How old *are* you, anyway?"

"So, what do we do?" Sk8rBoy William asked, for the first time looking not to Hansen for an answer, but to Mason. "We can't stay here forever, right?"

"No way," Christopher said from a sprawl on a nearby couch, eating handfuls of Count Chocula straight from the box while Inez *tsk-tsked* behind him. "We've already overstayed our welcome at your fine place of higher learning. Time to move on."

"You stay, you die," Mackenzie cooed, sweetly and grimly enough to bring a deathly silence to the room.

"Uh, so we go, right?" Richie asked at last, he too directing the question at Mason instead of Hansen.

"We go," Donn said, pounding the floor with the butt of his war-scythe.

"Yeah, I guess we go," Teddy agreed, though without the slightest hint of enthusiasm.

"We go," Sarah told them both, point blank. "We go as fast as we can, and as far as we can."

"*Chido,*" Alejandra harrumphed, one hand on her hip and the other on the hilt of her machete.

"And we go *together*," Becks said, smiling sweetly at her father.

"But how?" Diego asked with just the slightest hitch in his voice.

Mason looked to Hansen, and soon enough, they all were. There was only one way out. He knew it, Sarah knew it, and Hansen was smart enough to know it, too. Still, it just seemed right that Hansen should point the way, so he waited patiently while the man pretended to make up his mind.

"Building five," Hansen grumbled at last.

"You afraid, Gary?" Mason replied, throwing Hansen's own words back at him.

Hansen's trademark scowl suddenly returned in full. "You're an asshole, you know?" he huffed.

"Yes," Mason agreed without hesitation.

"And that monster truck of yours is a long way away."

"Her name is Gloria."

The scowl deepened.

"Chances are, we won't make it halfway to that... to *Gloria* before we're all killed."

"Chances are," Mason agreed again.

Hansen stewed for some time, then he said what everyone knew he was going to say.

"Alright then, building five it is" he grunted. "But just for the record, do you have the slightest idea just how we're going to accomplish that impossible feat?"

To be honest, Mason hadn't thought that far ahead, but now that the question was raised, he deposited a half-dozing Mackenzie into Sarah's lap and went to the window to see if things were half as bad as he'd imagined.

Shit...

They were worse. *Much* worse.

STAGE 3: BRAVO

Under normal circumstances, an alpha would settle into a vigil state once the sounds of human activity ceased. But these were far from normal circumstances. With so many creatures packed into the Quad, bumping together, jostling, lashing out at anything that might be perceived as prey, every single one of them was on high alert and charging at anything that moved. At any other time, the creatures tearing one another apart would only be a good thing, but with the swarm packed as tightly as sardines, every altercation just excited the bloodlust more.

The car barrier was still in place, but it might as well not have been. With the first wave crushed to a pulp, the rest of the swarm had a stepping stone, and they poured over the vehicles as if they weren't even there. And on the other side of the Quad, the wall of dead bodies that had been so carefully constructed was now torn asunder, and the hundred or so scattered corpses did nothing to stem the tide.

So that was it. The swarm had free and unfettered access from three sides, and they were using them all. And the ruckus they were causing was sure to bring more. Now, there were hundreds. By tomorrow? *Christ…!* To borrow a quote from a certain bug-hunting Marine Private, *That's it…! Game over, man! Game over…!*

And just for one last kick in the gonads, there were echoes there, too. Dozens of them, bumbling their way through the swarm like drunkards through a crowd and only agitating the alphas more. One of them in particular caught Mason's eye. He spared it a second and third glance just to confirm what he was seeing, but there was no mistaking the gold Rolex and the Armani suit. This was the one he'd clubbed over the head and Becks had finished off with a javelin through the eye. Armani had been down for the count, yet here he was, back up at the bell.

Gotta work on that forearm, Becks, he mused in his head.

Mason could feel everyone's eyes on him, but he said nothing as he tore himself away and padded across to the windows on the other side of the room. From there, he could look down on what they'd be facing in their drive for building five, and what he saw chilled him to the bone.

The buildings were a good forty feet apart, but though the northern end of the passage looked to be blocked by some kind of railing, a fresh wave of alphas was raging in from the east, straight down the concourse. So, the swarm wasn't just pouring in from three sides, it was gushing in from all four. End result? Goddam bloody mayhem.

There was a single door on the side of building five, but it was offset. Nothing like a straight shot. And without any-one on the other side to surreptitiously wedge it open, they would have to break it in under the full scrutiny of the swarm. He paced off the diagonal distance in his head and counted it as more than sixty feet. Sixty feet through the densest swarm any of them had ever seen, and without so much as a Sherman tank to their name. So to paraphrase Teddy, what in the flying fucking *Hell* were they going to do now?

Just then, Donn came up beside him, his big frame filling the corner of Mason's eye. The twenty-something punk planted the butt of his war-scythe on the carpet and uttered a low whistle as he looked down on the swarm, one hand lean-ing on Hansen's back-up pistol on his hip.

"It looks impossible," he said in a hush.

"So did crossing the Alps until Hannibal did it," Mason hushed back.

"Sure. Losing half of his army in the process," came the terse reply.

"Those were alternative facts, Donn. Fake news. Recent estimates put Hannibal's losses at something like eight percent."

Donn did the math in his head.

"Okay." he said at last. "So out of these fifteen people, which one are you willing to lose?"

"We just have to think outside the box," Mason told him, hoping he sounded more confident than he felt.

Just then, little Diego appeared on Mason's other side. He raised himself up on his tiptoes to get a good look at what was going on down below.

"Uh, Mister Mason...? Sir...?" he said as quietly as a mouse. "Instead of thinking outside the box, maybe in this instance we should go the other way."

"Huh?" Mason and Donn said as one.

"Well," Diego cocked one corner of his mouth in a semblance of a smirk, "instead of thinking *outside* the box, maybe it's time we started thinking *inside* that sumbitch..."

CHAPTER

XV

I t wasn't a horrible plan on the face of it.

After an hour of everyone offering their own input here and there, Hansen fully involved this time, it was actually raised to the level of almost shitty-ass. And an hour after that, after a whole lot of tweaking and massaging, wholesale destruction and rebuilding from the ground up, it attained the lofty heights of barely acceptable. But with no other choice and their backs against the wall, barely acceptable was the best they could hope for.

And yet, there was apparently one last sticking point.

"I am so sick of hearing about that *damn* book! Can you please tell me what's so important about a *goddamn* book?"

This was Hansen, back to his normal level of snark and still harping on that one point that'd wedged in his craw since the beginning.

"You have a problem with books?" Addison feigned concern. "If it makes you feel any better, Chief Wiggum, some of those books are bound to have pictures."

STAGE 3: BRAVO

As Hansen boiled, Inez spoke up as the voice of reason.

"Gary, books are mankind's way of handing down knowledge. Everything we've learned in the past five thousand years has been written down, just so we don't have to learn it again. Wouldn't it be a good thing to have some of those thousands of years of knowledge along with us to dip into when we need it?"

Not surprisingly, Christopher backed his mother's play.

"We can't be scavengers forever. Stuff'll run out eventually, right? Even canned food goes bad. There'll come a time when we'll have to know a lot just to keep going. I mean, does anyone here know how to farm? How to dig a well? How to refine gasoline? How to weave cloth?"

"How to hot-wire a car?" Richie threw Mason's way with a little side-grin.

"How to make bullets?" Alejandra added, effectively wiping the grin away.

"They're right, Daddy," Becks agreed, but her father dismissed it all with a snort.

"That's years away, sweetheart. When that day comes, we won't have to risk our lives trying to grab a few books on the run. When we really need them, we'll be able to waltz into any library in any city and just take what we need."

"Are you sure of that?" Mason asked him, pointedly.

"Of course! It's just common sense, isn't it? When a pack of wolves kills off all of their prey, they starve. It's as simple as that. Eventually, your so-called 'alphas' will run out of food, and that's it! No more food, no more alphas."

"Just a whole lot more echoes," Richie said, grimly.

Again, Hansen snorted the matter away. "They'll die off too. Eventually."

"Didn't they do that already?" Beverly hushed from the

sidelines.

Sarah leaned as far forward as the slumbering Mackenzie in her lap would allow and looked Hansen square in the eye.

"The fact is, Gary, apart from the obvious, we know nothing about this virus or how it affects the human body. We don't have the slightest idea how it alters the brain chemistry of those in stage 2, and we can't even *begin* to guess what it does to reanimate a corpse in stage 3. So far, it defies all known science and every bit of logic, so you can't sit there and say that you know how this will all play out, because you couldn't *possibly* know. *No one* could know. But maybe there is one book in all of existence that might be able to give us a clue."

As Hansen grumbled under his breath, Donn said, "I thought you already found the magazine you wanted. Isn't it the right one?"

"It is," she sighed, sagging back into her chair. "It's the one Jim Lambert told me about, and it makes me more certain than ever that he was on to something. But that article just scratches the surface. I need to see the *JAMA* report to know for sure."

"And once you get it, you can do something about it?" This from little Diego.

Sarah took her time answering, and when she did, it was with another heavy sigh. "Honestly, Diego, I have no idea."

A dark shadow swept across her features, and Mason knew that she was holding something back. But it didn't take a genius to figure out what. Even if she found her fabled *JAMA* report and it revealed every detail regarding the exact nature of the virus, there wasn't a damn thing she'd be able to do about it. A full team of scientists at the CDC with unlimited funds and equipment? Maybe. One woman stuck in the Dark

Ages? Not a fucking chance. But what would be the point of sharing that particular bit of news? After all, sometimes ignorance really was bliss.

"It's worth a few extra minutes," Mason concluded, once and for all. "The raid on the library will only be a diversion anyway. The objective is Gloria, and the only way to get to her is through building five."

"And you're sure that the best way to do that is by splitting up?" Teddy asked for perhaps the twentieth time. "Are you really *sure?*"

"I'm sure," he told her, trying his best to convey the confidence he wished he could feel. "As long as we all do what we're supposed to do, we'll be back together and out of this place before sundown."

"And where do we go then?"

Mason was about to answer, but Addison beat him to the punch.

"Any *fucking* where but here," he said, earning him an enthusiastic, "*A huevo!*" from Alejandra.

But they wouldn't make their move just yet, apparently.

"They're exhausted," Hansen told him, plainly, "They need chow and sack time. Three hours."

He was right. It was barely noon, and Mason felt like he'd been up for days. Some of the others looked even worse than he felt.

"*Two* hours?" he answered back.

"Three," Hansen repeated. "Plus one more to make preparations."

Mason didn't argue. It would still leave five full hours of daylight. Plenty of time to get everybody killed.

On that note, those with any energy left helped themselves to the stores of food and drink, and those who were too tired to eat either curled up in a chair or stretched out on one of several couches to get some shut-eye. And soon enough, the only sounds that could be heard in the place were the rattling of spoons against the insides of cans, and the occasional snore from those already lost to the world.

"I wish I could be like her," a tiny voice said, close to Mason's elbow.

He looked up from his can of peaches to see Teddy crouched at his side, nibbling on a handful of potato chips she'd stolen from one of the smashed vending machines. The 'her' to whom she referred to was obvious. Alejandra was splayed out on a nearby sofa, sound asleep and connected to the couch by a thin line of drool.

Addison appeared over Mason's shoulder then, slurping from a can of condensed milk.

"So do I, kid," he said in a hush. "But we'll get there. We'll *all* get there."

Or die trying? Mason added silently.

"You should try to catch a few winks while you can, Teddy," Addison told her, then he took one last swallow from the can and smacked his lips. "You know, whoever discovered the joy that is cow's milk must have been into some *seriously* weird shit."

Teddy giggled and proceeded to curl into a tiny ball at the end of Alejandra's couch with room to spare while Addison belched once and wandered off to find a place of his own.

In the renewed quiet, a somniferous little mewl from Mackenzie drew Mason's attention to her and Sarah, fast asleep in each other's arms, and despite the situation, or perhaps *because* of it, his heart melted at that idyllic little scene. With all of the madness of the world swirling about them, here were mother and child, wrapped in a blanket of love and peace and calm.

This is how it should be... he declared to himself. *This is how the world is supposed to work. This, right here...*

A sudden snort broke the reverie, but it was only Hansen in the middle of one nightmare or another. The man's head was flopped back and his mouth was hanging open, but that single snort was followed by no others, so Mason merely scowled daggers at the sleeping man and let him be. Then his eyes drifted over to Becks in the next chair, and his heart melted again. Dark, flowing mane framing an exquisite face. Beautiful long legs tucked lithely beneath her body as if that overstuffed chair offered all the room in the world.

Good *God*, she was beautiful! How he'd ever persuaded that gorgeous supermodel of a woman to join him for a cup of coffee at Starbucks that day was a complete mystery to him. And why she'd ever agreed to a second date was simply too unthinkable to imagine. Then, it had become more. And while he'd savored every minute of those days together, he had also been afraid for every one of those minutes that the days would inevitably come crashing to an end.

Surely, she'll wake up, he'd thought to himself more times than he could ever have counted. *One day, she'll realize that she could do so much better, and she'll be gone.* And after thinking those thoughts for long enough, he'd closed himself off to protect himself from the eventual hurt, and the words became real. After two years of his bullshit, she finally dumped his ass on the curb.

Now, he looked upon that face he never thought he'd see again, and he thought the words he knew he'd never be able to say out loud.

I'm sorry, Becks. I'm so sorry I made you leave me...

He deposited the half-empty can of peaches on the floor

and wiped the mist from his eyes, then he chanced to look Mackenzie's way and saw one big green eye half-opened and watching him. He leaned across the arms of the chairs and kissed her on the cheek, whispering, "It's all good, Mack," and once her breathing slowed and her half-lidded eye shut tight, he lowered himself back into his chair.

He dropped his chin to his chest and allowed his eyes to close, and his mind began to swirl with images. Sarah and Mack. Him and Becks. Becks and Hansen. Alphas and Echoes. Wilders and Creepers. And before he could make heads or tails of what he was seeing, he snapped awake to find Alejandra standing over him, spooning pudding into her mouth from a can the approximate size of a scuba tank.

"So we gonna do this or what?" she said, licking chocolate from her upper lip.

"Huh? What?"

He checked his watch. Three o'clock. *Christ!* He'd been out for nearly three hours.

"I guess you're only human after all, huh, Mace?" she quipped, wandering off with her keg of pudding and dodging all of Addison's efforts to help himself to a spoonful.

Fuck. He'd slept for nearly three full hours, but apparently no one had bothered to explain it to his body. His back hurt, his shoulders ached, and his eyes felt as if they'd been filled with gravel. And yet, when he surveyed the room, there was Hansen, not having had any more rest than he, yet fresh as a daisy and inspecting the troops as if it were the first day of boot camp. Twenty-plus years his senior, and the old man was showing him how it was done.

Fucking awesome.

He stretched hard enough to feel popping all along his spine, then he sluggishly pulled on his boots, hauled himself to his feet, and joined the others as they made preparations.

Four of the youngsters were hard at work on a crossbow-bolt assembly line. One of them had salvaged strips of hardwood from somewhere or other, and Donn and Christopher were busily whittling them into shape before passing them down the line. There, Mack and Teddy fitted each of the pointed shards of wood with little plastic crescents cut from plastic storage containers, fixing them in place with dental floss and glue.

"Will they work?" Mason had to ask.

In answer, Teddy cocked her crossbow and loaded one of her newly made bolts, then she let fly at the far wall. It carved a beautifully straight path through fifty feet of air, pierced a plaque of the founding fathers, and buried itself halfway into the wall.

"Okay, so they work," he shrugged. "May I?"

Teddy handed him the weapon with a grin, and he finally had his first close look at the crossbow itself. It was mostly pine from what he could tell – hand-sawn, hand-chiseled, and fitted together with glue and screws. The working end of the thing was a length of PVC pipe attached to thick nylon string, with a crescent-shaped foot-claw at the end to provide power for the draw. It was crude but ingenious, and as he handed it back, he did so with an appreciative nod.

"Very impressive. It beats the hell out of a chunk of rebar. But how did you...?"

She stopped him right there.

"It wasn't me, it was Kumiko," she said, the smile gone and her lips drawn tight. "I just picked it up. After."

There was that word again.

After.

The only use of the word *after* from this point on was suddenly made crystal clear. *After* was now a word to pinpoint the moment in time when someone died.

"Tupperware isn't nearly as good as feathers," she said, returning to her work. "But the curve of the plastic gives them a pretty good spiral."

Mason gave her a final nod and turned to go, but she suddenly reached out and grabbed him by the hand, freezing him to the spot.

"Please, Mr. Mason," she said, her eyes verging on tears. "Tell me everything's going to be okay?"

Christ almighty...

He closed both of his hands around hers and looked her directly in the eyes. "I'm sorry, Teddy, but I can't," he told her. "I honestly don't know if anything will *ever* be okay again. But I promise you that you are not alone. Whatever happens, we're all in this together. Do you understand?"

"I suppose," she allowed, but just barely.

"No, Teddy." Mason caught the girl's eyes before they could drop all the way to the floor. "I mean it. You're not alone anymore. We're all in this together. It's hard enough finding good people in this world, much less friends, and believe me when I say, even the most antisocial, misanthropic misfit doesn't want to be entirely alone. Take it from someone who never learned how to play well with others. If there's even one person in this life you know you can count on, then you hold on to them and you never let them go."

Just then, Becks emerged from the kitchen with Inez at her side, and just like that, he knew the solemn truth behind his words.

"Look around the room, Teddy. You have more true friends right now than most people make in a lifetime. These people will do anything for you. They will kill for you and they would die for you. Hell kiddo, when it comes to friends, you hit the jackpot!"

She smiled and sucked back her tears, then she reached up on her tiptoes and graced Mason's cheek with a kiss.

"Thank you, Mr. Ma—" she started to say, but she quickly corrected herself and told him sweetly, "Thank you, Mace."

Mackenzie didn't even bother looking up as she giggled, not quite to herself, "No more strays, my butt."

Teddy went back to her work station, giving Mackenzie a playful shove on the shoulder and receiving one in return, and as both girls giggled and shared secretive little hushes, Mason went to where Diego was sitting cross-legged on the floor. Before him were two empty shotgun shell boxes, a crystal fruit bowl nearly overflowing with gunpowder, and his fanny pack filled with .33 calibre slugs, the perfect size for a high-powered slingshot.

As he pried open the last of the shells with a paring knife, Addison swooped in to help himself to the bowl of gunpowder and began spooning it carefully into a plastic Pepsi bottle already filled to the brim with screws, and nails pried from whatever baseboards and doorjambs and electrical fittings he'd been able to plunder.

"No sense letting it go to waste," the man shrugged.

"Just make sure I'm nowhere around when you set that thing off."

"Trust me, Mace, if it actually comes time to use this bad boy, ain't nobody gonna be around to complain about the noise."

The thought was less than reassuring, but he let it go.

"Looks like we're just about ready," Sarah said, sidling up beside him and resting a hand on his shoulder as if it was the most natural thing in the world.

And as if it was every bit as natural, Mason reached up to give her hand a squeeze. "Looks like. You still alright with Hansen coming along?"

"Not really, but he's capable enough, and it's not worth a fight. Honestly, Mace, I'm more upset about leaving Mack behind."

"Sarah, if there's any part of this plan that you aren't comfortable with..."

"Oh please, Mace. I haven't been comfortable for a long, *long* time."

"You know Inez loves Mack like a daughter," he assured her," and Christopher and Addison are like two over-protective big brothers. And Alejandra..."

"Oh, Alejandra would take on the *world* for that girl," Sarah finished for him. "I know, Mace, I know. She'll be in the very best of hands. But I made a promise to myself that I would never be apart from her again, and here I am, leaving her behind yet again.

"Hey." Mason let go of her hand, but only so he could wrap his big arms around her. She buried her face in his chest, and he gently stroked her hair. "You're not leaving her behind, Sarah. You know that, and she knows it, too. You're only going to be a stone's throw away, and if we do this right, there'll be so many people packed inside Gloria by the end of day that you'll be *begging* for a little elbow room."

"Doubt it," she said, craning back her head to flash him a smile.

They held each other for a few moments longer, then Sarah gave him a loving pat on the chest and peeled herself away to go help Mackenzie assemble the last few tail-fins on the last few crossbow bolts, leaving Mason to wander over to where Inez, Becks, and a couple of the college kids were hard at work. Apparently, they had scavenged every blade they could find in the kitchen, including one particularly nasty-looking meat cleaver, and now, they were busily attaching individual knives to various lengths of wood.

"Look at this!" Richie declared, proudly presenting a six-inch carving knife strapped to a three-foot length of broom handle. "It's like a Roman gladius. Cool, huh?"

"You call that a gladius?" Sk8rBoy William scoffed, bringing up a rounded length of pine with a ten-inch butcher knife taped to one end and the meat cleaver to the other. "Now *that's* a gladius!" he crowed in his best Australian accent.

One last carving knife remained unclaimed, so even though he already had a sheathed knife on his belt, Mason helped himself to that last blade, slipping it into a belt loop as a just-in-case. Then, he pulled Becks aside to where the others couldn't hear.

"Becks..." he began, but quickly found himself struggling to find the right words, *any* words, to tell her the rest.

She reeled him in and threw her arms around his neck. "Mace, please take care of yourself. I didn't realize how much you meant to me before... before..."

She sniffled once, but only once.

"Oh, Mace, I am *so* sorry. It was all my fault..."

"Bullshit," he cut her off with a hush in her ear. "It was all me, Becks. I knew it then, and I know it now. I was mad at you for a while, but really, I was just mad at myself. If anyone's to blame, it's this big dumb asshole you kicked to the curb."

She attempted a protest, but he stopped her short and held her all the more tightly because of it.

"I love you, Becks. You know I'll move heaven and Earth to get back to you. But if anything happens..."

Now it was her turn to stop him short, and she did so with her lips pressed lightly against his. The kiss lingered, and when at last it ended, she gave him that familiar hair toss that had always brought him to his knees.

"You come back to me, Mace," she told him in no uncertain terms. "Promise me. You're a man of your word, so promise me you'll come back, and I'll believe you."

Christ, Becks... I might as well promise you the moon...

"I promise," he lied.

"I believe you," she lied back.

And with both lies hanging in the air, Mason tended to one last order of business.

"Becks, I have to ask you for a favor. Could you please look after Mack?"

"Oh, Mace, you don't have to worry about Mack. She'll be in good hands while you guys are gone. Why, Alejandra alone would..."

"No, Becks," he cradled her head against his shoulder, "I'm asking *you*. I trust every one of these people with my life, but I need to know that she has *you*."

The rest of the words went unspoken, but the message was clear. What he was asking went far beyond the next minutes or the next hour or the next day. In fact, it might go on for however long a lifetime amounted to these days.

"Of course," she told him, sincerely. "Of course I'll take care of her, Mace."

I promise... he expected her to add, but she didn't, and for that he was glad. That word suddenly had little meaning anymore.

She leaned back to flash him a smile. "Wow, Mace. I have to say, I never had you pegged as the family type."

She'd meant it to lighten the mood, but it couldn't have

backfired in a more spectacular fashion.

They had planned to start their own family once. A lifetime ago.

"And all it took was the end of the world," he shrugged. "Who knew?"

His attempt at humor lay beside hers like dead mackerel on the beach, and all that remained was a pair of naked, broken hearts.

"I'm sorry, Mace."

"I'm sorry too, Becks. But what happened, happened. Life goes on."

"Hopefully," she tacked on, grimly.

"Yeah," Mason sighed. "Hopefully."

With one last kiss, they reluctantly pulled themselves apart, and while Becks turned her face from the others, Mason went to where Alejandra was sitting on her couch and lowered himself down beside her. The vat of pudding sat beside her Tommy gun on the squat coffee table, while she ran a sharpening stone down the length of the machete held lovingly in her lap.

Alejandra didn't bother to acknowledge his arrival, but when he made the mistake of reaching for the spoon sticking up from the pudding, she cautioned him, "Mace, I'll tell you what I told Addison. You touch my pudding and I'll gut you like a deer."

He figured that she was probably joking, but decided it best not to test the theory. "You're pissed, right?"

"*No me importa.*," she shrugged, but her tone said otherwise. "You'd rather have that *tamarindo* watch your back, *como quieras*. It's your call, Mace."

"Ally, I'm not in charge here. In spite of what others might think, this is a democracy. We all have a say. *All* of us."

"A bunch of children and a grumpy old man," the girl scoffed, not taking her eyes from the stone singing its way down the blade.

"Hansen's right about one thing, Ally. There's no such thing as children anymore," Mason told her outright. "They're young, yes, and they haven't been through what we have, but they haven't exactly been sitting around playing Xbox, either. And despite whatever issues I have with Hansen, I know he's a good man. He's an insufferable, arrogant, blowhard dickhead, but he's an insufferable, arrogant, blowhard dickhead we can trust."

Alejandra didn't argue the point. She took her eyes off her blade long enough to shoot a glance at Hansen overseeing the last of the weapons assemblies, and Hansen happened to look over at just the same moment. The two shared a look that might have meant anything or nothing at all, then Hansen looked away and Alejandra returned to her blade.

"He's okay, I guess," she admitted at last, but with the added caveat, "You know... for a *gringo*."

"Someone call for me?" Addison's big head suddenly appeared from out of nowhere. "I hear *gringo,* and I come running. Hey, by the way, Ally, where did you find the pudding? It's just that I searched the kitchen from top to bottom and I couldn't find..."

Alejandra made a show of rolling her eyes and sighing heavily, then she paused the whetstone long enough to take one last spoonful of pudding and slid the rest of it down the table.

"Go ahead, *vato*," she said, resuming her chore, "I'm about to burst anyway."

Addison reached for the can, but then he paused with his hand in midair and with one wary eye on Alejandra. When and only when he was reasonably satisfied that it wasn't a trick and that she probably wasn't going to gut him like a deer, he snatched it up and eagerly dug in. With half of his face immediately covered in chocolate and his mouth filled to excess, he held the can out for Mason, but Mason graciously declined.

"No thanks," he said, noting Alejandra's playful smirk. "Apparently, I'm not worthy."

Sk8rBoy William and Richie happened to wander by just then, so Mason waited until they were gone, then he had a quick, furtive look around to make sure no one was within earshot, before saying, "So, what do you guys *really* think? Is it doable?"

"*Si*, doable," Alejandra said, though not entirely convincingly.

"Things are only impossible until they're not," Addison managed around a mouthful of chocolate. "Besides, it's not like we have a choice, right?"

"Same two as always."

"Sure," Alejandra said. "But in this case, only one of those is certain to end with everyone here dying a horrible, gruesome death. The other is only *likely* to end in everyone here dying a horrible, gruesome death."

"Comforting," Mason harrumphed, then his eye fell on Beverly standing at a window, looking out over the Quad with her twelve-gauge security blanket cradled in her arms, and his gaze hardened.

Addison followed his gaze as he shoveled in another mound of pudding. "She'll be fine, Mace. She's scared, is all."

"We're *all* scared," Alejandra reminded him, holding up her machete to check the keenness of the edge.

Addison dropped the spoon into the empty can and returned it to the table. "Not you, Ally. And certainly not Mace."

"Wanna bet?" they said together.

Alejandra finally sheathed the blade and picked up her Tommy gun. "*Vato*, fear is what makes you run from a bear instead of standing your ground. You show me a man who has no fear, and I'll show you a man who wouldn't last two minutes in this... this *locura*."

"Exactly right," Mason agreed wholeheartedly. "Fear is a superpower. It charges up the body and gives you that extra little edge. But if we succumb to that fear, we become a slave to it, and scared humans are capable of doing *monumentally* stupid things."

"And then they die," Alejandra summed up, emotionlessly.

"Or *everyone* dies," Mason corrected her. "That's why I want you two to keep an eye on Beverly."

"Keep an eye on her?" Addison squawked. "Whaddya mean, like a babysitter?"

Alejandra popped out the Tommy gun's magazine, checked that it was full, and slapped it back in place. "I'm no *niñera*, Mace. Maybe we should just lock her in a closet, huh? Or tie her to a chair."

Or maybe we should just shoot her...

Mackenzie's haunting words came back in a rush, and with them came the realization that that was exactly what had been swimming around in the back of his mind since the words had first been spoken. Put an end to it. Finish her now. Remove the weakest link in the chain and make the whole stronger.

But what then? Take out the next weakest link? And then the next? And then the next? Should he cleave his way all the way up the chain until only the strongest were left? But there would always be the next weakest link, wouldn't there? Inez. Diego. Little freckle-faced Teddy. Addison. Christopher. Eventually, even the Latina spitfire. And once he'd single-handedly hacked his way through the only friends he would ever have, where would he stop? Becks? Sarah? Mack?

"Never mind," he said, climbing to his feet. "Forget I said anything."

"*Chido*," Alejandra said as he left. "I already forgot."

Becks was off to one side, sharing a few last words with her father, and Sarah was on the other, doing the same with her daughter, so Mason took the cowardly path and went straight down the middle to Inez and Christopher.

Christopher had made some modifications to his hatchet, fitting a pair of boning knives opposite the blade, and another on the hilt for stabbing backward. Now, it had no grounds at all for being called merely a hatchet. With Christopher's lean muscles and quick reflexes behind it, it was a battle axe, pure and simple.

"Not bad, huh?" he said as Mason drew near.

"Not bad at all! Looks like you'll get them coming and going and everywhere in between."

"It's the in-between that worries me," Inez harrumphed. "Mace, I've been watching you make the rounds. If you don't mind me saying, you remind me a little of King Henry walking among his troops before the battle of Agincourt."

Inez. Sweet, loving Inez. As tacit mother of the group, it fell upon her to fret over every soul, and she did so with unwavering dedication. Still, she knew better than to ask what was worrying him. In fact, she probably knew it already, but sweet woman that she was, she was leaving the door open and letting him decide for himself whether to talk about it or not.

"Not quite the same, Inez. I believe Henry was in disguise, and if I remember my Shakespeare correctly, everyone in that camp was pretty much certain that they were on the eve of their deaths."

"Then it's not the same at all," Christopher said. "If anything, I'd say everyone here is raring to go!"

Mason said nothing, but he couldn't hide his trepidation from Inez.

"And maybe that's the problem," she said. "Children, marching off to war with pretend glee."

"These aren't children..." Mason tried, and failed.

"The hell they aren't, Mace! I don't care what Gary says or what you say or what these children themselves say, they are *children*, Mace."

"Every bit as young as your own child," Mason reminded her.

"Hey, I'm a whole year older than these kids!" Christopher protested.

"Wow, a whole year," Mason said, just under his breath.

Inez stepped directly up to Mason and took both of his hands in hers. "Hank Mason, you are one of the finest men I have ever known."

Mason attempted a protest, but she instantly shut it down.

"Now, hush. I know that you have the devil on your shoulder, and the world has not been kind to you. I get that. Believe you me. Christopher's father was the same way. He was bull-headed, opinionated, stubborn... *Lord*, that man was stubborn! Each and every one of God's creations has his or her own cross to bear, and it can be a woeful burden. My Barnabus spent his life standing toe-to-toe with the rest of the world, good and ready to give it the beat-down to end all beat-downs, but underneath all of that darkness and all of that pain, he had a heart of pure gold, just like you."

Not one to take a compliment easily, Mason retreated to his emotional failsafe.

"Barnabus?" he quipped.

Inez narrowed her gaze. "Something wrong with Barnabus?"

He kissed her on the cheek. "No, not at all. And thank you. Hey, maybe you're on the right track, after all. Gold *is* a cold, inert metal, isn't it?"

Just then, Mackenzie came running over, calling out, "Mace! Mace! Look! Sarah and I made it. Isn't it *awesome?*"

Her shadow was with her as always, so Mason greeted the big dog with a scratch between the ears before he took the thing from Mackenzie. It looked like a mad jumble of belts and blades and strips of cloth, but he figured it out quickly enough.

"Wow! You guys made this all on your own?"

"Uh huh!" She beamed a smile. "It's *awesome*, right?"

He tussled her mop of hair and smiled back, every bit as big. "Mack, this might be the most awesomest thing ever!"

They shared the sweetest of fist-bumps, the girl went running back to Sarah, and Mason turned back to see Inez wearing a decidedly cocky grin.

"You know another thing about gold, Mace?" she winked at him. "It melts pretty damn easy..."

This time, he merely shrugged.

He left Inez and her son to share a few final moments together, then he took one last good, long look at the troops. Sarah and Mack came to join him, then Alejandra and Addison, and as if an unspoken signal had rippled through the group, the rest of them began to gather around.

William and Teddy had their crossbows slung over their shoulders, a makeshift quiver with thirty bolts apiece across their backs, and a gladius in hand. Diego had his slingshot tucked in his back pocket, a bulging fanny-pack around his waist, and a knife as long as his forearm stuck through a belt loop at his side. The others all had their SBDs, and Mason was glad to see that his own people had shared their overabundant firearms. Now, everyone either had a gun on their hip, a rifle across their back, or both. Only Beverly was without an SBD, so he did her the honor of handing her his own purloined carving knife, and made no comment at all about the whiff of scotch he detected when she mumbled a quick, "Thank you."

At last, he decided that they were all as ready as they would ever be, so he retrieved his seven-foot length of rebar from the crook of the door and flung his knapsack over his back.

He gave one last look to Sarah, and when she nodded, he passed it along to the group.

"Alright, then. Like the man said, once more unto the breach, dear friends, once more! Now, let's get this shit done."

CHAPTER

XVI

It wasn't so much thinking *inside* the box so much as skirting the very edges of it. Diego had only been at Skyline for a semester, but his naturally inquisitive nature had taken him to every corner of the complex, and it was upon that unique perspective that all of their lives now depended.

The area behind buildings five and six was a designated smoking area, so classified because it was far from any public entrances to either building. In fact, it was a tiny corner of the campus that few people would even notice as they drove past on College Drive, and those that did wouldn't have given it a second glance. It was primarily a handicapped parking area, with two ribbons of asphalt branching off from it, running up to big overhead doors at the back of each building. These were their loading bays, noticed by few and ignored by all, but with this hidden little corner of Skyline lying a full seven feet below the Quad and accessible from above only by a narrow set of stairs, the math was obvious. This was the place to make their move.

Obvious, too, was the fact that they simply couldn't afford a replay of the Saint Valentine's Day Massacre. Though the swarm in the Quad was essentially bottled up, they were hardly alone. The area around Skyline was quite literally crawling with the dead and the undead, with untold hundreds well within earshot, so if this was to be done at all, it had to be done with absolute stealth.

Mason led ten shadowy figures down the stairs to the main floor, and there they were able to see close-up what they had already seen from the windows above. The Quad was literally filled to bursting with alphas. Mason had hoped that at least some of the creatures would have descended into a vigil state by now, but with so many packed so closely together, altercations were inevitable, and the scent of fresh blood acted like chum in the water. Every one of those sightless bastards was agitated. On alert. Ready to charge after any sound, human or not, and rip it to shreds.

One lone echo had somehow managed to weather the storm and was presently pressed up against a window at the far end of the hallway, but even as Mason watched, some random jingling of keys or coins in its pocket set two nearby alphas upon it. They lit into the creature with teeth and claws, and everyone on the opposite side of the glass had a completely unfettered view of the poor hapless thing being opened up like a can of tuna. But then, just as it began to sink from view, a third alpha joined in on the kill, and as Mason had feared all along, the wild thrashing of the three sent them off-balance, and one of the creatures smashed headfirst into the window. The glass held at first, but then a single ray shot up from the bloody spider web in the center, another crept slowly down to the bottom, and the whole thing suddenly gave way. The head came through, and everyone held their breath, but instead of the rest of the creature following and perhaps even starting a general invasion, it thankfully receded again as the creature was dragged off into the swarm.

A severed ear and tuft of scalp plopped to the floor, and Mason hurried everyone down one more flight to the basement.

There were no windows down below, so several flashlights stabbed on and Diego took over the lead, following the map he'd scribbled in his head. They crept in absolute silence toward the northern end of the building, farthest away from the Quad, and soon came to the offices of the Public Safety Department.

This was Skyline's campus security, and though only four officers strong, every one of the four had apparently done their duty right up to the end. According to Richie, one of the men had been torn apart while shepherding students to relative safety in those first few hours, and a second had been killed attempting to rescue a child from the clutches of an instructor turned feral. Both now had their place in the body wall. Mason himself had seen the shredded remains of a uniform on a slim female body heaved from the window of building six, so that left only one officer unaccounted for. At least, until now. That fourth officer had apparently stayed behind to man the radio and telephone right up to the last minute, coordinating between his own officers, the SBPD, and whatever had been left of emergency services. Now, he was the sole occupant of the command center on the basement level, sealed into a glass-fronted office, with a Bluetooth earpiece still clipped to one ear and a uniform hanging loose on an emaciated body.

A single scuff of someone's shoe was enough to awaken

the thing from its vigil, and it suddenly flung itself at the glass with a savagery belying its frail appearance. Several SBDs came up, and Clancy bared his massive teeth, but even as the creature clawed furiously at the glass, Diego remained calm and pointed mutely to the latticework of metal wires buried deep within the glass. It was reinforced. A high-velocity bullet might be able to pierce it, but a raging alpha never would.

The weapons were lowered, Mackenzie put a hand on Clancy's back to silence him, and Diego led them on. They passed through one last door at the rear of the office and found themselves in a large, empty space. A quick sweep of flashlights showed no one else present, so they all came together before a pleated metal wall on the far side of the room. But no, it wasn't a wall. It was a door. The big brother of every garage door in every home across the country. This was the loading bay, then.

They were there.

A regular-sized door sat a few feet away from the other – also metal, but with a tiny square of reinforced glass set into it at eye level. Alejandra stood on her tiptoes to have a peek, then she waved the rest of them in to take turns seeing what they were up against, and finally, Mason squeezed in beside Addison to have a look for himself.

It was just like every loading bay he'd ever seen. Precisely as high above ground-level as the deck of a truck, with a narrow platform of concrete jutting out a few feet, and metal steps at one end for foot traffic. But beyond that slab of concrete and those metal steps was insanity itself.

As Diego had described, there was the little handicapped parking lot, and just beyond that, the loop road running east to west. On the far side of the road was a vastly larger parking area to accommodate all of Skyline's students and staff, and past that was the suburban Hell that sprawled on for mile after mile. And in all of that vast open space, not a single square yard of ground was unoccupied.

There were hundreds upon hundreds of them, stretching all the way back as far as he could see. And besides a handful of cars abandoned on the road and in the parking lot, and one big old boat of a Pontiac with a handicapped sticker sitting dead center between buildings five and six, there was nothing else.

No body wall. No car barrier. No buildings. Nothing to slow the fuckers down.

Nothing at all.

No one had dared utter so much as a whisper since abandoning Fireside, but Mason had no need of words to know what they were all thinking.

It was suicide. Sheer, unthinking suicide. They would all be dead as soon as they opened that door.

If they somehow managed to open the door and pile through without the slightest breath of sound, they would be dead as soon as their feet hit the pavement. And if they somehow survived long enough to sneak a few steps into the swarm, they would be dead before they'd crossed a dozen feet. And if by some miracle they weren't immediately torn to ribbons, they still wouldn't be so lucky as to make it all the way to the other loading bay, nearly a hundred feet away. And even if they somehow accomplished *that* impossibility, they would then have to quickly and silently break through a door that was a carbon copy of this one – metal, with a little square of reinforced glass.

It was ridiculous to even consider. Impossible, by anyone's measure. Mason would be throwing his life away on a ridiculous venture destined to fail before it had even begun.

And with it, he'd be throwing away everyone else's life, too.

He checked his watch. It was 5:15. By 5:17, it would all be over. 5:17. Everyone he knew in the world would be dead by 5:17.

He tried to come up with the day's date, as if knowing exactly when all his friends had died might give him some peace, but as much as he tried to calculate backwards, he simply couldn't.

Was it still July? Were they into August yet? What day of the week was it? Friday? Monday?

It was a wasted effort. Days and dates had no meaning anymore. All they had was now. Still, one vestige of the old ways couldn't help but pervade Mason's thoughts.

Jesus, I hope it's not Monday... I'd hate to die on a Monday...

Addison fell back to let Sarah squeeze in beside Mason and have a look for herself. She said nothing, but her tightening grip on Mason's arm spoke volumes. Then Becks poked her head between the two, and she *did* speak, but in a hush low enough to have been a mere whisper on the breeze.

"You can't," she pleaded with both of them. "There has to be another way."

"There isn't," Sarah hushed back, and with one last gentle squeeze of Mason's arm, her fingers trailed down to his hand, their fingertips kissed, and she stepped away to leave him and Becks alone for the last moments they were likely to have.

And yet, Mason didn't say a word to Becks. In his mind, he didn't have to. Whatever he needed to say had been said, and for perhaps the first time in his life, he was at peace with himself. He reached out and found Becks' hand waiting for his, but they didn't linger there. That last connection made and his heart at ease, Mason released her hand and gave the signal, then he slowly and gently slid back the deadbolt.

STAGE 3: BRAVO

Most of the alphas were standing vigil, but it would only ever be fleeting at best. With every crescendo of roars and snarls from the Quad, a ripple went through this greater swarm, sending many of them into a probe and a few into full charge. Fortunately, the noise was enough to obfuscate the creaking of one rusty hinge as Mason eased the door fully open, but as the vantage point changed from that tiny square of glass to a full, unimpeded view of a swarm that seemed without end, he heard more than a few stifled gasps as the others gathered behind him.

He gave the floor a quick scan for debris, then he stepped soundlessly over the threshold and waited.

Seconds passed by without a single alpha taking notice, so he moved out of the way to let Sarah join him. Addison followed quickly behind, then Alejandra emerged with her machete drawn and fire in her eyes. Hansen came through next, with Becks trailing behind him. Hansen tried his best to position himself between his daughter and the swarm, but Becks would have none of it. She pranced to the far side of the platform with the grace of a cat, and stood in a semi-crouch, ready to launch her javelin or herself at anything that threatened.

Then the rest followed. Beverly, Christopher, Donn, Richie, little Diego. Then Mackenzie and Clancy emerged, and on cue, Clancy bounded down to the ground and set off into the swarm.

As expected, the swarm ignored the dog completely, but they did so now at their peril. Around Clancy's body was a crude harness constructed from leather belts and strips of cloth, courtesy of Mack and Sarah. And along both sides were affixed the strongest and sharpest knives of the lot. The dog was now a modern-day version of an ancient war chariot, and that big, beautiful beast wasted no time in wreaking his own special brand of havoc on the swarm.

He danced among and around alphas, sometimes coming so close that they could have reached down and touched him. But none of them did. Even as the blades cut into their flesh, they ignored the dog completely. Sometimes, the alpha suffered little more than a gash. Other times, a lucky slash of a ligament or tendon rendered the creature lame, slowing it to a hobble. And on those luckiest of occasions, the height of the alpha and the position of the blade was just right to sever an artery, and the wounded creature crumpled to the ground, bleeding out their last in that nameless little corner of Skyline.

On Mason's signal, the rest of them went into action, but this was no charge of the Light Brigade. This was a slow-motion infiltration, one cautious step at a time, and every one made in absolute silence. One by one, they either descended the steps or lowered themselves carefully from the ledge, and this was where a huge gaping hole had been left in the barely acceptable plan. The idea was for Mason, Sarah, and Hansen to make the crossing, and the others would simply be there to provide whatever assistance they could, and as Inez had described so perfectly, to 'thin the herd.' But the swarm itself was unpredictable. No amount of planning could tell everyone exactly where to go or what to do, so they all had to make their own calculations as they went and spread out whenever and wherever they could.

Mason went straight into the swarm, taking advantage of the narrowest of paths left open by Clancy's efforts, but it soon closed in around him and he suddenly had nowhere to go. A big male stood directly in his path, and two more were probing toward him. He held his breath and took a step back to let the first of the probers pass by within inches, but the other happened to stumble sideways on a broken foot at just that moment, and its new trajectory was bringing it directly toward him. With no room to sidestep the thing, he planted the end of his rebar between the creature's naked breasts with the lightness of a feather, held it in place for the two seconds required to let the swarm shift and open the tiniest of holes, then he gently guided it just far enough to the side that he could deke quietly out of its way.

He didn't have to look back to know that everyone was sticking to the plan. If they weren't, he'd hear it. One fuck-up was all it would take. One heavy breath, one grunt, one over-zealous *whack!* of a machete or a hatchet, and it was game over, man. Game over.

He knew Sarah was close behind. He could sense it. He could *feel* it. Five feet. Ten. No more than that. The woman moved without a whisper of sound, but he sensed her there right down to his bones. And he could feel Mack there, too. Twenty feet to the right and just a hair behind. And when he heard one alpha after another stumbling to its knees from that same direction, he knew exactly what that incredible little girl was up to. She was doing what she always did, confusing and disrupting the swarm. But she had upped her game, taking a page from Clancy's playbook and using what Sarah had taught them all about the most vulnerable places on a human body. Cavorting as silently and effortlessly through the swarm as a shadow, she was putting her knife to good use. The back of a knee here. An inner thigh there. And when possible, a quick slash across a throat or the back of neck.

Sarah had taught her well, and with her and Clancy working in tandem, enough room suddenly opened up to allow Mason a full three seconds to catch his breath.

He spared a glance high over his shoulder to four figures

hanging through two open windows on the second floor. Inez and Richie were there, each with a .22 rifle, and Teddy and Sk8rBoy William had their crossbows charged and ready. Those four were the artillery. If everything turned to shit, their combined firepower might be enough to pull a few asses from the fire. If not... well, the supplies inside would last just that much longer with only four mouths to feed.

As his eyes drifted down to the loading dock, his breath hitched in his throat when he caught sight of a flurry of ebony hair being entirely swallowed up by alphas. But then they seemed to part of their own volition, and another head appeared above the crowd. It was Christopher, coming to Becks' aid, and with both battle axe and the back end of a javelin to steer the alphas silently away, they were soon out of immediate danger.

Reassured, Mason spun back around and continued on. But scarcely had he taken another step when he realized how much trouble he was in. In an instant, he plotted every alpha in the immediate vicinity on a 3D map in his head, and what that map spelled was disaster. The way ahead was blocked, two alphas probing toward the Quad would be on him in seconds, and worse, a big bald fucker was probing toward him from the opposite side. In desperation, he planted the end of his rebar against the bald alpha in an attempt to steer it away, but instead of it riding the end of the steel around in an arc, the creature pegged up against it and remained fixed in place, clawing uselessly at the air and snapping its jaws without a hint of a snarl.

Damn! This was no alpha, he realized too late. This was an echo. It wouldn't be steered away, and it wouldn't be stopped. It would keep coming no matter what. He might be able to somehow duck out of the creature's way, but the thing would simply go after the next nearest human. Probably the human of whom Mason was rather fond, padding along a mere ten feet behind him.

He couldn't let the creature go, but he didn't dare take a swing and alert the swarm, so he did the only thing he could. He tensed his massive muscles, and with one mighty thrust, he punched the weapon into and through the creature's rib-cage. And as the horrible thing flailed about at the end of the spear, refusing to die, Mason calmly and coolly reeled it in, inch by bloody inch, until it was close enough to plunge his knife up through the bottom of its jaw and deep into the creature's brain.

At last, the thing dropped to the ground, but in the brief fraction of a second it took for Mason to pull the rebar free from its chest, the net closed in again. They were all around him – too close to even bring his weapon to bear. He side-stepped in the general direction of the Quad to keep pace with the advancing swarm and buy himself a second or two, but that was all he would ever have.

A second. Maybe two. No more.

He managed to create enough space to finally be able to bring up the rebar, but even as he envisioned a hard swing at the nearest pair of legs, connecting with another creature's chin on the upswing and a downward strike on a dainty little head, he also envisioned the aftermath of all those bones breaking.

Alright then, motherfuckers... You want stealth? Come and get it...

With his back against the proverbial wall, Mason set silently to work. He planted his rebar against a chest as thick as a barrel and plunged it through, and when the creature fell, he used it as an anchor as he danced sure-footedly around in a circle – spinning and slashing, spinning and slashing, spinning and slashing. Three alphas crumpled immediately to the ground, three more sprung leaks that would exsanguinate them in under a minute, and one little echo fell close enough for a quick stab through the base of its spine to end its thrashing. At last, he eased his rebar free with a barely audible *shhluck!* and used it to steer another away, and then another, but then a big, hulking creature came charging straight at him at a dead run, tearing a path through the swarm like a buzz saw.

It was almost on him. He tripped up one alpha and slashed at the knee of another to drop both bodies in the hulk's way, then he positioned his rebar like a spear and waited for the giant to come. But then a miracle happened. The giant stopped dead in its tracks and turned its blank, dead eyes to the sky, then it dropped to its knees, hovered there for a moment, and finally slammed face-first to the ground.

And that's when he saw it. A tiny red hole at the base of the giant's skull. And behind the giant, he caught just the faintest glimpse of Diego and his slingshot before the boy vanished back into the swarm.

He delivered another surgical slice to an old female just below the crotch, and had at the next with a swipe at its neck that sprayed a geyser of blood for the few seconds the creature was able to remain standing. With a quick peek beyond the swarm, he realized that he was nearly halfway there, but it gave him little comfort. If anything, the swarm was getting thicker. And even if he and Sarah and Hansen managed to make it all the way, there was still the problem of breaking in without bringing all of damnation down on their heads.

Oh, and by the way, Mace... he heard himself say inside his head. *Let's not forget that the place is overrun...*

Awesome. Fucking awesome.

But in a world where the best he could hope for was all of them only *likely* dying a horrible, gruesome death... he continued on.

He felt something grab his arm, and he swung around, ready to split the offending alpha open like a fish. Luckily, he managed to halt the blade just short of Sarah's navel. She said nothing, but pointed frantically back the way they had come. He could only catch quick little glimpses of the loading dock through all of the shifting bodies, but as he stitched those individual fragments of images into an overall picture, his blood froze in his veins.

Beverly and Becks were working as a team, and as evidenced by the scattering of bodies around them, they'd been doing their part. Becks' javelin and knife were both dripping with blood, and Beverly's carving knife was stained red all the way up to the hilt. But as Becks used the butt of her javelin to steer a probing alpha gingerly away, a tiny female echo stumbled out of the swarm and headed directly toward Beverly. But this was no ordinary echo. It had been a girl. Barely a toddler. Naked, save for a soiled pair of My Little Pony briefs.

Becks didn't see it. She couldn't have. But behind her, Beverly had stopped fighting. The knife hung loose at her side, her shoulders began to heave, and even from forty feet away, Mason could see sunlight glinting off a face wet with tears.

Seeing the impending disaster, Sarah turned to go back, but Mason stopped her with a hand on her shoulder and pulled her to his side. Unable to call out, they tried to signal Becks or Alejandra or Addison or anyone at all who might happen to look their way, but it was no use. Even the snipers didn't see it.

But just then, Mack flitted by a dozen feet away with Clancy on her tail. Mason signaled to the dog, and by sheer stroke of luck, Clancy happened to look over at just that moment. He stopped in his tracks and gave a little whine in Mackenzie's direction, and once the girl returned to his side, Mason sent them a series of hand signals while Sarah dealt with two overly-inquisitive probers.

But it was already too late. The toddler-echo was almost on Beverly, and the woman was making no move whatsoever to protect herself. And then she did the stupidest thing she could ever have done. She dropped her knife to the ground and fell sobbing to her knees as the little naked echo took its last, faltering steps. At last, she reached out for the echo as if reaching for her own dear lost child, and it was only when a set of tiny little teeth buried themselves deep into her wrist that the spell was broken.

Her gut-wrenching scream shattered the silence.

Then a single blast from her shotgun crushed it into dust.

CHAPTER

XVII

The entire swarm came alive, howling and snarling and charging across the open ground toward that hidden little corner of Skyline like rabid wolves descending on a wounded deer, and everyone was suddenly in a fight for their very lives.

Mason and Sarah hacked, kicked, punched and pummeled, but even as one alpha after another fell under Mason's sledgehammer blows or Sarah's surgical precision, others were there to fill the void.

At last, the two of them stood back-to-back and struck at anything that moved, but it was like trying to fight the tide. Wave after wave of alphas poured into that narrow little space of land, and now they were even starting to come down from the Quad in a cascade. Those that happened to come upon the stairs came racing down, tripping over one another, falling, tumbling head over heels and being summarily trampled into goo, but on the rest came.

Those that missed the stairs and came upon a metal railiing

they couldn't hope to understand were crushed to death by the swarm pressing in from behind, but the bodies piled up quickly, and the swarm finally crested the rail and started raining down from above. They dropped like stones, breaking bones, crushing skulls and snapping necks, but every broken body helped soften the landing for the next, and on they came.

Artillery! Mason screamed inside his head, and as if they'd been reading his mind, the four snipers suddenly opened up.

It was a replay of the Saint Valentine's Day Massacre, but this time on mute.

Mason detected the occasional hand clap of a .22 or the *twang!* of a bowstring, but the roar of the swarm drowned most of it out. He scanned the immediate vicinity and could see no evidence of alphas growing red freckles between the eyes or suddenly sprouting plastic-finned shafts of hardwood from their chests, but under the circumstances, he didn't expect to. The real fight was back there, at the very threshold of building six. That was where everyone would be retreating to, and where he'd instructed the snipers to concentrate their fire, should the need arise. They were his friends, yes, but all sentiment aside, if the swarm managed to breach the sanctuary, they were *all* done.

He forced the thoughts from his mind, and with Sarah at his back, he fought like a man possessed. He swung, he stabbed, he gored, he speared, and when two alpha skulls exploded as one to reveal Hansen's ugly mug behind, he focused his attention precisely there and fought twice as hard just to keep the man from being swallowed back up by the swarm.

At last, with both men hammering away at the same single point, the narrowest of paths opened up, and Hansen managed to squeeze his bulk through.

STAGE 3: BRAVO

And now, there were three.

For a full thirty seconds, they actually appeared to be holding their own, but Mason was under no illusions. The human body wasn't built for prolonged battle. Sarah was already starting to flag, and if their labored breathing was any indication, he and Hansen weren't far behind.

"Back!" Mason grunted, splitting a pretty little head in two and driving the back end of the rebar straight through a big male's eyeball until it struck bone.

"No!" Hansen howled between blows. "Forward!"

"They're in trouble!" Mason growled, plunging his knife into a neck that got too close. But before he could even begin to fight his way back toward building six, Sarah grabbed him by the arm.

"No, Mace..." she said, gasping for breath. "Forward..."

It stunk to high heaven, but deep down, he knew she was right. It didn't take a genius to see how the swarm had shifted. It was the gunshot. That single *damn* gunshot from Beverly's shotgun. That nuclear blast was drawing the whole swarm to that precise spot. If they tried to fight their way back, they'd run into an impenetrable wall of alphas and be ripped to pieces before they ever got close.

And she was right about the other thing too, the thing she didn't have the breath to say. They were no good to the others dead.

As much as it pained him to admit, their only way out of this mess was forward. It was their only chance. Because it helped him to turn his back on his only friends on Earth, he told himself that they weren't abandoning them, but that they were fighting for their own lives to save them all. And with that acknowledgement stuck in the back of his throat like so much rancid vomitus, he committed himself to keeping the three of them alive, no matter what.

He swept at a slender pair of legs, brought his weapon up in an arc that caught a young male under the chin hard enough to send its Giants baseball cap flying, then he brought the rebar down again, splitting a child-alpha's skull wide open. And with every swing, he took a half-step forward. And then another half-step. And then another, and another, and another. Over his left shoulder, Hansen was matching him blow for blow, and sticking to his side like glue. Over his right shoulder, Sarah was keeping up too, but her strength was clearly waning. So, with a few clipped words, Mason had all three of them take to spinning slowly about on their mutual axis, swinging and clubbing and stabbing at everything that moved, and all the while inching farther and farther away from their loved ones.

The scariest moment came when Mason's knife became lodged in a particularly robust ribcage, and with its handle slick with blood, he lost his grip as the creature crumpled to the ground. He made a desperate grab for the knife, but the swarm chose that moment to surge forward at just the wrong spot, and as hard as he fought to clear a space, he was forced to back off. Then he heard a shout from behind, and he forgot all about the lost knife.

"Mace!" Sarah howled. "Up here!"

They were at the big old boat of a Pontiac parked smack in the middle of the parking lot. Parisienne, by the look of it. Fifty years old, at least. A throwback to the good old days of gas-guzzling land-yachts that filled a driving lane from curb to dotted line.

He gave one last swing at an ugly pock-marked face and drove his fist into a random throat, then he spun around and bounded onto the car's hood and up to the roof to join Sarah.

STAGE 3: BRAVO

"Gary!" he shouted down, spearing one alpha through the top of its pointy little head and golfing two more aside to open up a few square inches of space. "Gary!"

Hansen reached up, and with his feet fighting for purchase and Mason hauling from above, he finally slid onto the roof like a mackerel.

It was a momentary respite at best, but from Mason's perspective, that old Pontiac was an island of calm in a storm-tossed sea. At better than five feet high and just as wide, the three of them huddled together in the middle of that island, wheezing and panting and gasping for breath as the storm rage on. Gnarled claws raked close to their feet and pounded away on all sides of the car, but with that brief interlude, they could all catch their breath. And better yet, from this new vantage point, Mason could finally get a clear look at what was happening back at the loading bay.

Barely a minute had passed since everything went to shit, and it was every bit as bad as he had thought.

If Beverly could have picked a worse time to let off a nuclear blast, he couldn't imagine it. With him and Sarah and Hansen already deep into the swarm, all seven of the others had waded in to do what they could to ease the pressure. Even now, he could see Addison's Nut-Buster flying and Alejandra's machete hacking away, but it wasn't at all clear if they'd be able to fight their way back to the stronghold. Then he spotted a battle axe and massive war-scythe arcing over the crowd, so he knew that Christopher and Donn were still in the fight, but they were deeper in the swarm and having a devil of a time. At last, Sarah pointed to where a path was appearing as if by magic through the swarm, and they both breathed a sigh of relief. It was the war chariot, cleaving its way back to the loading dock. They couldn't see Mackenzie, but Clancy wouldn't leave that little girl for all the world, so if the big, faithful hound was still going strong, so was Mack.

"She'll be okay," Mason panted to Sarah.

"I know," Sarah panted back, unable to say more.

Mason tried to make out Becks among the throng, but he couldn't.

As if on cue, Hansen stabbed a finger into the air, shouting, "There!"

Sure enough, there she was, but it didn't look good. Becks being Becks, she had gone to Beverly's aid. A dozen more alphas lay dead around them, so she had obviously been putting the javelin to good use. But even as she struggled to haul Beverly back toward the stairs, sobbing like a baby and cradling her bloody wrist against her chest, the swarm closed in.

Mason caught Richie's attention in the second-floor window and flashed him a hand signal, but even with all four snipers concentrating their fire precisely there, it would only buy Becks and Beverly a few more seconds.

"Leave her!" Hansen bellowed against the roar. "Rebecca! Leave her and run!"

Mason added his own voice, shouting, "Becks! Leave her! Go!" but he knew that even if she could hear them, she'd never listen. This was Becks, after all. She wouldn't leave Beverly behind any more than she'd leave behind a stray cat or a wounded bird.

"Becks!" he tried again. "Becks!" but all his shouting did was excite the swarm even more.

Becks had managed to drag Beverly to the bottom of the steps, but then she lost her footing and both of them dropped to their backsides, and even with the withering fire from the snipers above, the solid wall of teeth and claws and rage rapidly closed the distance.

STAGE 3: BRAVO

Hansen hushed one last, futile, "Rebecca..." then, all he or Mason or Sarah could do was watch her die.

But then the unthinkable happened. Just when death seemed imminent, Donn emerged from the swarm a full thirty feet away, and the three exhausted warriors clustered together on the hood of that half-century-old island in the middle of a raging sea had the distinct honor of witnessing the most heroic display of bravery and sacrifice any of them had ever seen before.

Donn sized up the situation in a heartbeat, and he immediately pulled his pistol, howling, "Over here! Come and get it, you sunzabitches!" He fired until his gun ran dry, dropping a dozen or more creatures, then he turned to his war-scythe, and through it all, he kept up the verbal attack. "Come on, assholes! This way! Over here, you ugly *motherfuckers!*"

The man was intentionally drawing the swarm to him and away from Beverly and Becks. It was heroism on a scale Mason couldn't even begin to imagine. Suddenly, all grew silent on the hood of the old Pontiac as three pairs of eyes watched a young man throw his life away. But even as Hansen drew his own pistol and took aim at the swarm closing in around their friend, Sarah laid a gentle hand on his arm to stop him.

It was over a second later. There was nothing anyone could have done. There was one last mighty swing of the war-scythe, then Donn was swallowed up the swarm, and there wasn't the slightest hint of a scream to mark his passing.

Mason looked back to where Becks was still struggling to get Beverly up the stairs. Donn's sacrifice had bought her time, but not enough. She reeled in a sobbing Beverly and backed up one more step on her rump, and that was when the swarm shifted again. Momentarily distracted, it now came at them in a surge, flooding toward the stairs. But just before it reached them, the *rat-a-tat-a-tat* of a machine gun split the air and a dozen bodies spiraled backwards, temporarily stemming the tide.

The diminutive form of Alejandra appeared out of the swarm and leaped onto the loading dock platform, turning her Tommy gun loose on the swarm, and as she mowed down the creatures down like grass, Christopher emerged, and then Addison, and they both swung high-powered rifles from their backs and added their own fire power to Alejandra's.

Just then, Christopher pointed into the swarm and they all redirected their firepower to cover Diego, just emerging into the daylight. Then he pointed again, and Clancy tore free from the swarm, just inches ahead of Mackenzie. Clancy bounded effortlessly up onto the platform, but Mackenzie was too small and was forced to take the stairs.

When she reached Becks, still struggling to haul Beverly up the last two steps, she didn't hesitate for a second. Both Sarah and Mason had a crystal-clear view as she pulled her revolver and pressing it directly against Beverly's temple, and before anyone could do a thing to stop her, that tiny little girl calmly and cooly pulled the trigger.

CHAPTER

XVIII

B y now, the swarm was beginning to lap at the hood and trunk of the old Pontiac, and as hard as Mason and Sarah and Hansen worked to bat them away, it was only a matter of time. The last image Mason had of Becks was of Addison and Alejandra grabbing her under the arms and all three retreating back into the stronghold with the others close behind, then he saw no more.

The gunfire from the loading dock was another double-edged sword. It created a veritable crush of alphas at the back of building six, but to the three on the roof of the old Pontiac, it was a godsend. As the swarm shifted, a gap opened up between the Pontiac and building five, so Mason hurled himself down and proceeded to widen the gap.

Still, it was no walk in the park. They formed up back-to-back-to-back again and fought for all they were worth, but there were several anxious moments when Mason seriously doubted whether or not they'd make it. But as their energy flagged, the big overhead door came into view behind the swarm, and all three of them redoubled their efforts.

They spun and they pivoted, they hammered and they stabbed, and through it all, they acted as a single entity. At last, Mason hopped onto the platform, hauling Sarah up after him, and as he batted at heads and Sarah kicked at anything within reach, Hansen strode casually up the stairs, even managing to throw them both a snide grin. Mason ignored the taunt, golfing a big bald head aside and clubbing a smaller one hard enough to drive the poor creature into the ground, then Hansen arrived at last to join Sarah in beating back the swarm, and he turned his attention to the door.

The latch plate was designed to keep burglars out, but the designers could never have envisioned a seven-foot length of solid steel with enough brains and muscle behind it to move mountains. Mason produced a tiny block of wood from out of nowhere and lodged an inch of rebar under the metal plate, and using the wooden block as a fulcrum and fifty pounds of steel as the lever, he leaned all his weight into it and felt the door move a fraction of an inch.

"Now would be a good time!" Hansen growled.

He reset the wooden block, planted his feet firmly on the ground, and tried again. He pushed on the rebar for all he was worth, but though the door creaked and groaned and threatened to give way, he had to stop when the wooden block began to crush under the weight.

"C'mon, put your back into it! Open the *fucking* door, asshole!" Hansen taunted him again. "Just think of it as my neck, tough guy! Maybe that'll do it!"

Mason reset the block and strained his muscles to the breaking point, and whether or not the image of his big hands wrapped around Hansen's neck gave him that extra bit of strength, at last there was a creaking and popping from deep inside the metal doorframe. He gave one last, hard shove and felt something give way, and the door finally cracked open to a petulant, "Ha!" from Hansen.

All was blackness inside, but even before the door was fully open, a pair of horrible dead eyes and a gnashing set of teeth appeared out of the darkness, and it was all Mason could do to plant a hand against the creature's throat to hold it at bay. He tried to bring his rebar into the fight, but there wasn't room, and with Hansen and Sarah both busy trying to hold back the swarm and no other help coming, all he could do was squeeze that throat for all he was worth.

Cartilage snapped as his fingers dug deep into the sides of the thing's neck, and still it fought, snapping its ugly teeth and raking at him with a pair of bloody, gnarled claws. He felt something come apart and his hand closed around a solid chunk of flesh, so he instinctively grabbed that handful of meat even tighter and pulled with all of his might. At last, he tore the entire throat away and tossed it to the ground with a horrible, wet *splat!* and it was only then that he realized his error. This was another echo. Even with its windpipe torn away and nothing more than a ragged, bloody hole between chin and chest, the creature kept coming, so he dropped his rebar to the ground and grabbed the creature by the ragged stump of its neck while using his other hand to alternatively bat its claws away and deliver sledgehammer blows to the creature's face.

It was a game he could never win. He was holding the creature off, but only barely. No amount of damage his massive fist could do would have any effect. The echo's nose shattered, its cheek collapsed into a concave mess, and still it fought. And now he could see other shapes forming out of the darkness behind it. More creatures. Alphas. Echoes. Dozens

of them, pressing up behind that one bloodied and torn creature blocking the doorway.

He went for his gun, but firing a gun now would only
bring the entire swarm down on them, so he went for his knife
instead, only to have his hand close around an empty scab-
bard. *Damn!* In the immediacy of the moment, he'd forgotten
that he'd lost it. With no other weapon at his disposal, he
reached all the way back to the rear pocket of his jeans,
wrapped his fingers around a most familiar shape, and in one
quick motion, he bowed the creature's head to its knees and
drove the sharpened tines of a stainless steel fork between its
first and second vertebrae, piercing its spine like an olive.

Immediately, a dozen claws came through the opening,
raking the air inches from Mason's face, and despite Sarah
and Hansen's best efforts, the swarm was already halfway up
the steps behind. So with fire all around and not a frying pan
in sight, Mason took the only course of action left open to him.
He hurled the paralyzed echo down the steps and grabbed his
rebar, then he barged his way into building five, stabbing and
hammering and kicking at anything that moved. He opened
up a few feet of space and soon found Sarah and Hansen on
either side. When they finally beat back the swarm enough to
make room, Hansen kicked the door shut behind them and
flipped the deadbolt, and from then on, all three of them
fought as they'd never fought before.

There wasn't a second to spare for digging out flashlights,
so they fought in the dark, and with no way of knowing just
what they were hitting or where, they kept up a running dia-
logue so the others would know where they were.

"I have the left side!" Mason called out above the roar.

"I'm on the right!" Sarah panted.

"I guess that leaves the middle for yours truly!" Hansen

gruffed, and Mason swore he heard a spiked bat whistle past, inches from his ear.

"No wild swings! Keep your strikes vertical!"

"Up close and personal. Just how I like it. Come and get it, you godawful *motherfuckers!*"

For several anxious minutes, it could easily have gone either way. More than once, Mason thought he'd felt his rebar crush a skull, only to have the creature rear back up and howl bloody murder, and there were times when he only became aware of how close the next alpha was when a clawed hand tore at his shirt. He stumbled over bodies and parts of bodies, nearly losing his footing several times, and with every awkward step, he imagined one of those corpses coming suddenly to life and tearing at his ankle with teeth and claws. And through it all, he fought on with a ferocity he hadn't known he possessed.

Hansen suddenly let out a sharp grunt of pain, and for one horrible moment, he thought that one of the creatures must have gotten to him.

Sarah called out, "Hansen, are you okay?" but there was no way either of them could help the man. Even now, Mason could feel hot breath on his face and claws tearing the air, inches away.

"I'm alright!" Hansen huffed at last. "Just watch your footing. This floor's slicker'n chicken snot!"

The man was three feet away and one step back, but the voice had come from lower down than it should have. So Hansen was on his knees, then. Or maybe he'd fallen on his ass. Either way, that momentary faltering had given the swarm an advantage, and he could hear them surging forward, straight down the middle.

"Hansen, stay down!" he shouted, and without waiting

for a response, he swung his rebar like a baseball bat, unleashing the full power of that seven feet of tempered steel.

Over and over he swung, feeling the weapon shudder with every strike. At last, Hansen huffed, "Hey, save some for me!" so Mason called out, "Clear!" and resumed clubbing downward with all of his might as if he were chopping wood.

With one last grunt, Hansen was back on his feet, pounding away with that spiked bat of his like a crazy man. "C'mon, you motherfuckers!" he howled between blows. "Come and get it! I'm your *goddam* huckleberry!"

Mason allowed the briefest of grins as he felt his rebar sink deep into a skull.

At last, the wave dwindled to a trickle, and a flashlight finally clicked on. It was Sarah, not ten feet away. She played the light from one corner of the room to the other, and after spearing one more alpha through the throat and clubbing another into pulp, Mason could finally see what they'd been up against.

The loading bay was barely fifteen feet to a side. Two hundred square feet, give or take. And in those two hundred square feet, perhaps thirty creatures lay dead or dying. One made a last grab for Mason's boot, but a quick stab from the rebar ended it in a splash. One other creature started to rise, but a surgical strike with a kukri shut it down for good. Only seven alphas remained upright, but now that there was light to see them by, seven new bodies were quickly added to the total.

Then they stood there, three blood-spattered warriors, gasping and panting away their exhaustion and their terror.

But this was no time for celebration. This was just the first rush. Schools didn't have a lot of locked doors, and battles weren't fought in a vacuum. Whatever was upstairs would have heard and was sure to come down, and it wouldn't take them long.

Hansen took the time to end one of the corpses as it struggled to its knees, and Mason dispatched two more twitching bodies with a jab through the cranium, then they all gathered together at the mouth of the hallway leading to the main stairs.

Barely had they stepped into the hallway when the second wave came in a rush. They clawed, they gnashed their jaws and they howled like banshees, and each and every one of them died in a most horrible fashion. Five. Ten. Twenty. Mason lost count before the fight was halfway done. And when this second wave finally slowed to a trickle, he pummeled one last skull to dust, wiped the blood of a dozen or more alphas from his face with his sleeve, and led the way over the jumble of bodies to the stairs that would get them out of this abattoir.

At last he could see daylight, and he gladly followed it like a moth to the flame. But then his nerves began to tingle, and he held up a fist, bringing them all to a halt.

Something was wrong. The roar from the Quad should have been muffled, but it wasn't. Not by a long shot. He crept up the last two steps and poked an eye around the corner, then he crept back down and whispered a few words into Sarah and Hansen's ears.

They were deep in shit, and it was about to get deeper. The way up to the main floor was clear enough, but most of the building's facade was made of glass, and the swarm had done its damage. All six massive windows had great gaping holes where some part of an alpha had broken through, leaving behind blood and gore and spider webs of cracks that radiated outward from the breaks in all directions. Worse, the two glass doors fronting the building were nothing but empty frames. Indeed, those open doors undoubtedly accounted for the huge number of alphas they'd had to battle to get this far, and Mason could only thank whatever malevolent god it was looking down on this hellscape, that the roar of the swarm had covered the sounds of battle as much as it had. But the crush of bodies in the Quad was rapidly filling the space left behind by the alphas that'd come down after them, and it was only a matter of time before another one or ten or fifty discovered the open door.

But there was no way back. Their only chance lay forward, so forward they went.

Mason took the lead, but then he felt a soft hand on his shoulder and turned to see Sarah's pretty face wearing an expression he knew all too well. He relented with a nod, and he and Hansen hung back as she went up alone.

It was a frightening thing to watch, but an endlessly fascinating one as well. The entire stairway was littered with broken glass, but the woman moved like a jungle cat. With one eye always on the swarm, she would tiptoe around the worst of it, and where no clean spot existed, she would sweep a few shards soundlessly aside before planting a toehold. Then she'd survey the ground for a full yard ahead, pick out the most advantageous spot, and toe a few more bits of glass away before bringing her foot down again.

Mason had seen this many times before. Both Sarah and Mack could move like spectres through a swarm as silently as kittens on a bed of down. Maybe it was their tiny feet, he'd often considered, or perhaps it was a female's lower center of gravity. But whatever the basis of their unique talent, he'd never been able to duplicate it. His two hundred plus pounds and size twelves didn't move the same way, and when he imagined how a flatfoot like Hansen would do trying to accomplish the same feat, his heart sank into his belly.

When Sarah reached the landing halfway up the stairs and was just feet from the open doors, she held her position with her kukri raised high, ready to strike, and waggled a pair of fingers down to Mason. Every bit of common sense he possessed fairly *screamed* at him to go ahead of Hansen before the clumsy ox could bring the whole house down, but he simply couldn't. He gave Hansen a flick of his head, and the ox started up.

The man could hardly be mistaken for a jungle cat, but he obviously knew his limitations, and he straddled the line just north of disaster. He followed in Sarah's footsteps as best he could, and when he couldn't, he held on to the handrail for dear life, used the toe of his boot to clear a reasonably bare patch of ground, and lowered his foot as slowly and cautiously as he could. It was like watching a water buffalo performing an adagio from Swan Lake, but much to Mason's surprise, the old man made it to the top of the stairs and the house still stood. Hansen struck a pose beside Sarah, his huge spiked club at the ready, and Sarah waggled another finger.

It was Mason's turn.

He started up, following in Sarah and Hansen's footsteps, but every lowering of his foot seemed to come with an accompanying crunch of glass or grit, and his breath caught on his throat every time. With one hand on the railing and the other clutching his rebar, he took one slow step after another, each one bringing him closer and closer to the maelstrom. A dozen footsteps and eight full minutes later, he stepped silently onto the landing, and Sarah pursed her lips in a silent sigh of relief.

But they were nowhere near safe. In fact, this was the most dangerous spot they'd ever been in before, bar none. The swarm was just feet away and hundreds strong, and there was absolutely nothing to stop them should they decide to storm in. All it would take would be one of them probing their way, and it would be over.

Mason looked around for something, *anything* he might use to block the doors, but it was no use. There was just too much damage and too many ways in.

The only thing they could do was let the swarm be and continue the rest of the way up. Mason nodded for Sarah to take the lead while he and Hansen covered her, and it was while he watched the swarm swirl and eddy just beyond all of those open doors that he saw it. Just twenty feet past the corner of the building. Big enough to tower over the swarm. Close enough that he could almost reach out and touch it. It was Gloria, that big beautiful Peterbilt, with the sun glinting off of her chrome trim like a guiding star.

For one crazy second, he imagined himself barging into the swarm and hammering a path all the way through to that big, beautiful truck. And then came an even crazier idea, why not? After all, it wasn't like he'd be amending a carefully laid-out plan on the fly, right? Whatever exceedingly dubious plan they'd hobbled together to get this far went to shit with one blast of a shotgun, so why not try?

He sized up the nearest alphas and plotted a route through and over that surging ocean of flesh, then he looked farther into the swarm and began to pick out those elements among them that would give him the best chance. Was that a gap? And those alphas moving in a cluster. Weren't they just a bit slower than the others? That big one had a pronounced limp. Broken leg, probably. And that other one was so near to death, it was barely able to raise a claw.

It was possible. If he moved fast enough and hit hard

enough, he might just be able to do it. And once he got to Gloria, he could come back for Sarah and Hansen, and they could all go save the rest of them. Mack. Alejandra. Becks. *Everyone!*

He had just about convinced himself to go for it when a hand like a steel trap grabbed his shoulder, and he turned to see Hansen's ugly mug wearing the deepest of scowls. They glared at one another for what seemed an eternity, then Hansen flipped his head in the direction Sarah had gone, and his scowl only deepened.

Apparently, whatever else Hansen was, he was also a mind reader. But in this case, the mind reader was right. He'd never make it. He'd be throwing his life away for nothing, and leaving his friends one more man short when they needed him the most.

A little embarrassed at being caught with his hand in the cookie jar, and a *lot* pissed off that it'd been Gary *Supercop* Hansen who'd done the catching, he returned every bit of the old man's scowl and then some. Then he flipped his own head after Sarah, and in the ensuing most ridiculously adolescent staring contest since the beginning of time, the two men took turns flipping their heads up the stairs and thinking up harsher ways to scowl.

At last, Mason acquiesced, but only just. He dropped the glare and the scowl and even gave Hansen what might have amounted to a nod, then he flipped his head up the stairs one last time. Hansen narrowed his eyes looking for tells and, finding none, he gave Mason one last glare that threatened all manner of horrific violence should he renege on their unspoken agreement, and he turned to make his way up.

Mason watched the swarm for any sign of change, but the surefooted water buffalo didn't make a whisper of sound. In fact, at one point he even spared a quick look over his shoulder, half-convinced that Hansen hadn't gone anywhere at all and that he was standing right behind him, waiting for him to do something stupid, but what he saw was Hansen and Sarah both at the top of the stairs, kukri and spiked bat at the ready and waving him on.

He looked across to big, beautiful Gloria one last time, and like a man turning his back on a dream, he spun slowly around and began picking his way through the minefield of broken glass.

CHAPTER

XIX

What'sa matter... Gettin' too old for this shit?"

The climb should have taken seconds, but five minutes later, Mason had only reached the halfway point. He happened to look up just then and saw a war-ravaged echo appear behind Sarah while her attention was elsewhere, but all he could do was wave and point and mouth silent words of warning up to her. Luckily, Hansen caught sight of the thing just in time and silently dispatched it with a knife through the base of the skull, but then more came.

In another world, Mason was already rushing to join in on the fight. In this world, though, with so many hungry ears a mere handful of yards away, he simply couldn't. And so, in the cruelest test of strength he could ever have imagined, he lowered his eyes, shut his mind off from both the swarm raging down below and the silent fight for survival going on above, and he concentrated on taking just one more step.

He could have kicked himself for not watching Sarah's ascent. If he had, he could have followed in her footsteps, but he hadn't dared take his eyes from the open doors. Then Hansen had followed and he hadn't watched him either, so now he was forced to pick his way through a fresh minefield. But wait. A clear patch, just at the edge of the next stair. Was that Sarah's doing? It had to be. He lifted a boot and prepared to mount that next step, but then he saw it. A tiny bit of glass, barely visible. Not trusting his big size twelves with the job of toeing the thing aside, he bent down, picked up that tiny fragment of glass between finger and thumb, and placed it as gently as he could a few inches away. Then and only then did he trust that spot enough to take that next step. And from then on, that was how he operated. He'd bend low, scour the step with his eyes, pick up each individual bit of debris, place them all gently aside, then up one more step. Then the next. And the next. And finally, after what seemed a lifetime, he took that very last step to the top and allowed the rest of the world back into his head.

Sarah and Hansen were still at work clearing the last of the echoes, and they were doing so without a breath of sound. Sarah was using her kukri with silent efficiency, and Hansen seemed to be doing alright with his knife, but having neither, Mason leaned his rebar against a doorjamb and tip-toed barehanded into the fray.

The closest was a girl. Teenager at best. San Jose Sharks t-shirt. Long, blonde hair matted with blood. One shriveled eye dangling against her cheek. The thing had been going for Hansen, but when Mason came close enough for his light to shine brighter than the other's, the echo turned and came directly at him, clawing the air and snapping its pearly-white teeth. He batted one claw aside and grabbed the other by the wrist, then he spun around behind the creature and craned the arm up its back until he heard it snap. Wrapping one arm around the creature's chest then, he planted a boot between its feet and pivoted his hips, and with the thing suddenly off-balance, he lowered it slowly and soundlessly to the floor, pinning it down face-first under a heavy knee. He grabbed a handful of hair and pulled it slowly back until he felt more than heard something pop in its neck, and still he pulled. At last, whatever shard of bone had broken loose in the echo's neck pierced its spinal cord, and all of the fight drained immediately out of the thing. The jaws continued to snap as he lowered the head to the floor, but the body would never move again, so he left the broken echo where it was and had at the next.

Female. Mid-30s. In life, probably tall, probably lanky, and if those long, bare legs stretching out from under that leather miniskirt were any indication, probably hot as hell. Now, most of its face was gone, along with a goodly quantity of guts and one entire breast. It came hobbling toward Mason on one high-heeled shoe, so it was an easy enough thing for him to get around behind it. He put a hand on each side of its head and gave it a sharp twist, then he lowered the ragdoll quietly to the floor.

Sarah was making quick work of a pair of echoes, dancing lightly around them until she was in the perfect position to deliver a killing blow to the back of each creature's neck, but she didn't see another one just emerging from the shadows. It was a big male. Linebacker type. Broad shoulders. Thick neck.

Mason launched himself into the thing and spun it around, and while its jaws gnashed uselessly at empty air, he grabbed the thing with a hand on each side of its head, drove a pair of fingers through each of its eyes, and didn't stop digging until he felt the ooze of brain matter squishing between his fingers.

With the last of the echoes gone, Mason reclaimed his re-bar and the three of them regrouped. The college library was dead ahead, and though its doors were made of glass, at least they were doors. They crept through as silently as ghosts and found two more echoes within. One was a college kid – big, muscular, but too hollowed-out to put up much of a fight. Hansen ended the big kid's suffering with a knife through the base of its spine. The other was female, more cadaver than echo. One stab of a kukri was all it took. Sarah knelt before the creature and read the name-badge pinned to a dowdy, old-lady dress. 'Mrs. Lancaster, Head Librarian,' it read. So, Sarah addressed her as such.

"I'm sorry, Mrs. Lancaster. I truly am. I'm sorry for every-thing that's happened, and I apologize for disturbing the sanc-tity of your library."

Mason thought he saw her wipe away a tear, but it might have just as easily been a bit of gore. Either way, he let it go.

"I'm sorry too," Mason said, then he proceeded to tear great swathes from her dowdy old-lady dress and use them to tie the door handles together.

At last, he collapsed to his knees, only to have Hansen come looming over him to say those very words.

"What'sa matter... Gettin' too old for this shit?"

It was typical Hansen, but this time there was no snark in it. And then the old man did something for which Mason was wholly unprepared for. Cop-of-the-century, self-righteous Detective Sergeant Gary *Bad-ass* Hansen actually reached down and offered Mason his hand. Reluctantly, Mason took it and allowed Hansen to help him to his feet, then he stood there in stunned silence, not knowing quite what to say.

Fortunately, Hansen said it for him.

STAGE 3: BRAVO

"Not bad, tough guy," he said. "I guess my old man was right. Even an asshole is good for *something*."

While Mason chewed on the words he wanted to say back, Sarah broke in with a few of her own.

"If you guys can handle the bromance without me, I have a book to find."

She descended on the old-fashioned card file beside a bank of dead computers and began thumbing through drawer after drawer while Mason and Hansen spread out to reconnoiter the rest of the library.

It was an expansive space, running the entire width of the floor from east to west. There were enough windows to let in every bit of daylight, and there were computers and work desks and easy chairs and couches galore. And there were books. Shelf after shelf of books. Sarah stopped thumbing and gave a silent fist-pump, then she disappeared into the stacks, and as she set about hunting down her elusive tome, Hansen perched himself at a window overlooking building six while Mason squatted down beside him to have a look at where they'd come from.

Mother of God...

He didn't think the grounds could get any more crowded, but he was wrong. If he'd had a pair of snowshoes, he might've been able to walk right across the swarm. But on the plus side, from this vantage point, they had a clear view into building six, and a quick head count confirmed ten souls present, so at least no one else had been lost when the plan went to shit.

Well, thank *Christ* for small favors. Two were enough. Hell, two were a damned sight *more* than enough!

"That place can't hold," Hansen said, plainly. "There's too many now. They'll mow the place down through sheer mass

222

of bodies."

"You're right," Mason had to agree. "But look at the bright side. *We'll* go before *they* do."

"Small consolation," Hansen gruffed, more at himself than at Mason. "This was a stupid idea. What the *fuck* were we thinking?"

"We were thinking of the only way to keep people alive, Gary. This was the best in an impossibly bad list of options."

"And now, even that shitty-ass option is gone, thanks to your... your *friend*. Now, *we're* over here, *they're* over there, and every single one of us is well and truly fucked. Goddam it to *Hell!*"

For the first time ever, Mason thought he saw something akin to fear in Hansen's eyes. But no... not fear. So what, then? Sorrow? A million regrets for a million things he'd either done or hadn't done? If Sarah was here, she'd know. One look at that face and she'd be able to read every tell the man ever had. But of one thing, Mason was certain. Something was clearly eating its way through Hansen's heart.

"I'm sorry about Beverly," Mason told him, sincerely. "I thought she'd be able to hold it together, but I was wrong."

"Hell of a time to find out. Some fucking leader *you* turned out to be."

"Hey, I'm just trying to do my best, same as everybody else. Believe me, I am no leader."

"I believe you," Hansen snarked, and for once, Mason took it gladly. "We have a big job ahead of us, tough guy. Between here and your monster truck are an approximate *fuck-ton* of '50s."

"We knew there would be. That's why we came up with Plan C, remember?"

"Oh, I remember alright. I remember saying how the whole

plan sucked cow shit."

"I didn't hear you come up with anything better."

"Why choose between a firing squad and a noose? So tell me, big man, do you really think you'll be able to get to your precious Tonka toy in one piece?"

To that, Mason could only say what he knew to be true.

"I'll either get there, or die trying."

For the first time ever, Hansen looked at him without hatred, without bias, and without the trademark Hansen scowl. He simply looked Mason square in the eye and said, "Well, you'd better get there, big man. 'Cause if you die trying, I'll have to answer to Rebecca, and that girl will have my you-know-whats for you-know-whats."

Any other time, Mason might have laughed. Now, he didn't.

"I don't doubt it for a second," he said, truthfully.

"I raised a tough little girl," Hansen said, and Mason couldn't help but see the distinction. Hansen hadn't raised a tough girl, he'd raised a tough *little* girl.

Was that how every father thought of his daughter? Was there ever a time when the girl stopped being a *little* girl? His mind went naturally to Mackenzie, and though she was certainly not his daughter, the question remained. Would the time ever come when he didn't see her as a *little* girl? If so, it would surely have been when that sweet little thing put a bullet through Beverly's skull. And yet, for some reason, it hadn't. So, maybe Hansen was on to something after all.

"We just have to let Sarah find her book, then we'll see what's what. But the good news is, if we *all* die trying to get to Gloria, you won't have to answer to Becks."

Mason could swear he almost saw Hansen crack a smile, but it might have just been gas. And just that quickly, the scowl returned.

"The book. The *damned* book. Tell me, big man, what is so *goddam* important about that *damned* book? What if all it says is that there's no way out of this mess? What if it says there's no way to fight the virus and no way to defend against it? What if it says that each and every one of us are destined to die, and that mankind is to be wiped off the face of the Earth forever? Will it still have been worth it?"

Mason answered without a moment's hesitation. "Abso-*fucking*-lutely."

The man searched Mason's eyes, then he dropped the subject altogether and picked up another. "So, what is it with you and Sarah anyway? Are you two... *together?*"

Mason released a heavy sigh. "Not that it's any of your business, Gary, but no, it's not like that. Yes, I love Sarah. I would do anything for her. I would kill for her. I would *die* for her. But no, we are not... *together*. I love Sarah. And I love Mack. And I love Becks. Let's just leave it at that, alright?"

Hansen mulled it over. "Alright, fair enough. I'll let it go. For now. But just so you know, big man, if you hurt my daughter again, I will most assuredly murder your ass."

On that point, Mason had no doubt. If their places were reversed, Mason would do the same without a second thought. But still, there was a point of clarification that had to be made.

"Just so you know, Gary, I got pretty damn hurt too. I don't know if she told you or not, but Becks and I were planning to elope. I know that every father wants to walk his daughter down the aisle, but honestly, is there any way you would've done that with *me* at the other end?" He registered Hansen's disgust and moved on. "There was going to be a quick stop at a little chapel in Haight-Ashbury with flowers and candles and harp music, then off to Phuket and a five-star hotel with a pool and a spa and a swim-up bar. It was going to be great. It was going to be *magical*. It would have been a fairy tale wedding we could tell our children about one day. And the very morning we were about to start our new lives together, she sent me a text saying that we were through."

"A text?" Hansen snorted. "Jeez, that's cold."

"Ya think?" Mason snapped, flushed with renewed anger. But as with all things in this new world, it didn't last long. "I blamed her for a while, but I was really just mad at myself. I know I treated her like shit, and she was right to kick my ass to the curb. But the one positive thing to come out of a world gone to Hell is that none of those things matter anymore."

Hansen shrugged. "S'pose not."

It was only two words, but they were a revelation to Mason. For the first time since knowing the man, he felt like he was talking to an actual person instead of the cardboard cutout of a tough, big-city lawman. And then it got weirder.

"I was going to retire last year, you know?" Hansen said, sounding almost human. "I had my thirty. I could've signed the papers anytime, but I couldn't leave the job. It was in my blood, I guess. Barbara begged me to hang it up. Kept saying that we owed it to ourselves. But I just went on making one excuse after another. Now, I'd give anything to go back and do things differently."

"A sentiment that could be carved on the tombstone of every human being who's ever lived," Mason harrumphed.

Hansen accepted the statement with a shrug, and in the awkward silence that followed, he narrowed his eyes at Mason once more.

"Harp music? Really?"

"It wasn't *my* idea."

As Hansen fought to stifle a laugh, Mason climbed to his feet and padded quickly across to a window on the far side of the room. From there, he could see the Peterbilt and the Mustang, but he could also see the swarm, and 'approximate fuckton' didn't even begin to describe it. The gunshots hadn't just drawn them in from the north, they'd brought them in from every point on the compass, and there wasn't so much as a stumbling block left to slow the bastards down.

He went back to Hansen and found him hanging halfway through the window, making hand gestures to someone across the way. Sure enough, it was Becks. When the communication was done, she nodded and flashed the 'okay' sign, then she waved at Mason and blew him a kiss, and he waved back and wished he was the kind of man who could do the other thing.

"I feel like Hasdrubal holed-up in the Temple of Eshmun," Hansen grumbled, dropping onto his backside on the floor.

Mason didn't get the reference, but he took a shot.

"Babylon?" he guessed, but wrongly, as it turned out.

"The great Carthaginian Empire. In 149 BC, Manius Manilius led a Roman army to Africa and laid siege to Carthage. The siege lasted two years, with the Romans battering down one wall after another as the Carthaginians retreated further and further back into the city. Ultimately, Carthage couldn't stand against such a powerful enemy. The city fell and was burned to the ground. After that, Carthage ceased to exist."

Mason couldn't help but see the parallels, but he held his tongue for now.

"Just before the end, nine hundred survivors, most of them Roman deserters, took refuge in the tower at the Temple of Eshmun. They tried to negotiate their surrender even as the temple burned, but the Romans weren't about to show mercy."

"So, let me guess," Mason harrumphed. "They fought to the very last man?"

"Not quite, no." Hansen shook his head. "One by one, those nine hundred souls threw themselves into the fire, including Hasdrubal's wife and children. They all died at their own hands rather than fall under the executioner's sword."

Mason harrumphed again. "Then they died for nothing," he concluded without a hint of mercy.

"Oh?" Hansen snarled. "You have a problem with a man dying with honor?"

"Honor, my ass!" Mason snarled back. "When a man faces certain death, he has precisely two options. He can lie down and die, or he can fight like hell and give it everything he's got right up to the last breath. He'll wind up just as dead either way, but only one of those options will let him take as many of the motherfuckers with him as he can."

In a thousand years, he could never have imagined Hansen's response. The man grunted once, then he said, "Well, maybe you aren't the dumbest bag of shit in the world after all."

Wow. A complimentary insult. In Hansen's world, that was akin to a French kiss. So, what were they now? Friends? Compatriots? The enemy of my enemy, and all that?

Thankfully, he didn't have to wonder for long.

"It's good to know you have a tiny bit of brain in that big fat head of yours, tough guy," Hansen gruffed. "Quite frankly, I had my doubts."

"Yeah, I got that."

"Oh, don't be such a sensitive little flower. In case you haven't noticed, big man, I'm not exactly a fan of the human race."

"Gee, I hadn't noticed," Mason muttered, not quite under his breath.

Hansen kept his eyes fixed on Mason, and rather than searching his face for tells, Mason had the distinct impression that the man was looking for the most vulnerable spot to plunge his knife. Ultimately though, Hansen sighed the matter away and turned his gaze to the floor.

"You know, my old man could do it all. He could fix the car, grow vegetables in the garden, build furniture... Hell, he even built his own house from the ground up. Me, I can barely hammer a nail. I used to be able to take care my old Chevy, you know, gap the spark plugs, adjust the timing, that sort of shit. But then they started making cars so complicated that I couldn't even change my own oil, and that's exactly what the billion-dollar companies wanted. They wanted me to give them even *more* of my hard-earned money, rather than be able to do it myself. I put my old man's refrigerator in the garage after he died. Forty years old, and that fridge still purred. Kept my beer as cold as ice. Upstairs, we had a fridge that told us when the milk was running low and a stove with more *goddam* computing power than it took to send men to the moon, and those fuckers broke down every two years like clockwork, and that's the world we made for ourselves. Our machines got smarter and our people got stupider."

Mason rolled his eyes, but Hansen waved it away.

"Oh, I know, tough guy. Every generation complains about modern technology and longs for the good old days, right? The music sucks and damn kids these days wouldn't know a hard day's work if it bit 'em in the ass. But all the grumpy old man shit aside, you know I'm right. Fifty years ago, would the world have crumbled to dust so easily? *Fuck,* no. But it was no grand conspiracy to make us so reliant on technology. We did it to ourselves and we were glad to do it. They made cars able to brake automatically, and it saved lives... so, bravo. But then our cars had to *park* themselves because it was just too damn hard to turn a wheel. Then they had to have lane-assist, because God *forbid* we maintained control of a motor vehicle enough to keep it between the lines.

"You know what I saw on that very first day, big man? I saw my neighbor from down the street piling his family into his brand new Lexus to make his escape, and they were doing just fine. Frank and Heather and all the kids got inside, all safe and sound, and they headed off to her mother's house or their summer cabin in the woods or wherever-the-fuck. But you know what happened next? A couple of '50s came out of nowhere and went charging straight at his car, and he stopped. He just stopped dead in his tracks as those '50s came tear-assing up the road. I couldn't for the life of me figure out why, but then it dawned on me. That brand new car of his had automatic braking. Can you believe it? I'm sure there was a way to shut the damn thing off, but who's gonna learn how to do that? It's a convenience and a safety feature, so why would anyone ever want to turn it off? So Frank sat there right in the middle of the road because his damn car thought he was going to run down a pedestrian. And then more '50s came, and before I could even think about helping, they tore that brand new Lexus apart where it sat."

This was one of those rare instances when Mason couldn't think of a thing to say. Somehow, *stupid died quick* seemed a tad cold-blooded, considering. So he said nothing.

"Hey, big man," Hansen gruffed. "How about you shove that massive melon of yours back just a bit, huh?"

Hansen ripped the closest chair cushion free and held it

in the air, and while Mason was still trying to figure out what the hell he was doing, there came a muted *thwack!* and the cushion was propelled backward. Hansen quickly reeled it in, and now Mason could see something sticking out from it. A short shaft of wood flanked by two curved bits of plastic. It was one of Teddy's crossbow bolts, but this one bore a passenger. A piece of paper had been tied to the shaft with a bit of string. It was a message, delivered as it would've been a millennia ago.

Hansen untied the paper and rolled it open. "It's from Rebecca," he said, and much to Mason's chagrin, he read the rest of it to himself first before deigning to deliver a condensed version to Mason.

"They're all okay, aside from Donn and that... that *Beverly* woman." He spat Beverly's name like a curse, and for the life of him, Mason couldn't find it in himself to disagree. "A few windows were smashed and some '50s tried to get in, but they were repelled. The doors are holding for now, and they're working on sealing off the second floor."

"They'll get it done," Mason said with absolute confidence, "they're all good people."

Hansen didn't deny it. In fact, he went so far as to say, "Yes, they are," before reading the rest of the message aloud verbatim. "Be careful, Daddy, and look after Sarah and Mace. We'll be ready in an hour. Addison says to let us know when you're coming so we don't think it's Jehovah's Witnesses knocking on the door and start shooting. Ha ha. Love you all. Becks."

He folded the paper neatly into quarters and shoved it in his shirt pocket as he sent a few hand signals across to his daughter at the other window. He finished with two fingers pressed against his lips, then he stood and declared in a huff,

STAGE 3: BRAVO

"Alright then. Sarah's had enough time. I don't care if she's found that precious book of hers or not, we are getting the hell out of here!"

As if on cue, the sound of crunching glass echoed up from below, and Sarah came barreling out from between the stacks.

"They're in," she said, just that simply.

CHAPTER

XX

Hansen cursed under his breath and ran to check the doors.

While he did, Mason looked for an out.

The roof? No. Even assuming that there was access from inside the library, they'd be going in the wrong direction. Getting to Gloria would be hard enough as it was. Getting to her from the roof would be impossible. Barricade the doors? Possible, but they'd never be able to do so in silence. They'd be telling the swarm exactly where they were. Not an option. Throw open the doors and try to stem the tide? Fuck that. It would be like trying to plug a thousand leaks in the Hoover Dam. For one agonizing moment, Mason once again considered taking on the entire swarm single-handedly, but once again, sanity trumped aspiration. And so, he made the only decision he could. He decided that they would stay precisely where they were.

He motioned for absolute quiet and ushered Hansen and Sarah to the farthest corner of the library. As they crouched together in a huddle, Hansen craned his neck to take a peek out of the nearest window.

"*Damn!*" he growled in a hush. "That monster truck of yours is only twenty feet out and ten feet down. I could almost *jump* that distance!"

Sarah scoffed the idea away. "And if you tried, you'd fall twelve feet short and break both your legs."

"*Damn* it!" Hansen pounded his leg with a fist. "If I wasn't so pig-headed, Mace, I'd have let you bring that Tonka toy right into the Quad!"

Well, son of a bitch. Hard-ass Hansen admitting a mistake was astounding enough, but he'd just done something even more spectacular. He hadn't called Mason 'asshole,' or 'big man,' or 'tough guy.' He'd actually called him *Mace*.

"It was the right..." Mason began, but he quickly cut himself off as the first of the probing alphas appeared on the far side of the glass. It continued on past the doors, but as always, what started as a trickle quickly turned into a flood. First one, then three, then ten, then twenty, then too many alphas to count. And just that quickly, the second floor was overrun.

No one on the other side of those simple glass doors failed to understand just how precarious their position had become, least of all Hansen.

"Okay," he growled, rising to his feet. "We have to go. Now!"

"Hey!" Sarah hushed, grabbing him by the belt and unceremoniously yanking him back down. "You're not going anywhere!"

"Get your fucking claws off me, you *cunt!*" Hansen growled, batting her hand away.

"Gladly!" Sarah hushed, but instead of backing down, she came nose-to-nose with the man. "As long as you sit the *fuck* down and shut the *fuck* up, my claws won't come anywhere near you. But understand this, Hansen... If I think for even a second that you're about to do something stupid that'll get us all killed, this *cunt* will put a bullet straight through that ugly fucking head of yours."

As the vein on Hansen's neck pulsed a brilliant red, Mason readied himself. *Which will it be?* he wondered. Will it be the usual verbal tirade, or would the man actually be stupid enough to try to lay a hand on Sarah with Mason right there beside her? Either one was sure to end badly. The former might earn Hansen a quick choke-hold and a lengthy nap. The latter would positively make the sleep eternal.

But for the second time in as many minutes, Hansen surprised him.

"Quite so," he said, barely above a whisper. "Apparently, I am not immune to the occasional rash decision brought on by fear. I'm sorry, little la..." He stopped himself, and restarted with what appeared to be a truly sincere, "I'm sorry, Sarah."

The immediate crisis over, Sarah returned to form.

"Don't be," she said, dismissing the entire thing with a shrug, "No harm done." She cast a quick eye toward the doors, adding a breathy, "I hope..."

"Nevertheless," Hansen insisted, however grudgingly, "I used inappropriate language in referring to you as a cunt. Cunt is a term I normally reserve for the lowest dregs of your gender. You are not a cunt, Sarah. You might be a bitch, but you are most certainly not a cunt."

"Gee... thanks," Sarah said, deadpan.

Just then, an alpha thundered into the door, shaking the glass in its frame and making all three of them back farther away, slowly and silently. They eased down between the stacks until they could go no farther, then they huddled to-gether in the deepest, darkest corner of that abandoned li-brary.

"Barbara always said that my mouth had a way of run-ning faster than my brain," Hansen confided to Sarah in a whisper. "My wife, Barbara. She was forever trying to get me to see the good in everyone. In all honesty, I never saw it, but I pretended to. For her."

Sarah took the man's hand in hers, saying sweetly, "She sounds like a good woman."

Hansen started to pull away, but ultimately, he didn't. He simply sat there, content to share the touch of another.

"She was. She was a fine, *fine* woman. She and Rebecca were my whole world. They were my strength and my con-science."

Mason's heart suddenly tightened, and he didn't have to wonder why. Hansen wasn't doing it deliberately, but he might just as well have been talking about three other people Mason knew rather intimately.

"I'm sorry," he told the man, honestly. "I didn't know Bar-bara well, but she was a fine woman indeed. I'm very sorry for your loss."

He'd gone too far. A man like Hansen was built for nei-ther consolation nor maudlin displays of emotion, and Mason should have known it. The man pulled his hand free of Sarah's on the pretense of satisfying an itch behind his ear, and with that most tenuous of bonds broken, his entire demeanor changed. Gone was the misty-eyed widower, and back was the hard-assed Detective Sergeant *Grab-'em-by-the-balls* Han-sen.

"Enough of this bullshit. Plan B is shot to shit, so we go with Plan C. Rebecca said an hour, but we won't last that long.

So are we going to make a move on your monster truck, or do I have to do it myself?"

It was too much. Something else was eating away at the old man. Something beyond his daughter's life hanging in the balance, and even beyond the loss of his beloved wife. It was no one's business but his own, so Mason let it go, but he didn't let go of the other thing.

"We can't alter the plan now, Gary. Becks said an hour, so we go in an hour. They'll need that much time to barricade themselves in. Until then, we conserve our strength. We're going to need it."

Hansen clearly wasn't happy with the judge's decision, but he conceded the point with a grudging nod. And now, confined in a library with one person he barely knew and another he outright despised, Hansen looked up at the rows of books, then to the floor, and then he busied himself with picking the odd bits of lint off of a shirt already heavily stained with mud and blood and gore.

At last, when the silence became too awkward even for him, he chucked his chin toward Sarah and told her plainly, "That girl of yours is one tough little monkey."

Sarah considered the statement with a sigh, allowing a semi-committal, "I guess."

If Hansen had any scruples, he would've left it there. But he didn't.

"I bet she saw something in that *Beverly* woman no one else was willing to see, am I right?"

Sarah's back stiffened. "As a matter of fact, that sweet little girl suggested just yesterday that we should cut Beverly loose."

"Smart girl," Hansen harrumphed.

"Then she suggested that maybe we should just shoot her."

STAGE 3: BRAVO

"*Very* smart girl," Hansen harrumphed again.

"And today, she did just that. A few short weeks ago, that sweet little girl was playing with dolls. Now she's perfectly capable of putting a bullet in someone else's brain. So yes, Hansen, I guess she's become a tough little monkey. Is that what you wanted to hear?"

Hansen looked her square in the eye. "As a matter of fact, yes! It means she's a survivor. And more to the point, it means that *my* girl's chances of surviving this shit just got marginally better with someone like that watching over her."

"Someone like *that?*" Sarah snapped, but Hansen waved it off.

"Oh, I didn't mean it like that. You know what I meant. Hey, most people die in this world because they can't let go of what *was* and wrap their head around what *is*. Now, I'm an asshole from way back, so it was no big thing for me to go from 'me against the world' to 'me *versus* the world,' you know? But Rebecca doesn't think that way. She couldn't! Oh, she can finally take down a '50 if she has to, same as she might be able to take down a rabid dog. Under the right circumstances, she might even be able to do the same to a person, and I stress the word 'might'. But your daughter..."

Sarah skewered the man in place. "My daughter... *what?*"

"Oh, c'mon, Sarah. No offence and all. It's a compliment! All I'm saying is, Mackenzie is different. She's smart. She sees things the way they are, not how they were. In a strange way, I suppose the younger the kid, the easier time they'll have adjusting to the new paradigm."

"And what paradigm is that?" Mason asked, already knowing the answer.

"Why, kill or be killed, of course," Hansen said, just that simply.

"Survival at any cost?"

"Damn straight! Same as always. So the questions is, why did you keep that *Beverly* woman with you? I mean, really, if Mackenzie could see the signs, you would've too, right? You had to know she was... unstable."

Ain't no psychiatrists in the 'poc'lypse... Mason thought to himself.

"That poor woman went through hell," Sarah snarled. "She had her child ripped from her arms and thrown to the swarm, for *Christ's* sake!"

"Well, boo-fucking-hoo!" Hansen cut her off with a huff. "We've *all* been through the same shit, haven't we? We've *all* lost someone, right? Hell, there's not a person left alive on this shitball of a planet who hasn't suffered a loss of some kind. So don't you dare excuse the fuck-up someone makes today because of whatever shit they went through before."

Sarah looked about ready to explode, but Mason settled her down with a gentle hand on her shoulder.

All at once, he knew the burden Hansen carried, and he understood the nature of the dark cloud hanging over the man. Still, it was none of his business. It was Hansen's cloud, so it was entirely his decision whether or not to bring the rain. And after looking back to the books and to the floor and everywhere else but at Sarah, the old man finally did just that.

"I killed her," the man hushed, more to himself than to anyone else. "I killed Barbara. My wife. The love of my life. She was counting on me to keep her safe. I was her husband, her protector, and I failed her. I'm a cop. I should've seen it coming, but I didn't. All of a sudden, the road was blocked and we had nowhere to go. Then the '50s came. Twenty. Fifty. Dunno, maybe more. I backed off and tried to find a different way out of the mess, but it was the same everywhere. I kept trying, kept moving, but with Barbara screaming and Rebecca crying, all I could think was 'Get there! Get there!' I tried one way after another, then I took a wrong turn and came up against a massive roadblock, and before I could get turned around, the '50s came again. And then more. And then more. Before I knew it, they were piled so thick around the car, I couldn't budge the fucking thing. Then one son of a bitch rammed the passenger window with his big fat head, and the window cracked. And with so many of the fuckers pressed up against both sides of the car, the glass finally shattered. They reached in and started to drag her out..."

A tear threatened the corner of his eye, but he willed it away before it could form and told the rest as if he was giving his testimony on the witness stand.

"I couldn't stop them. I grabbed for her, but she was already gone. I fired a full clip and killed enough of the fuckers to open up a hole, then I saw her lying there on the ground, screaming and crying as more of those monsters tore into her. So I loaded another clip and took down a dozen more, then I used the last round in the clip to end her pain. I murdered my wife as our child looked on. I shot her in the head and I saw her brains splatter, and I left her there in the middle of the road..."

Jesus Christ...

What was it that Becks had said? It was quick? Well, apparently it wasn't quick enough. And Becks had seen it all. Every gruesome detail.

Not knowing what else to say, he said the first thing that came to mind.

"It was a mercy, Gary. You know that."

"Of course it was," Sarah cooed, taking Hansen's hand once again. "There was nothing you could have done."

240

But again, it was too much. Hansen pulled away from Sarah and sneered the matter into nothingness.

"Oh, please! Spare me your sentimental Oprah bullshit. *I* fucked up, *I* watched the love of my life being torn apart, and *I* put a bullet in her head. I have to live with it for the rest of my life, but dwelling on *that* shit won't get me through *this* shit. When I can afford to mourn Barbara properly, I will, I promise you. When that time comes, I will bawl my eyes out like a tiny, little baby and be appropriately inconsolable. But *now* ain't that time!"

Mason couldn't disagree with the sentiment, but it was too cold. Too callous. Too cruel. He knew it, and judging by the look on Sarah's face, she knew it too. Deep down inside, even Hansen had to know it. But Gary *Hard-ass* Hansen could never be seen as just another man, could he? For all of his life, he'd had to be Dirty Harry, John McClane, and Robocop, all rolled into one. All grit, zero emotions. But those emotions were there, alright. He was carrying the weight of that horrible event like a millstone around his neck, and sure as shit, he felt every single damn ounce of it.

"So I say again," Hansen concluded, though with no enthusiasm at all, "that girl of yours is one tough little monkey..."

"It's her world now." Mason finally said aloud what he and Sarah had only ever hushed to each other when no one else was around. "Hers and Teddy's and Diego's and the rest of them. You're right, Hansen. Kids adapt easier, and though I hate the idea of what they'll have to become and what kind of lives they'll have to lead, at least they will *have* a life."

"And long ones at that." Hansen nodded, adding the almost off-handed postscript, "Hopefully."

Hopefully...? Mason scolded the old man inside his head.

STAGE 3: BRAVO

Don't you know about hope yet, Gary? Trust me, when that bitch cuts, she cuts damn fucking deep.

CHAPTER

XXI

T he cover was stark white, with the letters *JAMA* written across the top in bold script. Beneath were the words *The Journal of the American Medical Association*. Mason saw the thing sticking out of the back of Sarah's jeans, but it couldn't possibly be what she'd been looking for. It was too thin, too inconsequential. With all of the importance she'd put on finding it, he'd expected something akin to a sacred tome, not the latest issue of *Harper's Bazaar*. And now, as Sarah crouched around the corner to check that the doors were still secure, Hansen saw it too.

"Is that it?" he scoffed, turning up his nose. "Is that your *damn* book?"

"It is," she said, leaving the thing precisely where it was.

"And now that you've found it, would you mind telling me what was so *damned* important about finding it? Is there a secret incantation inside those pages that'll end all this? Are you gonna bring back pepperoni pizza and Monday Night Football, Sarah?"

STAGE 3: BRAVO

Sarah said nothing, and as far as Mason was concerned, she didn't have to. Hansen's snarky tone aside, that report was her business and hers alone. If she wanted to share anything about it, she would. If not, so be it.

Sadly, Hansen was not so accommodating.

"Young lady, I'm no fool. You say that something is important to you, fine. As long as it doesn't put lives in danger, we will all go out of our way to help you acquire it. But don't give me that same tired old line about finding a way to stop this insanity in its tracks. Forgive me for saying so, Sarah, but you're just not that good! *Nobody* is! I'm sure you're as clever as all hell, but you're not going to come up with a cure for a global pandemic using spit and duct tape. So tell me, Sarah, what was so vitally important that you simply *had* to get your hands on that little white book?"

Again, she said nothing, and again, she didn't have to. Mason had known the reason right from the start – from the moment she'd brought to whole thing up – but it was none of his business. At last, though, Sarah pulled that too-thin magazine from the back of her jeans and collapsed cross-legged to the floor. Then she took a deep breath, released it slowly, and handed the magazine to Hansen.

"I was at work when it all started," she admitted to the man, however painful the memories. "When I realized how bad it was, I should have left, but I didn't. Mack was home, and a good woman was looking after her. She'll be alright, I kept telling myself. Ain't nothing gonna hurt my little girl. But Mrs. Dobson was infected, and toward the end, she changed. Mack was able to get out of the apartment in time, but she couldn't escape the virus. She'd been infected, too, and that sweet, blind little thing had no other choice but to wander through the streets all on her own, trying to get to me." She wiped away a single tear and continued. "Fortunately, Mason found her, and he protected her. He stayed with her even though she was already in stage one."

To his credit, Hansen kept his snotty comebacks to himself. He simply looked from Sarah to Mason and back again, and kept his big trap shut.

"I expected her to turn at any minute." Mason picked up the narrative, he too reliving the pain of those awful first days. "I knew nothing about the disease, but I held on to the one thing I *did* know. With every virus, some people are immune, and some people can be infected and still get better. So, I clung on to that one possible future. I *hoped* that that little girl would live."

Sarah reached out for Mason's hand, and he took it gladly.

"And she did!" Sarah declared through a smile, though another tear broke loose and streaked her cheek. "She lived! She got better! Somehow, her immune system was able to fight off the virus!"

"But..." Hansen said, leaving the word hanging in the air.

"But I know from personal experience that not all recoveries are permanent. Some viruses return with a vengeance, and this was no ordinary virus to begin with. So I had to know. One way or the other."

As it turned out, Hansen was human after all. Gone was Robocop, and in its place, a loving parent. He averted his eyes from Sarah and began flipping random pages in a magazine that he hadn't a hope of understanding.

"So, what does it say? Could the damn thing, uh... *return with a vengeance?*"

No one hung on Sarah's next words more than Mason. He held her hand as tightly as he ever had, and prepared himself for the worst. Tears welled up behind Sarah's eyes, and like a dam bursting, they began pouring down her cheeks, but just as Mason thought that his worst fears were realized, Sarah beamed the broadest grin the world had ever seen.

"No!" she gushed as she threw her arms around Mason, and they hugged as if they were all that tethered each of them to this world. "She's okay, Mace," she cooed in his ear. "She's okay."

"Oh, Sarah," Mason hushed back. "Thank God... Thank God..."

Even Hansen wasn't entirely unaffected. Though he made a show of stoic indifference, Mason thought he caught the man hiding a sniffle as he stuck his nose between the pages.

"So, it's like the measles," the old man stumbled through his words, "Supermeasles, I guess. One per customer. Well, good. Good for her." He cleared his throat and plunged on. "But what else does this *damned* book say? Where did it come from? Was it terrorists? How do we fight it? And most importantly, can the rest of us still be infected?"

A full minute later, Sarah peeled herself away from Mason, but she didn't let go of his hand. And in that darkened library, surrounded by the dead and the dying, and with a horde of barbarians quite literally at the gates, Sarah told them everything she knew about the end of the world.

"No, it wasn't terrorists. As a matter of fact, the virus was created as a *cure*, not a disease."

"A cure?" Hansen scoffed. "A cure for what, *life*?"

Instead of answering, Sarah raised the open question, "Have either of you ever heard the word 'nanotechnology'?"

They both nodded.

"Little machines," Mason said. "Micro-sized."

"Yes." Sarah gave his hand a squeeze. "Little machines. Micro-sized. Modern science theorized for decades about nanotech. Tiny, impossibly-small robots that might one day kill cancer cells, remove plaque from clogged arteries, repair damaged organs molecule by molecule. But the problem always was, how do you build a machine smaller than a human cell? Well, we've been getting better at making things smaller and smaller, so it looked like it was just a matter of time. After all, think about the lowly transistor. Back in the days of vacuum tubes, a radio was as big as a kitchen cabinet. Then came radios that you could carry around in your back pocket, thanks to a few transistors taking the place of those vacuum tubes."

"I had one of those as a kid," Hansen admitted, almost sheepishly.

"And later on, you had a smartphone. Those early radios had a whopping four transistors. Do you know how many transistors are... uh, I mean *were* in that smartphone of yours, Gary?"

Fortunately for Hansen, Sarah answered her own question.

"Three to four *billion!* That's billion with a 'b'! So okay, clearly, we were getting better at making things smaller. But there was another problem. One nanobot would never be enough. A single patient might require millions or billions of them, all dedicated to a particular task in order to have any noticeable effect, and how do you mass produce millions and billions of microscopic machines? It seemed like it might not happen for another century or more, but then someone came up with a brilliant idea. Concentrate all of the money and technology and effort to build just one, then bond the tech to a virus. Well, a *reovirus*, actually."

"Reovirus?" Hansen flipped the magazine's pages even more feverishly. "Reovirus? Whassat?"

STAGE 3: BRAVO

"It's called an *orphan* virus. One of several harmless viruses found in the human digestive system. They call it an orphan because it's not associated with any known disease. Now, a virus isn't alive, understand. It's just a package of genetic material wrapped in a protein shell. It reproduces by subverting a healthy cell and injecting it with its own DNA, and that cell then goes on to reproduce a few million copies of the virus. So the idea was, if they could create a single microscopic robot and somehow bond it to an orphan virus, maybe the body's own cells could become like tiny factories, with each one churning out millions upon millions *more* microscopic robots."

"Lunatics," Hansen gruffed, "playing God."

Sarah didn't argue. Not exactly.

"Maybe so, but at least she was trying to be a *benevolent* god."

"She?" Mason did the math. "Ah, the lady in white. The one on the cover. *Chan*, was it?"

Sarah nodded. "The science was sound and had *incredible* potential. Think of it – an army of machines all programmed to destroy harmful pathogens, repair damage, rebuild lost function. With one injection, they'd be able to regenerate spinal cords, reconstruct optic nerves, repair atrophied muscles. Every disease known to man could be eliminated in its initial stages. Eventually, even aging *itself* might be reversed. Every cell in our bodies would be continuously rebuilt by billions of microscopic robots, all dedicated to the single task of repairing and maintaining the machinery of our physiology. Theoretically, nanotech could keep a human body alive indefinitely. Can you imagine living ten lifetimes, Hansen? A hundred? A *thousand*?"

Mason could plainly see how excited Sarah was getting,

and he couldn't blame her one bit. She was back in *her* world now – back in the world of science and medicine and everything pre-apocalypse. And even though she just so happened to be describing the step-by-step destruction of the whole world, he said nothing, lest he take from her these few fleeting moments of her old, happy life.

Sadly, Hansen was not so charitable.

"One's plenty," he growled, still flipping pages like he was looking for the crossword puzzle at the back of a TV Guide.

Sarah was undeterred. "Patient A was a young boy. Eight years old. He developed a brain tumour deep in his cerebellum. A medulloblastoma, far too deep for surgery and too advanced for chemotherapy or radiation. I had to read between the lines, but I'm guessing that the child's father was *very* rich and *very* influential. It would have cost billions, and to get it done as quickly as they did, undoubtedly some laws would have been skirted, and some corners cut. But in the end, Chan and her team managed to create the tech, then they went on to perfect a technique to bond the tech to a virus."

"And they put it in the boy," Mason said.

"They did." Sarah nodded, enthusiasm fully intact.

"A human guinea pig," Hansen scoffed. "So, did it make him one of those... *things?*"

"Not at all!" Sarah fairly beamed. "In fact, the procedure worked perfectly! The tech was programmed to eliminate every last cancer cell and repair all of the damage to the cerebellum and brain stem, and that's exactly what it did. It was a monumental success! The boy's recovery was so astonishing and so rapid that he was released within the month. After all, no one anticipated any kind of complications..." Here, Sarah's excitement vanished in an instant. She swallowed hard and turned her eyes downward as if in prayer, and she added, sourly, "But Darwin knew better."

She took a deep breath before continuing. "The rest of this is conjecture. Understand, the *JAMA* report ends with that initial success, so this is nothing more than an educated guess at what happened after. But it's probably as close to the truth as we'll ever come. I can only assume that while the technology was doing what it was programmed to do, the virus followed its *own* programming, courtesy of Mother Nature. You see, every new generation of every organism on Earth throws out random mutations. Those that benefit the organism are passed on to future generations, and those that don't, die off. That's evolution. We all learned about that in high school. A random ape is born with an extra cubic centimeter of brain mass, it's better able to survive and procreate, and a few million years and hundreds of thousands of mutations later, *voilà*... Homo sapiens. Well, even though a virus isn't technically alive, it follows the same rules. It throws off countless mutations in every generation. Some stick, some don't, and believe it or not, some of those variations actually turn out to be beneficial to the human body. But sometimes, they turn out to be quite deadly."

"So what you're saying is," Hansen summed up in his own way, "the whole world ended because one doctor tried to fix a broken boy."

"Well, obviously I can't be sure, but it makes sense. Look, viruses mutate. It's what they do. A virus endemic to one species throws off a single mutation in a billion that allows it to jump the species barrier, like the so-called Swine flu or Avian influenza. Or a crow carrying H5N1 dies and falls into a pig sty where one of the pigs is already infected with H1N1, and like two separate armies attacking a common enemy, they share information, swap genetic material, combine, mutate, recombine and mutate again *ad infinitum* until one lone virion manages to slip through a human immune system's defenses. I can only assume that Patient A passed the technovirus to someone else, and they passed it to someone else, and so on and so on. It might have spread to thousands or even *millions* of people, and they would have never known they carried it unless someone looked at a blood sample through an electron microscope. The only sign that they'd been infected at all would be a complete *absence* of medulloblastoma. So, it went undetected, and eventually, the virus must have either mutated on its own or come upon a host carrying another type of virus. It became deadly, and it became airborne, and from there it was just a short hop on a 747 to global pandemic."

Mason stifled a gasp. A short hop on a 747. His return flight from that horrible week in Thailand. He'd told Sarah all about it. Blindness. Panic. Rage. An emergency landing. And all of it ending with a man in a suit biting into the face of a rescue worker.

Jesus... Was that the short hop? Had he actually been there to witness the beginning of the end?

"Clearly, a precious few must have been immune even then," he heard Sarah say through the pulse thundering in his ears, but the words gave him little comfort. He tried to speak, but the words lodged in his throat.

Sarah put her other hand on his cheek and told him in no uncertain terms, "And those precious few should consider themselves extremely fortunate to have been given a second chance at life. Just imagine what good might come from it."

He nodded and managed to force a smile, but the reality of it shook him down to the core. Here, he thought he'd escaped the thing thanks to his natural aversion to humans. But in reality, he'd been in the thick of it all along – elbow to elbow with those first few hundred lost souls.

"And what makes someone immune to a brand new disease?" he asked, trying to keep his voice steady.

Sarah shrugged. "Chance. Genetics. Luck of the draw. Divine providence, if you prefer."

"I don't," Mason admitted, feigning a grin.

"You make it sound like it was inevitable," Hansen snorted, breaking into their reverie. "Like one virus or another was always destined to come along and take us down."

Sarah answered honestly. "Well, the tech adds a new wrinkle, but there are more than a trillion trillion *trillion* viruses on Earth. They're the oldest organisms on the planet, and they'll probably be the last to go. They've adapted to changing conditions since the Earth cooled. They evolve *continuously*. It's what they do. It's how they're programmed. We humans were very lucky for a very long time. The last major outbreak was over a century ago. In 1918, the Spanish flu killed a hundred million people. Almost as many as the two World Wars combined. At the time, it amounted to five percent of the world's population."

"Okay, I get the whole mutation and Darwin shit. After all, I'm living it! But tell me, Sarah, how the hell can a virus turn an otherwise normal human being into a raving, bloodthirsty maniac?"

"Actually, that's the only question I can answer with any kind of confidence. With all of the patients we treated at Trident, the one thing we were able to learn was that the virus systematically destroys all higher brain functions. It starts with the visual cortex, here in the occipital lobe," she pointed to the back of her head, "then it spreads to the rest of the cerebrum. When all higher brain functions are gone, so is the human. No thought, no cognition, no pleasure, no pain. All that's left is the alpha, and all it knows is to feed."

Hansen abandoned the *JAMA* report entirely, throwing it on the floor. "And just what kind of *magical* virus can resurrect a dead body, huh? Answer me *that*, if you can..."

She shrugged again. "Well, now we're back to conjecture, but think about that first case, Patient A. That young boy had a tumor deep in his cerebellum. The tech was programmed to eliminate cancer cells and repair damage to that specific area. Now, the cerebellum is the part of the brain that regulates movement, so it must be that when the body dies, the tech keeps working, keeps repairing, keeps rebuilding. But not the whole brain, because technology can't evolve like organics. The tech was programmed to rebuild non-functioning neurons and axons in the lower brain, specifically the cerebellum and the brain stem. It wouldn't have the programming to repair anything in the cortex or neocortex."

"It fixes just enough to make the dead move."

"Exactly right."

"To infect others?"

"To *reproduce*. The tech and the virus are one, so the tech rebuilds..."

"...So the virus can go walkabout," Mason finished the thought for her.

Sarah nodded grimly and went on. "The initial outbreak was airborne, and it infected a *huge* majority of the population. The last we heard from the CDC was that perhaps as much as ninety percent of the population had been affected. But then, the virus changed again. It became vector-borne in a single generation. That's amazing enough, but that new adaptation gave it an *unprecedented* delivery system. Some viruses infect through a cough or a sneeze, like influenza. Some remain virulent on a handrail or a doorknob for several days. Norovirus, for instance. Some require direct contact and will lie in wait long after the death of the host until a loved one touches a cheek or holds a hand. Ebola is the perfect example. In the case of this... this *technovirus*, it doesn't have to lie in wait or hope for surreptitious wind currents. It can actually *propel* an echo toward a potential new host."

"Like marionettes," Mason concluded. "Puppets. With the virus as the puppet master."

"I can only assume that it's present in every drop of bodily fluid. Saliva, blood, sweat... Human skin is actually a good barrier against viruses, but if the skin is broken and even a single virion is able to enter the blood stream..."

Mason looked at his hands, then to the faces of the others, all splattered with blood. But before he could find the words for his fear, Sarah put his mind at ease.

"I know, Mace, I know. I worried about that too, but if it could pass through mucous membranes, we'd have caught it by now. It must require direct access to the circulatory system."

He breathed a heavy sigh of relief.

"But your girl, Mackenzie," Hansen interjected. "She was sick, and she fought it off."

"Yes, Mack was infected by the airborne strain, and her immune system was able to put up the right defenses. Who knows? Perhaps *millions* would have recovered under normal circumstances, but blindness in a world of predators isn't exactly an asset. We'll never know how many might have survived that initial outbreak, but I can tell you that no human immune system on Earth would be able to fend off the technovirus in its vector-borne form. Those little bastards start replicating immediately, and they have their own personal

747 in the form of sixty thousand miles of arteries and veins in the human body."

"Well shit..." Hansen snarled, looking decidedly sick to his stomach as he kicked the *JAMA* report back to Sarah. "Fat lot of good *that* does. But tell you what... if I ever come across a good-looking Asian lady in a white coat, I believe I'll gladly wring that cunt's neck."

CHAPTER

XXII

Mason checked his watch.

"Almost time," he said, slipping the knapsack off his back and dumping its contents on the floor.

To anyone else, it might have looked like a load of laundry, but it was hardly that. This was every jacket, shirt, and towel the college kids had been able to find in the Alamo to fashion themselves a few makeshift beds. Now, every bit of it was tied together end-to-end, just like a number of bed sheets in a certain hospital an eternity ago.

Hansen tiptoed back to the window overlooking building six, and while he was gone, Mason hushed quietly to Sarah.

"Sarah, this *technovirus...* once it's in you, it's *in* you, right?"

"Mace," she told him, stroking his cheek lovingly, "even if it was on that plane, you're okay."

Reluctantly, he took the hand from his cheek, but he didn't let it go. "I wasn't talking about me," he hushed, leaning so close to her that their lips nearly touched. "I was talking about Mack."

All at once, Sarah's back straightened. "What are you saying, Mace?"

She wasn't angry. She couldn't be. Not with him. But he'd clearly plucked a nerve. A nerve that she'd probably already worried into a frayed mess.

"I might have been immune, but Mack was infected. She had that *thing* in her, this... this *technovirus*. It was in her brain. Rebuilding. Rewiring. So all I'm asking is, is the thing still in there?"

Sarah pulled her hand away, and for the first time ever, she looked at him with something akin to anger. "We're not having this conversation," she said, but as she made to rise, Mason pulled her back down.

If it were anyone else, Becks included, there would have been indignation. Harsh words. Maybe even a slap across the face. But this was Sarah, and this was Mason. Sarah gave a single huff, then she took his face in both of her hands and kissed him warmly on the lips.

"Mace, you're the sweetest man in the world. I know how much Mack means to you, and believe me, you mean every bit as much to her," she kissed him again and hushed in his ear, "and to me."

"But..."

"Mace," she quieted him with a look, "she's okay. It's good news. Drop it."

Mason struggled for the right words, *any* words, and finding none, he finally gave up and simply drank in the warmth of this wonderful woman he'd known for a few weeks and for a lifetime.

The implications were clear. Were those little machines still inside Mack? Yes, undoubtedly. Was there any way to get them out? No, not a chance. Were they still at work, rebuilding, rewiring, reconnecting? Maybe, maybe not, there was no way to know. But if they were, was there the slightest possibility that those new connections might result in an alteration of mood or behaviour? It was anyone's guess, but there had to be a chance.

Or maybe it was just as Mason had imagined it. Maybe Mack was just wise beyond her years and adapting like mad to survive in this living Hell. And even if the technovirus was still at work and helping her along with a swift kick to the brain stem... so what? Who cared about the means as long as the end result was a Mack who still drew breath?

And that's where he left it, even if it was only in his own mind. Mack was alive. Period. Done.

"I have more good news." Sarah cocked a grin as she reached into her pocket. "Look what I found. It's not an iPod, but it still works."

It was a wristwatch. A man's. She must have taken it from one of the corpses while Mason was occupied elsewhere. It looked like one he used to wear himself. One with an alarm. Not exactly uncommon in the days before everyone carried a smartphone. She cut several feet of cord from the window blinds and tied the watch to one end, and now it was perfect.

Mason watched Hansen throw a few more hand signals across the way, then he held up the chair cushion and got his reply. He unfurled the message, read it, checked his watch, then he tossed a few more signals – a thumbs-up and a final kiss – through the window, and tiptoed like an ungainly rhinoceros back to the others.

"Five minutes," he said. "Get ready. I'll give you a ten second countdown."

They moved to the window overlooking the Peterbilt, and

while Mason secured one end of the makeshift rope to a conveniently situated bookshelf, Hansen and Sarah saw to the window itself. It was thick, double-paned, and unlike the windows on the west side of the building, it didn't open, so they had no other choice but to break it. But rather than throwing a chair through the thing and ringing the dinner bell, they took a decidedly more surgical approach.

Starting at the top corners, they each placed a soft-covered book against the window and used the butts of their pistols like hammers, thumping the glass in incrementally harder blows until it cracked and gave way. Then they moved across the top and down the sides, chipping a few inches of window away as they went. The crowd below stirred, and some of the alphas directly against the building became enraged by the bits of glass raining down from above, but before long, Hansen caught the bulk of the window in his arms and the way was clear.

As Mason cleared the last shards from the frame, Sarah scurried two windows away and repeated the process to open a hole at the bottom corner. Hansen raised a pair of fingers and she set the watch accordingly, then she tossed it through the hole and threaded the line carefully through her fingers until it hung just above the heads of the tallest creatures below.

Now, it was Mason's turn. He gave the makeshift rope a few sharp tugs, tossed the end of it out the window, and climbed up onto the ledge. Hansen raised a single finger, Mason acknowledged it with a nod, and as that last minute ticked away, he tucked his fifty pounds of rebar through a belt loop and studied the swarm, mapping the best possible route through the ungodly mess.

Here, an older alpha next to a hobbled female. There, a

child. Beyond it, a big male dangling its guts like an apron. Closer to the truck, a pair of females, ravaged by the swarm. Hansen began a whispered countdown from ten, and all other thoughts left Mason's mind. All he knew was the rope in his hand and the swarm swirling below. When Hansen reached six, he turned his back to the swarm and took the first few steps down the side of the building.

He finished the countdown in his own head and took a single step down for every tick of the clock. When he reached the count of three, he could feel claws batting at the back of his shirt billowing down as if it were a piñata. He held fast, took a deep breath, and ticked off the last two seconds with a familiar aching in his gut.

Two... one... *Now!*

An almighty explosion shook the Quad, then the tell-tale *rat-a-tat-a-tat* of a machine gun echoed between the buildings, punctuated with single shots from high-powered rifles.

This was Plan C, conceived as a last-ditch play and spotty as all hell. But truth be told, Plan B wasn't much better. The original idea was that they'd get to Gloria from here the same way they'd gotten here from building six – namely, a slow-motion crawl through the swarm. It was iffy enough on the face of it, but after Plan A went up in flames, it took Plan B right along with it.

It was Sarah who'd insisted they have a Plan C, just in case.

For all intents and purposes, that ridiculous crossing between the loading bays should have been do or die. If Plan A failed, they should all have been torn to bits, and there would have been no point in even imagining how they'd get from building five to the truck. But Sarah was too cautious and too smart to leave it at that. And so, Plan C. It was their Hail Mary play, and this time, it really *was* do or die. If Mason fucked up now, the Peterbilt would remain parked in that spot forever, and Skyline would soon sport thirteen new corpses.

He tried to see what was directly below, but dangling at the end of a bat-rope from the side of a building didn't allow for a great view. Still, he tossed his head from side to side to get an idea of the immediate area, and when he saw a general surge toward the explosions coming from the Quad, he let go of the rope and dropped into the unknown.

Immediately, he was beset on all sides. He had his rebar out in a flash and clubbed two alphas into mush with a single swing, but he couldn't move. Whatever spurious route he'd mapped out in his head had dissolved away with the detonation of the Pepsi bomb and subsequent hail of gunfire, and all he could see now was a solid wall of teeth and claws closing in from all sides.

But then came Sarah's next miracle. A metallic *ding-ding-ding* began to chime from the wristwatch at the end of the string, and just enough alphas were drawn to it that a hole opened up in front. Without a moment's hesitation, Mason widened the hole with a few prodigious swings of the rebar, then he picked out the path of least resistance through the swarm and did what he did best.

Every swing of the rebar was like a buzz saw through jelly. With no time for subtlety, Mason targeted every skull in his path, turning one after another into hamburger. Blood spewed, bone fragments flew, and on more than a few occasions, a lucky strike detached the skull entirely and sent it sailing away, pinwheeling a trail of gore over the swarm.

He stepped on fallen bodies to gain a few extra inches in height, he directed his blows so that each fresh corpse fell into the paths of others, all the while he thought of only one thing...

STAGE 3: BRAVO

Get to the damn *truck!*

He heard Hansen's voice in his head, *It's only twenty feet out and ten feet down!* but two minutes had already passed and Gloria was still half that distance away. So he fought on for all he was worth. Then the watch stopped chiming, and he fought even harder.

He heard glass shattering from above and Sarah shouting from the far end of the second floor, and as a portion of the swarm took off after her voice, something massive crashed to the ground only a few feet away from Mason. It was one of the library's bookshelves. It must have weighed eighty pounds, but Hansen had somehow man-handled the thing through the window and flung it right where it needed to be. One alpha was knocked unconscious and two more wound up pinned beneath it, and as the crush of bodies was temporarily stymied by this new barrier, Mason took advantage of those precious extra few seconds.

There was no time to distinguish between the creatures, and no time to plot a course. He merely bashed away at any body part that presented itself and did his best to catch another on the backswing. The entire seven-foot length of rebar ran slick with blood and gore, making his hands slip several times, but he never let go. He simply tightened his grip and had at the next. And the next. And the next.

At last, Gloria loomed up, big and beautiful, a few feet away. He threw himself into two big alphas between him and it, nestled his back against those ten gorgeous tons of Detroit metal, and swung madly away.

With the gunfire from the Quad, Sarah hurling down abuse, Hansen hurling down things of a more substantial nature, and Mason fighting like a man possessed, a gap finally opened up and he was able to sidestep to just below the passenger door.

But now, there was another problem. As soon as he turned his back on the swarm, they'd be on him. He redoubled his efforts and managed to beat back the swarm enough to allow a full half-second to grab the handle, but even as the door swung open, his felt claws at his back and another grabbing hold of his shirtsleeve. He gave a backwards donkey kick and heard a satisfying *crack!* as the hand fell away from his sleeve, then in a moment of pure desperation, he spun around, drew his pistol, and fired pointblank into the swarm until the clip ran dry.

At last, he hurled himself through the open door even as a dozen claws raked at his ankles and feet.

He fell to the floor of the truck and kicked at one claw after another to hold the creatures at bay. But with every one he kicked away, more were there to take its place.

One particularly massive alpha began to haul itself up onto the step, so Mason leapt onto the passenger seat and thrust his rebar straight through the creature's throat. As the body pulled free and dropped onto the swarm, he made a grab for the door handle, but the swarm surged again and there were suddenly a dozen hands and arms in the way. He reloaded his pistol and emptied it, reloaded and emptied it again, and when his last clip ran dry, he took to swatting viciously at the claws with the butt of the gun, just to buy himself that second he needed to make a grab for the handle.

He was holding his own, but it was a deadly game of whack-a-mole that was bound to end badly. He couldn't get the door closed with hands and arms in the way, and no amount of injury made those unfeeling claws withdraw. But then, the rules changed again. All of a sudden, there was a sound like hailstones on a tin roof, and alphas began dropping to the ground, one after another after another.

Up above, Sarah and Hansen were doing what they had to do. With salvation so near and yet so far, they had turned to their guns to keep Mason alive. But they were ringing their own death knell in the process. The only thing keeping the swarm from overrunning the library was a thin sheet of glass and strips of dowdy old-lady dress, and all of that gunfire would be whipping the swarm into a frenzy. Every bullet those two fired was one more tick of the clock... and time was quickly running out.

He took a last desperate swing at two alphas who'd somehow escaped the fusillade, then he lunged for the door, and with claws grabbing at his very sleeve, he threw all of his weight into it, swinging it shut.

But no! It hadn't closed all the way! At the last second, a single alpha had reached through, and now a dainty little arm was trapped between door and frame. And with the door unable to close, a multitude of fingers immediately appeared around the edges of the gap and succeeded in widening it enough to let more claws and arms squeeze through. With no room to swing the rebar and his pistol empty, he once again reached for his knife, and once again he cursed himself for losing it.

Bu then, even as the door threatened to be wrenched from his hands, he had an epiphany. He groped blindly beneath the passenger seat, hoping that the thing was still there. And it was! His hand closed around a pair of rubber grips, his thumb popped open a snap, and out from under the seat came another one of Sarah's Hail Marys.

It was a Desert Eagle .50 calibre pistol, courtesy of Magnum Research Inc, and a would-be survivalist who'd locked himself safely away in his 4x4 with tons of supplies and an infected child. Mason had found the pistol early on, but he'd only used it once. The recoil was so intense that his arm had ached for days afterward. He was all for getting rid of the thing, but Sarah wouldn't allow it. So under the seat it went, waiting for the unlikely day when that unwieldy monster might just save their collective asses.

He pressed the muzzle directly against the dainty forearm and pulled the trigger. The report was like an explosion inside Gloria's cab, but it was worth the ringing in his ears to see the offending limb quite literally blown in half. As a dead claw flopped to the floor and the ragged stub of forearm slithered away, he pressed the gun against the next arm and fired. And again. And again. And again. And as the last claw crumpled to the floor like a dead tarantula, he once again threw all of his weight into pulling the door closed, and at last there was a muted *click!* as the latch snapped into place.

He was safe for the moment, but there wasn't even time to catch his breath. He could still hear muted gunfire through the gongs ringing in his ears, but he realized with a fresh wave of dread that none of the swarm around the truck were being hit. That could only mean one thing.

He looked up through the windshield and saw Sarah and Hansen with their backs against the window. They were still shooting, but they had changed the direction of their fire. Now, they were shooting *into* the room.

Shit!

He jumped across to the driver's seat and toggled the key. There was a single hesitation as Gloria coughed out two days' worth of neglect, but the engine finally caught and Mason jammed it into gear. He swung the wheel wide and watched a dozen creatures careen off both sides of the cowcatcher, then he slammed it into reverse and ran a dozen more into the ground. With one last spin of the wheel and a heavy foot on the accelerator, he manoeuvred the big truck directly below the broken window, then he rolled down the window and shouted at the top of his lungs, "Sarah! *Jump!*"

Sarah motioned for Hansen to go first, but she quickly lost the argument. Hansen gave her one good, hard shove, and she flew through the window, landing on Gloria's roof with a *thud!* Mason dug a spare .50 caliber clip from under the seat to the accompaniment of a mad scrambling from above, then Sarah called out, "C'mon, Gary! Jump!" and he looked up to see Hansen's big back framed in the window. The man took four more shots, and with his gun now empty and the swarm inches away, he leaped through the window and hit the roof hard. A pair of legs briefly appeared over the windshield as he lost his footing, but they quickly scrambled up and out of view, and Sarah pounded on the roof.

"Go, Mace!"

Any other time, he would have floored the accelerator, but he couldn't with two passengers perched so precariously above. So instead, he feathered the pedal to pick up speed slowly, and this simple bit of caution very nearly spelled their undoing.

The first alpha thudded down to the long, wide hood of the Peterbilt like a sack of potatoes. And then came another. And another. Realizing at last what was happening, he hollered, "Hang on!" and pegged the gas pedal to the floor.

In the mirror, a steady stream of alphas continued plummeting to the ground as they blindly followed the sounds of their prey, but they were no longer a concern. Three alphas were stubbornly clinging to Gloria's hood, and even now, one of them was scrambling up the windshield to the roof. Mason screeched the truck to a stop and climbed halfway through the window, Desert Eagle at the ready, but there was no need to fire.

Up top, Hansen was on his back with the wind knocked out of him, but Sarah was still on her feet, having ridden the truck like a champion surfer. And with her gun blazing three perfectly-aimed shots in the span of a second, one creature went tumbling over the side, another somersaulted backward over the cowcatcher, and the third slid lifelessly down the windshield, trailing a hideous streak of gore.

Mason tucked the pistol in his waistband and threw a grin up to Sarah.

"Are you enjoying the view from up there, or would Madame rather come in?" he quipped, earning him a beleaguered groan from Hansen and a big smile from Sarah.

It was no easy feat getting Hansen through the window. In Mason's mind, helping the man in feet-first as the rest of him flopped around on the roof was rather like watching a whale giving birth in reverse. Finally though, the man crumpled to the seat and dropped to the floor, and Sarah followed him in as gracefully as a swan.

"Hi, sailor. Going my way?" She beamed a grin at Mason, but there was no mirth in it. She took her place in the passenger seat and patted Gloria's big, flat dashboard. "Long time no see, sweetheart. I've missed you terribly."

And with that, they were off.

Mason spun the wheel, tossing the dead alpha off to the side and crushing several more to pulp, then he carved a wide, circular path through the swarm to come around at the Quad with as much speed as possible. Bodies flew left and right or were crushed beneath the Peterbilt's wheels, but Mason only increased speed. He ploughed through the swarm like a sickle through wheat, then he rounded the corner into the Quad, and his heart skipped a beat.

Christ! There are hundreds. No, *thousands!*

The entire Quad was a rolling sea of alphas. As many as fifty might have been blown to bits by Addison's Pepsi-bomb, but the void was quickly being filled in, the gore of all of those deaths trampled into an unrecognizable goo under a hundred feet. Atop building six, Christopher, Addison, and Alejandra were raining down Hellfire, but at the first sight of Gloria, the three of them ceased fire and scampered back across the roof, and everyone's salvation suddenly rested in Mason's hands alone.

With Hansen on his knees between the seats and Sarah trying to hang on for dear life even as she rummaged through the supplies in the sleeper cab, Mason dropped his foot to the floor and charged headlong into the swarm. The cowcatcher did a good job of keeping bodies from piling up under the wheels, but it wasn't long before Gloria started skidding from side to side like a drunkard on ice. So Mason feathered the gas when need be, opened the throttle wide when he could, and above all else, he didn't allow the truck to lose one iota of momentum, lest the crush of bodies close in and pin it in place.

He did everything he could to keep the truck moving as the roar of that big, throaty diesel engine whipped the swarm into an absolute frenzy. He swerved, he spun, he circled around and doubled back, but no matter how many bodies came apart on the cowcatcher or were crushed under Gloria's wheels, the creatures never stopped coming. They roared, they clawed, they howled, and they charged at the truck from every direction at once, so around and around he drove, not once taking his foot from the accelerator.

Sarah came out of the sleeper cab and threw a handful of fresh clips to Hansen, and as she climbed over him into her seat, Mason couldn't help but notice that she'd collected something else from their stores besides ammunition. The homemade holster strapped to her thigh was relatively new, but the thing inside of it was an old friend. She'd found that sawed-off shotgun on the very first day, and it had saved her bacon more than once. She dumped a box of shells into her lap, stuffed her pockets full, and threw Mason a nod.

The crazy circling of the truck had the swarm charging every which way in utter confusion, but enough of a space finally opened up that with one last spin of the wheel, Mason was able to bulldoze his way between buildings five and six and shudder to a stop directly beneath the open window.

He keyed off the ignition to silence the roar, crawled back through his driver's window, and all but leaped onto Gloria's roof.

The bottom ledge of the window was chest-high – easy enough for an active man to haul himself up. But Mason was no ordinary man, and he was presently fueled by fear, rage, and one hundred-proof adrenalin. He planted one hand on the sill and vaulted cleanly through while Sarah and Hansen clambered up to the roof after him.

Plan C had clearly taken a heavy toll. With the detonation of the Pepsi bomb and the subsequent hail of gunfire, the swarm had torn through the doors of building six and flooded the lower floors. All that held them back now was a jumble of tables and chairs and couches blocking the main stairwell, but it wouldn't hold them back for long. Even now, one end of the barricade was failing, and it was only the concentrated effort of nine desperate souls pushing back against it that kept the swarm from pouring through.

Only Mack and Clancy were hanging back. Wisely, the girl knew she'd be of little help at the barricade, so she was doing the right thing. She had her .22 at the ready for the inevitable moment when the walls fell. She caught Mason's eye as he appeared, but where any other child of ten might have rushed to greet him, she merely nodded, smiled, and sighted down the barrel of her gun.

Sk8rBoy William saw him as well. He shouted, "We can't hold them!" and far from the tough-ass kid he'd pretended to be before, Mason saw him now as what he really had been all along – a teenager scared half to death.

Mason charged at what he perceived as the weakest point in the barricade and threw himself into it beside Becks, using every ounce of muscle to wrangle it back one more inch.

"All you kids, *go!*" he grunted through the strain. "Becks, get these children clear!"

Becks was barely more than an arm's reach away, but she had to holler just to be heard above the roar.

"I can't! Ally, take the kids!"

The Latina spitfire may have been tiny, but she wasn't exaggerating when she grunted back, "*A poco?* I don't think so, *chica*. I think you need me right where I am!"

"Addison!" Mason tried again, but all he got back was, "Uh, yeah... kinda busy here, Mace..."

Sarah was only then clambering through the window, and even though she couldn't have heard the conversation, she jumped right into action.

"Teddy! Diego!" she howled, waving her arms over her head to get their attention. "William! Richie! C'mon! Move!"

None of them budged from the barricade, so she tried again, rather more emphatically this time.

"Teddy! Diego! Get your asses over here, *now!*"

In Mason's mind, an ordinary mother would have called to her own daughter first. Hell, an ordinary mother would have grabbed her daughter by the scruff of the neck if need be and hauled her bodily from the place. But Sarah was no ordinary mother, and Mack was no ordinary girl. No, Mack was right where she needed to be, and so was Clancy. If and when the walls fell, that skinny little .22 and that massive hound might once again be the only things standing between the rest of them and death.

Diego and Teddy looked to Mace, and he flicked his head. All at once, they peeled themselves away from the barricade and ran to Sarah, and as she lowered them through the window down to a waiting Hansen, she called out again.

"Richie! William! You're next! On the double!"

Sk8rBoy William steadfastly refused to go, and only a hard shove from Mason got Richie moving, but the kid had barely taken a step before he caught Christopher's eye, and he all but threw himself back into the barricade.

"I'm good!" he shouted, straining every muscle against the swarm. "Christopher! Get your mother out!"

It was an infuriating act of mutiny, but Mason couldn't help but respect the two a little more because of it. In truth, he didn't mind the trade-off of Richie and William for Christopher and Inez. After all, the two big sophomores had double the strength of the other two combined. But the mutiny didn't end there. Christopher balked at the very suggestion of abandoning his friends, and Inez downright refused.

"Don't you be telling me what to do, young man," she huffed at Richie. "And don't you *dare* refer to me in the third person when I'm standing right here!"

Richie managed a strangled, "Sorry, ma'am..." and in any other situation at any other time, Mason might have laughed. But with the situation as dire as it could ever be, he instead took a small wooden chair that was doing nothing to support the barricade, and he all but threw it at Richie and Christopher and Inez, all huddled together in a knot.

"Get the fuck out!" he fairly roared with anger. "All of you! William, you too! We can't hold them! Go! That's an order!"

The four of them exchanged looks that might have said a million words, but they still made no move to go. But then Hansen hoisted himself through the window and charged at the barricade, throwing all of his two hundred pounds of weight into it and snarling at Richie and William.

"You heard the man! Get the fuck out!" he roared, then he nodded to Inez and told her plainly, "Inez, my dear, please see your son safe. And if these other two give you any shit, just pick 'em up by the ears and drag their sorry asses out."

"Like children?" Mason heard Inez quip, but whatever Hansen said in reply was lost in the roar of the swarm.

Inez pointed wordlessly at the window and held that position until all three youngsters reluctantly abandoned the barricade, and while the three of them jockeyed to be the last to go, Inez put a hand on Hansen's arm. Her lips moved in a whisper only the two of them would ever share, and as Hansen released a heavy sigh and Inez turned to follow the other three out, the whole world suddenly collapsed.

CHAPTER

XXIII

Mason saw it coming.

With only him, Hansen, Alejandra, Addison, and Becks left to hold back literally tons of rage, the outcome was inevitable. The five of them were simply no match against the swarm. It wouldn't be long.

The other defenders must have known it, too. Alejandra shared a look with Addison, then she looked past him to Hansen, and their respective silence spoke volumes. Becks might have used those last seconds to say a few parting words to her father, but with him at one end of the barricade and her at the other, there was simply no chance. She looked up at Mason and mouthed a few words, and even if he hadn't been able to read her lips, the look in her eyes told the tale.

I love you...

Mason's heart skipped a beat at those three words he hadn't heard, but before he could even begin to mouth them back, there came a crashing and splintering of wood, and Alejandra's shrill cry of, *"Mierda!"* as the whole left side of the barricade crumbled away.

To Mason, the collapse happened in quick little images of death. He saw Christopher shove Richie through the window and grab Sk8rBoy by the shoulder to toss him through next. Then there was an image of Addison and Alejandra hopping back and turning their guns loose. Then the big body of Gary Hansen filled his entire field of view as the man charged toward his daughter. And at just that moment, the rest of the barricade collapsed directly on top of Mason, and all he knew was the weight of a thousand elephants crushing him to the floor.

It was almost too much. With no room to expand his lungs, he only stayed conscious through sheer force of will. He was on his stomach, with his arms pinned between chest and floor, but it was actually a lucky break. If he'd been on his back, he wouldn't have had the leverage, and if his arms had been anywhere but directly under him, they would've been useless. As it was, the task was nearly impossible, but he somehow turned his wrists enough to plant his palms squarely on the floor, and summoning every ounce of strength he had left, he pistoned his massive arms and crawled to his hands and knees, upending the table that had fallen squarely on top of him and throwing alphas in every direction. With most of the weight gone, he gave one final push to his feet and threw the table backwards, knocking a dozen more alphas to the ground and plugging the hole for the one precious second he needed to get his bearings.

Sarah was at the window. Inez was beside her, looking as if she had just seen the face of the devil himself as she fumbled to get her gun free. Mack and Clancy had dissolved back into the swarm and were doing what they did best – namely, eluding the swarm as easily as shadows and sowing utter confusion while they took them down by the dozens. Christopher and Alejandra and Addison had their guns out and were unleashing holy Hell on the swarm, and Hansen was with Becks, but they were in trouble. Hansen was trying to get her to her feet, but some part of the barricade had fallen on one of her legs, pinning her down. And through it all, alphas charged and raged and clawed at anything that moved.

With his trusty rebar left behind in Gloria and his knife gone, Mason had only one weapon left. He drew the colossal Desert Eagle from his waistband and took aim at a pair of alphas tearing toward Hansen and Becks. Again came the explosions, and two skulls were nearly atomized. Then he targeted three more alphas charging after Mack, but before he could pull the trigger, Sarah dropped all three of them with as many shots. She took down three more, then her pistol ran dry and she turned her shotgun loose, pumping and shooting, pumping and shooting, and blowing great gaping holes in the swarm with every blast.

The explosions from Sarah's shotgun were easily matched by the thunderous *boom!* from Mason's Desert Eagle, and every pull of the trigger from that monstrous handgun was accompanied by the most incredible spray of gore. Such was the awesome power of the weapon that oftentimes, the bullet would pass straight through one alpha and into another, taking them both down. And at least once, a bullet actually passed through *two* alphas and still retained enough kinetic energy to drop a third.

But even if Mason'd had a thousand clips, it would never be enough. The barricade was utterly gone and the swarm was pouring through in a flood. He shot until his last clip ran dry, then he dropped the gun to the floor and grabbed whatever he could find to fight the raging horde.

STAGE 3: BRAVO

One of the tables used for the barricade had splintered into a dozen pieces. One of the splinters looked enough like a 2x4 to catch his eye, so he snatched it up and swung away.

One swing took off the top of a head. The second caught an alpha squarely behind the ear and sent it spiraling through the air. A third pounded a groove into an unruly mat of hair. A fourth shattered a jaw.

Again and again he swung – pounding, bashing, clubbing at every alpha within reach, and still, it wasn't enough. Even with a constant hail of bullets, and Mack and Clancy creating their own brand of mayhem, it wasn't enough. At last, Sarah ran out of shells to feed the shotgun, and a sudden surge in the swarm had Alejandra and Addison backpedaling toward the window, firing as they went, and Mason knew the end was near.

Alejandra made a desperate grab for Hansen as she retreated, but he shrugged her off and redoubled his efforts to dislodge his daughter's leg from the debris.

"Hansen!" Alejandra howled at him. "Hansen!"

But the look on his face said it all. He would never leave his little girl. Not for anything.

Alejandra dropped a spent magazine to the floor and slapped in her last fifty rounds, and with a single jut of her chin Addison's way, they both stepped up on either side of Hansen and laid into the swarm with unbridled fury.

Every shot that she and Addison made hit home, but the mad jumble of bodies did little to stem the tide. The swarm poured in relentlessly, and the time finally came when Mason could feel claws on all sides. He turned and swung and turned and swung, then knowing that he was losing the fight, he took one last fury of swings and made for Becks.

Hansen was digging at the tangle of debris for all he was

worth, and he was making some headway, but he would never be able to get her out in time. In seconds, Becks would be dead. One second after that, Hansen and Alejandra and Addison would follow. And one second after that, the rest of them would die.

So it was all or nothing. Do or die. Literally. Everyone he knew in the world was about to be torn to pieces, and he had precisely one chance in all of Hell of affecting the outcome.

He caught Christopher's eye and flashed him a signal, and as Christopher and Inez concentrated their fire on the swarm surging up the stairs, he swung away at the rest in an absolute rage. He caved in the side of a skull and bashed in a face on the backswing, then he brought the 2x4 down on another alpha's head and caught another in the jaw on the way up. But as those creatures fell, others appeared.

Then others.

And then, more still.

He threw himself into a pair of alphas, bowling them over, and leapt to his feet to bash two more to their knees. A kick to an ankle. An elbow to a throat. A punch to a breastbone. An elbow to a jaw looming over his shoulder. A downswing to a forehead. An upswing to a jaw. A thumb gouged in an eye.

Now, he was a street-brawler, fighting for far more than just his life. He pounded and kicked and punched, over and over and over, just to buy Hansen those few seconds he needed to get Becks free. And as if the universe had taken note and chosen to reward him for his efforts, Becks' foot suddenly popped out from whatever had been holding it, and she and her father turned their fury on the swarm.

They could have run. They could have turned their backs and hightailed it to the window and made their escape. But they didn't.

Hansen drew his pistol, Becks retrieved her javelin from the floor, and together, father and daughter fought for all they were worth. And in a singular moment of absolute clarity, Mason realized why.

They were fighting for *him*. They were putting their lives on the line for *him*. The woman who had ceased to love him was standing shoulder-to-shoulder with a man who outright hated him, and they were risking everything they had... for *him*.

Mason didn't need the added motivation. With death pouring in on a thousand feet, he swung away like a madman. One more down. And another. And two more. And as the pile of bodies grew around him, the swarm was forced to stumble blindly over them, giving him just enough of an edge to be able to pound the life out of a dozen more.

But he was only human, and the swarm had no such limitations. The entire Quad was funneling though a pair of shattered doors and up those very stairs, and no force on Earth would be able to stop them.

With Sarah keeping the path clear with her kukri, most of the college kids had made it through the window. Only William remained, but just as he was about to follow the others through, Inez's .22 rifle ran dry, Addison dropped his empty weapon and went for his SBD, and the last of the college kids bravely swung his crossbow off his back and joined the battle.

He had half a quiver left, perhaps fifteen bolts, and he made every one of them count. He cocked, loaded, and fired in a blur, taking down one after another after another with an expertly-aimed shot straight through the heart.

"Mack!" Sarah called to Mackenzie over the roar, and whether it was the tone of her voice or the realization that the war was already lost, the girl complied.

She tripped up one last alpha and took down two more with a pair of handclaps, then she signaled to Clancy, and the two of them charged for the open window. Clancy bounded effortlessly through, and Mack followed him out like a tiny gymnast, then Sarah grabbed Inez by the arm, screaming at the top of her lungs to be heard over the bedlam.

"Your turn, Inez! Go!"

But the woman would have none of it. Not if it meant leaving her son behind.

"Christopher!" she howled. "Christopher!"

Dutifully, her son ran to her, and it was in that split second of arguing over which of them would hang back long enough to see the other safe that the end came. If Alejandra could have magically produced one last fifty-round magazine, it might have bought them a few more seconds. But it was not to be.

"*Mierda!*" she cursed, dropping her Tommy gun and drawing her machete. And just like that, their time was up.

The defenders collapsed back toward the window as a unit, but this was no orderly withdrawal. It was all they could do to hack and slash and stab and kick enough to keep from being overrun.

"We can't!" Hansen growled between pistol shots, and there was no need to say more. Mason had already done the math.

It was simple. One person through the window at a time, with the rest fending off the swarm. At some point, it wouldn't be enough. Mason put the number at three. Two could never hold them back. Three might. So once they were down to three, that was it. No more would be getting out after that. Once they were down to three, it was game over, man, game over. And so, he coldly and emotionlessly decided which two people would die alongside him.

Again, the math was simple. At any other time, he would want Sarah at his side. But not now. Not with Mack in the equation. No, it had to be Hansen and Alejandra. Addison was good, but Ally was better.

"Becks! Go!" he shouted over the roar. "Sarah! William! Addison! Get the fuck out!"

But the point was moot, ultimately.

Mason caught the briefest glimpse of Inez pushing her son through the window to safety, but before she had the chance to climb through after him, a horrifying shriek filled the air, and Sk8rBoy William staggered backward, one hand clutching the side of his neck as a torrent of blood streamed down the front of his shirt.

Mason hadn't seen it, but one misstep was all it had taken. One single misstep. And whether it had been claws or teeth, the kid was now dead on his feet. He'd either bleed out, or the virus would take him. There was nothing anyone could do. That brave, frightened, stupid college kid was a dead man walking.

Despite the obvious, Inez howled, "William!" and rushed to his aid.

She should have known better. Hell, she *did* know better. But where she should have been making her own escape, that *damned* motherly instinct of hers sealed her fate every bit as tightly as the boy's.

Sarah made a grab for her, but then two alphas came at her in a rush, and it was all she could do to fend them off. Addison did his best to come between her and the swarm, but with the loss of William's crossbow, the right flank suddenly fell – and with it, their last hope. The swarm poured through the breach in a wave, and descended on William and Inez like a pack of rabid dogs.

Addison and Alejandra made a desperate attempt to save them both, but their daring wound up doing more inevitable harm than any theoretical good. With their momentary mutual lapse in judgment, the line collapsed entirely.

It wasn't their fault. Mason knew that. And anyway, how long could they have held on. Ten more seconds? Five? Two? They were never going to win this fight no matter what they did. Hell, maybe it was even better this way. Get it over with. No more fighting. No more running. Just a quick and painful exit from this shit-hole of a world.

"Mace! Mace!"

It was Sarah, calling to him from somewhere behind. Her voice was shrill, frantic. He'd never heard her like that before, but then again, he'd never died with her before.

He wanted to call back to her, to tell her to save herself, and that it was alright that he was about to die, and to tell her a thousand more things. But he was fighting so hard just to delay the inevitable that he couldn't spare even that much energy. And so he'd die without telling her all of those things. And he'd die without telling Mack the thousands of things he wanted to say to her. And he'd die without telling Becks the thousands of things he should have been telling her all along. So he boiled down all of those thousands upon thousands of things into the most important words he would never get to say, and he spoke those words inside of his head.

I love you all...

At last, Alejandra and Addison beat back the swarm enough to reach Inez, but by then her shrieks had stopped, and it was no wonder. What those things had done to her and William in that handful of seconds was simply awesome in its brutality. Flesh torn. Eyes gone. Abdomens ripped open. Guts spilled out.

"Mace! Mace!"

It was Sarah again, shouting at the tops of her lungs. As he turned and fought and turned and fought, he finally managed to catch the barest glimpse of her through the crush of bodies. She was trying to fight her way through to him, but a kukri could only do so much, even in Sarah's hands.

He took a swing at a pair of skulls to buy himself another second, and at last he was able to gulp enough air to holler back to her, "Go!"

But still she fought, slashing and stabbing and hacking her way into the swarm, so Mason summoned enough energy for one more word, knowing that that single word would speak volumes.

"Mack..."

Sarah fought on for a few more futile seconds, but the point was finally reached when the implications of that single word came face to face with an impenetrable wall of teeth and claws, and Mason saw her turn to fight her way back to the window. He stole just enough quick little peeks through the fighting to know that she'd made it, but Sarah being Sarah, even as she climbed through the open window, she managed to save his ass one last time.

"Mace!" she howled, half in and half out of the window and whacking furiously at scores of claws just to be able to deliver the message, "Mace!" she cried. "The roof!"

Fuck! The roof! *Idiot!*

Fortunately, he didn't have to translate for the others. Addison pushed Alejandra ahead and followed at her heels, and Hansen took two more quick shots at a pair of skulls before joining them at a run.

"Far end!" Addison shouted between pants. "Left! Ladder!"

It was enough. The layout wasn't dissimilar to the Alamo, so Mason led them unerringly to a small storage room at the back of the building and to a ladder running up one wall. There was no door to buy them time, so without preamble or apologies, he threw Alejandra onto the ladder and gave her a prodigious shove with a hand on her backside, and she started up, though not without the muttered curse, *"Hijo de puta..."*

Next up was Addison, and he needed no encouragement. He scrambled up after Alejandra like an overgrown monkey, and caught up to her before she'd even reached the hatch. And now that it was only him and Hansen left, Mason sized up the situation in an instant. Hansen was sucking wind. He was exhausted. The only thing keeping him upright was the mile-long stick he carried up his ass. At twenty-plus years his senior, the old man should be the next to go. But above all else, the man was a cop. True blue, right down to the core. They could argue and threaten and bully one another 'til the cows came home, and the end result would be the same.

Mason launched himself up the ladder.

And none too soon. Barely had he reached the halfway point when the swarm came bursting into the storage room with a roar and proceeded to tear the place apart. In a fit of panic, Mason stopped and had a look down, afraid that the old man had been one step too slow and that he would have the ignominious honor of watching Becks' father being ripped to shreds, but he was pleasantly relieved to see Hansen's big, ugly mug hovering just behind his knees.

"Take a fucking picture," Hansen snarled up at him. "It'll last longer."

STAGE 3: BRAVO

He double-timed his ascent and rolled out onto the flat roof beside Addison and Alejandra, all of them wheezing and panting as if they'd run a marathon. Alejandra took one look at Mason and suddenly jumped to her feet, rushing back to the open hatch.

As Hansen's head appeared, she sighed, "*Qué cabrón...* Glad you could make it, *tamarindo,*" and helped him the rest of the way out.

Then she was flat on her back again with Hansen laid out beside her, both of them panting as if there wasn't enough air left in the entire world.

"I thought you were dead meat, *tamarindo...*" she managed between breaths.

"Not yet, *peleonera...*" Hansen panted back. "*Moriré cuando esté listo.* I'll die when I'm good and fucking ready..."

CHAPTER

XXIV

Even above the roar of the swarm and the building being torn apart just a few feet below, the sound of Gloria's big Cummins diesel engine cranking to life was unmistakable.

Mason picked himself up and half-ran, half-staggered to the edge of the roof overlooking the east side of the building. Sarah had waited there behind the wheel just long enough to know for certain that no one else would be coming through the window, and now she was driving away.

But she didn't go far. A dozen or more alphas had blundered through, falling onto the truck, so she carved a path through the swarm with a few quick loops around the Quad to shake the hitchhikers loose, then she pulled to a stop just far enough away that she could look up through the windshield to the roof of building six.

The setting sun glinting off the glass made it hard for Mason to see, but he thought he could make out seven distinct heads pressed up against the windshield. Seven heads. All present and accounted for. Well, mostly...

It could have been worse. That's what he told himself as he collapsed back to his knees and held up a hand to tell those below that they were okay, that all four of them had made it to the roof. Sarah waved back, and he could just make out a long mane of ebony hair cascading suddenly downward beside her. It was Becks. She was crying. She had her face in her hands, and she was crying. Then, that beautiful head was pulled closer to Sarah, and an arm went around her shoulder. And as the sun continued down behind his back and the glare on the glass gave way to shadow, there was one single moment when he could see everyone clearly. Sarah. Mack. Becks. Richie. Teddy. Diego. And there in the center, being comforted from both sides, was Christopher. Seven heads. Seven people. Seven friends he thought he'd never see again.

Then the sun dipped below the crest of the building, and they were gone, just like that.

But the truck remained. The engine was keyed off, but there it sat... so near and yet so incredibly out of reach.

Addison appeared beside him, breathing hard and thumbing his glasses to the bridge of his nose. "Did they all make it? I mean... well, you know what I mean."

"Yes," Mason told him plainly.

"Thank God." Addison breathed a sigh of relief. "But *Jesus!* Poor Inez. And that William kid. I didn't really like the guy, but *Jesus!*"

And with that, Mason came up against a familiar old foe. Before this whole shit-storm started, he rarely gave a damn about any*one* or any*thing*. To paraphrase Caligula, if all of humanity had but one neck, he'd have gladly hacked it through. But then came Mack. And then came Sarah. And even while humanity's neck was being hacked through by the cruel sword of fate, he'd learned a new way to look at those few who were left.

Poor Inez? No. Inez was dead. Her troubles were over. She'd been a kind and gentle woman, but she got stupid, and she was dead. Poor *Christopher* was more apropos, but even that rang somehow untrue. Christopher would mourn his dead mother, so pity be to him. But Christopher was still alive, which was more than could be said for most. So, upon whom should one heap one's pity in this fucked-up bizarro-world hellscape? The living? The dead? Those creatures caught so horribly between the two? *Christ*, maybe the whole idea of pity should be laid on the ash-pit of history along with the rest of mankind's extinct, self-indulgent bullshit.

He struggled for something to say that wouldn't make him out to be a monster, and finding nothing, he merely shrugged.

"Is Rebecca alright?"

It was Hansen, coming up from behind. Even if he hadn't spoken, his big, flat feet were unmistakable. But this wasn't his usual stride. It was slower. One heel scraping up gravel from the roof. And other footsteps, too. Alejandra's, almost in lock-step, but slightly off. So, apparently Hansen wasn't Superman after all.

When they reached the edge of the roof, Ally lowered Hansen to his knees and asked him gently, *"Esta bien, tamarindo?"*

"Estoy bien," Hansen replied without a hint of his usual snark. *"Gracias, peleonera."*

"De nada," the girl said, almost sweetly.

Mason eyed the man from top to bottom. "Are you hurt?"

"Don't you worry about me," Hansen gruffed back. "If I slow any of you down, you have my permission to leave me behind."

"Do we have to wait until you *actually* slow us down?" Addison half-joked, earning him a huff from Alejandra.

And there they sat, four castaways looking down upon a ship they could never reach, bobbing in a storm-tossed sea.

"Now, that's what I call a rough day," Addison sighed.

"We've had better, but it could've been worse."

"A *lot* worse," Alejandra agreed. "I have to say, there were times there where I thought we were all goners."

"You're not alone," Mason admitted back, however reluctantly.

"Honestly, the only time I thought we were done for was that business at the loading dock," Addison chimed in. "After that, I knew we were invincible."

"Most of us," Hansen reminded him, grimly.

"Yeah." Addison hung his head. "Most of us."

"That was some bad shit, alright," Alejandra sighed.

No one said a word about Beverly or about the sweet little girl who'd put a bullet through her brain, and the subject was quickly dropped.

"Did Sarah find her book at least?" This from Addison.

"She did," Mason said, and with Hansen snorting and grumbling in the background and tossing in the odd, "Mad scientists," and, "Playing God," to punctuate his general disgust, he did his best to give them an accurate though exceedingly abbreviated account of the parts of Sarah's tutorial he'd understood. They listened with equal parts rapt attention and disbelief, then they each summed up their feelings in their own way.

"That's fucked up," Alejandra sneered.

"But it's pretty cool, right" Addison said, a little too excitedly. "They sound like Borg nanoprobes!"

Ally turned her sneer on him and he beat a hasty retreat. "But yeah, it's *totally* fucked up."

By now, the sun was almost gone and the truck was lost in shadows, and still they sat. Then twilight turned to dusk and ultimately to utter darkness, and they sat there still, each of them picturing in their minds both their deepest hopes and their darkest fears.

"How do we get down?" Alejandra asked at last. "I thought every building was supposed to have a fire escape. Isn't it like a law or something?"

As the resident keeper of all manner of useless trivia, Addison answered.

"Actually, external fire escapes have become almost obsolete now, thanks to improved building codes."

"Well, good for the fucking building codes. *Puta madre*, what are we gonna do? Parachute down?"

"Don't worry, *peleonera*," Hansen assured her. "You'll be back in your muscle car soon enough."

"Oh yeah? You got thirty feet of rope I don't know about?"

"Trust me," Hansen said in as gentle a voice as he might ever have used. *"No te mentiría."*

Silence for several long moments, then Alejandra hushed back a single word.

"Okay."

Mason inched back from the edge and laid down on his back, making himself as comfortable as possible on a bed of tar and gravel.

"We won't be going anywhere tonight. Better get some shut-eye while we can."

"Deal!" Addison said, and proceeded to beat them all to it. He curled up in the comfort of his sweater-vest and was asleep in seconds.

"Alright," Hansen gruffed, and there was considerable shuffling about as he and Alejandra did what they could to settle in on Mason's other side.

"*Tienes el sueño ligero?*" he heard the old man hush.

"*Supongo. Por qué?*"

"*Tengo apnea. Si sueno extraño, despiértame,* okay?"

"Okay," Alejandra hushed, and almost immediately, everything grew quiet atop that deserted island.

Mason could almost tune out the roar of the raging sea, as he let the darkness envelope him, but as his eyes adjusted to the absolute pitch-blackness, he realized that it wasn't so absolute after all.

Stars.

Jesus *Christ*, the stars!

The sky was as it must have been a million years ago. Before smog. Before electric lights. Before jumbo jets. Long before man and his infernal 'civilization.' Mason was no stranger to the night sky, and he'd had occasion to gaze up at it from some of the remotest places on Earth, but it had never been like this.

Never.

No wonder those early humans had bestowed such wonder and magic upon the heavens. The sky was alive! A million stars were out, and with the moon yet to rise, each one of those millions were as clear and as bright as a diamond. And there, a brighter star glowing red. Was that Mars? It had to be. And he could even make out little smudges of light lost among the stars. Nebulae, maybe? Distant galaxies? Christ, was it possible that he might actually be looking upon things as far away as other galaxies?

All of a sudden, the Earth felt very, very small. A tiny

fleck of sand, adrift in a cosmic ocean. And with that, Mason's mind expanded to fill the cosmos.

Was there life out there? Was that star-speckled ocean perhaps *teeming* with life? Other worlds? Other beings? Other so-called civilizations? If so, would any of those civilizations ever know about this tiny fleck of sand? Would any of those beings on any one of those countless worlds out there ever look down upon the Earth and say, 'There was man here, once'?

And what of the Earth itself? Would a single trace of this once great civilization remain in a hundred years? A thousand? A million? When some other intelligence rose up to take man's place, would there be a single one among them who would know what had come before? And if so, would they care?

His eyes drifted back to the glowing red dot, and he pictured that world in his mind's eye.

Mars. There had been water there once. Warmth. Air. Life, probably. Now, it was dust and rocks and ice. But among all of that dust and all of those rocks and all of that ice, there was something else there, too. Maybe not life, but certainly *proof* of life. Proof in the form of metals and wires and glass lenses that some intelligent creatures had dropped in on the red planet from time to time. In a million years, all of those things crafted by man will have dissolved into the Martian soil, but wasn't there still proof of this life elsewhere?

A crescent moon began to rise over the eastern horizon. The moon. Earth's companion in her voyage across the vast cosmic ocean. That beautiful, desolate world had given early man comfort and had lighted his way through the dark. Now, it would be mankind's legacy. In a million years, proof of man would still exist in her endless vacuum. The ridiculous flags of a divided people would have bleached away to nothingness, but proof of their existence would remain.

It was a comforting thought, for what it was worth. But even as his body grew numb and his eyelids began to droop, he couldn't help but wonder if this failed experiment in natural selection deserved to be remembered at all. Perhaps it would be best, after all, if mankind and all traces of its so-called 'civilization' were expunged completely from history. They'd had their chance, they'd fucked it up, and they'd self-destructed. The entire species wasn't even worth a footnote.

Suddenly, he couldn't keep his eyes open any longer. He felt himself drifting away into the endless cosmos, but it took only a single word from Hansen to snap him fully awake again.

"Mace?"

"Huh?" He sat up with a start, one hand on his empty holster.

"Easy there, big man. We're okay. Stand down."

Despite the reassurance, Mason ran his eyes across every inch of the roof, paying special attention to the closed hatch hidden in the darkness. As satisfied as he could be under the circumstances, he lay back down, though not without a grumble.

"I'm trying to sleep, Gary. Do you mind?"

Hansen ignored him. "I have to ask you something, tough guy. How come when I'm stuck in some impossible situation with no way out and death all around, I always have to suffer through it with your ugly fucking mug as company?"

Mason didn't give it too much thought.

"Fate? Karma? Hell, Gary, maybe the universe just loves fucking with you. If you want out so bad," he threw a thumb over his shoulder toward the edge of the roof, "have at it."

Hansen snorted what might generously be considered a laugh, then he fell silent again. But just when Mason thought he was done...

"I tell ya, tough guy, I've been on ships in the middle of the ocean on a calm, moonless night, and I've never seen a sky like this."

Grudgingly, Mason replied, but just barely.

"Yeah? No shit."

Silence for nearly a minute, then Hansen broke it again.

"You know, some people just rub each other the wrong way. No big deal, it happens. Hell, a whole *lot* of people rub *me* the wrong way. But sometimes, people just get off on the wrong foot. It was like that with me and my old partner, Frankie. Frank Chow. We hated each other from the get-go. You know how it is. Nothing in common, two completely different people. But Frankie turned out to be a hell of a cop and one of the best friend's I've ever had. We were partners for eight years. I was pallbearer at his funeral."

Mason stowed the wisecracks and told him, sincerely, "I'm sorry. Was he killed on the job?"

"Cancer," Hansen huffed the word as a curse. "Thirty years old, never smoked a cigarette in his life and ran three miles a day. Then one day, poof!"

"I'm sorry," Mason said again, even more sincerely.

Another silence, long enough that Mason began to think the old man had finally fallen asleep. The moon was bright enough now that he could make out a little more than just the old man's silhouette. Alejandra was out like a light beside him, her pretty face tucked into his chest and his arm around her shoulder. Hansen must have been just as exhausted as she, but no, he wasn't asleep yet.

"The guy worked out constantly. Never ate meat. Took

care of himself like no man I've ever known. I used to kid him that he was going to be pretty damned embarrassed lying in a hospital bed one day, dying from nothing. Then he did just that. He died. Cut down in the prime of his life. Left a wife and two kids. *Damn*, he was a good man!"

This time, Mason said nothing, knowing enough to let Hansen work through his pain. But soon enough, that pain began to double back around.

"You know, I hated you the second I laid eyes on you," the man said, just that plainly.

"I know," Mason replied, just as plainly.

"I hated you because I knew the kind of man you were. And when I saw how you treated Rebecca, I hated you even more."

"I know," Mason said through a heavy sigh. "So did I."

Another silence. Prolonged this time. Alejandra uttered a somniferous little grumble, but Hansen stroked her hair as gently as he might a kitten, and the grumbling stopped.

"And you know what, Mace?" Hansen said, quieter now. "Now that I've come to know you, I *still* hate you."

"I know," Mason sighed again.

Despite the words, Hansen reached over and gave him a pat on the shoulder, though it felt more like a punch.

"Oh, you're not such a bad man, I guess. It took the whole world going to Hell in a hand-basket, but I can see that now. Believe me, I've met some of the worst human beings on the planet, and you wouldn't even rank in the top fifty."

"Uhh... Thanks. I guess."

"Bah! I tell you, tough guy, I've met some of the worst scum this society has ever churned out. Murderers. Rapists. Men who'd do things to kids... *Fuck!* Well, I tell you what. That shit changes a man. Seeing that shit day after day, it truly does change a man. When you spend your life looking at the worst this world has to offer, you eventually start seeing the worst in everyone."

"I can understand that," Mason told him, honestly.

"When I was barely out of my blues, I arrested a man who'd killed his wife and baby. Carved them up like a Thanksgiving turkey. Blood fucking everywhere. No one could take a step in that shitty little rat-hole without stepping in the stuff. So, you know what I did, Mace?"

Mason shrugged.

"What I did was, I got that fucker to confess, I booked his ass, and then I threw my shoes in the garbage. *I* signed on to that shit. My wife and daughter didn't. Well, maybe Barbara knew a little of what she was getting herself into, but Rebecca never had a choice. And worse, she never knew the man I used to be. The only father she's ever known was the man I'd become. The man this world had already turned me into. While all the other fathers were taking their kids to birthday parties and having little fucking tea parties and reading bed-time stories, Rebecca's old man was out in the streets, rubbing elbows with garbage."

Suddenly, Mason felt almost sorry for the old man. Not much, but enough that he felt obliged to tell him, "Becks never minded, you know? She was worried about you getting hurt, but she was always proud of you. In fact, you were kind of her hero."

Hansen gruffed a laugh. "Oh, shit! That must have pissed you off to no end."

"Now that you mention it..." Mason harrumphed. "But honestly, Gary, you did a good job. You raised her right. The only mistake she ever made was falling for the wrong guy, and she remedied that mistake rather decisively."

STAGE 3: BRAVO

"Well, I suppose she could have done worse," Hansen admitted, though not without obvious discomfort. "But you're giving me too much credit. *Barbara* raised our daughter. I just stuck my head in from time to time. Thankfully, though, we were of a mind when it came to children. The last thing we wanted was to raise an elf."

Mason searched his lexicon database and came up empty. "Uh, elf?"

"That's what me and Frankie called them. ELFs. Entitled Little Fucks. Back then, we'd come across one every once in a while. After Frankie died, that's all I ever saw. Entitled little fucks. Society owes me... My mommy told me I was special... *Jesus!* We raised a generation of entitled little fucks. Pussies. Weaklings. And where are any of those ELFs now? *Christ*, maybe Darwin had it right all along."

"So you're saying that parents should have been tougher on their kids? Spare the rod and spoil the child? Seriously?"

"Oh, don't get your ovaries in a knot, Princess. All I'm saying is, we didn't do that generation any favors by putting them on a pedestal. Believe me when I say that no one ever loved a child more than Barbara and I loved our little girl. We *showered* her with love, but we also taught her that the world wasn't going to be handed to her on a silver platter. She could be anything she wanted to be, and we'd support the hell out of her, but she'd have to work for it. She'd have to work hard, she'd have to have a mind of her own, and she'd have to *use* it."

"And the first thing she does is fall for an asshole." Mason forced himself not to laugh. "A wise man once told me that no father will ever like any man who dates his little girl. It must have pissed you right the *fuck* off when you saw the kind of loser *your* little girl picked."

"Now that you mention it..." Hansen gruffed, but he couldn't hide the hint of a chuckle. "Oh, I could've given you a chance, I suppose. I should've known that Rebecca was too smart to fall for anyone as completely worthless as you appeared to be. Uh, no offence and all."

Mason said nothing. Once again, Hansen wasn't saying anything that he hadn't already heaped upon himself.

"Yup, she could've done worse," Hansen said again, then he actually reached across and gave Mason a genuine pat on the shoulder. One that might not even bruise. "Mace, you're doing a noble thing, taking care of your friends at any cost. In my book, that makes you a good man."

"You sure, Gary? At least you had an excuse for turning into an asshole. I've been an asshole my whole life."

"I'll take your word for it." Hansen almost-chuckled again. "But if it takes an asshole to keep his friends alive in this clusterfuck, then you just go ahead and be the biggest asshole the world has ever known."

"Biggest asshole wins the prize?" Mason quipped, joylessly.

"They usually do," Hansen returned, matter-of-factly.

"So, it's down to survival of the fittest?"

"It's down to survival, *period!*" Hansen gruffed, loudly enough to earn him a somniferous, *"Qué es..."* from Alejandra, but he stroked her hair again and hushed, *"Nada, querida. Vuelve a dormir..."* and she quickly fell back to sleep.

"Survival at any cost?" Mason hushed, barely above a whisper.

"One man alone? Maybe," Hansen hedged. "But a man looking out for his loved ones? Abso-*fucking*-lutely."

"Well, you might have to remind me of that from time to time, Gary. You know, just in case I start to get soft in my old age."

"For as long as I can, Mace," Hansen sighed, suddenly sounding as exhausted as he should be. "But for now, I need some shut-eye. I'm dying over here."

"Fair enough," Mason concluded the conversation, and thankfully so. But then he felt a second pat on the shoulder and Hansen's voice returned, albeit slowed and softened with fatigue.

"Bravo Zulu, big man. Bravo Zulu."

Mason understood the terminology. It was one hundred percent Navy. Bravo Zulu. In Navy code, it meant 'Well Done.'

Mason didn't know quite how to respond, so he went with his go-to and said nothing. But Hansen apparently had a few last words that needed saying before sleep took him completely.

"There were eight of you to start," he hushed, barely awake now. "If we die on this rooftop, seven will leave. So, whaddya think, Mace. Was it worth it?"

Mason thought about it long and hard, and at the end of it all, the best he could do was quote a friend.

"Every minute in this living Hell is a risk," he said into the darkness. "What difference if we risk our lives here or there?"

After some deliberation, Hansen allowed a simple, "Good answer," and said no more. Soon enough, the old man's breathing grew deep and long, and Mason knew that he was nearly asleep. But not entirely, as it turned out. He managed one last, "Bravo Zulu, big man..." then he really was asleep.

As Mason gazed up at that shining red dot and at those millions of stars and at the great spine of the galaxy just now peeking up over the edge of the world, his thoughts turned from the infinite and back to his own little corner of that tiny flake of sand.

Was it worth it? Was any of it? Was it worth keeping Becks and the others alive, just to keep them alive? Was it worth any of them surviving, knowing the kind of world they'd have to live in? The questions were unanswerable. But then Mack's face appeared in his mind's eye, and then Sarah's, and then Becks', and he knew.

Hell *yes*, it was worth it. Every hour or minute or second he was able to keep those incredible people alive was worth it. He was an asshole, yes, but he was the kind of asshole who would do whatever had to be done to keep Becks and Sarah and Mack safe, and that was enough.

As he gazed up at the heavens, at all there was and all there is, and all there ever would be, he heard Hansen's last words ringing in his ears.

Bravo Zulu, big man. Bravo Zulu...

Well done.

CHAPTER

XXV

There were dreams. Always, there were dreams. Most of the time, the freak show world of alphas and echoes intruded, bleeding one into the other, but every once in a while, there was a different kind of dream.

Not tonight, though.

Mason and Becks were together. His apartment. She was laughing, and so was he. They were happy, content just to be. And in a heartbeat, it all changed. Becks turned away for the briefest of moments, and when she turned back, it was with the cold dead eyes of an alpha. A foamy red spittle bubbled up at the corners of her mouth, and she suddenly launched herself at Mason. He tried to hold her back, but it was like trying to wrestle a mountain lion. A double handful of claws raked across his face, and he howled in pain. Unable to see through the haze of blood, he propelled himself backward along the couch. But it was already too late. The claws tore his chest open, and he felt hot, acrid breath against his neck...

He bolted awake, one hand on his empty holster and the

other at his own throat.

Jesus *Christ*!

The rooftop was still in shadow, but there was enough light from the rising sun to see that they were alone on the island. And with most of the swarm having been lulled into a vigil state during the night after the sounds of humans had ceased, it was almost even peaceful. Mason took the rare opportunity to lie perfectly still for ten minutes or more and let the last ghosts of the nightmare fade slowly and naturally away, then he sat up and took stock of the situation.

Addison was curled into a knot on one side of him, and Alejandra and Hansen were on the other. Ally's head was resting on the old man's chest, and he had one big arm around her. It was almost adorable to see. Less adorable was the service pistol in Hansen's other hand, safety off and one big, meaty finger inside the trigger guard. Not exactly safe, but these days it was better unsafe than sorry.

Ally still had her machete, and Addison his Nut-Buster. Good. He had left his own SBD back in the Peterbilt, but he'd somehow clung onto a chunk of bloodied 2x4 during the escape. Not great, but it'd gotten him this far, so not bad. The other three still had their sidearms, but if he remembered the previous night's events correctly, two of the three were empty. Only Hansen was still packing, judging by the one mag still in the double pouch on his belt. But his pockets were empty, so thirteen rounds was all the firepower they had between them. That, plus whatever the old man had left in the clip. One, maybe two more. And that was it.

He climbed to his feet and conducted a rather more personal inventory.

His back hurt. Understandable. So did his neck. Also understandable. A twinge in his right arm, all the way up to the shoulder. Recoil from that *damned* cannon. A tweak in his left knee. He must've wrenched it during the melee, but no matter. Slight cramping in his legs. Beginnings of a headache. Early warning signs of dehydration, undoubtedly. He hadn't had a drop of liquid in over twelve hours, so it was to be expected. The others would be in the same boat. Hansen would have it worse. Addison, too. Ally was younger and fitter and had less body mass, so she'd be a few hours behind.

He padded over to the edge of the roof as quietly as he could and looked down. Sure enough, the Peterbilt hadn't moved an inch. The Quad was still dark, but he could make out enough to know that Sarah and the others couldn't have had a very pleasant night. The swarm must have clawed away at Gloria for an hour or more before losing interest. Her sides were painted red all the way up to the windows, and at least one intrepid alpha had managed to climb onto Gloria's back to leave bloody graffiti all over the side of the cargo box.

A tiny hand suddenly appeared from the darkness of the cab and pressed against the windshield, then a tangle of red curls appeared, and Mack's little face appeared over the steering wheel. She looked up at him and smiled and waved, and Mason smiled and waved back.

He tried to count back the number of days since he'd first met that remarkable little girl, but it was impossible. Weeks, certainly. A month? Maybe. Maybe it'd been a month, but it couldn't be much more than that. And yet, it seemed a lifetime ago. And in a manner of speaking, he supposed that it probably was.

Was it worth it? he heard Hansen ask inside his head again, and this time the question didn't even warrant an answer.

Dimly, he remembered Hansen saying something about

not being the man he used to be. Well, he wasn't alone in that regard. Mason wasn't the man he used to be, either. Close, but not quite. And the catalyst for that change was that little green-eyed girl smiling up at him just now. But Mack had changed, too. And so had Sarah. And so had Becks. And so had they all. Whether it was for better or worse, only time would tell. If he was still around in a dozen years, he might wish he could come back to this precise day and steer those individual trajectories a few degrees one way or the other. But with neither time machine nor crystal ball at his disposal, all he could do was hope.

Mack's lips moved, so he knew she was talking. More probably, she was whispering. Someone else was awake, then. Sure enough, Sarah's face appeared over the girl's shoulder, and she looked up. But no smile this time. Just the pursed lips and furrowed brow of someone breathing a sigh of relief. Then, there came a flurry of hand signals back and forth.

All okay?

Yes. You?

All okay. Any way down?

Working on it. No rush. Wait there if you can. If not, go.

Mack delivered the final signal.

We're staying.

And that was it. Mason gave the OK sign, then quite against his nature, he put his fingers to his lips and sent down a kiss. To his delight, not only did they not laugh, but each of them echoed the gesture back, sending up kisses of their own. And as they receded back into the shadows, Mack tucked safely in Sarah's lap, Mason turned his attention to the impossible.

Ultimately, there was only one way to get down. Nobody was going to like it, but there was no other way. Anticipating the reception his plan was likely to get, he sat cross-legged on the roof and wracked his brain until the sun grew hot on his back. Then, he reluctantly laid a hand on Addison's shoulder, rousing him from a deep sleep.

"Huh?" Addison grunted, rubbing the heels of his palms into his eyes and fishing his glasses out of the neck of his sweater-vest. "Dude, I was having the best dream ever! Selena Gomez was an Orion slave girl. Green skin, scanty panties... You couldn't have waited five more minutes?"

"Sorry, buddy," Mason replied, somewhere between mildly amused and utterly appalled, "But unless you want to stay up here for the duration, we should get our respective shit together before the natives get restless again."

"You know what, Mace?" Addison grumbled. "People might like you more if you woke them up with a blueberry muffin and a latté instead of doom and gloom."

Mason ignored the comment and moved to rouse the others, but just as he was about to shake Hansen awake, Addison stopped him.

"Maybe you should let him sleep a little longer, Mace. He's an old man, and he's been through a lot."

"We've *all* been through a lot," Mason huffed.

"Again," Addison shrugged, "stressing the word 'old.'"

Mason relented, and instead tapped Alejandra on the arm.

The only thing worse than a hungry Alejandra was a tired Alejandra, so he withdrew his hand as if he'd just poked a sleeping bear, and on cue, the girl raised her head, wiped a line of drool from the corner of her mouth, and snarled at Mason and Addison both.

"What the fuck, man?" she growled, then she looked down at a still-sleeping Hansen and dutifully lowered her voice. "Gloria still downstairs?"

Mason nodded.

"You got a way to get down?"

"I think so."

"Am I going to like it?"

"Nope."

"Figured."

She peeled herself away from Hansen and took special care in laying his arm back down on his chest gently enough so as not to wake him. She made an attempt to wipe away a puddle of her own drool from his shirt front, and failing that, she climbed to her feet and began making her way around the entire perimeter of the roof as quietly as a mouse.

"Am *I* going to like it, Mace?" Addison asked, hitching his glasses high up on his nose.

Mason mulled it over. "No, but you won't hate it nearly as much as Ally."

"And Hansen?"

"Let's just say that it will be a slightly less... *respectable* exit than he's probably used to."

"Uh oh," Addison arched an eyebrow. "I don't like the sound of that."

Mason left it there. Addison was a smart man. He could work through the math every bit as well as him.

Just then, Hansen sucked in a great lungful of air, startling Addison enough to make him jump. The old man stirred and opened his eyes, and with a quick look to see Alejandra gone, he sat bolt upright and brought up his pistol. But the quick movement took its toll, and he was suddenly wracked with a coughing fit that he muffled as best as he could in the crook of his arm. When he could breathe at last, he looked to where Alejandra was still circling the roof, and he relaxed. He thumbed the pistol to safe, returned it to his holster, and used the crook of his arm to muffle another deep, phlegmy cough.

"Damn," he said at last. "Still here, huh?"

"I know how you feel," Addison joined him in a grumble. "I keep hoping that I'll wake up back in my one-room apartment, with the Buckholtzs arguing over my head, the stench of Mrs. Constantinescu's cooked cabbage filling the halls, and those bastard Tomlinson twins blasting their cartoons through the walls."

Hansen regarded him as he might regard a two-headed cow, and said nothing.

"I'm just sayin'..." Addison mumbled quietly to himself.

Presently, Alejandra scampered noiselessly back and squatted down in front of them.

"They're pretty quiet right now," she hushed. "If we're gonna go, now's not a bad time. You got those Batwings of yours, Addy?"

"Ally, I told you. Batman has a Bat*wing*. *Singular*. Man-bat has *wings*. *Plural*. It's an entirely different thing, see?" He looked to Mason and Hansen and added a quick, "But that's just comic books and not relevant to the situation. I'm surprised at you, Ally!"

She scowled at him and offered Hansen a jut of her chin. "And how are you doing, *tamarindo*? Still with us?"

"Barely," he said, muffling another cough.

"Yeah, you slept pretty rough. You make a lousy pillow, old man."

They shared a smile.

"I warned you." Hansen shrugged.

"*Cierto*." Alejandra shrugged back.

"*Lo siento*."

"*No seas*."

Hansen choked back one more cough and turned to Mason. "You got a Plan D in that big, fat head of yours, tough guy?"

Back to your old self, I see... Mason said silently, but aloud he only said, "Sort of."

"Well, that's encouraging," Hansen gruffed, looking not at all encouraged. "Does it involve getting more people killed?"

Mason said nothing, and his expression didn't change, but Hansen immediately attempted to wave the harsh words away.

"Bah! That was a stupid thing to say."

"Yes, it was." This, in no uncertain terms, from Addison.

"Damn fuckin' *right*, it was," Alejandra growled at Hansen from point blank range.

"I apologize," Hansen told Alejandra, then he repeated it to Mason. "I'm sorry, Mace. I'm not exactly a morning person. And I believe I might have mentioned something earlier about my mouth running faster than my brain."

"S'alright," Mason lied, eager just to be shut of the whole thing.

Alejandra looked like she might have a few more choice words to say, but Addison steered the conversation elsewhere.

"Okay, so the way I see it, we can't go down the way we came up. And without a Bat*wing*," he stressed the word pointedly to Alejandra, "we'll have to scale thirty-plus feet of sheer wall." He crawled the few feet on hands and knees and hung his head over the side. "Gouge hand and foot-holds as we go? If we had a hammer or pickaxe, maybe. Drive in some kind of spikes to hang on to?" He looked around the roof and finally picked at a loose bit of aluminum flashing where the tar and gravel ended. "Naw. Glider? Big-ass suction cups? No, you know what? What we really need is..."

He stopped talking, and his face gradually contorted into a mask of horror. He looked up at Mason, and Mason nodded.

Yup, Addison was a smart man, alright. That big nerd could do the math every bit as well as him. Apparently, though, Alejandra was a step behind.

"Someone wanna fill the rest of us in?" she said, scowling from one of them to the other and back again.

Addison and Mason shared an awkward look, and Addison shrugged. "It's your plan. *You* tell her."

Mason hemmed and hawed for as long he dared, then he came clean.

"Ally, we need a rope," he told her and Hansen both, then he took a beat before adding the rather more pertinent, "Or at least something *like* a rope."

It didn't take long. They'd both been there for the preparation of Plan C. Mason gathering up the odds and ends that'd made up the makeshift beds. Him, tying them together. But with that particular something-like-a-rope currently hanging from a window one building away, there was only one option left.

"Shit!" the girl cursed, horrified. "Our clothes? You want our *clothes?*"

Before Mason could answer, Addison confided to him in what was undoubtedly supposed to be a whisper, "Dude... just FYI, I'm kinda goin' commando here..."

"Oh, fuck *that*, man!" Alejandra howled. "No way! No way, Mace! I don't mind showin' what I got, but I ain't hanging on for dear life to somethin' that's been soaking up Addy's ball-sweat for who knows how long. No way!"

"Hey, it's been like a day!" Addison tried to defend his

honor, but then he thought it over and had to admit, "Alright, maybe two. *Three*, tops."

"Dude," she screwed up her face at him. "Don't you chafe?"

As Addison turned a brilliant shade of red, Mason stepped in.

"It's the only way, Ally. Four pairs of pants will get us close, and your leather jacket will help. Your shirt won't help much, so you might as well keep that." He ran a calculating eye up and down Addison's pudgy body, adding, "Maybe you can do something with your sweater-vest, Addy. You know, to cover your, uh... your..."

"Oh great," Addison harrumphed, deadpan. "I'm going to fall to my death from the roof of a college wearing a diaper. Awesome."

Alejandra hid a cute little laugh.

"And suddenly, the issue of ball-sweat doesn't seem like such a big deal!"

Through it all, Hansen remained silent. Under normal circumstances, Mason would have welcomed that silence with open ears, but these were not ordinary circumstances, and his silence was deafening. He regarded the man closely, and as old as he was, Hansen looked as if he'd aged twenty years overnight. He was exhausted, laboring for breath, and though the sun had barely risen, his pale skin glistened with sweat.

Mason began to feel an all too familiar churning is his belly as he lowered himself to his knees so that he might look the man square in the eyes.

"You don't look so good, Gary," he said, outright.

"S'pose not," Hansen replied.

The two men looked at each other, and whether they'd seen something in one another's eyes or in their hearts or in their souls, it was clear that they both understood it all.

"When?" Mason asked, just that plainly.

"Basement," Hansen replied, just as plainly.

"I thought we had a deal about being completely honest." Mason feigned scorn.

"I lied," Hansen said, forcing a crooked smile.

Mason's shoulders slumped, and all he could offer was a hushed, "Well, shit."

When Hansen was done muffling another cough in the crook of his elbow, he gave Mason the barest of nods. "Shit, indeed."

It didn't take very long for the others to catch on. With all they'd been through and all they'd seen, it didn't take long at all. But there was no lamenting, no donning of sackcloth and throwing of ashes, and no offering of words that would mean less than nothing. They simply gathered closer around Hansen and gave him what little they could.

In her best impression of a head nurse, Alejandra said, "Show me," and Hansen dutifully gave her his hand.

It was the smallest of scratches. No bigger than a paper cut. But it was there.

"I fell over one of the fuckers and landed hard," he told her. "I tried to break my fall, and something stuck me. I don't even know what."

Alejandra inspected the wound closely, holding it right up to her eyes. It was so minor. So inconsequential. The kind of wound that might not even have bled. But it wasn't the blood getting out that did the damage. It was what got in.

"It looks like nothing! Are you sure? How can you be sure?"

The question didn't need answering. They'd all seen the signs before. Hansen was ashen grey. Sweating. His breathing growing rougher by the minute.

She took one last shot at it. "It could be the flu or some-thing. You don't know."

"I do," he told her plainly, turning his injured hand around to take hold of hers. "I wasn't sure at first, but I am now. It feels different. *I* feel different. I started to feel it last night, but by the way our... *friends* downstairs kept trying to murder my ass, I held out a tiny bit of hope that I was wrong. But I wasn't. I guess it just took a little longer for the fuckers to work their way through an ornery cuss like me." He attempted a wink and added, sweetly, "I knew you'd wake up if anything... happened."

"So, what? You expect us to just leave you behind now? Sarah's a nurse. Maybe she can..."

Hansen stopped her right there. "Not a chance, *peleonera*. And no, I don't expect you to leave me behind."

She spared a quick glance to the gun on his hip and looked him square in the eye. "What are you thinking of do-ing, *tamarindo?*"

Hansen sucked in a shallow breath as if he was inhaling glass shards. "I'm thinking that I have to go. I left my car dou-ble-parked downstairs."

"And what then?" Ally stuck out her chin.

"Then, you can all keep your pants on," he said.

It was a poor attempt to lighten the mood, and Alejandra was having none of it.

"And what *then?*" she asked again, her chin quivering ever so slightly. "You just gonna drive off into the sunset like some kind of big fucking hero or something?"

"Something like," he said, simply.

Even with his body stiffening and wracked with pain, he managed to lean forward and give her a gentle kiss on the cheek.

"*Otro lugar, otro tiempo,*" he hushed in her ear. "*Larga vida, peleonera.* Have a long, happy life."

She rested her forehead against his, and whatever else they had to say passed silently between them.

Alejandra swept back an errant lock of hair as they parted, but it didn't fool anyone, especially when she used the ruse to draw a thumb across her eye and it came away wet. She looked to Mason in desperation, and he let his expression confirm the inevitable.

She looked back to Hansen, and her eyes suddenly filled with tears. "I don't want you to."

"Hey, kiddo," he cooed to her, "shit happens. Just promise me that you'll do what you can to keep these idiots alive, okay? Whatever it takes, *querida*, that's what you do."

"*Claro*," Alejandra said, sucking back her tears and sticking out her chin. "I promise, *tamarindo*."

He laid a gentle hand on her cheek. "My name's Gary."

"I promise, Gary," she said, sweetly.

"*Gracias*, Alejandra," he said back, every bit as sweetly, and perhaps even more so.

Another cough boiled up from deep within his chest and exploded out, wracking his body from top to bottom. He muffled the cough as best he could in the crook of his elbow, and when it finally subsided, Mason could see that his sleeve was soaked through to the skin.

"I can feel those little fuckers setting up their little fucking factories," he managed. Barely.

Mason said nothing.

"Help me up..." Hansen panted, and immediately, three pairs of arms came to meet him.

They hauled him to his feet, and Alejandra propped herself under his arm to steady him. He patted her on the shoulder, and she flashed him a sad smile.

"I don't want you to," she said again.

"I know," he told her through a throat full of gravel.

They all helped to keep him upright as he led them to the hatch, then Mason put the toe of his boot to the thing, and they all peered down into bedlam.

"*Mierda...*" Alejandra gasped.

"*Si. Mierda,*" Hansen echoed, barely above a hush. "Mace, try to explain it to my little girl?"

It was in the form of a request, but it wasn't really. It was a demand, and it encompassed so very, very much. He wasn't telling him to explain to Becks how her father died or that he loved her or that he was doing this for her. He was telling him to explain to her why her father couldn't say goodbye to the one person he loved with all of his heart. And Mason understood completely. That hard-assed son of a bitch might have guts of steel, but one look at his daughter's tear-stained face would destroy him.

"Alright." Mason nodded.

Yes, he would explain it... *after*. Another *after* to pinpoint another moment in time when someone died.

And that was it. No last words, no more goodbyes, no more anything. They helped him step into the hatch and find his footing, and then they let him go. He felt his way down the ladder and reached the bottom with no reaction from the alphas standing vigil, and then he was gone.

No one said a word. They all padded slowly across to the front of the building and waited, and a few short minutes later, Hansen emerged. As far as the swarm was concerned, the man was invisible, but instead of just weaving his way through them, he was doing so much more. With a click of a cheek here and the barest whisper of a human word there, he was playing Pied Piper, leading the swarm out of the building to clear the way for the others. It was one final act of bravery, and it didn't surprise Mason one little bit.

The man didn't look up. He didn't dare. He simply made his way around to the far side of the building, leading the bulk of the swarm to the battered and beaten car barrier.

Only one creature came close. It was Mason's old friend with the Armani suit and the Rolex. Hansen planted a hand on its chest and shoved it back, and Armani didn't so much as gnash its teeth. The old man crawled over the barricade on his belly, slid awkwardly through the open window of his cruiser, and took the precaution of rolling the windows closed before keying the ignition.

The car started on the first crank, and the swarm went crazy. They howled and they raged and they charged the car from every direction, but Hansen sat in place for the better part of a minute and let them claw away.

And at last, he pulled the car forward and headed off, just like that.

Most of the creatures were elbowed aside by the rein-forced bumper, some fell under the wheels, and a few intrepid alphas managed to claw their way onto the hood of the cruiser, but Hansen pulled away from that last bastion of humanity as easily and casually as a man on a Sunday drive through the country. He bounded over the curb and hit the road, and as the car chugged away from Skyline at an alpha-friendly ten miles an hour, he finally hit the siren.

It was the dinner bell to end all dinner bells. Alphas came out from every corner of the complex and from everywhere else, tearing after the cruiser, and Hansen led them on their not-so-merry way. The car finally rounded the football field and hit Skyline Avenue, and with one quick double-tap on his horn as a final farewell, Hansen wheeled left, leading the swarm north into suburban Hell.

Mason ushered the others down before the siren faded away completely. A few alphas had been left behind, but they were so broken and wasted that it took little to finish them off. Mason reclaimed his cannon of a pistol from the floor, Addison and Alejandra slung their empty rifles across their backs and gathered up all of the other discarded weapons, then they each spared a few moments to gaze upon the bodies of their fallen.

He hadn't known Sk8rBoy William for long, so his torn body didn't mean much. But Inez was another story. He'd gotten to know her, and he knew he would feel her loss deeply. But now was not the time for such things. The three of them turned their backs on what was left of their friends, and without a single word or a single tear between them, they passed down the stairs and through the shattered doors, out into the Quad.

Even with the swarm gone, Gloria hadn't moved an inch. Sarah was too smart for that. None of them could have witnessed the exodus, and they mightn't have been able to detect the starting of a car engine from so far away, but none of them could have missed the wailing of a police siren. And still, Sarah had kept the Peterbilt exactly where it was as the Quad emptied out around them. She was far too smart to let Gloria's roar compete with the siren.

At last, the doors opened and seven people piled out to meet three others, weaving a cautious path through a battlefield strewn with bodies and parts of bodies.

Becks arrived first and threw her arms around Mason, then she looked beyond him, and her chest heaved.

"Mace?" she asked, and with one last desperate look for the man she knew would never come, she buried her face in his neck and cried without making a single sound.

"He saved our asses," Addison told her in a hush.

"Damn *straight* he did," Alejandra said, patting Becks on the shoulder as she passed by.

Mason stroked her long, black mane and told her honestly, "He was a good man, Becks. I know that now. You were right to be proud of him."

She released him, wiped one last tear away, and managed to fake the semblance of a smile.

"Gee, Mace," she said, her voice hitching once and only once. "And all it took was the end of the world."

Mack and Sarah approached with Clancy at their side, and Becks welcomed them in with a hand on Mackenzie's tiny shoulder. Mason gave Clancy a scratch between his ears and found a spot between a flurry of curls to kiss Mackenzie on the top of her head, then he took Sarah into his arms and hugged her as tightly as he ever had. Behind her, Christopher was standing at arm's length from the others. Richie, Teddy, and Diego were close by, but they were giving him room. Mason shared a look with Christopher, and whether that look said it all or that they were both afraid of where any words would lead, it was enough.

The siren continued to fade away to nothingness, but just as the last faintest whisper of the wail hung in the air, Mason either heard or imagined he'd heard the short, sharp crack of a gunshot. With that, he reeled Becks in, and the three of them clung to each other as if they'd never let go.

Without a word, the entire group started back to the Peterbilt. But just as they neared that big beautiful truck, Alejandra and Addison corralled Teddy and little Diego under their arms and peeled away, picking their way through the mine-field of bodies toward the Mustang.

"Too crowded in there," Ally called back. "And ain't no way I'm leaving my ride behind!"

They watched them all the way to the Mustang, and only once all four were safely inside with doors closed and locked did they turn back to Gloria. Mason climbed in behind the wheel, Sarah took her usual spot in the co-pilot's chair, Mackenzie and Clancy squatted between them, and Becks, Richie, and Christopher took to the sleeper cabin. And for the first time since they'd crossed into San Bruno, Mason took a deep breath, releasing it in a hush.

When they'd first arrived here, there had been only the stains of old blood to mark the struggle for survival. One day later, the place was a charnel house. Hundreds of bodies occupied the place now, with four of their own among the number. So what had they accomplished? Trading a few lives for a few others? They'd come with eight, and now they were ten. So, was that it, now? Was it all about the math? Was the sum total of their existence going to forevermore be measured by a body count?

Was it worth it? he heard Hansen ask again.

Becks leaned forward and rested her hand on Mason's shoulder, and just as the last time, the question didn't warrant an answer. As for the rest of it, he could only replay some song lyrics he might have heard a lifetime ago.

There ain't no time to wonder why, Whoopee! we're all gonna die...

He keyed Gloria to life, and still he sat there, looking out at the tangles of bodies all around. But then one of the bodies stirred and began to crawl its way back its feet, and then another, and another still, and Richie said from behind, "Uh,

Mace? Maybe we should go, huh?"

Mason couldn't agree more, but just as he shifted into gear and spun the truck around, a familiar figure stumbled into view, directly in front of the Peterbilt. It was Armani – one side of its skull caved in, one cheek stained an ugly black with the goo that had oozed from a destroyed eyeball, and that damned gold Rolex still dangling from its wrist.

Even as he heard the Mustang growl to life, he sat there watching Armani stumbling over the countless bodies.

"Hey, Sarah?" he asked as casually as he could.

"Yes, Mace?"

"Ummm..." He struggled until he found something approximating the right words. "Those little micronaut things... they can die, right?"

She mulled it over. "Well, technically they're not alive, so..."

"But machines quit working, right? Like, if I smash a toaster with a sledgehammer, you could say that I'd killed it."

"I suppose," she said, rather noncommittally.

"And a virus isn't alive either, but they can be killed too, right?"

"Uh... sure, I guess you could say that."

He took a deep breath before he asked the next question.

"So what kills a technovirus?"

His words hung in the air for some time, then Richie piped up from the back, "A bullet to the head seems to do the trick."

That answer suited Mason just fine, but ever the scientist, Sarah couldn't let it go at that.

"No, Richie, a bullet kills the *host*, not the technovirus. I don't even know if..." She cut herself short and looked out at the gathering echoes, and as her body grew tense and her hand went automatically to her pistol, she muttered an ominous, "Oh, dear Jesus..."

Armani was getting closer. But now, it wasn't alone. No fewer than a dozen echoes were stumbling their way toward the truck, and twice that many were stirring. He looked to the body wall and saw three of those ancient corpses struggling to crawl out from under the heaps of others.

It couldn't be. It couldn't. But it was.

Armani was dead. He'd killed it himself. Then Becks had killed the echo it had become with a javelin through the eye, deep into the brain. Armani had died twice, yet here it was.

An old female echo thumped into Gloria's flank, and Mason looked down to see her. Clean hole, just above the nose. Ragged. Torn. One of Alejandra's .45 calibre slugs. He looked to another and saw a skull opened up like a hard-boiled egg. And another, with multiple puncture wounds from a spiked bat. And another, its mouth filled with goo from a shot that had gone up through its jaw and into its brain.

"Sarah?" Mackenzie hushed.

The girl crawled into Sarah's lap, the others leaned out from the sleeper cab, and together they gazed out upon the wakening swarm.

They should all be dead. Not even an echo could sustain the kind of damage they were seeing and keep on going. But they were.

Sarah had said it herself. When the body dies, the tech keeps working, repairing, rebuilding. But only now did they understand the full meaning of those words. Only now did they get it.

Those little fucking machines didn't have an off switch.

The Mustang's horn sounded, making them all jump. A hushed round of nervous fake-laughter, and Mason pulled the truck forward, crushing Armani to a pulp and rolling effortlessly over dead and undead alike. He pulled up beside the Mustang just as Addison rolled his window down.

"Dude, are you seeing this?"

Mason didn't answer. He called down, simply, "Stay close," then he pulled ahead of them and made his way back down the concourse.

He expected to hear Alejandra's music start up from behind, but it didn't. They drove on in silence, the Mustang tucked tightly against Gloria's backside.

When they emerged onto Skyline Boulevard, Mason threw an imaginary salute toward the North, then he wheeled the Peterbilt South.

EPILOGUE

I t was almost dusk by the time they got there.

Three days of rough travel. Three days of bashing road-blocks aside and picking their way through an endless maze of surface roads. Three days of eating and sleeping in their vehicles. Three days of pissing into bottles or huddling next to the truck with their pants around their ankles to do more. When they had the time and the space during those three days, they would park the vehicles with their noses to-gether and take advantage of an hour or part of an hour to share a semblance of a meal together. But then the swarm would inevitably come, and they'd be back in their vehicles to do it all over again.

By the time they found the little homemade stand with the hand-painted sign, the sun was low on the horizon. Addi-son and Diego unlatched the gate and swung it open, then they latched it again and retreated to the Mustang to follow a trail of dust kicked up in Gloria's wake.

As always, Mason plotted the surroundings as he went. On one side, an open field carpeted in strawberry bushes. On the other, two acres of fenced property including the house, an oversized utility shed, and a full acre of overgrown lawn. No alphas. One echo pinned against the far side of the fence.

Another, bumbling through the strawberries. No goats. No pigs. No chickens. Daniel's pickup parked against the porch. Bloodied. Dented. Driver's window cracked.

He keyed the engine off and let Gloria's momentum carry them the last thirty yards. When the truck eased to a stop and set about pinging away its heat, Mason popped the door open and climbed out with Richie and Christopher on his tail. The air was scented with the sweet smell of strawberries, but behind it was the sickly-sweet stench of death. Sarah cracked her door open to release Clancy and Mackenzie, and as they ran off to play on the grass, she and Becks came out together.

It was quiet. Too quiet. Gloria was many things, but subtle, she wasn't. They'd have to have heard, but no one emerged from the house or from the shed or from the fields beyond.

Mason took one step onto the porch, and a slender hand suddenly appeared out of the darkness within the house, pressing against a glass panel high up on the front door. It retreated for a moment, then it returned and clawed a ruddy stain down the glass. Then a howl arose from within, and the door shuddered as something wild thrashed away at the other side.

He turned his back to the door and looked out at Mackenzie and Clancy taking turns chasing each other around, frolicking through the grass and mindless of anything else.

"We could stay here for a while, Mace."

He'd barely heard Richie's voice as he stood there watching the girl and her dog playing so gaily through the grass. If he lived a thousand lifetimes, he might never be able to imagine a better picture. They were free. They were happy. They were everything Mason could ever hope to see. But it was an illusion. A single frame of beauty in a horror movie from Hell.

"He's right, Mace," Christopher said, dissolving that single frame of beauty into nothingness. "We could clean them out and stay for the night. Maybe even longer, what with a fence and all."

Yes, they could. They could burst through the door, guns blazing and rebar swinging. But then what? Dig a pair of graves, side by side? It wouldn't end their suffering, it would only delay it, and not even an unrepentant asshole would get any sleep knowing that they were out there, clawing their way back up through six feet of dirt.

But they could do it *right*, couldn't they? They could use whatever gasoline was left in the pickup to burn the bodies completely and kill the little fuckers once and for all, right? Hell, they could even give the two of them a Viking funeral and set the old Walton-mobile ablaze before sending it rolling through the strawberry fields. But then what? A meal of someone else's food and a sleepless night on someone else's bed?

"No," he said at last. "This is their home." And that ended the discussion.

By now, Teddy and Diego had joined in on the fun, taking turns chasing Clancy around and being chased by him in return. It was a crazy game of tag, with Clancy always 'it.' They ran and they laughed as if they didn't have a care in the world, then Teddy emerged from the grass and tagged Alejandra, saying, "You're it!" and with the briefest of scowls and a mighty, "Oh no, you didn't!" the Latina spitfire tore off after the others, calling out, "I'm gonna getcha!" as she chased all of them around in endless circles.

Sarah and Becks came up onto the porch and did their best to ignore whatever was clawing at the door. They took their places on either side of Mason, and he put an arm around each of them.

"Fresh air, relative safety and enough strawberries to choke a horse," Becks sighed, "I could get used to this."

"Don't," Sarah replied, and that was that.

They watched the game of tag for a few minutes more, then a breathless Mackenzie tore out of the grass and made straight for the porch, and before Sarah knew what hit her, a pretty little face broke into a wide smile and hooted the words, "You're it!"

Cheerfully, Sarah abandoned the porch and chased after her daughter., then Richie and Addison joined in, and it became a free-for-all. Then Becks took Mason by the hand and hauled him from the porch, and it was all he could do to grab Christopher by the collar and drag him along too.

And with the sun dipping below the horizon, echoes gathering at the fence and a wild young thing raging just beyond those paper-thin walls, those ten lost souls let the rest of the world slip away.

If only for now.

About the Author

KEN STARK was born in Saskatchewan, but has called Vancouver home for most of his life. He was raised on a steady diet of science fiction and disaster movies, so it seems right that his first published book series be about the zombie apocalypse. In his spare time, Ken tries to paint like Bob Ross and play poker like Doyle Brunson, but results suggest that he might have got it all backwards.

Tweet Ken @PennilessScribe
Website: www.kenstark.ca